LAND OF YOUR POSSESSION

On the terrible night when Coventry loses its cathedral, Lizza is comforted at the loss of her daughter by Krystof, the Polish refugee. Her marriage crumbling, she heads home to South Durham. It is safer from enemy attack than the cities, but Priorton has its own dramas. Beatrice, Lizza's sister, is slowly emerging from the trauma of a rape. Beatrice's son, Alex, toys with the affections of young Josie. Josie herself, just fifteen, is growing up too fast... And Lizza, awaiting the birth of her new baby, is irresistibly drawn to Krystof whom Fate brings again to her door.

LAND OF YOUR POSSESSION

LAND OF YOUR POSSESSION

LAND OF YOUR POSSESSION

by
Wendy Robertson

British Library Cataloguing in Publication Data.

Robertson, Wendy
Land of your possession.

A catalogue record for this book is
available from the British Library.

ISBN 0-7505-0814-3

First published in Great Britain by Headline Book Publishing
Ltd., 1994

Cover illustration by arrangement with Headline Book Publishing
Ltd.

Published in Large Print December 1997 by arrangement with
Headline Book Publishing Ltd.

Magna Large Print Books
Long Preston, North Yorkshire,
England.

Magna Large Print is an imprint of
Library Magna Books Ltd.
Printed and bound in Great Britain by
T.J. Press (Padstow) Ltd., Cornwall, England.

British Library Cataloguing in Publication Data.

Robertson, Wendy
   Land of your possession.

A catalogue record for this book is
available from the British Library

ISBN 0-7505-0814-0

First published in Great Britain by Headline Book Publishing
Ltd., 1994

Published in Large Print December, 1995 by arrangement with
Headline Book Publishing Ltd.

Magna Large Print is an imprint of
Library Magna Books Ltd.
Printed and bound in Great Britain by
T.J. Press (Padstow) Ltd., Cornwall, PL28 8RW.

For J.O and A.J.R
The long and the short of it.

I

Lilies

I have forgot much, Cynara! gone with the
    wind,
Flung roses, roses, riotously, with the throng,
Dancing, to put thy pale, lost lilies out of
    mind...
        Ernest Dowson, *'Non Sum Qualis Eram'*

CHAPTER 1

Lizza King's hand tingled as the glass under her finger scraped across the glossy surface of the wooden table, swerving to a stop on the letter **F**, scrawled hastily on a scrap of paper torn from the margin of the *News Chronicle*. She held her breath as the glass swung in successive arcs, to the **I**, then the **R**, then the **E**, then the **S**, then back to the centre.

She took her hand off the glass and shook it to get rid of the tingle in her fingers. 'FIRES,' she said.

Mrs Callaghan, the sweat glowing on her upper lip, sat back with satisfaction. 'There, you see, Mrs King! Sure, there's no way I could push the glass! Wouldn't you feel me push? What was it you felt?'

'A kind of tingling.'

'There! Didn't I tell you?'

'What does FIRES mean?'

Maeve Callaghan shrugged her plump shoulders. She was more interested in the magical process than in the mere facts that emerged. 'What did we ask?'

' "What will happen next?" That's what we asked,' piped up Josie, Maeve's daughter, who was thin as a twig, the sticky smudges on her grubby face giving her a childish look which belied her fourteen years.

13

'Fires?' Maeve rubbed her full bosom with a lingering hand. 'Well, there's been fires already, from the bombs, fires all over the city. Sure, there'll be more of them before we're through. That's of no great import.' She grinned a slightly wolfish grin, her front teeth just a bit too large. 'How about the Fires of Love? Is your Mr King a passionate man, Mrs King? Sure, he always looks a very cool customer to me, riding the street on his bicycle, in his white mackintosh. Cool as a cucumber.'

Lizza's chair scraped back over the linoleum as she pushed herself away from the table. Now she was regretting her impulse to call at Mrs Callaghan's on her way out. 'What about Mr Callaghan?' she challenged.

'Theo?' Some of the colour faded from Maeve Callaghan's face, highlighting the livid bruise on the eye and the right cheek. Her laughter barked out without humour. 'Fires long since damped down there, darlin' girl. Long since! In my book, isn't marriage just the scrawniest pig in the silliest poke?'

'Mammy!' said Josie, scowling.

Her mother shook her head as though to dislodge a gnat from between her brows, then laughed her usual open laugh. 'Another question, Mrs King!'

Lizza joined in the laughter and, leaning forward again, placed her finger on the glass beside theirs. 'Ask it my fate, Mrs Callaghan.'

Maeve's face assumed a trance-like expression developed especially for these occasions. 'Spirit of the glass, we ask you the fate of Lizza King.'

It spelled out CASTLE.

'Wait!' said Maeve.

Then it spelt FIRES again. They kept their fingers on the glass. Then came PAINT. Then CHILD. Then DEAD.

The baby inside Lizza executed a somersault. She stood up. 'Silly games. I've no time for silly games, Mrs Callaghan.'

Maeve curved her fingers and scooped the battered scraps of paper into a little pile. She went to pick up her own whimpering baby, Anne-Marie, and sat with her on the battered couch.

Lizza had delivered Anne–Marie two months before. The midwife had crashed into a police car in the black-out and arrived half an hour too late, wheeling her twisted bike, the buckled wheel squeaking at every turn.

Maeve made a knuckle and let Anne-Marie grab it with eager gums. 'It's only a wee bit of fun, Mrs King.' She waited till Anne-Marie quietened, removed her knuckle, plucked a cigarette out of a tin case and lit it up, staring at Lizza through the smoke. Then she said cheerfully, standing up, 'It doesn't mean a thing. And anyway, isn't that your own little one I hear outside?'

When she saw them, Rebecca parted her pursed lips, opened her mouth so wide as to make a cherry-black hole and bawled even louder.

Maeve Callaghan leaned over the pram chuckling. 'It's a good pair of lungs she's got on her, Mrs King,' she said. Rebecca started to cough in the wreath of cigarette smoke.

Lizza's gas mask clattered against the rubber on the high chrome handlebar as she leaned over and tucked in the pink knitted blanket yet again. She smiled and stroked Rebecca's round cheek until the coughs and the crying subsided. 'And a good temper, Mrs Callaghan, to match the hair.'

Rebecca was hiccuping now. Her brown eyes widened with conscious appeal under the lazy auburn curls that straggled across her broad white forehead.

'She'll break a dozen hearts before she's finished,' said Maeve thoughtfully, moving her own baby from one hip to the other.

Lizza looked up at the clear autumn sky. 'That's if she gets the chance.'

Maeve followed her glance. 'Jerry didn't bother last night. Maybe he's forgotten about us. Isn't London a juicier target?'

'According to Roland, there's plenty plums here in Coventry. All those aero-engines. He says Jerry'll be back for them. You can be sure.'

Maeve put a finger to her lips. ' "Careless Talk", Mrs King, you know what they say about "Careless Talk!" '

As she tucked Rebecca's blanket around her again, the war weaved its way through Lizza's head like a clinging vine. Ever since the summer she had listened to the thrum-thrum of the planes, seen the dazzle of tracer bullets across the Coventry sky, heard the thrump and boom of bombs falling in the spasmodic air-raids. By

16

now, however, the routine of warnings, the rush to the air-raid shelters and the clatter of their own ack-ack gave her, in her optimistic moods, an illusion of protection, a feeling of control.

There were still dances and the pictures. Queues most nights. Up till this last rush of work in the factory, Roland and Lizza themselves had gone dancing every Saturday. Roland loved to dance. Lizza was proud of her husband's grace and his tall fair looks as he steered her expertly through the soldiers and their girlfriends, through the women dancing together, moving round the floor as though they were the only two in the hall. They had learned to dance in a little studio in Bradford; it was in that twenty-foot space that their sturdy boy-girl friendship had imported the sensuality that turned it into love. Even then, Roland had cut a different figure, with his cultured voice, and stories of his father sailing the high seas on the other side of the world.

Smiling at this thought, Lizza nodded cheerfully at Mrs Callaghan and walked on into town, forgetting the Ouija glass and its dire warnings.

She always relished this walk down avenues of modern houses, set in rows of four fronted by neat little gardens, their bright doors illuminated by panes of coloured glass. Creaking slightly as they turned, the high wheels of Rebecca's pram gathered leaves blown down by the recent autumn winds. In one garden dogs barked; in another, three children played: two girls throwing a red ball into the air, a boy with

17

his arms open wide, dive-bombing the girls from all angles.

Lizza took a short cut between two houses, down a lane which divided two lots of back gardens. The tell-tale hump in many gardens proclaimed the individual air-raid shelters. Some of these structures were very crude, the turf thrown carelessly over the heap of earth. Lizza's favourite was the one planted up by its owner with shrubs. Except for the odd bright berry on the sprawling cotoneaster, this hump was bare and leafless now, but right through the late summer it had quietly glowed with the small bobbing heads of rusty chrysanthemums.

Within ten minutes she had reached the narrow streets of the city centre. Here commercial buildings dominated the houses, some with timbered upper storeys and narrow windows. Lizza had a sense for old places and here she could feel the grandiose echoes of the medieval merchants for whom they had been built.

When he had first brought her to this city, Roland had laughed at his wife's delight at the sheer antiquity of it all. 'It's just old buildings, dearest Lizza. This is the twentieth century! The good things about this city are the factories, the factories! Have you seen the size, the capacity? Like nothing I've ever seen.'

She had scowled at him. 'The mills where I first worked in Bradford, they were that big and bigger. Filled with great looms. And they were ugly too. And so were the pit sheds back home in Durham. And the hospitals where I

18

worked before we were married. Maybe you need buildings that size to make your aeroplanes in, but *they* won't be there in three hundred years. Buildings here in this row, they've stood three hundred years, and'll stand three hundred more. William Shakespeare could have stood here!' At that time she had been very pregnant with the twins, but she still drew herself up to her full height and declaimed Rosalind's speech from *As You Like It: 'Beauty provoketh thieves sooner than gold...'*

He had glanced round at the bustling crowd, laughed, and put one gentle hand over her mouth. 'Shush now, love, or you'll have us both thrown in the loony bin.'

'Well then,' she grinned, 'with my training I'll know just what to do, won't I?'

That night, they had made love in the devious way they had evolved to accommodate Lizza's bulky shape. Then, he had asked her to speak as Rosalind again for him. 'I like it,' he said sleepily, 'the way you can stream the old words like that. I liked it when I first met you. A little Geordie girl spouting the words of Shakespeare.'

She had punched him then. 'Too big for your boots, you are. I knew it was a mistake marrying a lad who'd been to public school, even if he kept running away from it. We do have books up there in the North you know, and we haven't boiled our young for breakfast for years.'

'Hey, watch where you're going, missis!' The pram had ground to a halt, its front wheels tangling with the sandbags piled up outside the steps of the Guildhall. The policeman helped her to pull it free and touched his helmet as she thanked him.

He leaned over the pram to chuck Rebecca under the chin. 'Fine baby, missis. Got two of me own at home. Older, like, but seems no time since they were in reins like her.' He glanced at the sky. 'God will that they may live to a ripe old age.'

She followed his glance towards the empty sky and shook her head, then smiled at him and wheeled on. As she turned down a narrow street her destination reared before her: a bay window with a faded board over it, painted with a windmill and the words 'Windmill Café' etched in scratchy gold leaf.

She unclipped Rebecca and carried her into the dark interior of the café. Three of the small round tables were occupied by pairs of elderly ladies. The waitress, a middle-aged woman with grizzled hair, smiled and pulled across a scratched blue-painted high chair to the table in the bay window. Lizza strapped Rebecca in and gave her usual order—tea with a scone for herself, scone with milk for Rebecca. The waitress shook her head at the mention of the scone, but, as usual said she would try to squeeze one out of the cook for the baby.

Rebecca beamed, looking round like a prima donna for the expected adoring attention. This came almost instantly in the form of a fat white-haired woman in the opposite corner who started to play peek-a-boo with her.

Lizza leaned down to scrape around in her bag. Rejecting the Ethel M Dell she chose the new C.S Forester that Roland had brought in for her. *Captain Horatio Hornblower,* an adventurer of the Peninsular War. She took the cup of watery tea in her hand and settled down for a good read.

At the end of the first chapter her mind wandered, as it often did, to her mother. No question she would disapprove of Lizza's habit of slinking out of her neat suburban house every day, to read her books in the neutrality of a café. Ma would be slaving away in her County Durham house, fighting the tide of pit-dirt, a battle in which she was always just about victorious.

Lizza fished in her bag for the photograph her sister Beatrice had sent her. She smoothed the wrinkled surface; the severe face looked back at her. Alice Bremner was standing in a cross-over apron beside the back door of the house in Bracks Hill, looking fiercely towards the camera, a brush in one hand and a bucket in the other. On the back of the photograph, Beatrice had written in her neat hand, *'Ma says these are her badge of office. Ha ha!'*

Weapons of war, thought Lizza. Her mother looked more like a soldier on the alert, than some skivvy, some house slave.

But she had not come to help Lizza with her battle when the twins were born. When the first twin, quickly christened Barbara by the midwife, died, Roland's aunt had come, taken one look around at the cluttered kitchen, sniffed, and

21

said, 'You need someone of your own here, my dear. Can your mother come?'

After that first twin died Lizza had hoped with all her heart that Ma would come to help her, to give her some comfort in the little suburban house. Even in her desolation over Barbara, she savoured the thought of having her mother to herself for the first, the only time ever.

But it was her sister Beatrice who came from County Durham. Beatrice rendered the house spotless in an afternoon. She made bread from flour she had brought in her case and little pasties from a scrap of meat she found in the pantry. But she did not touch Elizabeth, the surviving twin. All the time she was there she averted her gaze from the basket with its delicate load.

One night in bed, Roland had commented to Lizza that Beatrice was a great help but she didn't seem to care for baby Elizabeth at all.

'It's because of Alex,' said Lizza.

'Alex?' Roland frowned. He had met Alex, Lizza's cocky seventeen-year-old 'brother', several times on their rare visits North. He knew that Alex was Beatrice's son, a fact tacitly understood but never mentioned in the house at Bracks Hill. Lizza herself rarely talked about her family.

Lizza put out the light and snuggled down until only her nose showed above the blanket. She spoke into the dark. 'I was at the house in Bracks Hill when Beatrice did the deed, or it was done to her. She came in, face bruised, clothes creased and blood on her ankles. My mother bundled me into the front room. And I

22

listened at the door as their voices rose and fell and our Beatrice started to sob. Then I heard the clanking of the tin bath being heaved into the kitchen, I pushed at the door but it wouldn't give; Ma'd thrust the back of the settle under the sneck. I had no idea what had happened or that she "fell wrong" as a consequence. I was young, remember. And that house was built on secrets. Then, by coincidence, I was visiting there nine months later when she had the baby on the scullery floor. It was a shock. I hadn't realised she was carrying. I'd teased her about putting on weight.'

'Didn't Beatrice tell you how it happened?' Roland felt her hair move as she shook her head.

'Beatrice said nothing to me, just trudged round the house in her quiet way. I was just back from Bradford. I'd had my hair bobbed for the first time and was wearing this new leaf-green coat. At that time there were no common words to use between us. To explain it. To share it.'

'She'd been attacked?'

'I don't think I realised it then. She kept her secret. Funny, though, that it was me who saw the baby burst from her on that visit. Not Ma. There was no time, I've never seen it quicker. It was me, funnily enough, who gave him his name. I'd been reading about the adventures of Alexander the Great, even read Beatrice a bit of the story as she lay in bed. Beatrice told Ma she wanted him named Alexander. I think Ma was pleased. Alex—like Alice, see? Maybe that's why she took to the baby, took him over. I don't know. From that first day she was in charge. He was hers.'

By now she was rigid beside him, reviving again her chronic anger with her mother, which was now mixed up with losing the first twin and her mother not coming to her aid.

He stroked her hair. 'There'll come a time for you to forgive her, Lizz, for sending you away like that.'

'The hymn calls them dark satanic mills. I cried, you know, but she never saw the tears. Why send me and not one of the others? I've thought of that plenty times since. Our Bernard said I was the middle one, and not much use in the house. And cheeky with it, they said. That put me outside Ma's magic circle; Renee and Beatrice stayed close: good girls.'

With Beatrice in the house in Coventry, Lizza had concentrated on little Elizabeth. The twins had been five weeks premature. If she could get this surviving baby to term she knew it would be all right. Elizabeth was tiny and perfect, and sucked surprisingly well. Her twin sister Barbara had breathed only long enough for the midwife to christen her, but Elizabeth had insisted on staying, had fought for her chance.

Beatrice had stayed in Coventry four and a half weeks.

One night when Elizabeth seemed fine, Mrs Callaghan had come in to mind her while Beatrice and Lizza went to the pictures to see a Charlie Chaplin picture. Lizza watched the little strutting figure with fascination, forgetting

24

for a few moments the baby at home and the one she had lost. When they got back from the pictures, Mrs Callaghan said the baby had been good as gold, a little angel.

The next day Elizabeth died. She had nearly, but not quite, survived. That was when, despite all the wordy and seductive childhood lessons in Chapel, Lizza knew with absolute certainty there was no God.

Rebecca was born, fine and healthy, just a year later. It was an easy pregnancy and a straightforward birth. She had been good, a true delight from the day she was born, walking and talking early. In the many hours of playing with and watching Rebecca, some of the hurt in Lizza's heart healed, but whenever her thoughts strayed to little Elizabeth, who had fought so hard, she still felt a dart of physical pain.

Now, sitting in the Windmill Café, with her hand keeping her place in her novel, with Rebecca in the high chair opposite, burbling away at her captive audience, Lizza repeated under her breath the words which had shocked Roland so much. 'I cursed God. I dismissed him from the universe, when my little doll, my Elizabeth, died.'

Alice Bremner smoothed out the letter which had arrived with its Coventry postmark and handed it to Beatrice, who sat down at the table to read it.

'Read it out, Beatrice.' Firelight glinted on the bright fender and on Alex's red hair as he lay on the clipped mat in front of the hearth, warming his pale face.

'Lazy tike,' said Alice, 'move over, will you? I need to get at that oven.'

'Go on, read it, Beatrice!' Alex closed his eyes, letting Lizza's words about the latest air-raid flow over him. He could see the flight formation of the aeroplanes high in the sky. He could hear the dull, heavy roar of the big Heinkels, different to the noise made by British planes. He could hear the ack-ack guns and the crashing thud of the bombs; he could see the flare of the fire lighting up the night sky.

...And down below, all this noise and flaring fires! If I stretch I can peer under our black-out and see the jagged gap where three houses stood at tea-time. The Callaghan's house next door had a shaking but it is still more or less intact. They'll be trekking back here in the morning with their two prams, picking their way through the rubble to see their walls still standing even if the chimney pot is a bit skew-whiff.

What Roland calls 'the midnight shift' has been around: dark people of shadows, who root around in the wreckage for things they can sell or barter. Scavengers for the enemy. Brave in their own way, I suppose, lurking out there before the all-clear. Our other neighbours will trek back to nothing but bricks, plaster and splintered wood. And three books, gaping open, their pages dotted like confetti all across the road.

But not this house. His bombs will not get this house. I know it.

'By, our Lizza can't half put a letter together,' said Alex.

Beatrice shook her head. 'They should go in to one of the big shelters. They're foolish staying in the house.'

'Safest place, under the stairs,' said Alex. 'Didn't you read it in the papers? We go under the stairs, don't we?'

'It's not the same. There's no raids up here. The odd bomb dropped off, maybe...'

'You read too much, Alex,' interrupted Alice. 'Head filled with rubbish.'

He stood up and leaned over to pick a hot scone from the tray in her hands. 'Now you don't mean that, Gram.'

He took his grandmother's pride for granted, just as he accepted the fact that Beatrice scrubbed out three shops every week to pay his modest fees for the grammar school. Weren't they rewarded when he did so well in his exams? Wasn't he the first person in the family to go to the grammar school? Wasn't he doing it for them?

He bit into the scone and chewed noisily. 'Anyway, we're getting those Jerries now. They say Mr Churchill sent our lads across to rub Hitler's nose in it soon. Probably in planes they make down Coventry, with a bit of luck.'

'Shh, Alex. That's Careless Talk. You know what they say!'

He leapt to his feet and, very elaborately, looked in the fireside cupboard and peered through the pantry door and turned round grinning. 'No Nazis in there.'

Beatrice laughed. 'Get on with you.'

'We'll knock on their back doors, those Jerries, Beatrice, you watch! Our lads'll get across there and thrash them. Give 'em half a chance.' He paused. 'Give me half a chance...'

'You can shut that talk right here.' Alice's tone was wintry now.

'Aw Gram, I wanna...'

'You can want all you like. You stay at school...' The scones bounced as she clashed the baking tray on to the table.

'School's a waste of time. Those Jerries...'

Then she smacked him hard across the face, twice: once one way and then the other. 'You're doing nothing, going nowhere, I tell you.'

Beatrice looked on in silence. Alex rubbed at his reddening cheek in astonishment. Jonnie once had told him that she had a hard hand, but he had never felt it before.

'Now,' said Alice, her voice sharp as flint, 'the pair of you can get up the Street. They says there's fish at Snowballs and corned beef at Smiths. It'll take queuing.'

Beatrice stared at her quietly for a moment, then went for her coat, pulling Alex from the room with her.

When they had gone Alice sat on a hard chair, stared at the fire, then lifted her head to the large sepia photograph on the wall. 'They're doing it again, Tom. They sucked you away into the mud, your blood in that foreign earth. Now they've got our Jonnie, the little one, the one you never saw, that grew to be your double.

Now he's the dear Lord knows where, behind barbed wire as good as dead. Now this one, this very last one, this *lovebegot*, is aching to go. Aching for it. Aching to leave...me.'

Then she put her hand before her narrow face, so that even the sepia shadow of the dead man on the wall could not see her tears.

CHAPTER 2

In the black pearl-light of the early morning Roland King jumped off his bike and pushed it through the tall factory gates, along with the hundreds of others who were reporting for work. The faces around him were white and creased from the long hours at work, and the exhaustion of many nights diving in and out of the shelters, in and out of bed. He sometimes thought that the war would be over before any of them got two decent nights' sleep in succession.

The voices that greeted him were cheery enough.

'Now mate!'

'How goes it, Rollie?'

'See they had a bit of crack over your way last night, Rollie!'

Having deposited the bike in the bike shed with the hundreds of others, Roland went through the large workshop down to the Test Shop and to his own wired-off cubby-hole, feeling, as usual, the order and satisfaction of work flooding his being. He loved the dusty smell and clanging sound of the factory: the buzz and bustle of people settling down to work. Then came the clatter and roar of machines doing their bit, drowning out altogether the sound of mere humans. His nostrils filled with the distinctive smell of grease and dust, fire and petrol, which was for him the smell of the future.

He had fought his father long and hard to achieve the privilege of getting his hands dirty when he worked. He had listened to hours of rhetoric about a wasted public-school education, and complaints that if he wasn't going to sea couldn't he at least be something interesting like a lawyer or a doctor?

He shrugged himself out of his raincoat, folded it neatly, and put it with his rucksack and trilby in the small cupboard he had fashioned under his bench. From the back of the cupboard he took a roll of stitched sacking which contained his oiled tools. These he unpacked carefully and laid in a line on his bench. In his early days at work he had been the butt of some jokes on account of what was seen as the fussy, domestic way in which he went about his job; he had had to endure mutters about the influence of women. But the quality of his work soon wiped out the mockery; apprentices who had learned their trade under him were going over that same neat ritual preparation in all of the major aero-factories in Britain. They too would have been extra busy since the spring.

He smiled sometimes at the jibe of the

'influence of women'. In fact his methodical approach had been inspired not by his mother, who had died when he was born, but by his father, a merchant captain. The house had been run by the Captain's sister, timid lady-like Aunt Mary, who scampered obediently around the house, pursuing the ship-shape routines he insisted on in his home. Meal-times were *at the Captain's table*. The kitchen was fitted and ordered like a ship's galley. Spring-cleaning was organised like a campaign for a sea battle even when the Captain wasn't there, for he left *closed orders...*

Roland's relationship with his father was like that of a midshipman with a kindly but authoritarian captain. He admired his father much more than he loved him. But now he was worried about him. He leaned against his bench and frowned. As far as he knew, the Captain was at present somewhere in the Atlantic with a merchant convoy. But he had not heard from him in two months and his heart chilled as he listened obsessively to the wireless reports of submarines attacking merchant vessels, of men adrift for days at sea. He kept this thought from Lizza, of course. She had enough on her plate, coping with Rebecca and the house, the queuing and the bombing.

And now she had this new baby on the way to think about.

'This is no way to win the war, Mr King!' boomed a voice behind him, strongly accented.

He pulled the canvas cover from his lathe and turned to smile at Pieter Vann, his development manager. 'You're right there, Mr Vann.'

The Dutchman's name was not really Vann; he had once told Roland his name was Van Something-or-other, emitting a sound that was like a man swallowing his own epiglottis. So he shortened it to Vann. Anyway, he'd added drily, his name sounded too German to be tolerated, nowadays.

Pieter Vann leaned over and rubbed a finger through the grease on the tool, which was in its final stage of completion. 'Nice piece of work, Mr King.' The tool was for a flexible aircraft gun-mounting, to which Roland had made his own specific modifications. 'Improves the movement; safety too. If it comes up to scratch in the tests.'

Roland nodded. 'It will. Saves one life, it's worth it.'

Vann bit his bottom lip. 'Each little life counts, Mr King. Every single one. Thousands have died.'

'You're right there. Every life.' Roland smiled in quiet sympathy. Vann had been in England eight years now. He lived alone.

Roland changed tack. 'We'll have this tool done, ready for trials by the end of today, don't you worry, Mr Vann.'

He worked through the day with characteristic quiet concentration. Even at dinner-time, he sat with one hand on the tool as he ate his sandwiches, ignoring the gaggle of men having a quick game of cards at the end of the section.

At twenty to seven Mr Vann approached him again. 'Now, Mr King, are we done?'

Roland banged his head as he brought it away from the lathe, emerging to see the foreman's grinning face.

'Yes, Mr Vann, this is the last of this lot. Just that last adjustment.'

'You're getting praise from upstairs for this development, I must tell you.'

'We all do our bit. Some of these lads haven't been out of this place more than eight hours a day in the last six weeks. We're all driven.'

Pieter Vann clapped him on the shoulder. 'We'll need that and more, Mr King. Losing too many planes over France, cracking Jerry on the coast there. And all those down here in the summer in the big battle. Cracking Jerry,' he repeated, rolling the words round his palette.

It was funny to hear Pieter Vann, in his Dutch accent, saying 'kreckin' Yerry' like that, with such relish. There had been mutterings on the section when he first came: the lads thought that the feller might be a Jerry himself. But they had been slowly won over by his courteous manner, and the trickle of information about the invasion of Holland and the deportation of all his family under the Nazis.

'Well, Mr Vann, as I said, they're just about ready for test now. I'll be needing my next project.'

Vann stroked his unshaven skin. 'Mmm. There's a feller arriving on Monday with modified plans for a new tool. Something to do with petrol-feed. You'll be getting that. So there's no reason why you shouldn't finish now,

Mr King. But we'll need to be here at six on Monday?'

Roland laughed. 'Same as usual, you mean!'

Workers in other parts of the shop had also been given a signal and were pulling on jackets over their overalls and caps down on their heads. In seconds, the section was cleared and they were all clattering towards the big doors, gas masks bouncing on their hips, hands in their pockets, rooting for their cigarettes and matches.

Roland, dressed for exit himself, strolled to the door with Vann. He turned towards the older man. 'Any news about your family, Mr Vann?'

The other man shrugged. 'There is my nephew who got to North Africa, I've had a letter from him. Five months ago he had one letter from my mother and my sister, his mother, then nothing. I have heard nothing.' He paused. 'They are taken, I am certain of it.'

'It must be hard, not knowing.'

Vann's chest gurgled with a sigh which was almost a sob. 'Harder for them, Mr King, harder for them.' He coughed. 'This new man who will come on Monday with the designs, he brought them from over there somewhere. A foreigner. He may know something.' His voice was neutral but his thoughts were with his mother and sister, also over there somewhere.

By the time Roland was at the end of his own street he had thrown off the weariness of the day and the depression brought about by momentarily sharing Pieter Vann's loss. Before going into the house he pushed open the garage door and pulled the canvas cover from his Morris. The car was shining clean and in perfect condition, but up on blocks for the duration. He ran a skilled hand over it in the semi-darkness and sighed. The war would be over when he drove that again with Lizza by his side and Rebecca—no, Rebecca *and* the newcomer, whom he hoped would be a boy—in the back seat. He pulled the canvas back and tied it neatly down again.

Before he put his key in the lock he battered cheerfully at the glass-paned door, shouted, 'Where is everybody?' then strode through the graceful little front room into the kitchen.

Rebecca, sitting in her high chair with jam on her face, crowed with delight and held out her arms. Lizza, curled in an armchair beside the fire, her nose in a book, stood up, smiling faintly. 'I heard you looking at the car again. No one's going to steal it, you know. You're early!'

Roland picked up Rebecca and started to lick the jam off her face. 'One lot finished. New tool project on Monday, so the good Lord Vann let us off before seven.'

She looked towards the gas cooker, a new one bought just before the war which her sister Beatrice had thought was a miracle from heaven. 'There's nothing ready. There's soup from yesterday.'

He sat down, the energy draining from him a little. 'No matter, Lizza. The soup from yesterday and a bit of bread will do me

35

fine.' He smiled across at her. 'I'm two hours early after all.' He appreciated the steady way Lizza dealt with the uncertainties of the long, unpredictable hours of his work. Some of the men had hell to pay when they turned up yet again so late. Or their wives were out, jawing with other women, or even men. It was true that Lizza was fiery and could flare up. That was one of the things he liked about her. But normally she would read her books, play her endless and elaborate games with Rebecca, tend her garden and keep the house neat. Later, when Rebecca was finally in bed and they were sitting at the table eating the soup made by Lizza from her own vegetables (surprisingly tasty, reheated), the air-raid siren went. Stubbornly refusing to hurry, they finished their soup, then Lizza went up for Rebecca and brought her down, bundled in her blankets.

Lizza and Roland didn't trek out of town as did the Callaghans and some of the others, looking for barns and hedgerows for protection. On the very first raid, they had gone into the big shelter on the Crescent. That didn't suit Lizza at all. As she explained to Maeve Callaghan, 'Me, I never did like to be so close to people. And Rebecca didn't get her proper sleep. I've always been quite firm about her sleeping hours. Roland says it's my nurse's training but I think it's just common sense.'

Of course she had to disturb Rebecca a bit to get her down into the narrow space under the stairs which Roland called the cellar. But the child hardly woke up at all. She just lay across Lizzie's arms like a piece of seaweed. The new baby, stirring about inside Lizza, was much more wakeful, absorbing into its brain Lizza's restless worry, her battened-down instinct to flight.

Roland took the bombing in his usual calm stride. More than once Lizza had thrown a pot at his head in sheer frustration at his lack of panic. In violent rows, she accused him of insensitivity, hiding away from the death that was around him.

If he was at work during a raid, he did shifts as fire warden there and usually stayed till the all-clear. When he wasn't at work, after doing his round as an air-raid warden, he would return to the house. Then, sitting under the stairs with a torch, or bravely up at the kitchen table, he would make his charts, complete with date, type of aeroplane, frequency and target. The next day he would check his facts as he went to work on his bicycle, wobbling round the potholes, the crevices and rubble. When he came home at night he would take an india-rubber and rub out errors and replace them with verified facts, inked in. Then he would add new data about the particular street, the particular building which was hit. His next task was to add small figures of men and women, like bundles of sticks, in rows like soldiers. These were his dead.

Lizza did not need her hospital text-books to see that in the wild chaos of death, fire and great explosion this activity gave Roland a sense of shape, order and control. His neat graphs, his lines of little men, his codes of time and plane-type, gave him a quiet man's sway over those giants; those wizards up in the sky who, like Thor, could cast thunderbolts into lesser people's lives.

He had gloated with uncharacteristic glee at the early victories at sea. How neatly they responded to both his desire to defeat the Germans and his perpetual concern for his father out there in his convoy, at the mercy of the elements and the rapacious German U-boats.

Lizza thought Roland was lucky. His work, of which he talked so very little, involved making engines for machines, which in their turn could wreak their own thunder-and-lightning damage on the enemy's bus-stops; on his churches, his children. She knew that Roland had his way of getting back at them, those boys in the sky.

She fretted that she herself had no way of fighting back. She could not work in the hospital to help return the wounded to full health, to fight or guard some more another day. Any chance of hospital work had stopped when she got married. No question, then, of married women continuing to nurse.

They would have taken her back now, of course, it being war-time. But now there was Rebecca to see to, and this new one coming. Reasons, she was told, for her to be away from the city. Pregnant women and women with small children were to be evacuated. But she wouldn't go.

She looked at herself in the small mirror that she kept in her cubby-hole under the stairs.

Brave or foolish, she insisted on staying there, pottering away, reading her books, playing with Rebecca. Roland nagged her about it. 'You're hard, Lizza, hard!' he would say, only half laughing.

'Hard? You don't know about hard! My mother, she's hard. Couldn't be soft, I suppose, with five young children, and her husband a war hero in the Great War. A dead one of course. The Great War? The war to end all wars? Now the Germans have either killed our Jonnie or got him in some prison camp. The war to end all wars? That's a laugh now, isn't it?'

This evening, Roland put her oil lamp on its little shelf by the camp-bed and heaved the radio with its heavy batteries on to the floor beside the cellar door. 'There. You've got your book?'

She pulled *Captain Horatio Hornblower* from under the pillow.

'Right, there now, I'm off.' Roland pulled on his scarf and his warden's helmet and then bent down to kiss her hard before he shut the cellar door. She listened to the slam of the front door, then settled down to read in the tiny circle of light afforded by the lamp. She wondered if they would come tonight, the boys. The city was always ready, but sometimes the planes went on, not bothering to stop. The serious bombing had happened only four or five times.

Of course they could be up there now, those boys, even younger than her brother Jonnie, with their fingers on the levers that could drop all hell on this city, this fine city, her adopted home which was older than Shakespeare.

CHAPTER 3

Josie Callaghan tucked her skirt up tightly into her knicker legs. A year ago she would have tucked it into the top of her knickers, but not since the blood came. She had waited for the blood such a long time. Every girl in her class had started before her. She was fourteen before she had her first show. But now she tucked her skirt up, not down, and without glancing around at all made a handstand against the wall. She stayed there quite still, looking at the world through a curtain of tangled black hair.

She could see Number Thirty-four opposite, with its smashed chimney at the bottom of her view and its front door at the top. From this angle the tape that criss-crossed the windows might have been drawn on to the glass in pencil.

'Bloody-bugger-bloody-bugger-bugger...' she chanted, enjoying the heat of the blood running to her head and the feeling of immunity rendered by her inverted position.

'Jo-sie!'

With difficulty, she turned her head and encountered the bright eye of little Rebecca King. ' 'Lo Rebecca!'

'Josie?'

'You're wondering what I'm doin' aren't you? Upside down like this? You call it a handstand,

40

Rebecca. An' when you do one, you can say anythin' you want...swear...curse...'

Rebecca's eye vanished from the gap in the fence, and her whole head appeared above it, beside that of her mother.

'I'd watch that, Josie,' said Lizza King. 'The blood running to your head'll make you feel dizzy.'

Josie dropped to her feet and rocked giddily from side to side until she found her balance. 'So it does, Mrs King.'

'And what d'you think you're doing, teaching my baby to swear? Swearing's a sign that you've got no proper words in your head.'

'Aw sorry, Mrs King!' Josie wasn't worried. Mrs King was the odd one. Nose in a book half the time. Sometimes not knowing just which world she was in, never mind what time it was. A woman like that doesn't worry about a bit of old swearing. 'But I was topsy-turvy. It doesn't count then. Nothing does.'

Lizza laughed. 'I hadn't heard that one, Josie. You've made it up.'

'Indeed I have not! It is so. Me grandma told me, many a time.'

Old Mrs Callaghan was the first member of the family Lizza had met. They had moved in one day, and the next day Lizza had half dragged, just about carried the old woman home, having discovered her in a drunken stupor by the bus-stop on the Crescent. She had listened to the old woman's babble, half familiar from her hospital days. There, the old women had been mad rather than drunk, but

41

heaving them about felt just the same, as did her instinctive sympathy for the childlike quality of some old people, inside and outside asylums.

She was about to leave Mrs Callaghan at her doorstep when the old woman suddenly clung to her and begged her to come in. She was anxious that her son would get on to her for coming home in this state. 'Won't he give me trouble for spending me own savings on a wee bottle of comfort in these hard times? Just like his dad! He'll give me a clout for causing trouble! Ah, dear girl, if you're there he'll hold off.'

So Lizza had gone with her into the house, which seemed full of shiny things and strange colours, and stiflingly hot from the fire piled high at the back of the fireplace. She'd wondered briefly where they'd got their coal, whether they knew there was a war on.

A colourful, unkempt woman, heavily pregnant, was leaning back in a chair, a faintly grubby child playing at her feet. The man coming towards her was spotless, his face shining clean, his glossy hair combed straight back, his immaculate shirt in sharp contrast to the brown fold of skin that lay against its snow white collar.

Theo Callaghan had been all charm with Lizza, bowing over her hand as he shook it. But the next day, when she saw Mrs Callaghan, the old woman had an ugly red weal on her cheek.

'Mrs C! How did that happen?'

The old woman put a black-nailed finger to her cheek. 'Ah, Mrs King, didn't I, like a silly old woman, fall against the scullery door?'

Lizza had stayed silent then. However, after that she began calling at the Callaghan house to chat with the old woman, letting Mr Callaghan know she was keeping an eye on her. It was no hardship. She enjoyed the old woman's talk: the comic tales of her youth were often on the edge of indecent, and the funnier for it.

And she got to know Maeve Callaghan, equally laconic and funny, but quite timid; Josie Callaghan, thin as a bird, now this mysterious mixture of child and woman who still did handstands against the wall; and Liam, wide-eyed and solemn, who played serious ball games with Rebecca; and, in passing, Mr Theo Callaghan, always charming and polite with her, who sent a shiver down her back.

It was the old woman who called on her the night Maeve had her baby, saying Theo had gone for the midwife but hadn't returned and wasn't the baby very much on the way? 'Bein' a nurse, I thought you could do the trick, Mrs King!'

'But babies! I know nothing about babies! It was old women I nursed, Mrs Callaghan. Mad old women!'

The old lady chuckled. 'I thought you had the touch. But anyway, come, won't you? I can't manage meself.'

So Lizza had delivered Anne-Marie, her own experience in having the twins and Rebecca standing her in good stead.

The midwife came half an hour late, wheeling her buckled bicycle. 'Police car banged into

43

me in the black-out,' she said sourly. 'Doing more damage than the blessed Germans, this black-out.'

A month later it had been Maeve Callaghan who came for her, to ask her to lay out her mother-in-law. 'She asked for it specially, Mrs King. Said you knew all about old women.'

So Lizza had laid Mrs Callaghan out. She completed her tasks lovingly, handling the body with respect, as she had for the old women in the hospital. She combed out the pretty silver hair, patted powder on the cold, badly bruised cheek, and put the veined hands together. The nails still had dirt beneath them.

She was surprised at the sadness she felt. She had known the old woman so briefly before she died. She wondered if she would feel like this when her own mother died. In the brief months of their acquaintance she had discovered all about Mrs Callaghan's childhood in the West of Ireland, her violent husband, now dead ('Dare I say thank the Lord? It was him or me!') of some digestive complaint; about her life with her easy-going daughter-in-law and the son who had taken over his father's routines of violence.

Compared with this, Lizza's own mother was a closed book. She knew nothing of her mother's past, of her youth. Her mother's mouth would close tight with disapproval, curl with contempt, at the slack sound of nostalgia in her neighbours' voices.

Now, in the street, Josie was shaking her head in Lizza's face, to get her attention, 'So, Mrs

King,' she was saying, 'if you don't mind, I'll do it again. I do three of these handstands every morning, and don't you know it does me the world of good?'

Lizza laughed, and put Rebecca down again so she could continue to peer through the fence.

Carefully, Josie executed the two more handstands, muttering the swear words until they had finally lost their power, then stood up unsteadily, pulling her skirt down and smoothing it with her grubby hands. Then she picked up the three balls she had placed in the purple shadow at the bottom of the wall and balanced them on her hands, before she started to play three-baller against the wall, chanting her song to help the rhythm:

Whistle while you work.
Mrs King made you a shirt
Hitler wore it
Goering tore it
Wasn't he a twerp?

A neatly manicured hand reached over her head and plucked away one of the balls, spoiling her rhythm and making her scatter the other balls over the pavement.

'Dad! What's that for?' she scowled up at him and bent down to pick up the balls.

'I've been shoutin' you for five minutes.' He hauled her to her feet, keeping his hand on her upper arm. 'I've told you before, you come when you're called.'

45

'I never heard.'

'You never do.' He fingered the flesh above her elbow. 'I've told your mother you're short of a smack.'

She pulled her arm away and kept her eyes away from him. 'What is it you want?'

'You're to come and get your brother and take him off for a walk. Your mother's tired.' He marched her into the house where her mother was sitting in her usual chair, a whimpering Liam at her knees.

'Here's the girl. Playing outside, deaf as a post as usual,' said Theo Callaghan shortly.

Maeve struggled to her feet and gently pushed Liam across to Josie. 'Take our Liam across to Swanswell pond, Josie. He likes it there, even if the water's black with soot now. No need to take Anne-Marie. Isn't she asleep upstairs like a good girl?'

Liam ran to Josie's thin-armed protection. Maeve eyed her husband then made her way towards the door to the staircase.

He looked at his watch and turned to his daughter. 'The boy needs a good walk, to melt his temper. No need to be back before four.'

He shepherded them out and locked the door behind them before turning to follow his wife upstairs.

Josie knocked on the door when she came back at half past three, but there was no answer. She had walked with Liam by the Swanswell and Liam had caught the attention of two passing soldiers. One started to play ball with the child and the other started to talk to Josie, whispering

things to her which made her grab her brother
and run.

So she sat on the step and sang into Liam's
ear:

Roll along Mussolini, roll along,
You won't be in Abyssinia long
You'll be sitting on the plain
With a bullet in your brain
Roll along Mussolini, roll along...

Lizza liked the fizz and risk which seemed to
sizzle through the wall from the house next door.
When she told Roland about the upside-down
swearing, his face remained glum.

'You want to leave them alone, Lizza. They're
scruffy and...improvident.'

'He's a clerk at the council, Rollie, and she's
a sweet woman, kind...'

'Oh, he's tidy enough, I grant you, but she's
a slattern...'

She batted him on the shoulder, quite softly.
'You have it the wrong way round. It's the man
that's a slattern and she's one of the kindest
people... Oh, Rollie, the only thing you can
make meaning out of is those old machines.
With people, you don't understand a thing.'
Her hand fell to her side and she sat down
and picked up her book. 'Oh, get on with your
graphs, I thought the tale about the upside-down
girl would amuse you.'

She tried to remember whether he had been
like this before the war, humourless and...old.
She didn't think so, but she couldn't be sure.

47

That was all a long time ago. So hard to remember.

With her book loose on her lap she thought back to one morning after one of the summer raids, when Josie had come to her door, thin as ever, looking younger than her fourteen years. 'Can I come and see the baby, Mrs King?'

Lizza had opened the door wide and followed Josie into the kitchen. 'Here she is.' She smiled down at Rebecca. 'But she's not really a baby any more, Josie. You're a big girl, aren't you, Rebecca? She's trotting around by herself really well now, Josie.'

Josie heaved the willing Rebecca on to her lap and looked Lizza in the eyes. 'I saw the arm of a baby, Mrs King, this morning, when I was poking round after the raid. A little arm, smaller even than Rebecca's here. Brown. It smelled like cooked meat. There in the rubble. Then they collected it and it wasn't there any more.' Her thin lips were pressed hard together and she looked up at Lizza through narrow eyes.

Lizza put her arm across her stomach where her own new baby was executing a forward roll.

'So why don'cha go in the big shelter, Mrs King?' urged Josie, reaching the object of her visit. 'Or out in the country into a barn like Mammy and us do?'

'The babe'll be all right, Josie. Both of them. Rebecca and her little brother or sister lying in here. Believe me, I know it. I just know it. You don't have to worry about us.' And she had looked at the skinny child with her long

48

eyes and narrow folded mouth, who was now her friend.

'And that Josie's a good girl,' she said now to Roland's bent head.

'The girl? She runs wild. Never clean.'

'She's very fond of Rebecca. And me.'

'So am I. But I wash myself every day.'

'You're never here. She keeps me company.' He put his pencil down. 'She's just a child.'

'I have to make do with who's here. You're never here and Theo Callaghan keeps his wife shut in when he's home. Without Josie I might just as well be invisible. I miss things, Rollie. I miss...people. My old ladies.'

'Mad old women!' he snorted. 'Is that what you want, to go back to one of those mausoleums and play Florence Nightingale to a bunch of mad old women?'

She jumped up, glaring at him in pure hatred. 'What's happened to you, Roland? Whatever it is, it's...'

He stood up. 'The war's happened to us all, Lizz. But it's you who have stayed in that cocoon of yours, reading and dreaming your way through it as though it were some play.' He sounded formal. Like a schoolmaster.

'I could do something. I could go back to nursing.'

'You can't. You know there's Rebecca and this new little one on the way. You're dreaming again. Not in the real world.' He ducked, but her book still caught him in the corner of his eye and he yelped in pain. When he got his head back up again she had gone and he could hear her clashing about in the bedroom, then the gurgle and grind of the gas geyser as she ran herself a bath.

Lying in the steam, Lizza thought of Roland, the shining boy she had married. In those days he had loved her dreaming and praised her for her kindness to the old women. How could things—the war, growing up, working at fever pitch—have changed such a boy to this sensible adult, as far away from her as the stars from the sun?

She closed her eyes. People, she thought, were like shoes which you wore to your own shape. Then some bits wore out and you patched them. And to keep going you had to keep patching them. But sometimes they were more patch than shoe, changed from the original in every respect. As they turned out, you wouldn't choose them in a thousand years.

CHAPTER 4

Early on Sunday evening Pieter Vann laboured up the road on his bicycle to ask Roland to go to the factory with him. A new tool needed setting for Monday morning. Lizza was not disturbed. These out-of-hours calls were not uncommon. Roland's ability to turn his hand to anything in the factory was legendary.

At the door, Roland put his cheek against Lizza's hair. 'I could be two, three hours, love.

50

You go to bed.'

'Take care!' Lizza leaned against the door frame, the black-out curtain behind her. She watched the two men cycle away into the coal-black night. Roland, in his light mackintosh, was swallowed into the thick blackness of the unlit street, which joined the starless sky on an unmarked horizon. She put her hand to her throat, feeling proud of his own quiet heroism and at the same time guilty about her waning feelings towards him. She looked upwards. No moon tonight either. She thanked the fates for that, having given up thanking God for anything. No moon tonight. No sirens. No raid.

She was turning to close the door when she thought she heard a sound beyond the rickety fence. 'Is that you, Josie?' No response. She shivered. The night was cold and, now, perfectly still.

She closed the door behind her and went through the front room into the kitchen. She stirred the fire and then sat down to complete the letter she was writing home. Home? What was she doing, even now after so many years, calling it 'writing home'!

...went to the pictures and saw *The Wizard of Oz* with Judy Garland. It started in black and white and ended in bright colour. You would love it, Beatrice. Lovely songs. And the idea that in our dreams we can be in quite another place. We need to dream of brighter places just now. It is so dark inside and out...

'What a lovely sight it is, Mrs King, to see a pretty woman writing in the light of a single lamp.'

Her pen clattered to the floor. She stood up. 'Mr Callaghan. I didn't hear you, did you knock?' He smelt of smoke, hops and sweat: the aura of a drunken man.

He smiled and sat opposite her on the armless chair beside the fire. 'Your front door swung back again, I should think, after you seen your husband off. Gone to his work, has he?'

With exaggerated care, she put the letter on to the bookshelf beside her. 'He'll be back soon. Any minute.'

'Now isn't that strange? I'd have sworn I heard him say a couple of hours. Must be my mistake.'

She leaned down to pick up her pen from the floor and then sat up in her chair, her back straight. 'Yes,' she said, casual now, 'it must be your mistake.' She looked him in the eye. 'Was there something your wife wanted, Mr Callaghan?'

'No, I'd not quite got home yet. But when I heard that soft voice of yours at the door I had the great urge to come and...thank you for all that kindness to my mother. I never got you thanked. She was a foolish old woman...'

'I thought she was a fine lady. Lots of spirit...'

'Ah, she was a sly old brewer. Could grease herself into anybody's good...'

Lizza stood up. 'She was a fine lady,' she

repeated. 'Now Mr Callaghan, I've jobs to do, and my husband will be back soon.'

He stood up and started to pick up her ornaments one by one: the small pottery pieces of ladies from history she had accumulated in her time in Coventry. She stood watching him, her hands clenched behind her back.

Callaghan's smooth white hand finally grasped a fine pottery figure of a lady in Regency costume, which she had bought just the week before in the big store in town.

'Now here we have a fine lady. A lady indeed.' He dropped the figure like a stone from his hand, scooping it up again an inch from the floor. Then he held it up again, ready to drop.

'No!' she lunged towards him to rescue the lady.

This time the Regency lady shattered as he dropped her, properly this time, on the lino. He leapt towards Lizza. In a second he was kneeling over her, clear of her body, with one hand across her throat.

'Mrs Callaghan...' she gasped.

'Bitch of a wife, no good to me, might as well give a rag doll a seeing to.'

'My baby. The baby...' She wriggled and fought.

He yanked her skirt up to her waist and his eyes flicked down as he reared up so he could see the white thigh, the pull of suspender. 'That's it, see? Bit of fun and no harm done. Already up the stick.' The oil had vanished from his voice, replaced by the rough edge of the streets.

She strained against the arm over her neck. 'No! Stop!'

He stopped her open-mouthed cry with his lips and his slimy, beery tongue. She thought she was going to choke.

He pulled back and laughed. 'Dying for it, stuck-up bitch! Knew it when you walked in our house. Dying for it!' He was fumbling for his fly. 'That wet-willie man of yours don't know his arse from his elbow. All you need is a man's loving care.'

She looked down and saw the pulsing thing, narrow and hard, glistening at the tip. He had to take his other arm from her neck to wrench at her knickers; she used this opportunity to heave herself out from under him and leap to her feet as he unbalanced and crashed to the floor where she had recently struggled.

She grabbed a kitchen chair and forced herself to smile as he scrambled to his feet. She held the chair, legs outward, like a lion tamer. Feeling behind her she found the knife drawer and grabbed the bread knife. 'Put that little thing away,' she laughed hoarsely, 'it's too small to be out.'

He lunged towards her and she crashed a chair leg into his face, raising a livid weal on his cheek. 'Don't think I won't do it. I've felled twenty-stone madwomen in my time, and they, poor things, were filled with the strength of seven devils.'

He laughed faintly, one hand up to his throbbing face, the other fumbling vainly with his unbuttoned fly. 'Now, Mrs King. Don't take

54

it too hard. Wasn't I only showing you you were an attractive woman? Wasn't I only trying to show sympathy for...'

She jabbed again. 'Out!'

Keeping his back to the wall, he edged round the room and vanished through the middle door. The knife still in her hand, she followed him, locking the door behind him, and leaning against it for a few seconds.

She shook herself and leapt into action, whirling through to the kitchen, carefully putting the chair in its usual place by the table. Then, taking every single ornament which Theo Callaghan's hand had touched, she smashed them on to the lino beside the Regency lady.

'Mammy, a bomb a bomb?' Rebecca was standing at the top of the stairs in her nightie.

She looked up at her. 'No, no, love. There was an accident. One of my pottery ladies is broken. You jump back into bed. I'll be there with you in no time.'

She returned to the kitchen, took a brush and swept the heap of shards on to the shovel. She hesitated before she unlocked the back door and negotiated the black-out curtain to tip the loaded shovel into the bucket she kept in the enclosed back porch.

She looked up at the sky and her heart sank. It was peculiarly light now. The heavy cloud had parted and the moon was low and bright; the stars were hustling for space in the sky. Back inside, she made herself a cup of tea and sat up at the table.

She started to shake.

Greater than the anger, the feeling flooding through her was guilt. How could Theo Callaghan know about her and Roland? How could he know that since the death of the twins they had made love with conscious intent only rarely, including the time that, thank the fates, had brought them Rebecca? How could he know about the times she turned to Roland, only to be gently and wordlessly turned away? How could he know about that fading of early passion, to be replaced by an abstemious and platonic love which she valued, but which left her body, her very senses aching? How could he know this feeling which she could not share with anyone? She shook her head at that thought.

Was she so open? Such a trollop? She rubbed her eyes, willing the tears to come, but they wouldn't. Then she jumped, as the familiar sickly wail of the siren assaulted her ears.

As she was collecting Rebecca from her bed she peered from her bedroom window and watched the Callaghans bustling away down the street with their prams loaded up with Anne-Marie and Liam, surrounded by pots and pans and precious things in parcels: Josie and her mother pushing the prams; Mr Callaghan marching on ahead, using his umbrella like a gentleman's walking stick.

Within five minutes her own air-raid routine was complete, with Rebecca in her under-stairs bed, Lizza's own little lamp lit and her book opened at her place. She would be on her own. Roland would stay at the factory all night now, fire-watching.

Pushing the incident to the back of her mind, she made herself look at the thick book in anticipation. She was working her way for the second time now through the adventures of Becky Sharp in *Vanity Fair*. She liked Becky, even if she was a bad girl. She knew how to survive. And Becky knew about war too, in her own way.

After reading for half an hour Lizza closed the book, keeping her finger in her place, and looked down at her sleepy daughter, her own Rebecca, named after the girl in Thackeray's novel. Rebecca felt her attention and opened her eyes, smiling up at her. She stroked the round cheek.

Lizza was pleased that she had not cried. She wouldn't give that foul man the satisfaction. And anyway, rape, or near-rape, was nothing to what was happening now to this town and this country, with bombs fracturing families, and shredding children; fires melting homes. She would not tell Roland.

She opened her book again and read on.

Roland gave Pieter Vann a leg up the ladder through the skylight. Then they made their way to the watching post, treading carefully along the extended guttering. To their right the roof rose at an angle; he wondered, in passing, how the squiggle of camouflage, which looked like hieroglyphics from down here, could really look like rows of houses from the air.

They put down their rucksacks and gas masks and settled down on the little wooden stools at the watching post. They didn't need their glasses to see the flare of fire on the southern perimeter of the city, but thankfully, there was nothing closer. Roland made a note of it in his notebook.

Pieter had lit his pipe, and Roland sat back with his own pipe as comfortably as he could, letting the fruity aroma meander over him.

'And how is your father now, Roland?' Pieter's voice came with an extra effusion of smoke.

Roland smiled towards the glowing tip of Pieter's pipe. The foreman had met his father once, when the Captain had been on leave and had come to the factory in search of his son. The two older men had had a long conversation about the Dutch seafaring tradition, becoming amicable acquaintances on the spot. 'The Captain? I don't know, Mr Vann. He's in a convoy somewhere in the middle of the Atlantic. Or was. I haven't heard from him in weeks.'

He could feel Pieter shake his head. 'Those merchantmen are the brave souls. Out there with little or no protection.' He paused. 'And your own family? How do they take the raids?'

'My wife's fine. From County Durham, you know. Hardy types. They're used to danger up there. Met it with the mines for hundreds of years. So she's sensible about all this. And if she's all right little Rebecca's all right. And we're expecting a new addition in the spring.'

He shot forward as Pieter clapped him on the back. 'Well done, my boy! Such an optimistic thing in these times.'

'Did you...do you have children, Mr Vann?'

Pieter took the pipe out of his mouth and knocked it against the rough wood framework of the open-sided hut. 'There were no children. My marriage was only brief.' He sighed. 'I had a son. He died in her arms, then she died. Long before the war.'

Roland, honoured at the confidence, went further. 'Your mother and sister...'

'Are taken as I thought. I had a letter from my nephew in North Africa. He had a letter smuggled out by an American, from a friend of theirs, a Catholic. He saw them loaded on to trucks like cattle. He said they sent their love.' He took a determined suck at his pipe. 'And not to worry.' He stood up, leaned against the makeshift handrail, and put his glasses to his eyes. 'See that flare, Roland? Nearer now? Not far from that crescent near you, I'd think.'

Roland peered into the blackness. 'No. Too far to the east.' The sky, punctuated here and there by bright light, was now suddenly full of the heavy drone of engines, passing over but dropping nothing. Picking up his notebook to make a note of the number, and the type, he said a quick prayer for Lizza and Rebecca, under the stairs in his neat little house.

'Oh Lord take care of them.' He often breathed little prayers these days; when there was nothing else he could do, it seemed like something. He wouldn't tell Lizza, of course; she scorned prayers, saying they were as much use as children chanting fairy-tales. Since the bad experience of the twins she had hardened

59

against all that prayer stuff. He had had to battle to get Rebecca christened at all. There were times when he felt he was a stranger to Lizza; she had changed. Once she had been funny, had been funny and clever. A bit of a dreamer always. She needed her books, her stories, like some people needed food. But somehow they had taken her from him on a cloud of her own imagining. He sometimes felt she had gone from him just as surely as the soldiers who were every day now leaving their loved ones, never to be the same again.

He glanced at the foreman. 'Don't you think time's overdue for the Americans to be in with us, Mr Vann? I was certain they'd join after we hung on so well after the Battle of Britain and the Germans didn't invade. I was certain! But they're dithering like a maiden aunt—*will she, won't she...*'

'We need them. They'll be in, my boy. Any day. And that'll make the difference. That'll show this madman... Otherwise he'll get here to this land and he'll... But the Americans will come. They have to. They'll show this madman, believe me...'

The next morning, at half past seven, there was a knock on Lizza's door. She opened it to Josie, standing there in the drizzle, Liam huddled to her side.

'Can we come in, Mrs King? We're locked out. Mummy and Daddy had a big row in the barn and didn't he go bowling off to work with the house keys, saying we were to stay out as

60

he wasn't having,' she paused dramatically, '*a whore and her brats* soiling up his house.'

Lizza opened the door wider. 'Come in, come in.' She peered into the damp wall of rain behind them. 'Where's your mother then?'

'Oh, she's way behind. Didn't he give her a good belting and her leg's lame now! I brought all the heavy stuff and Liam on my pram, she only has Anne-Marie on hers. But she'll be hours yet.'

It was half an hour before Mrs Callaghan arrived, limping badly and white as flour dough. Lizza put her on the sofa in the front room with her leg up. 'How could he do this to you, Mrs Callaghan, how could he do it?'

' 'Cause the man's a raving lunatic, that's why. Some man in the pub had given him a black eye and he turned on me,' said Mrs Callaghan wearily. 'I wouldn't perform there on the straw where the children were, so he gave me a beating. With his blessed umbrella if you please.' She lifted her skirt and showed the purple weals caked with blood.

It took Lizza half an hour to clean Mrs Callaghan up and dress her injuries. Then the baby started to cry and Josie fed her from a grubby bottle while the two women had a cup of tea.

'Why do you take it?' said Lizza.

' 'Cause women always do, I suppose. The men always want that one thing and the women is too tired or too hating to give it, or not wanting another little 'un, so instead they get a beating. Instead of *it*, I suppose. They

61

make their mark on you in another way. But I suppose my legs are only this bad because he came for me and this time I got in first, with the umbrella. Then he seemed to go berserk. Grabbed the umbrella and...well...you see. I did it because the littl'ns were there, see?' She sipped her tea. 'Don't look so worried, Mrs King. It could be worse. He brings a wage in. White-collar job. Too good for me, or even his old mother, God rest her soul. According to him, that is. And at least other women aren't a problem. I'd trust him to the other ends of the earth with women. Who would have him? But in all the other things he's an evil bastard. Evil.'

Lizza buried her nose in her cup and thought this was yet another reason for not telling Roland about the attack.

The Callaghans stayed all day. The little house seemed to shrink even smaller as Lizza kept tripping over Liam or tucking in the screaming baby or answering Josie's questions.

In the late afternoon, there was an air-raid warning and Lizza insisted they all stay, that they shouldn't set out for the fields again. So she tucked Mrs Callaghan and the young ones under the stairs with Rebecca and huddled herself under the kitchen table with Josie.

Roland came back just before the all-clear, tripping over the two prams in the front room in the dark. Under the kitchen door came the beam of the little lamp. He could hear children snoring.

'God almighty, what's this, Lizza?' he roared.

He was assaulted by a babble of voices, an

emergence of bodies and an exhalation of sweat coming out of the kitchen.

'Mr King, me daddy beat me mammy...'

'Mr King, your wife kindly offered us shelter...'

'Roland, Mr Callaghan locked them out...'

Exhausted from one shift at work succeeded immediately by a night watching for fires across the city, he looked from one to the other, blank-faced.

'I've just come to get changed,' he said coolly to Lizza, 'a wash and a freshen up and then I'm needed back at work. There's this new man coming, the Pole.'

He picked his way through the mess of alien people and objects in his own kitchen, and made his way up the stairs.

Maeve Callaghan turned anxiously to Lizza. 'Mrs King, I'm sorry if...'

Lizza laughed. 'He's tired, Mrs Callaghan. Always on his mountainous horse when he's tired. And could you find it in you somewhere to call me Lizza? We've all survived together here, after last night. We might all be dead. And I can't go on calling you Mrs Callaghan.'

Maeve grinned broadly and went back into the kitchen. 'As long as I don't have to call Mr King anything but that. It'd be like calling His Holiness Paddy. Now would it be too forward of me to make us all a cup of tea?'

Upstairs in the bathroom, Roland heard the great spurt of laughter and his anger at the invasion increased. He would have given anything to put his weary head down on the bed and luxuriated in a few hours' sleep. But now he had to go to the factory and meet this Pole, who had drawings from Germany for the new tool. He pulled his cheek flat to shave without cutting it. He couldn't think the Germans would have got further than themselves on the fuel feed: he had seen fragments from the crashed planes. But... His mind filled up comfortably with speculation about the tool, and Lizza and her rabble of visitors vanished from it entirely.

CHAPTER 5

Roland turned off his lathe and peered through the mesh wall, watching as the stranger came down the line. He was tall, broad-shouldered, but he walked lightly, his narrow body carrying little weight. He had slightly heavy features and odd hair, a kind of thick patchwork of auburn and black. His suit was loose-fitting, though well cut, and he carried a soft grey trilby. A battered rucksack was slung across his back. The stranger drew more than one glance from the turbaned girls as he walked beside the stocky figure of Pieter Vann.

Pieter Vann squeezed into the narrow space beside Roland's bench. 'Here is Roland King, Mr Sobieski.' Roland noticed the hand was soft. No engineer, this. 'He will be in charge of the project on this new tool for the petrol feed and

64

will assess the potential of the other tools.'

Krystof Sobieski clicked his heels and bowed slightly before he shook hands with Roland. 'An honour to meet you, Mr King. Mr Vann has told me you are a gifted engineer.'

'You are an engineer yourself, Mr Sob— Sob—?'

'You must call me Krystof. I myself have trouble saying names like "MacNamara" and "Hindhaugh".' He said them perfectly. 'And no, I am not an engineer, nothing so useful. I am an artist. For a month or so employed,' he smiled thinly, 'under some duress, as a copyist in a plant in eastern Germany.' He dropped the rucksack on to the bench and started to open the top. 'Before I started my long walk...'

'We'll look at the papers in my office.' Pieter Vann picked up the rucksack and shepherded the two men back along the shop and up the steps to his scruffy heaped-up office.

He sat behind his desk. 'Now, Mr King, I need you to work on the spec for this new mounting with...Mr...er...Krystof. They must be precise. Steel's short anyway. Then we can get them into production. They'—he always called the Ministry 'they'—'want the mounting developed, tested on production models by Christmas. Always they want things yesterday.'

'Will there be time?' Roland looked at Krystof.

The Pole shrugged. 'I would not know. I have said I am no engineer. I just watched the tool being developed in their factory, so I might be some help. Here—I've a sheet here which is my

65

drawing from memory of the men working.' He tipped out the papers and spread them across the desk. 'They—your Ministry people—took the original ones.'

Unlike the usual detailed geometric planning designs, this drawing seemed to leap from the page. The steel tool almost glittered among the looping cables. At one side of the drawing, beside the lathe, Krystof Sobieski had incorporated an image of a worker, who was lovingly polishing the new tool with an oily rag. He was wearing dungarees and had a shock of fair hair and long, blunt-ended fingers.

Roland laughed. 'My counterpart. He'll be a Jerry then?'

'No. That is Anton, from Czechoslovakia—transported to work there from prison, like me. He vanished after the tool was finished. I never saw him again.'

Roland whistled. 'How d'you get here then?'

'I walked.'

'What?'

'Walked. Got away from that factory. An evil place; a torture chamber. The women...' He paused. 'I walked through Germany, Italy, Hungary, through France, where the French had me in prison, then on to Marseilles. Then to England.'

'You make it sound easy.'

Krystof shrugged. 'Your people thought it too easy although many beside me did it. They had me telling the story again and again. But many have done similar journeys. And worse things happened to others.' He laughed. 'You might say it was worse when I got here, finding the right person to show these drawings to, then convincing him that I wasn't a spy or a Nazi *plant*. I had ten nights in jail here, where it was worse than in France. Then weeks in a place with *more comfortable* chairs, *more comfortable* questions...'

'You speak good English,' said Roland, frowning. 'A kind of English.'

Krystof laughed. 'What you can hear is your county of Devon. My own grandmother came from Devon, the daughter of a sea captain. And always we had nursemaids from there...'

'Well, all that's over now,' said Pieter, as he stood up, the manager again. 'I've work to do on the shop floor. You settle in to work here with Roland. Lock the door behind me. No one but you to see those drawings.' He looked at Roland. 'I need to have that spec ready to act on by the end of the day, Roland.'

'You'll have it, Mr Vann.' Roland smiled slowly. He was intrigued by the task, and by the Pole whose grandfather, like his own father, was a sea captain.

'Well, look who's here!'

Josie was peering sideways through Lizza's net curtain as a firm knock resounded through the house. Lizza was clearing the crumby residue of the morning meal from the kitchen table. Rebecca and Liam were still sitting up to the table, eyeing each other over butterless slices of bread, spread with Lizza's precious wild damson jam.

Maeve Callaghan shuffled across to the door and opened it to her husband. 'What is it, Theo?'

He waved a brown envelope in her face. 'I'm called up, Maeve. Seems they've removed my exemption. I need you round there to help me get ready. I'll have to do my bit. There's no question,' he added virtuously, 'of me trying to get out of it...'

Lizza was standing behind Maeve now. He returned her stare with bland indifference. She folded her arms and put up her chin.

'Called up?' chuckled Maeve. 'Well, there's a turn up. How long is it you've been wriggling on that hook? I tell you what, Theo. Why don't you go across and put on that kettle. Me and the littl'ns'll be there in no time.'

She shut the door behind him.

'You'll go to him?' said Lizza. 'After he did that to you?'

'Won't I?' said Maeve, grinning. 'I'll go there and give him some dinner, I'll iron his clothes and maybe even give him what he wants, tonight.' She was pushing items at random into one of the prams, on top of the sleeping Anne-Marie. 'And then, pretty soon, I'll hand him over to Jerry. And, God forgive me, I hope they sort him out. No fate is bad enough,' she said calmly. 'They can have the old bugger. I'll have my house and my bed to myself for the first time in sixteen years.'

That afternoon, Lizza had to queue in three shops to get fish and a tin of corned beef and some off-coupon second-hand material which had lined some old stage curtains. She would send the material home to Beatrice, who was good at the sow's-ear-into-silk-shirt routine.

She came into the house cold and miserable, unwilling to face the post-Callaghan mess and an unlit fire. There was a letter from Beatrice on the mat. She forced herself to light the fire, settle Rebecca with a drink of milk, and make herself a cup of tea before she allowed herself the pleasure of reading it.

Dear Lizza,

Thank you for your package of buttons and embroidery silks. Where do you get these things? I've some upholstery webbing so I'll make you an embroidered belt fastened with those two nice little leather buttons. It will dress up that brown wool dress of yours a treat.

Things here are as you would expect. Ma still works like there's no tomorrow, even though I do the house. Makes broth to take to old Mr Gallagher and the Roberts twins, both of which are laid up with flu. (Mr Gallagher's grandson is in trouble over a pig. He got two and fed them with slops contributed from the street. One was properly sold in the market. The other he got permission to slaughter and duly did. Now a man from the council says he may only use what would have been his ration and he cannot either sell or give the rest away. There's been a few midnight visits to that house, I can tell you.)

Ma knits and alters clothes for the orphans down in Carhoe Orphanage. Goes down there often as not to deliver them. One day I'm sure she'll pinch a couple of orphans and bring them home. She needs babies and children around her so she can always be the queen bee, the eternal provider. And Alex is no good to her now on that count. He's bigger by the day, all taken with the war and those aeroplanes. He goes on about the Navy, says they train pilots, too. Talking of that, it seems a plane coming down from a Glasgow raid loosed a bomb on Carhoe Co-op just last week. It blasted all the back of the buildings, where the butcher's department keeps the beast before the slaughter. Said you could smell roast beef for hours afterwards. I went down and saw it burning. There was a man beside me carrying twins in a kind of sling made from a woollen shawl. They would be about three. I thought of you, Lizza. No people hurt of course. Not like where you are. Alex and Ma continue to be at daggers drawn. He is determined to join up and she is determined he won't. If anything, one is as bad as the other. No word from Jonnie. I must say he is a big miss here, being the cheerful one. There was a letter from our Bernard in Cornwall, digging away there for victory. They are all well. Young John and Kit are good scholars like their dad, and you. But James is not walking though nearly two. Lazy like his ma. But no word from Renee in Scotland. But she was never a letter writer. Not like you. I often think of you and hope that you take every care so that no damage comes to you and yours.

Your sister
Beatrice

Lizza smiled as she folded the letter back into its envelope. At least Bernard, in his reserved occupation, was safe with that slattern wife of his and his three boys. As safe as any miner is, fathoms down below the earth. And Renee, dependable Renee, who had followed her miner husband to Scotland, never did write. She would be taking even this in her sturdy stride.

She was still smiling when Roland finally got home at nine o'clock. The house was shining clean and she had a corned-beef hash keeping warm for him, over steam.

She took his coat from him. 'You look tired.'

He sat and put his elbows on the kitchen table, his chin in his hands. 'Long day, Lizza. Doing specs for this new tool. I told you this Pole—his name is Krystof Sobieski—he brought plans for this tool from Germany, and can you credit it, Lizza, he walked here? His grandfather—no, great-grandfather, was a...escaped the Nazis, not once but twice, walked through Germany, through France, and then...' His speech was slurred with exhaustion.

'Whoa!' laughed Lizza. 'Slow down! Eat your dinner. Take a breath and then you can tell me about this wonderful Pole!'

He had finished his meal and was stretched out on a chair before the fire, when he looked round the spotless room bereft of sprawling and wriggling bodies. 'Where are they? What happened to the ubiquitous Callaghans?'

'They're back home. The ubiquitous Mr

Callaghan came to collect them. Apparently he's to be called up. Escaped it so far, but they've caught up with him.'

He laughed shortly. 'They'll run riot all together without him in there.'

She stood up and started to clash the dishes into the sink. 'He's a hateful man, Roland. A monster. He did—does terrible things to her. And...'

'And what?'

'Nothing. There's a letter there from our Beatrice. Apparently they've dropped a bomb on Carhoe Co-op. No one hurt.'

He sighed. 'Any bomb up there's an aberration. Much safer than here. You should be up there, Lizza. Out of all this...'

'No,' she said. 'I'm better here with you.'

She finished the washing-up and came to sit opposite him by the fire. 'Now you can tell me all about this wonderful Polish person. What did you say his name was?'

She looked across and he was fast asleep, head to one side, and mouth slightly open.

She had pushed him upstairs, undressed him and hauled him on to the bed before she realised that there had been no air-raid warning. No siren. No raid. She got into bed beside him. Tonight she would have had time to tell him about Theo Callaghan and the attack, to tell him what she had felt, and how, in the light of all these other things that were happening, a mere attempted rape was nothing.

'Is that it, Roland?' she said into his unconscious back. 'Is a mere rape nothing

72

at all beside all the other things that go on?'

She looked at his back with resentment and, easing herself up in bed, took her small notebook out of the drawer in the bedside table and started to write.

I am invisible to him, a convenient shadow in his life. He worries about his war and his planes; he comes back and eats my dinner, sleeps on my chair, in my bed.

She allowed the anger to flow through her, clenching her teeth; her knuckles showed white around the pencil. Then the rage was replaced by guilt.

I'm lucky to have him here; he could be away in some unknown place. He could be in hospital like others after the so-called glorious retreat from Dunkirk; he could be dead, buried in some mass grave off the Dunkirk beach; he could be behind barbed wire somewhere like Jonnie.

But he was here beside her, snoring gently. Exhausted. Dead to the world. She put her pen away, fighting back the desire to write something about Maeve Callaghan and how lucky she was: Theo going off, away, so that she had her house, her chair, her bed to herself.

Later, twisting in sleep, she seemed to be wrestling again against the oppressive weight of Theo Callaghan, fighting him off, raging silently into the face above her. She forced one hand up and managed to strike a blow at the face, which became pale and sprouted a dark moustache. The eyes shone and a voice which did and did not come from the mouth started to harangue her for hating England and not being able to do this for England. 'Lie back! Lie back!' the voice roared. In spite of herself she was aroused. Then the mouth opened and a great stream of noise emerged.

'Lizza! Lizza! Wake up!' Roland was shaking her and her ears were filled now with the wail of the siren.

She groaned. 'Not again, not again.'

'Get Rebecca!' he mumbled, his lips not yet awake. He was pulling on his trousers over his pyjamas. 'Get up! Get up!'

It turned out to be a false alarm, but by the time she knew that she was wide awake under the stairs, reading the story of Brer Rabbit to a tearful Rebecca.

This time when they came back to bed, Roland was wide awake, roused by the running in the streets, the shouting and the final relief. He pulled her towards him and she felt his lips slide from her cheekbone to her soft neck.

She pulled away.

'What is it, Lizza?'

'It's this bloody war, that's what it is.' She turned over and pulled her knees up towards her chin.

He fitted himself round her from behind and

74

put his arm across her, over the bedclothes. 'We're all right, though, Lizza, aren't we, in spite of this bloody war?'

She would have liked, then, to tell him about Theo Callaghan, but she couldn't.

'Mmmm.' She felt him relax against her as he dropped again into his instant sleep.

After ten minutes she got up and went to the window and lifted the black-out curtain. The street was enveloped in velvet darkness. Above the roofs the moon rode high and bright; ineffectual drifts of cloud, like skeined wool, pulled their way across its surface. No wonder there had been an alarm. Someone somewhere would be getting it.

Words spilled from her mouth in a whisper: '...*make guilty of our own disasters the sun, the moon, and the stars*'. Now where had she read that? She sighed. It came to something when you saw a bright moon and cursed it.

This time when she went back to bed she went straight to sleep. She dreamed again of Hitler but this time his face broadened into the comic face of Charlie Chaplin and she was chasing him round the kitchen, finally managing to set fire to him with the new patent lighter she had on her cooker. At this, he put out his arms and raced away, mimicking flying, just like the boys in the street when they were playing at being the RAF dive-bombing the Hun in the Battle of Britain.

CHAPTER 6

'Bremner!' The voice roared into Alex's ears.

'Yes, sir?'

'Answer the question!'

'What question was that, sir?' Alex blinked over the shiny navy backs and bony bristling craniums of his school-mates at the pockmarked, moustached face of 'Callah' Herring, his history teacher.

'The question was, "Can we call the Industrial Revolution a revolution?" '

'I can't see that it matters, sir, what we call it.'

The bristled heads turned and eyes peered first at him, then at Mr Herring, shining in anticipation of another set-piece battle.

'And how might that be, Bremner?' Herring lowered his forehead so that his tiny chin vanished and his eyes bulged, giving him the fish-like appearance that had resulted in his nickname, 'Callah', after the street-call of the herring-sellers.

'Why, sir, the only point about the Industrial Revolution is whether now we're at the stage where we can make enough guns and bombs and planes to beat the stuffin' out of them Nazis. The war's in the air now. The warriors are the pilots. Some only a year more than us...'

A low cheer went around the class.

Callah's face went dull red. 'You may boast a crude logic in your statement, Bremner, but in fact it is ignorant, ill-informed and frivolous. Come out here.'

An anticipatory ripple went round the class. They liked a good beating. Three swipes on each hand from Callah's thick cane made Alex flinch, but he didn't cry out. He came back down the narrow aisle, his stinging hands under his armpits.

Herring adjusted his sleeves and beamed around, happy as he always was after giving whacks. 'Now, gentlemen, before we return to the powerful forces of change in the eighteenth century, may I say one word about war? There may be arguments that this war we're at is just and that the enemy is the enemy of civilisation and justice...' No eye met his. Heads were sunk on hands. '...but let me tell you there is no romance in war. It is not a Robin Hood world. War is about the fracturing of flesh and the death of innocents. In the last war—called, if I remember rightly, "the war to end all wars"—I have seen it. I have done it. There is no romance in it. Do not underestimate what men are being called to do in the name of England... Now, may we return to the significant matter of the Industrial Revolution?'

The red swelling on Alex's hands had developed to black bruising when he got home that night for tea. His hands lay loosely on the table while his grandmother muttered her usual prayer at the end of the meal. Then Beatrice grabbed his hand as he reached across the table for one of her fatless sponge cakes and turned it over. 'What's this?'

'Fractured flesh. Got it off Callah Herring. For cheeking.'

She dropped the hand and picked up the canvas belt she was embroidering for Lizza.

'You should curb your tongue. What was it this time?' His grandmother was stacking the dishes in a neat pile on a tin tray.

'About the war. Not to take it lightly. About fractured flesh and things.'

'You should listen to him. He was there in the last one. Quartermaster in the Royal Welch...'

'This is different. It's not the trenches. I'm sick of hearing about the trenches. This time it's fast tanks and submarines. Heinkels and Spitfires.'

'You're just as dead. Flesh just as fractured.' Alice Bremner picked up the tray and moved across to the scullery door.

'If everyone felt like that, old Adolf'd be in here tomorrow in his jack-boots.'

'We stopped the Kaiser last time. That was supposed to end it all. Now look at it. Seems like there's no difference.'

'Defeatist talk. The authorities'll get on to you about that. It could lose us the war. We all have to do our bit. You two are keepin' the home fires burning. I'm doin' nothin',' he said defiantly.

Beatrice looked up from her sewing. 'I'll be called up meself soon, for the factories. Bombs are the last thing I want to make, like. Anyway,

78

you do your fire-watching on the school-roof, Alex. Every other night.'

It had been fun at first, clanking around those forbidden areas at night with big boots and a tin hat, making tea on a little primus stove. It had been fun, watching the planes go overhead, on their way north or south, checking which were theirs and which were ours. One night he had been stuck up there with Callah Herring. At one o'clock the teacher had gone off to do his very assiduous round. A single plane had gone over and Alex had danced around the roof, yelling and shouting, 'I'm here, you bastard Hitler-loving squirt, here! Come and get me!'

But the hum of the plane's engines had faded as it went further north to wreak its damage on the banks of the Tyne. And Callah Herring came back and pretended he had not heard his pupil's outburst.

Now he said to Beatrice, 'Fire-watching? That? When will we ever have fires up here? Now down where our Lizza is, you'd be some use, being a fire-watcher!' He paused, then proceeded with some deliberation, watching his grandmother out of the corner of his eye. 'No bloody use here. Them Nazi bastards might be interested in Tyneside and Teesside. Or Hartlepool or Sunderland. Or heaving Glasgow a big'n. But here? Bloody waste of time. The bastards aren't interested in us.'

'Stop, Alex,' warned Beatrice.

But his grandmother was on him, brandishing a long broom handle. 'Stop that filthy language. Stop it!'

He stood up. 'I'm tellin' yer, Gram, I'm not goin' back to that school. Bastards like Callah Herring...'

His mouth closed as blows rained on to his shoulders, the bristles scratching his face. He let three land, then wrested the broom from his grandmother and leaned it neatly against the pantry door. 'You shouldn't waste your energy on me now, Gram. We're not supposed to waste energy. Don't you know there's a war on?' Then he dodged out, slamming the door behind him. He opened it again and stuck his head into the space. 'Like I say, Gram, I'm not goin' back to that school. Never again.'

He walked down the backs, whistling his personal promise to hang Hitler's washing on the Siegfried Line. The allotments, when he got to them, were spooky in the growing dark. Most of them were well dug over for the winter. One or two lean-to greenhouses had signs of life in them, shadows of old men and women tending their pots and nurturing their winter shoots. Beatrice was good on their allotment. Made sure they were never short of vegetables. She took 'Digging for Victory' seriously.

He made his way to his Uncle Jonnie's patch, now being kept up by Beatrice, undid the string latch to the shed, and squeezed his way in. He dropped the black-out on the little window, struck a match to light the storm lantern on the top shelf, and pulled the rubber sheeting off an object he had been staring at with fascination for some weeks now.

'Now, you beauty,' he said.

80

In the week since Theo Callaghan had left, his wife seemed to have grown two inches, and shed pounds and years in equal proportions.

Lizza eyed Maeve's high heels and the gravy-browned legs with the artful line mimicking a seam. 'You're looking smart, Maeve!' She opened the door wider to let her neighbour in out of the drizzle.

'Well, shouldn't a girl make the best of herself in these God-forsaken days?' Maeve collapsed on to a hard chair, kicking off the left shoe and rubbing her ankle, then stretching her leg out to view it appreciatively. 'That gravy browning is a mixed blessing. Had a hungry dog licking away at me ankles the other night. A four-legged one too. Anyway, now himself is away I can put a speck of make-up on without being raped in me own bedroom.'

'Was that why you...'

'Went like an old woman? Well, it'd have taken a nun's habit to keep him off you. Even then...' Her voice tailed off. 'But you wouldn't want to hear that with that fine feller of yours, I suppose...'

Her tone invited confidence, but Lizza resisted, and changed the subject. 'So where are you going dressed up like a dog's dinner?'

'The matinée at the Savoy. They say *Goodbye, Mr Chips* is on, but I don't know that it'd be back so soon. That Robert Donat, though, don't you like him? Don't you go for him? But then you don't need to. You've got your own Robert Donat at home.'

Lizza grinned, refusing again to be drawn. 'So are you going on your own for this romance with Mr Donat?'

'Nah. No fun. I'm going with Mary O'Connel, who I talk to after mass on Sundays. She's a saint. Isn't her man away on minesweepers, and isn't she on her own too? I thought a trip to the pictures would cheer her up.' She pulled her shoe back on and stood up, wiggling her heels to get comfortable. 'The thing is, Lizza, would you keep an ear for next door? It just needs an ear. Isn't Josie there, the little mother, and quite capable?' She leaned towards Lizza's mantelpiece mirror, licked her finger and stroked her darkened brow upwards. 'I'll be back at tea-time, ready for the Trek.'

'I'll keep an ear for them,' said Lizza.

Maeve kissed her on the cheek and Lizza smelled the slightly antiseptic smell of Evening in Paris. She squashed the disloyal speculation as to whether it really was the sainted Mary O'Connel who would be the cinema companion. Or if it were her, was she really such a saint after all?

Maeve had gone just ten minutes when Josie was at the door with a screaming Anne-Marie in her arms and Liam hanging on to her skirts. Rebecca shouted down from upstairs, where she had been having her afternoon nap.

Lizza put down her book. 'Come in, Josie. It's open house here.'

Josie thrust the screaming Anne-Marie into her arms and leapt up the stairs two at a time, calling behind her, 'I don't know why Mammy leaves the baby with me, I can't do a thing with her. I'll get the little'n for you, Mrs King.'

All through the afternoon Josie and Lizza played gin rummy while Liam and Rebecca rolled around in their private battle on the floor. Anne-Marie, fed and changed, slept peacefully in her pram. Barely concentrating on the game, Lizza thought about the war. This is what it was, really. Well. Half the time. This was what the war was, half the time. Boring. Hours of waiting, desultory activity, waiting for the now almost inevitable siren, then the routine flurry of activity, the routine waiting, the routine all-clear. No such thing as a good night's sleep...

'Mrs King! Mrs King! It's your drop!' Josie's pale face was glaring into hers.

Maeve Callaghan got back at six, her face scrubbed clear of the bright lipstick and with tidemark stains round her ankles where the painted seams and the gravy-browning stain had run in the rain. She shepherded her flock cheerfully out of the door. 'Sure, there was no need to have them in here, Mrs King. Josie is a big girl, quite capable...'

They had just reached their own door when round the corner of the street came a sorry figure: a tall fair boy in a belted school Burberry, his fair hair plastered down on to his head so that it glowed like a bulb in the early evening light. He was pushing a motorbike which had one flat tyre and groaned its objection at every turn of the wheel.

They watched without a word as he wheeled the bike up Mrs King's garden path and knocked on her door.

Lizza came to answer, thinking Josie had forgotten something, and beamed when she saw him. 'Alex!'

He winked and grinned. 'Now, Lizza! Here I am to help you rub that bastard Führer's nose in it.'

She pulled him inside and peered past him at the motorbike, then smiled at the watching Callaghans, who hurriedly closed their door. 'You came on that, Alex? What...?'

'Jonnie's. He left it in the allotment shed. I had to pay through the nose for petrol from this lad whose dad's on the Black.' He removed his sodden coat and his teeth started to chatter.

She took the coat and hung it round a hard chair in the front room and led him through to the kitchen fire. She went into a cupboard and pulled out a towel.

'Here. Dry off while I make you some tea.'

The kitchen door opened and Josie's head popped round. 'Mammy says could you lend a couple of spoons of sugar, Mrs King? We're out of rations and she's no good without her cup of sweet tea before the Trek.' Her round, bright eyes took in the boy by the fire.

Lizza grinned. Life was getting less boring by the second. 'Come in, Josie, if that's what you're after. This is Alex Bremner. My brother. Alex, this is Josie.'

Alex came out from under the towel, his fine pale hair sticking up like a halo. He grinned. ' 'Lo, Josie.'

' 'Lo, Alex.' She stayed by the door and

84

finally dragged her eyes away from him to watch Lizza carefully spooning three teaspoons of sugar into a screw of paper.

Lizza smiled at her. 'Alex is come down here to get in spitting distance of Hitler. It's too quiet for him up North.'

Josie returned her glance to the boy, who, still grinning, was unbuttoning his shirt now. She grabbed the sugar and fled, but not before she heard the laughter pealing out behind her.

CHAPTER 7

Lizza put Alex in Rebecca's little bed, and Rebecca herself had to sleep in the cot, which had been scoured and polished, then left under a clean sheet till the new baby came. Lizza had first bought the cot at an auction for the twins, but neither had ever slept in it. In her four and a half weeks on the earth, little Elizabeth had been tucked into a dressing-table drawer more appropriate for her size.

The night he arrived Alex went to bed at the same time as Rebecca and, there being no siren, slept through till morning. His snores were audible right through the house.

Lizza told Roland about the arrival of her nephew when he came home from work at midnight. There was little reaction; she wasn't even sure whether he had heard her. In bed she tried again, saying that Alex arriving like that reminded her of Roland himself, arriving at Bracks Hill on a motorbike in 1926, to take her back to Bradford, after she had moped at home right through the General Strike. Roland sighed then, and reached out, pulled her to him. Then he put his chin on her shoulder and dropped off to sleep.

In the morning Roland was off to work before the rest of them were up: Rebecca and Alex still lay fast asleep in the back room. Lizza stayed very quietly under the sheets, listening to Roland's whistle as he scraped the black off his toast.

At eight o'clock Alex leapt down the stairs and enjoyed a gigantic breakfast, eating four of the potato cakes Lizza had made from her own potatoes, and wolfing the last rasher of bacon in the house.

'I expect you've brought your ration book!' said Lizza absently, concentrating on guiding Becky's hand, with its spoonful of mash, to her mouth.

He smiled across at her, his perfect teeth gleaming. 'In the bag, Lizza. And six pounds that I've saved. You can have that if you like.'

'Where did you manage to accumulate that much?'

He shrugged. 'Delivering groceries for Mason's. Other jobs for people. Gram wouldn't take any of it. You can have it if you like.'

She brandished the spoon. 'Keep it! You'll need it. We might be short of a lot of things, with rationing and this push for work. But money isn't one of them, with all this blasted overtime. So, what do you think you'll do in Coventry, when everybody's running away from here?'

'Find what it's like in a front-line town. In the thick of it. Thought I'd get a job in one of the factories, while I was waiting.'

'What is it you're waiting for?'

'Well, I'll be eighteen on November the fourteenth. Then I'll join up. Is there just one more of these? They're smashin'. Thought the legend was that you couldn't cook.'

'It's the war. We're all driven to desperate measures.' Lizza gave him her last potato cake. 'What does Ma think of you coming here?'

He shrugged. 'I don't know. She's been dead against any mention of me joining up, for months. Always seeing me dead on the field of battle. So I didn't tell her. Left her a note. We had this big row yesterday. No, the day before.'

'A row?' She had always marvelled at Alex's easy acceptance of the exceptional love and care offered him by his grandmother: his sheer lack of self-doubt. Her mother had given this boy an unconditional love, a love denied to her own grown-up children.

'Well, we did have this row over me calling the Nazis "bloody bastards". She whacked me with the broom.' He pulled his shirt to one side and peered down awkwardly to see the bruise, then grinned back across at her. 'I don't know whether it was the "bloody" or the "bastard" that was the problem. The "bastard" probably. Truth hurts.'

'Does it hurt you, Alex?'

He stood up and wiped his mouth with the back of his hand. 'Can't say it does. Me Gram has always been good with us. The good mother, you might say. But it's Beatrice sitting and saying nowt that sometimes gets me. I can't ask her about him. Just as well slit me throat.' He went and peered through the net curtains, his back to her. 'Do you know who he was, Lizza? Did you meet him?' His voice was muffled.

'Well, as you well know, Alex, I wasn't there. I was slaving over this weaving loom in Bradford.'

'You came home, though.'

'Yes. And I knew something had happened.'

He turned his back to the window and faced her. 'What happened? You know what happened.'

She thought of Theo Callaghan forcing himself on her and knew finally what had happened to Beatrice was rape. But that was just what she couldn't tell Alex. 'I think it was a secret thing. A love affair that went wrong. Beatrice never said. And I had to accept her secret.' Her eyes slid away from his bright stare towards Rebecca. She picked up a cloth to dab at Becky's potato-smeared face. 'It's all in the past, Alex. We are what we are.'

He shook his head. 'Maybe you're right. But it's easy for you to say...'

'That's where you're wrong, Alex. It's been easy for you. In that house, the centre of the universe for those two women. Never putting a foot wrong. Going to the grammar school...'

'I got there myself. I passed the exam.'

'So did I, but I still couldn't go. Our Bernard did too. And he couldn't go. Now here's Ma trying to hold you to her. Couldn't wait to get me away, though. At fourteen. As young as Josie next door...'

'Is she fourteen, that Josie?' Alex unclipped Rebecca from her chair and balanced her, squealing, on his head.

'Yes. A bit more, I think. And even Maeve Callaghan wouldn't let *her* go. But I was let go...'

'Me Gram would know you'd cope.' He lifted Rebecca down and swung her round.

She laughed. 'That's what Roland always says. And our Bernard. You all protect her.' She held out her arms for Rebecca, who jumped into them. Lizza heaved her up on to her own shoulders and slowly swung side to side.

He pulled on his crumpled school Burberry. 'Maybe we're protecting you. Where would you rather be, Lizza, here with Roland and Rebecca, or back there like Beatrice, right under me Gram's thumb?'

She put her head on one side. 'Ah, now I see what I missed! All that wisdom they teach you at the grammar school. Makes you sound like an old man at seventeen. And where might you be off to, in your fine top coat?'

'Can I borrow your bike? I want a ride round the town. To see round this place a bit. See the bomb damage.' He banged her forearm with his knuckle. 'That's wisdom for you! Know thine enemy!'

She laughed. 'The bike's in the garden shed. And the back tyre needs blowing up. Haven't used it much lately. There's more pram than bicycle these days, in my life.' She winced at her own self-pitying tone.

She smiled up into Alex's young face. She should have sent him straight home to safety, with a flea in his ear. But she knew she didn't want that. She was pleased to see this boy; to laugh at his careless talk, relish his jaunty style. She was clinging on to him like a lifebelt. Anything to break the boredom. Anything. Even a young boy on the loose, casting around before climbing into some cockpit to be blown to bits in the deep blue sky.

On the street, Alex flung his long legs over the saddle and commenced his careering progress towards the town centre. He relished again, as he had on entering the city, the endless streets, cheek-by-jowl with factories and workshops painted with their weird camouflage. And the scurrying people. He thought of the turbulent energy of a bee-hive near Bea's allotment, kept and tended by an old man from Bracks Hill.

At first Alex looked in vain for dramatic craters in the roads, streets of collapsed houses. Then he did come upon one block of bombed houses, close to a factory wall, which had been made good with tarpaulins and plywood. He stopped and braced himself with one foot on the dusty ground either side of the bike. Three walls of one section remained; ribbons of wallpaper

90

lifting in the cold air. Around the hollow square, the fences and gates were still standing. One gate was secured by a neat string tie. Behind the fence, spars of ragged wood poked their way out of the heap of rubble, on top of which was a glass rose the size of a dinner plate in an untouched frame of wood.

Alex leaned his bike against the fence and started to clamber up the mountain towards it.

'What yer think yer doin' there, mate?' came an odd deep voice from behind him.

Alex turned guiltily, lost his footing, and ended up at the bottom of the heap, clutching the glass window. He lifted his gaze resentfully into a half-familiar face.

'What yer think yer doing?' repeated Josie Callaghan in her normal voice. She jumped off her bike, throwing up her leg so he could see her knickers. She stood there in front of him, her skirt shrunken and ill-washed, her grey wool socks round her ankles.

He peered past her into the empty street. 'You're the lass that lives beside our Lizza an't yer? What're you playin' at, like?'

'Just keepin' a check on yer, ain't I? Says on the wireless to keep a sharp eye and ear for strangers...' She watched him thoughtfully as he stood up and dusted the fragments of red brick from his coat. 'So what was it you was doin'? Thievin'? There's a law against looters, you know.'

'Just thought I'd take a look round...' Alex's face burned. He had been caught wrong-footed in more than one way. Even his voice sounded slow and lame beside her sharp tones. 'Thought there might be something useful...'

She hooted. 'Do they know nothin' where you come from? There ain't nothin' left, twelve hours after Jerry smashes a place. Everything loose gets taken. Clothes. Ornaments.'

'I thought there was a law against it?'

'My mammy says there's another law. *"The Lord helps those who help themselves."* ' Her eyes narrowed. 'You wanna see where I keep my stuff?'

Alex stood up and with dramatic care placed the window-frame up against the collapsing fence. Then he brushed the fine dust off his coat. 'What stuff?'

'The stuff that gets left. The stuff that nobody wants.'

'Where is it?'

'I'll show you.' She was up on her bike again, throwing the words back at him. 'And bring that glass window! We'll keep it.'

Not sure what she meant by the 'we', he clambered back up on his own bike and, steering clumsily with one hand because of the window, followed her.

Josie stopped at a house whose roof had been tightly covered with tarpaulin and whose downstairs windows had been elaborately boarded up. The glass over the door was etched with the name 'Beaconsfield'. She looked up and down the empty street then quickly unfastened the gate and wheeled the bike down the path and around the side. She parked the bike in a covered lean-to between the house and the outhouses, then fiddled with a window and opened it.

She watched Alex park his bike and place the window-frame on the ground. 'Give us a bump up, mate,' she said.

He looked at her, frowning.

'Here, put your hands like this,' she said crossly, linking her fingers together in front of her. He obeyed and she put one foot in his hands, her hands on his shoulders, he caught a glimpse of knicker and she was through the window. Her face popped up again. 'Now go round the back. And bring that window with you.'

The door was open by the time he arrived. She peered behind him. 'Get in! Get in!'

'Come on! Come on!' She continued her harassing chant as she led the way upstairs, leaping two stairs at a time, the worn-down heels of her shoes flashing before him.

She pushed open the door to the gloomy back bedroom and he caught a glimpse of her knickers again as she squatted to turn on the single-bar built-in electric fire. He stared at the shining chrome. He had never seen a fire in a bedroom before.

She grinned up at him. 'The electricity should be off, but it ain't.'

There was a single bed in the corner covered with a wild variety of limp cushions. Crowded on the floor were objects and items of every kind: broken hammers, blunt chisels, chipped jugs, cups without handles, battered pans, torn books, a bedside lamp with no flex, a picture without a frame, a frame without a picture and a radio without valves.

Alex started to laugh. The room reminded him of a magpie's nest up behind the shed in Bea's allotment. Near the bee-hive when he came to think of it. 'Where d'you get this lot, then?'

'Where d'you think? Houses all across the town.'

He shook his head, pleased now to see this bossy girl's actions as childish; restored in his own mind to being the older and wiser of the pair of them.

'I always wait twelve hours.' She picked up a cracked meat dish and turned it over, fingering the flowered rim. 'I always wait twelve hours. When nobody comes for them I pick'm up.'

He collapsed on to the cold sticky lino by the fire. 'Must've taken some collecting, this lot,' he said, only half teasing.

She grinned. 'You bet. It takes a full day after a raid.'

'What about school?'

'School?' She sniffed, scornfully. 'Haven't been since the summer. I'm always down here.'

'Who else comes here then?'

'Just me. I climbed in one day and thought it'd make a good...' She paused.

'Den?' he said, suddenly relishing the childish word.

She straightened up a chisel beside its neighbour. 'That's kids' stuff.'

'We, me friend Len Torrass and me, we had a den a few years back...'

'Where was that?'

94

He laughed. 'Don't laugh, mind! It was halfway up an old pit heap, made of an old spready bush that was already there and some pit timbers we dragged near a quarter of a mile.'

'How old were you?'

'Twelve. Len Torrass was fourteen. He's in the Merchant Navy now. Or was. His ma had notice he was missing at sea last month. U-boat sank them.'

Josie walked around the room, pulling at the bedcover and peering through the taped-up windows. She lifted up the looted window-pane with the rose and leaned it against the taped frame. 'There, you can see it better against the light,' she said with satisfaction. 'Come and see!'

He hauled himself to his feet and peered through the red glass of the rose, and the dusty criss-cross of sticky tape, into the bright October day. He could feel a heat coming from her, and a faint smell which reminded him of washday dinners.

She leaned away from him so she could look him in the eye. 'Do you swear?' she asked.

'I do sometimes.'

'What do you say?'

'I say "bloody" sometimes. And "bastard". Usually when I'm talking about the Nazis.'

'Do you say these?' She mouthed a word into his ear, followed closely by another.

He went brick red. 'They're mucky words. You can't say them. You're a lass.'

She laughed. 'So I can. I can say them when

I'm up on my hands against the wall, and I can say them in here, in this house. This is no-man's land. Left behind by the cowards who lived here before. Belongs to me now.'

Alex felt powerless. He felt his hands and feet were too big for him. He felt like a country fool against this sharp city kid. He also felt like he felt when it was nearly dinner-time at home and his Gram's meat pies were throwing out their wonderful flavour, making his nose, his whole body itch with hunger.

He distracted himself by conjuring up a question. 'Have you seen a bomb drop? Not just heard it, like, from the shelter, but seen it?'

'Course I have,' she said scornfully. 'September. Tea-time. Hadn't even got home for tea and down he comes in daylight.'

'Who?'

'Jerry dive-bomber. What a pilot! One minute he wasn't there and the next'—she put out her arms and was the plane—'he was flying through the cloud'—she turned round and round—'twisting through cables off the barrage balloons.' She hopped to one side, then the other. 'Zigzagging through our bullets, then wham! Direct hit on the Standard. Fires, explosion...' She spread out her arms, flopped herself hard on to the bed, shaking her hands and feet in a frenzy.

He put a hand towards her shoulder but she twisted herself away from him and leapt back on to the floor. 'Then he lit off back up through the clouds and that was it.' She breathed out slowly and squatted beside the fire, clicking the heavy steel switch. 'You have to go now. I've things to do.'

All he could do was leave. Back on the pavement he lifted the front of the bike and stood on one pedal until the wheel whirred to a start, then looked up to see the girl's narrow face staring down at him through the criss-cross tape at the dusty window. She had taken down the rose window. He wondered what had made her do that. His rose window.

He put his head down and pedalled like mad. She was just a little kid, pinching things. Pinching his rose window.

That week Alex went three times to Beaconsfield. He was never there more than three minutes before Josie would turn up, having followed him all the way from Lizza's. They talked in a desultory fashion, about Josie's collection and the Trek.

'What do you do? Sleep under hedgerows?'

'Nah. There's this barn up a narrow pathway that I found. Used to have hay but's half empty now. My dad talked to the farmer, who couldn't say no, there being a war on. But he ain't happy. Sure, he's livid half the time.'

'You know, you talk funny?'

'*I* talk funny? And you speak the King's English, I suppose?'

'Nah. Half the time you talk like your ma, kind of half Irish: "begorrah" and all that. And the other hand you talk this "ain't" this and "ain't" that, like the kids in this town.'

'You'll talk like that soon, and when you get

97

in to drive those aeroplanes you talk about, it'll be "what-ho chaps!" like it is on the newsreels. Say it.' She poked him in the ribs.

'What ho, chaps!'

She shrieked with laughter and started to leap around the room like a monkey.

He caught her by her narrow shoulders and made her stand still. 'Give me a kiss,' he said.

She folded her lips tight and shook her head.

He bent down and put his lips on her hard cheekbone. How soft her skin was there. Even softer further down on her cheek. She turned her head; her tight-shut lips met his and a bolt of lightning shot through his brain and landed somewhere in his solar plexus. His hands tightened on her shoulders and he tried to pull her towards him.

She pulled away so she could look more clearly into his face. 'Do you know, they kiss sometimes with their mouths open?'

His white skin went bright red. 'The lads say that...'

'Can we have a go?'

His hands came down and grasped hers tight. 'Nothing spoiling. But you have to close your eyes.'

She closed her eyes, and put her mouth, slightly open, towards him. He brought his mouth towards it and felt the unimaginable softness of her lips on his. The tip of her tongue started to tease the inner edge of his lips. The sweat was pouring down his back.

She pushed him from her. 'There. What do you think?'

'What do I think? I...'

'Did you like it?'

'Yes. I...where d'you...'

'Everybody knows...' she said scornfully.

'Can we do it again?'

'No. Another time. Let's sort these things.'

But that day when he pulled her out of the pantry window he kept her against the shadowy wall and pushed himself near so that he could feel her enticing little body close to his.

'Give me one of those kisses,' he pleaded.

'Oh, well, ain't you the keen one,' she giggled, putting up her lips and closing her eyes.

Within a week Alex and Josie were open in their comings and goings, watched by Lizza and Maeve Callaghan from their respective houses. One day Maeve Callaghan (taller in her ankle-strap shoes and well made up now, her wild hair in a snood, her generous figure completely under the control of a good corset) stopped Lizza on her way to the Co-op. 'Sure it's nice to see the young ones getting on so well don't you think, Lizza? You wouldn't think there was a war on.' She laughed heartily.

Maeve's interest brought Lizza up short. Up till that point she had watched the sweethearting of the young pair with the kind of benevolent detachment she brought to the films she enjoyed so much at the Roxy. But Maeve's interest made it real and she saw afresh Josie's thin child-like form, her child-like clothes and her frequently unwashed face.

'Doesn't it trouble you, Maeve?'

'Trouble? Sure the trouble in this world is not

99

enough love, Lizza. That old Theo, may he rot in hell, or Germany or some other place, he banged me about cause he hated me, not cause he loved me. And that Adolf Hitler never had a day's love in his life. I swear it...'

Lizza was irritated at the sentimentality. 'But that doesn't happen on its own, Maeve. That love. There's consequences. Babies. Marriages that are at best a set of benevolent habits; at worst a place where terrible things happen...' Her voice trailed off as she met Maeve's bold eye.

'Ah, that's it, don't you see, Lizza? You have to stock up the good times, savour them. Then they become a treasure in the head when the times become hard. Don't you see it? Oh, I know, nowadays Theo is a beast, not deserving to walk on the earth. But he was wonderful when we were courting, so anxious to please. So attentive. And there was another boy before, called Rory...'

'So is that all there is, Maeve? A brief flowering, a little true love? And the rest is enduring the consequences.' In her mind's eye Lizza could see Roland's turned back.

'But there are other chances, now, don't you see, Lizza? The order is changing. Sure this war is a terrible thing, but...'

But Lizza had barged past her with the pram and was striding along, tears blinding her eyes.

That night at tea she told Alex he was spending too much time trailing around the town with Josie. The girl was a child, he should find friends of his own age.

100

'They're all at work or at school in the day.' He glanced at her through the corner of his eye. He and Josie had been much further than a kiss at Beaconsfield that day. 'And Josie isn't that young. She knows her way round. She's a lot of fun.'

She picked up his plate. 'She's a child. I expect you're behaving yourself, Alex.'

He turned to look at her. 'Better than my father did, you mean? Whoever he was?'

She shrugged. 'If you like.'

He stood up and threw an arm around her. 'Leave it alone, Lizza. She's a funny girl. Older than she looks. We are getting on. Life's short. I'm not going to war without...'

'Without what?'

'Knowing what it's like to give and take that much fun. No chance of it at home—Gram as cold as a cucumber and our Beatrice even worse, wrapped up in ice.' He felt her shoulder relaxing under his grasp. 'Can't see much of that warmth here either to be honest,' he said softly, ' 'cept between you and little Rebecca here...' Then he kissed her on her cheek and he could have done anything—robbery, murder, arson—and she would have been on his side.

She pushed him away, smiling wryly. 'Go and dig me some potatoes from the patch, will you? And don't think you can charm the birds off the trees, because you can't.' He went off whistling, knowing that that was just what he had done.

Before the siren went that night Alex raced back to the house to find her. 'I want to go to the

Trek, with Josie and her mam and Liam and Anne-Marie. You don't mind, Lizza?'

'Would it make any difference if I did?'

He grinned, and later gave her a thumbs-up signal as she watched him help Josie push the second pram towards the end of the road into the dusk.

Later that night Roland crawled in beside Lizza, on to the makeshift bed under the stairs, mug in hand.

'Ouch, Rollie! You're freezing!' Lizza had been awoken by the sound of him stumbling round the kitchen making tea.

'Lizz. You awake? Would you like some of this tea?'

She cradled the mug in her hands. 'I've been trying to have a word with our Alex over spending too much time with Josie Callaghan, Rollie. They're running wild through the town, those two.'

'Lots of children are. Some of them are not bothering with school. Parents like me working all the hours...' He yawned.

She put away his cup and placed her hands on his shoulders. 'Do you know what I've been thinking about, Rollie? Those first days after you'd run away from school and I thought you were too toffee-nosed to be my friend? And how you found me back in Durham after the Strike and took me back to Bradford? And what friends we were, even though we were young. Younger than Alex.'

He outlined her pale face with his finger, then drew it to him and kissed it. Her lips quickened under his and her arms went tightly round him. 'Roland...' she said.

He pulled away. 'I'm sorry, sweetheart, so sorry. I'm dead beat. A hell of a day today and it'll be worse tomorrow...'

Her hands came down by her side and she shuffled further down in the bed, her face turned away from him. He pulled the cover almost up to his eyes as he always did and fell asleep within a minute.

Hours later, when the nightlight had flickered to nothing and the space was pitch black, she felt his hand stroking her arms and her legs over her nightdress, then him pulling at it so he could get contact with her skin. She felt his mouth over hers, then on her shoulders and her breasts, then he was inside her and she was chorusing with him gasps and groans of short-lived relief. Then it was over and she wondered if she had dreamed it. She knew she hadn't. Both Rebecca and this new baby had been conceived in the very first such dream-like contacts. And Rebecca here and this baby, leaping around inside her now, were all too real.

The all-clear sounded and Rebecca cried, and, as was her custom, crawled into bed between them for five minutes before they hauled themselves into full wakefulness.

Alex returned from the Trek at eight o'clock and threw his rucksacks on Lizza's kitchen table. With a magician's flourish he pulled out an odd parcel of cabbage leaves containing four eggs and an old, stringy and very dead chicken. 'I thought after our big discussion about life

103

yesterday, me Auntie Lizz deserved an egg for breakfast.'

Rebecca in her high chair laughed and clapped. Lizza reached across and tousled the auburn head. 'You need a job, Alex. There's too much bad in you, to lie around waiting for events.'

The thought firmed up as she said it. Alex seemed set on staying now. Roland could find him a job at the factory. That shouldn't be too hard. Then she thought about her dream-like contact with Roland in the early hours. It had been no dream, but like other similar incidents they would both conspire to treat it as though it were. Within the conspiracy was the heresy that, delightful though those moments were, they were about need, not desire. And that it could have been anyone lying there beside Roland in the makeshift bed.

CHAPTER 8

'What's he like, this Polish feller who's working with you?' said Lizza, casting around for a subject that would hold her husband's interest for more than two seconds before he went to sleep in his chair.

Roland had come home slightly early from work. The tool had been completed and was going for tests. For a few days the only work would be repairs, cleaning and planning. Then back into maelstrom.

'I like him, but he's a bit hard to read. Old, perhaps more than forty. He's clever,' said Roland. 'You'd like him, Lizz. Reads novels at the break instead of eating.'

'What does he read?'

'Wouldn't know. English. Edgar Allan Poe was one. And *Wuthering Heights*. Some have leather covers.'

'His English must be good. What does he actually *do*?'

'Well, he's no engineer. He helps me with some straightforward stuff, and does a bit on the line, now and then, runs about for Pieter Vann.'

'So everything's going all right over there?'

'Some of the chaps are not so happy with all the overtime. We get lectures now and then from a man from the Ministry. He doesn't half go at them. You know, "Don't you know there's a war on!" Things like that.'

'Is that all he does, then, this Pole?'

'No. He draws. Men at work, that kind of thing. Management's talking about a war-time record. None of his stuff leaves the factory, though. It goes in Mr Vann's safe.'

'So. He doesn't have much to do with you at all?'

'Well, he sits and has his break with me. And keeps an eye on what I'm doing. He saw the original tools, in Germany, and has this eye, because he's an artist. So Vann thinks he might spot something if there's something amiss when I was finished. He wouldn't, of course, in my view. It's all about measurement.'

Lizza lifted up the skirt she was stitching and looked at the line of stitches on the hem. Beatrice had made it 'blind' for Rebecca, from some old striped material in their mother's trunk, and sent it with only the hem to do. It would fit perfectly, as did all Beatrice's 'blind' offerings. 'I was thinking, Rollie. It's time our Alex got work.'

'He's had his playtime, has he?' Roland laughed, trying to light his pipe yet again.

'Well, he insists that spending time with Josie Callaghan is all right, but the boy has too much energy. And she's a sparky little thing. I like Josie. She's unusual. But she's like a tinder box waiting to spark. And he has too much time on his hands. Would there be something for him to do, some work for him down there at the works?'

Roland puffed away, watching the red glow with some satisfaction. Lizza fought down the desire to grab the pipe from him and throw it into the guttering fire. Before the war she would have viewed this patient pipe-filling with some affection. She had bought him his first pipe when he was just twenty-one. But the affection in her seemed to be draining away, and with it all of her tolerance. Now it just got her goat that he kept her waiting, like some child at school, for an answer.

'Don't see why not. He's brainy but he's no skills, of course, but they're putting everyone on production. Even women now!'

'Even women!' The protest came out more

106

weakly than she meant. 'Women are working like that all over England and doing as good a job as the men ever did. Don't you ever listen to the wireless?'

He put up a protesting hand. 'Sorry! Sorry!' But it was an automatic apology; there was no real heart in his voice and she was angry with him. She was so angry she could have hit him.

But she let it go. 'About Alex, Roland...'

'Yes, yes. The boy can come in with me tomorrow.' He sucked at his pipe and picked up the evening paper. 'I'll be off at six-thirty, so you'll need to kick him out of bed.'

Alex, already intimidated by Lizza's husband with his quiet demeanour and cultured speech, got himself up early the following morning and was ready to go off in the dark by six-thirty. The two of them rode in silence through the early morning bustle of the factory road, Alex using Lizza's bike, which he had now tuned to perfection.

Roland got Alex through security on his own say-so, and kept the boy with him at his bench until Mr Vann came around. While they waited, he and Krystof cleaned off the bench for the next job, and set about cleaning the tools. Roland had to field questions from the boy about the tool that they had just finished, and Krystof fielded questions about whether he knew any of the famous Polish pilots who had fought in the Battle of Britain.

It was quite a relief when Mr Vann did come along.

Roland pushed Alex forward. 'This is my wife's...younger brother, Mr Vann. He's from the North. Just out of grammar school, so he's no duffer. I thought with these labour shortages you might find a spot for him.'

'Turn your hand to anything, young man?'

Alex dragged his gaze away from the heavy machinery and the elemental objects which he knew would one day fly in the sky. 'Yes sir, anything. Sweeping up. Anything.' He looked the thick-set man straight in the eye. 'I'm a quick learner.'

Mr Vann, like many people on first meeting Alex, was charmed. 'Well, bring your things.'

Alex turned his hands out.

'You bring nothing? Oh, well, follow me.'

Roland and Krystof watched them walk side by side down the line.

'He is a fine boy...' said Krystof quietly.

Roland looked at him sharply. 'Do you have children of your own, Krystof?'

He smiled thinly. 'I had two sons. One would be as old as the boy there. We wished to send them to America in thirty-seven, to safety you see? Their mother is Jewish and has relations in New York. She would not go herself. But the train, on the way to the harbour there was a crash... You see, my friend, it is not only the war...' He suddenly looked wretched.

'My own father's missing now.' Roland had no idea why he blurted that out. Perhaps one terrible thing balancing another. He bumbled on. 'He's in the Merchant Navy. His ship went down.'

They stood awkwardly for a few seconds, then got on with their work in silence.

Half an hour later Mr Vann came along to tell Roland he had set the boy on sorting packing materials, where he shouldn't do much harm. He looked across at Krystof, now making a sketch of a perspective down the line from Roland's booth. 'So how is the hostel, Krystof?'

Krystof shrugged. 'There is a war on. Too many people and too few spaces. One has to endure.'

Mr Vann shook his head. 'I've had my own experience of such places. Even now I am only in a small room in someone else's house. But at least there my landlady does the good home-cooking. Even with the rationing.'

There was a pause.

'You could come to my house to eat, at least!' said Roland.

Krystof looked up from his sketch pad.

'There'll be another early finish tonight, won't there, Mr Vann? The steel for the new jobs won't be here till tomorrow, or even the next day. Come home to tea, Krystof!' Roland was warming to the idea by the second.

'I don't know, Roland, your wife...'

'Lizza, my wife that is, is sick of me rolling in with nothing to say. And she's a reader like you. And for somebody who says she can't cook she does wonders with those vegetables of hers.'

'In that case, Roland...' Still clutching his notebook, Krystof brought his arms to his sides, clicked his heels and bowed his head. 'I will be honoured.'

Mr Vann looked from one to the other, like a mother proud of her clever children, and hurried off.

After work Alex raced on ahead of them on his bike to warn Lizza of the visitor. Roland walked his bike, and Krystof Sobieski, a slightly longer way home. The evening was chilly but bright and clear and there was not a cloud in the sky.

Lizza's day had been catapulted into action by the postman, who knocked on the door to deliver two parcels and two postcards for Alex. She read the cards. One was from her mother. *'Many Happy Returns of today, Your Gram, Alice Bremner.'*

Beatrice had filled her card with small neat writing.

Dear Alex,

Best wishes on your eighteenth birthday. The house is quiet without you and some of your friends have called to ask about you. Your grandma is like a 'woman off'. Please please don't do anything without letting us know.

Love, your Beatrice

Lizza stood the cards side by side on the tile fireplace. They were both hand-coloured scenes, probably bought years ago, of Durham Castle. The fourteenth of November. She had forgotten the boy's birthday. So, it seemed, had Alex, in the rush of things. It must be a funny anniversary for Beatrice. A poignant anniversary of a difficult event, which had been preceded nine months before by the worst event of all.

Josie saw the cards when she came in and commented on them. She laughed her wicked laugh when she heard whom they were for, and poked at the parcels to try and guess what they might be. 'What do you think, Mrs King?'

Lizza poked at the parcels. 'The fat one's a jumper knit by our Beatrice. The clangy one'll be a tin with a cake made by his grandma. Probably a cherry cake. She's famous for them.'

Josie licked her lips. 'Ain't there no rationing up there?'

'Oh yes there is. But you should see my mother's store cupboard, from before the war. And they can get the odd egg. And Beatrice does a deal with the bee-man at the allotments for honey. And somebody will kill a pig and pass around the bits. It's against the rules, but...'

Josie hung around all morning and in the afternoon walked into town with her. Lizza always enjoyed the bustling centre of town: Broadgate, with its shops and now its brand new big store. And within sight, the spire of Holy Trinity and the more distant mass of St Michael's Cathedral. Broadgate still retained its bustling sense of self-importance, despite the shortages that made the shop windows sparse, and the occasional hazard of sandbags.

Lizza bought a tiny birthday card from a paper shop, some handkerchiefs for Alex and a new lace collar for herself from the big store. Josie looked around the shop with interest,

111

ignoring the frosty glances of the neat sales-ladies who whispered to each other at the sight of this urchin on their pristine premises.

'I ain't never been in here since it was finished. It's like a church.' She wrinkled her nose. 'There's a funny smell.'

'That's newness, Josie. The smell of the future,' laughed Lizza. 'New paint, new wood, new polish. There's probably no finer shop in England than this. Certainly not where I come from.'

Josie drew her finger along the counter, making a nerve-splitting squeak. A tall sales lady with her hair in a neat roll right round her head moved purposefully towards her. Lizza grabbed Josie's arm and pulled her out.

She buckled Rebecca back into the pram. 'You're a bad'n, you, Josie Callaghan.'

Josie grinned and rolled her eyes to the back of her head. 'D'you see her, that woman? Sure, you'd think she owned the place.'

They made their way out of Broadgate through the narrow alley that broadened out to give way to the stone bulk of Holy Trinity. Josie stopped dramatically and swept her glance right to the top of the spire and then across to the lurking weight of St Michael's Cathedral. 'God, this place is full of churches.'

Lizza smiled. 'Have you been inside any of them?'

Josie shook her head. 'Not my kind of church. My mammy would've had me whipped if I'd have crossed the threshold. What about you? Have you been in them?'

112

Lizza nodded soberly. She had gone into the cathedral at Beatrice's urging, the day before Elizabeth died, although they didn't know it then. They had been on their way to the pictures to see Charlie Chaplin. 'Come on, Lizza. Let's just have a look!' Beatrice had urged. 'Say a prayer for the bairn.'

Lizza had sat in a seat towards the front, amid the heavy medieval splendour, and thought hard about baby Elizabeth and her fragility; the nearest thing she could do to praying. Beatrice beside her was on her knees. Her head, with its old-fashioned bun at the nape, was bowed low over her hands. There in the deep peace of that place which seemed to speak of eternity, Lizza had at last allowed herself to hope.

'Is it nice inside?' Josie's voice intruded.

'It's very old. And kind of permanent. Like the temples of the Aztecs.'

'And what might they be?'

Lizza grinned. 'Come on, ignoramus, I'll take you for a cup of tea.'

She took Josie to the Windmill Café where, having negotiated the new sandbags at the door, they had weak tea and small dry biscuits.

Josie loved it. 'Sure this ain't half a swanky place, Mrs King. Do you come here all the time?'

'A lot.'

'On your own?'

'Well, there's Rebecca.' She was buckling her daughter into the high chair. 'Usually I bring a book and read it.'

The elderly ladies looked on in disapproval

113

as Josie put her elbows on the table, held her cup between her two hands and leaned forward. 'You're a queer one, ain't yer, with your books, Mrs King? An' yer good-looking enough not to be a book-worm. So I can ask you this. Were you ever in love?'

Lizza felt a thousand years old. '*Was* I? Was I? Why d'you want to know?'

'Well, you were the only one I could ask. Mammy's no good for this kind of thing, an' yer might as well ask a bar of soap as ask me dad. So I was wondering, how d'you know how you feel if you don't know how you should feel?' Josie's eyes gleamed straight into hers.

'Well, I think you know when you are. Are you saying you're like that about Alex?'

'Nah. I just like him. But girls aren't supposed to like boys, like a buddy, as the Yanks say, are they? But I was thinking, what if this just liking is being in love? Like it is in *Gone With the Wind* and that? How would I know?'

'Well,' said Lizza slowly. 'I think I like Roland like a friend. Like a buddy you might say.'

'How old were you when you met him?'

'Fourteen, fifteen. Your age I suppose. We were friends.'

'Did he kiss you?'

'Mind your own business,' said Lizza sharply.

'Well,' said Josie airily, 'Alex kisses me and he wants to do it all the time. And I like it. But like I said, is it being in love?'

Lizza stirred vigorously, watching the sugarless tea swirl in her cup. She would let Alex get his birthday over and have a very strong word with him about Josie. Then she started to wonder if she had, ever, been in love.

'Mrs King?'

'You're too young, Josie, too young for any of this. Leave it alone,' she said crossly. 'All this sloppy talk. Don't you know there's a war on?'

'Ah,' said Josie wisely. 'But without love how'll there be any future, any *after-the-war*?'

Lizza drank up. 'Anyway, it's time I was home. I've a letter to write.'

Josie left her in the town centre saying she had things to do, but she would see her at tea-time because she wanted to give Alex his present.

Back at the house, Lizza put Rebecca to bed and settled down to write a letter addressed jointly to her mother and Beatrice.

...Alex has settled down surprisingly well here, and is little bother. Don't worry about him. He can take care of himself. He seems to enjoy being in the 'big city'. It's so different here. Like it is a different land. Roland's trying to get Alex a job at the factory. It will be sweeping up or something, but he will be 'doing his bit'.

He talks about joining up, and if the day comes when he decides to do it, there's no way any of us can stop it. But be sure I will let you know. Roland is working very hard at present; they're building more and more aircraft, but there are still complaints that some of them won't do enough—won't work seven days a week, twelve hours a day. I *have* to think it's all to the good, that it will help our boys, as they always say. Thank you Beatrice for the lovely skirt for our Rebecca. I turned up the hem and it fits a treat. It was a lovely idea to embroider those little cherries on the tuck. I put it with that woolly jumper you knit her and she looks like something off a Pears Advertisement. I hope you're well and are not missing Alex too much. He's quite safe here...

'Lizza! Lizza!'

She covered her letter with her hand as the same boy was hurtling through the door. 'He's bringing the Pole home to tea...' Alex gabbled on about Krystof and how wonderful the factory was and how they were going to fix him up with his own identity card and how they thought Roland was a genius there...

Lizza put a hand over his mouth to stop the flow of words. 'The Pole?'

'Krystof Sobieski. He's living in a hostel but he's coming here to tea. Roland sent me on, told me to tell you he'll be here in five minutes...' His voice tailed off as he caught sight of Josie grinning in the doorway with Rebecca on one arm and a rough brown paper parcel in another. ' 'Lo, Josie, fancy seeing you here!' he grinned. He held his arms open. Rebecca jumped into them and he kept his eye on Josie over the child's head.

'Happy Birthday!' The girl thrust the parcel towards him.

'Birthday? I forgot!' One-handed, he unpicked

the string, and out fell a piece of metal with some German writing on. He grinned at her.

She nodded. 'A bit off an incendiary, I think. Happy Birthday. Got it from a house...' He leaned across Rebecca to try and kiss her.

Suddenly the kitchen was too full of bodies for Lizza. 'Out! All of you. If I've got to do tea for some foreigner, I need some space. You can get your other birthday things after tea, Alex.' It was an order, not a request. 'Out you go! Take these two babies to see your ma, Josie. And send them back in twenty minutes.'

She shut the door behind the three of them and, like a scouring wind, cleared books and papers off the surfaces, pushed toys into cupboards and washed down the table. Then she turned on the oven, put on a pan to make the Oxo gravy which she mixed with corned beef from the larder cupboard and a basinful of mashed potato. She thrust in a handful of dried parsley from her garden and sprinkled it with salt and pepper. Then, hesitating, she broke the last one of Alex's precious stolen eggs, stirring it carefully into the potato. Working at speed, she divided the mixture into chunky cakes and put them on a greased pan in the oven. She put on a pan to boil and put her own small, scrubbed-clean carrots into the bubbling water. Then she spread her best cloth on the table, the best knives and forks and side plates and stood the chairs at proper right-angles to the table.

Finally she raced upstairs to wash her hands and face and put on a dark green blouse, now hurriedly trimmed at the neck with the new lace collar from the big store. She looked in her mirror and desperately brushed her hair into a tidier kind of bush.

She was just coming down the stairs at the front when she heard the back door click and the murmur of voices in the kitchen. She took a deep breath, walked through and smiled into the face of the stranger.

Almost instantly she was looking at thick black hair with patches of auburn as he bowed over her hand. 'So kind of you to welcome a stranger, madame...' She had never heard a voice like it; located somewhere deep in his body, but soft, almost like a woman's.

She pulled away her hand too quickly. 'I'm called Lizza. Please call me that.'

He smiled. 'Elizabeth, like the queen. Elizabeth.' Her heart jolted as, in that deep soft voice, he spoke her baby's name.

'No! Elizabeth died. My name is Lizza,' she protested.

'We can wash our hands in here, Krystof.' Roland, shepherding their visitor towards the kitchen sink, smiled reassuringly at Lizza. 'Something smells nice, Lizz.'

Lizza shrugged, keeping her eyes away from the foreigner. 'Just the corned-beef ration. And my carrots.'

Roland was washing his hands at the sink with his usual care. 'I was just telling Krystof about your vegetables, Lizz.'

Lizza handed him a towel. 'I just do what our Beatrice tells me in her letters and the vegetables come up out of the earth.'

'Lizza's family, Krystof,' said Roland with unusual enthusiasm, 'can do anything they set their heart on. Sew, cook, wallpaper, mend shoes and clocks. And write, Lizza here can write! You never saw such letters. And recite! Do you know she can say the whole of Shakespeare by heart...'

'Roland, will you shut up!' She handed the towel to Krystof. 'Take no notice of him, Mr Sobieski.'

He rubbed his hands vigorously, then returned it to her smiling. 'He has a great deal to be proud of, Lizza. And please, please, it is Krystof.'

At that moment Alex returned with Rebecca and the room was full of bodies again. Josie had gone on the Trek with her mother, who had had one of her premonitions. She had urged Alex to come but the temptation of talking to Krystof was too strong and he refused.

Busy with the enlarged and much more elaborate meal than usual, Lizza was left with little time to reflect on the surge of energy which was welling up in her, except to ascribe it to racing around the house before the two men got in.

Alex opened his presents and expressed his gratitude with charm, shaking hands with the men and kissing Lizza on the cheek. He put on the jumper which Beatrice had knitted for him, put his nose in the cake tin sent by his grandmother and said, 'Cherry cake! Smells like Bracks Hill!'

The supper went smoothly. Rebecca was on

her best behaviour, crumbling cherry cake in her high chair, and Krystof was commandeered by Alex, who asked him what it was like working for the Germans, and burrowing out the detail of his subsequent long walk to freedom. 'We crossed Slovakia in the falling snow with the help of smugglers. Then Budapest; Zagreb; Italy; France.'

'What did you do there?'

'Well, for a time I was fighting with the Polish forces for the French. Then caught and in prison in Germany and sent to the factory with my Czech friend, then I escaped and got out back to France. Then in prison again, escaped again. Then Marseilles for a time. Then a British warship to come here.'

Alex whistled. 'How could that happen? The Nazis letting someone escape?' He scraped the last of the corned beef from his plate.

'They're not supermen, Alex. Not as efficient as the legend they set about. These were ordinary soldiers and there was confusion.'

'So you fought them, when they invaded your country, and in France, too?'

Krystof laughed wryly. 'Yes, in my own country we all fought—artists, musicians, butchers, bakers. Anyone who could hold arms, carry an axe. And there were some brave encounters. But it was like a dog fighting a flea. My wife was taken. I saw Warsaw, saw my land taken. Saw it engulfed by flames. I was...' He coughed.

'There was no preventing them,' said Roland.

Krystof looked at him over his last forkful of corned-beef cake. 'That is one view,' he said politely. 'There are those of my countrymen who think...'

Roland opened his mouth to defend his government when the air was ripped by the familiar, ever-chilling sound of the air-raid siren.

Roland and Lizza exchanged glances.

'It might be another false one,' she said.

'Take no chances, Lizz. I keep telling you, take no chances.'

She looked around the table, her glance taking in the still face of Krystof Sobieski. 'Too many of us for under the stairs. We'll have to go to a proper shelter.'

'Go to the big one on the Crescent. I'll see you on my way. My watch at the factory tonight.'

There was a scramble while they prepared for what might turn out to be a whole night in the shelter. Roland dashed upstairs for his fire-watching gear. Alex zipped up Rebecca's siren suit over her jumper and new skirt, gathered together bread and flasks and the last of the cherry cake, and put them in his rucksack.

Lizza pulled out blankets and pillows from their permanent position under the stairs. Krystof insisted that he would carry these so that all Lizza had to carry was Rebecca and their gas masks.

As they parted company from Roland, Krystof offered to go with him to help with the watch at the factory.

'No, wouldn't be allowed. You stay with Lizza and Rebecca.'

As they came round a corner into the dark scramble of the main street, the siren faded and they could hear a sound like the distant rumble of thunder.

'That must be them?' said Alex.

'That's them,' said Krystof, his face white under his dark hair. 'Hurry!'

There were crowds on the pavements and wardens yelling at them to hurry along.

'Crikey!' said Alex as a great spurt of flame leapt up on their far left and another in the middle distance. Rebecca screamed. The noise was joined by the clangour of the fire engines careering on their way. They heard the swish-swish of an incendiary nearer at hand and the ominous plop as it reached the hard surface of the road; they hurried on.

'There's ours!' said Lizza, as they heard the ack-ack guns open up and the distant thump of bursting shells.

'Ours? Our guns?' said Alex, marching on, shaking with a combination of fear and delight at being in the middle of it all at last.

Another lick of fire leapt into the sky to the right and the whistle of falling bombs shrieked into their ears. The extent of fire lifted the cloak of darkness from the city, rimming the edge of the hurrying people with rosy halos of deceitful beauty.

The traffic was building up on the road, the steady throb of car and motorbike as they left the city counterpointing the noisy fire engines, ambulances and Home Guard vehicles still making their steady way into the stricken town centre.

The warden was collecting groups of people together and hustling them across the road to the big shelter. Lizza's little group waited ten minutes to get across the road before they could join the end of the queue. As they got nearer the entrance, the smell of wet clothes and bodies, the residual foistiness of bedding kept only for this purpose, became stronger; Lizza's stomach began to heave and Rebecca's grip round her neck became a stranglehold. When they finally started to go down the steps the little girl started to fight and scream for her daddy.

Lizza turned and fought her way back out with her shrieking child, ignoring the shouts and curses of the people who were in her way.

She stood, trying to calm Rebecca, waiting while Alex and Krystof struggled to back their way up the steps out of the shelter.

The three of them stood side by side on the pavement. Rebecca whimpered in Lizza's arms. 'I want to be in my own house,' shouted Lizza grimly. 'We'll just have to squash in under the stairs.'

Alex looked up into the clear sky with its bright moon, and at the flames which seemed now to fill the whole of the world. And he heard the continuing throb of the aeroplane engines. He knew what he wanted to do. 'Will you be all right with Krystof, Lizza?' he shouted. 'There's Josie and her mam out there on the road. I want to find them.'

Lizza looked up into the dark eyes of the

stranger. 'I can take care of...'

'We will take care of each other, Elizabeth and I,' said Krystof grimly. 'You go to your friend, Alex.'

Alex started running down the street, here and there battling with people in his headlong haste. As he ran, a great tongue of flame lit up on his right, another to his left. He could smell the cordite and hear Rebecca screaming again behind him.

Krystof and Lizza looked at each other. An ear-splitting explosion far to their right spurred them into action.

'The gasometer!' shouted Lizza, pushing Krystof with her shoulder. 'Come on!' she shouted over the din, 'the sooner we start, the sooner we get there...'

As she spoke, there was a great crash on their right and a building crumbled, throwing up a great cloud of dust which settled on their hair and their clothes. The glare of the fires was blocked out for a second. Then an explosion thudded in the distance, more fires flared, and they set off to run.

CHAPTER 9

Outside the shelter, the rosy dazzle of fire had restored the evening to full daylight. At first Krystof and Lizza, with Rebecca on her back, made slow progress. Like Alex, they were running against the tide of people, who were still flowing past them in the direction of the various public shelters, or to further destinations outside the city. Around them the storm from the sky raged, bombs screaming down on all sides, the crack and thunder of collapsing buildings set against the crackle of the flaring fires. Beyond the buildings, the red sky was made sullen by the mixture of black dust and smoke emitted from the collapsing city below.

The people they passed were mostly heavy-laden: a baby in his pram was protected by an old tin bath; one man in a dark suit was sheltering his wife and two children with a vast black umbrella punctured by shrapnel to the state of a ragged colander; three women were wandering along the roadway in a daze, one with a tin washbowl on her head, two still in pyjamas and dressing gowns; lucky escapers from a shelter which had just had a direct hit.

A brilliant flash cut the air ahead of them, then their ears were pierced by the whining sound of the bomb and the unmistakable *thrump* as it hit the ground. A billowing wave of dense dust made Rebecca double up against her mother with coughs and sneezes. Lizza herself was deafened by the boom of the explosion.

They paused to let the dust die down. Lizza changed Rebecca from her back to her front. Then, cautiously, they started to edge round a deep crater which, ten minutes before, had been a public house. An ambulance was nose-down in the crater. Its driver was now slumped across the bonnet, eyes still gleaming with the shock

125

and fear which were his last living emotions. Beside the ambulance, under the chaos of glass and wood and brick, Lizza caught a glimpse of red soil, like a wound in the earth's crust.

They tiptoed past the gaping hole, closing their ears to the moans and shouts emerging from the rubble.

Lizza hesitated.

'Come on! Come on!' said Krystof. 'People are on their way to help. See! They're running! Come on, Lizza! Or you will be the one to be blown up next! And little Rebecca!'

Plunging into an alley to avoid the invasive heat from a factory on fire, they tripped over hoses and in one place had to plodge through water where the main had burst. A kitchen chair was swinging precariously from an overhead wire. The smell of cordite, sizzling wood, blistering paint, leaking gas and something resembling cooking pork burned its way into Lizza's nostrils. The bombers overhead continued their implacable drone. All around them explosions of light were succeeded by seconds of dense darkness; their ears were filled by the whistle of falling bombs and the ominous rattle made by incendiary baskets as they swung around, sending their small parcels of fire in every direction.

In one street they had to thread their way, crunching on broken glass, through tramlines which had reared up into the air like the front legs of a stallion; in another street they passed a bus chugging along, complete with conductor: a sight denying the chaos with its spurious appearance of normality.

Rebecca sagged, heavily unconscious, in her mother's arms. Lizza leaned up against a wall, whose hot stones instantly repulsed her. 'Ouch!'

Krystof dropped his bags and his burden of pillows and packages, and took the child from her. He patted Rebecca's face till her eyes opened again. 'There, little sweetheart,' he shouted into her ear over the crashes and hisses, the drone of plane engines. 'Wake now! Wake now, sweetheart. Come on now, you can be a robber-lady!' She sat in his arms, wide-eyed, as he hurriedly took out a coloured silk handkerchief and tied it round the lower part of her face. 'Now the robber-lady may ride on her horse.' He adjusted his rucksack and lifted her on to his shoulders, pressing his chin down to hold her hands while he picked up the bags again.

Breathing hard, Lizza looked beyond him to the city, now illuminated to the brightness of day; the fires, impelled by the November wind, were leaping from building to building. In the middle of all that smoke and flame was the big store where, just today, she had bought the little lace collar; the Windmill Café where she had had tea with Josie; the picture house where she had seen Charlie Chaplin, that time, with Beatrice; the high spire of Holy Trinity and the spire and the medieval weight of St Michael's. Now, high above them, at the point where the rim of light from the flames started to fade, the dark night sky was criss-crossed by searchlights and cut through with tracer bullets.

'Come on, Lizza! We must move!' urged Krystof. They hurried on. At one point they passed some firemen who were yelling at each other that the water had gone, there was no water! The fires would have to burn. They would have to burn.

Then two figures in uniform loomed up at them through the dust. 'Get off the street, get off the street, won't you?' bawled one. A dull crump and the deadly suck of air to their left heralded yet another explosion. They watched as one warden dropped like a stone, and the other kneeled at his side, reaching in vain to loosen his collar.

Krystof dropped a bag to the ground and grasped Lizza's hand in his. 'Come on, Lizza, come on!'

His pace as he dragged her only finally slowed when they reached the end of Lizza's street and saw her little house with its bright door intact.

They looked back in the direction from which they had come. One noise had subtracted itself from the cacophony.

'Our guns!' said Lizza. 'They're not shooting any more.' The tracer bullets no longer scored the sky. The ack-ack no longer bred its false comfort. The whistle and thump of bombs still filled the air around them; the hum of the planes still crossed the sky in systematic squares, as though the pilots were tracing graph paper in the heavens. The scream of rescue traffic and the forlorn ringing of the bell of a waterless fire engine still added their layer of sound to the dense night. But there was no ack-ack. Now they did not even have the sound, the illusion, of protection to hearten them.

Lizza unclasped her hand from Krystof's and ran towards her house. 'Come on! Come on!' It was her turn now.

Inside the house the light switch did not respond. She felt around for her little oil lamp, lit it and led the way to the small space under the stairs which Roland called the cellar. 'In here, in here!'

They tucked themselves into the narrow space and pulled the door to behind them. The massive wedge of sound modified to a distant clamour and she relaxed, cuddling Rebecca to her, comforted by her child-like smell.

Then she felt the arm of the stranger around her shoulders. She started to tremble. Krystof muttered softly in his own language, stroking her hair and Rebecca's arm. Finally, 'It is all right, you are all right...'

She closed her eyes for a second and slipped away into unconsciousness. When she came to, Rebecca was playing at her feet with a knitted fireman doll made by Beatrice, and Krystof was pulling at something in his rucksack. He lifted a small folder towards the smoky light of the oil lantern.

'What's that?'

'These are drawings I made in Warsaw, Elizabeth. On just such a night. The night they destroyed my beloved city, polluted my land.' He undid the string on the folder and put it in her hands. She leafed through the drawings. They showed a city on fire. Tongues

129

of flame moved around buildings and people with formalised beauty; a castle in outline pulsed with fire; city walls lay black against a flaming sky; a group of people sheltering under an overhanging wall looked out, their faces strained and fearful.

He looked at her. 'We share this, you and I,' he said.

She looked at Rebecca, now finally curled asleep between her legs, clutching the knitted fireman. Dried tears made white tracks in the thick black dust down the child's round face. The blouse and the little skirt made for her by Beatrice were crusted with thick red mud.

The house shook. Lizza flinched back into the wall and put a hand over Rebecca's head. Krystof took the folder from her and thrust it back into his bag. He smiled at her in the dim lamplight. The house shook again and he reached out to pull her close. 'All we can do,' he said simply, 'is take care of each other.'

She pulled away, breathing heavily. 'It's too hot in here. Too crowded.' She could feel sweat beading on her upper lip.

His arm tightened. 'We are all we have, just at this moment, Lizza.'

She relaxed against him, her back against the wall. Unbelievably, she slept again.

She woke again and shook her head, pushing wisps of hair back up into the round band. She wrinkled her nose against the dank paraffin smell. 'I was asleep. How could I? How long...Rebecca!'

'About twenty minutes.' Rebecca was sitting

130

on Krystof Sobieski's knee, playing with her woolly fireman. 'The child awoke.'

She relaxed against him again, then sat up. 'Can I have another look at the pictures? Those drawings of yours?' Anything to keep her mind away from the droning engines, the distant crashing sounds.

'In the rucksack.'

She took the folder carefully into her hands and turned over the fragile single sheets. She had to peer very closely to make out the dramatic background of the castle, the dark hurrying figures; the rearing figure of a man in a soft cloth cap holding up a rifle; the predatory low-flying aeroplane; a woman crouched in a corner with a baby in her lap and her arms round a small boy; the bright bold face of a young woman in a stylised halo of flame.

She looked across at him. 'Who's this?'

'My young niece. Her name is Katya. The house of my wife's brother—her father—had gone. Where he or his wife was she did not know. So she took shelter with me.'

'This was during a raid?'

'See that arch above us? We sheltered under it for three hours.' Lizza could feel his bony frame shake slightly. 'All we could do by then was watch. So I took out my pencils and drew. I wished for a record.'

'You always have these with you?'

'I have carried them ever since. Those men at your government house in the country looked at them, of course. But since then, no one.'

Holding it delicately with the tips of her

finger and thumb, she turned another sheet over. 'They are so fragile.'

'If I survive...God willing, if I survive, they will survive. In the peace I will paint the images. And exhibit. Then people will know what it was that took my city, my land. What it felt like.'

Carefully, Lizza closed the little folder. She held it close to her and relaxed against him. In minutes, despite the storm of noise around them, they both slept.

They were catapulted to wakefulness by an explosive pressure which flung them like rag dolls against the roof of the cellar, then back against a wall. Then the house cracked and splintered and, the very walls screaming, it fell to pieces around them.

She lay against the wall, quite blind for a second. The house was down. She knew that. And she and Krystof, this stranger, were locked together, facing each other in the darkness, their bodies folded together like sardines. Inside her, the new baby squirmed and tumbled, responding to her confusion. She knew Krystof would feel that movement and wondered if he would realise...

It took minutes of careful blinking and rubbing to get her eyes open; her face was caked in a thick dust which the blast had driven into every crevice. She finally forced open her eyes to see Krystof. His own eyes gleamed at her from his dust-caked face.

'Are you all right?' His white teeth sparkled in the blackness.

'My head aches and my foot feels as though

someone's sewing it on with hot needles,' she mumbled, still half conscious. She reached out. 'I can move my arms, though.'

Then the storm at the back of her befuddled mind struck. 'Rebecca!' she shrieked.

She put out her hands as far as she could and all she encountered was wood and brick. She could feel Krystof doing the same thing.

His voice was in her ear. 'Nothing here!' he said hoarsely.

After two minutes of desperate fumbling her right hand did clasp something. It was a small piece of cloth. She pulled it towards her face and touched it to her lips. Her tongue traced the embroidered flower which Beatrice had stitched on the tuck on Rebecca's new skirt.

'It's her skirt, a bit of Rebecca's skirt,' she muttered. 'They've killed her. She's dead.'

'Sssh, sssh,' he whispered. 'She could be quite safe, Lizza. She could have wandered off. Safer out there than in here.'

She fingered the cloth, 'But...'

'Sssh,' he whispered.

She relaxed against him, half fainting. Instantly she was inside a dream which rehearsed again the incidents with Roland earlier in the day. This time she was saying to him, shouting to him across a wide void, 'Roland, you're a stranger. We know nothing of each other.'

'But we're friends!' He was yelling it, his mouth open wide as a cavern. Then he was at her side and they were making love standing up. But when she looked at his face it was that of Krystof Sobieski. She opened her eyes and found herself nuzzling up to him, this stranger in her house.

She pulled back as far as the confined space would allow. 'I was having a dream,' she said, 'a bad dream. They had killed Rebecca and I was...'

'It's all right, Lizza, it's all right.' But he was shaking and she could feel the tears on his cheeks.

'Rebecca?' she whispered.

'She got out. I'm sure of it.'

But she rubbed the piece of fabric slowly between her finger and thumb, not sure at all that Rebecca had got out.

Alex pushed his bike through the line of hurrying walkers. The lightly burdened people in the column—those who had fled with small bags packed with their insurance and ration books, their wallets and purses—were far ahead. He pushed his way through that straggling end of the line. These were people who clung more fiercely to their cumbersome worldly goods. They were doggedly trudging along with sacks over the crossbars of bikes, goods piled on prams and bogies. He passed an old man with a row of medals on his chest, being pushed along in a makeshift wheelchair by a white-faced middle-aged woman with dyed red hair and high-heeled shoes. Even at the very outskirts of the city they were all still having to negotiate the razor-sharp shrapnel fragments underfoot and the random trap of bomb craters. And in some, people got bogged down, where the road was gummed up with mud where the plaster from the broken walls had mingled with water from the broken mains pipe.

Finally the crowd thinned out and the roadway improved. Now Alex could mount the cycle and snake in and out of the line. He found the Callaghans at the very head of the pram- and bogie-pushers. They were down, now, to a single pram. Josie was carrying Liam, and Mrs Callaghan was doggedly pushing the pram at a kind of fast trudge. Baby Anne-Marie was barely visible under the pile of blankets and bags of goods.

Above them the bombers droned on. Around them was still the splash of fire. He slowed down his bike to walking pace and moved in alongside them.

'What're you doing here?' The wide grin on Josie's face belied her sour words.

They all ducked as there was a thudding explosion to their right. 'The Pole's looking out for our Lizza and the baby, and Roland is fire-watching and I thought...' He lifted the tear-stained Liam out of Josie's thin arms and put him on the crossbar of the bike and wobbled along beside her. '...I might be some help here.'

'We were managing...' said Josie.

'Shall I go back?'

She shook her head soberly. 'No. I need you. I'm buggered without the pram.'

There was a thudding on their right. Then they could hear the rattle of a plane not far overhead. The sound of gunfire was followed by screams behind them.

Quickening her fast pace, Maeve looked across at him grimly. 'Could you put our Josie on the crossbar as well, me darlin', and make off with her?'

He got back up in the saddle and leaned back, 'Gerron, Josie!'

She looked at her mother. 'No. I...'

'Won't you get yourself away, little one? Jerry'll have us one way or another but, let it please the Mary the blessed mother, don't let him have all of us.'

More gunfire crackled behind them. 'Gerron, lass!' said Alex. 'Do as you're told!'

Then she was in front of him, clinging desperately on to the wriggling Liam. He set off, riding alongside the hurrying Maeve. 'I'll get on, Mrs Callaghan. You follow on. We'll get the barn nice and snug for ye...'

'You go!' urged Maeve, ducking, and they heard the smooth whine of another low engine. 'Get away, will yer? Won't I see you there nice and snug? Get on, me darlins, and don't look back!'

Alex pedalled as he had never before. The sturdy bike made good speed despite the heavy weight it was carrying. The twisting lanes soon took them well ahead of the column. Then they ducked, as yet another plane, or perhaps the same plane coming round again, flew low over them. Alex's blood froze at the rattle of the strafing gun and further screams from people in the columns.

'Stop! Stop! That'll be our mammy!' Josie

struggled and the bike wobbled. Liam let out a great wailing cry.

'Bastard! Bastard!' yelled Alex, as he straightened up the bike, pedalling furiously. 'No stopping, Josie, no stopping! Your ma said not to look back. That's what she said.'

Fifteen people had already taken up residence in their barn when they arrived. One man was feeding a camp fire with a broken door and the others huddled: wet steaming bundles round a fire. Alex wheeled the bicycle into a corner where he felt it would be safe, while Josie, with Liam in her arms, elbowed her way to the front of the crowd. 'Give way, will ye? This wee boy's got pneumonia...'

They waited there all night. Like the others in the barn, they were subdued. Josie stayed by the fire, her face implacable, clutching Liam to her thin body. Alex hung about by the door, watching with disbelief the pulsing red glow in the distance which was the city he had just left.

As more people crowded into the barn he asked each one if they had seen a...well...plump Irish lady with a baby in a pram. But the newcomers shook their heads. With so many people out there, it was impossible to say, they said.

At the factory Roland spent the night fighting fires alongside friends and strangers, including brigades brought from outside the city. Normally they worked in fours; tonight it was in twos, and he was pleased to find himself assigned with

137

Pieter Vann. Time and again a fire would be put out, only for another plane to come over and relight it. More than once the water failed. Pumps were blown up, pipes were punctured, vehicles were burned. Dodging the snaking hoses being hauled by the men from the Dudley fire brigade, he and Pieter Vann used trolleys to wheel his lathe and his test bench out into the big yard. Looking to the sky, he thought it was a vain action. The gear was in just as much danger out here, when you thought of it.

They paused at the door as they returned. Then, apparently from nowhere, a huge ball of fire gathered itself together and shot into the air. They were thrown back by a great blast which seemed to rip the building apart. In the chaos which followed they could hear the screams of men caught in the collapsing walls. They waited for the dust to settle and went in. The roof was open to the sky. Great sections of glass and steel ceilings were lodged at awkward angles on the shopfloor. Machines were welded to the walls. Roland set to again with Pieter and the others to put out the scatter of new fires and lift masonry for the rescue squad.

They worked on steadily for hours, responding to each emergency as it arose, occasionally reporting back to the Control Centre shelter for new instructions. There was a succession of panics as the water stopped and as they ran out of sandbags. But the water came on again sporadically and an army lorry arrived with half a load of sandbags. They did what they could.

Roland had no sense of time passing but he was suddenly aware that the threatening pink reflection of fire was mixing with the natural light of the early morning. And the sound had changed. The bombing had stopped. There was no droning, no screaming, no thud of explosions, no crack of disintegrating buildings. He stood up and stretched his back. Around him, other men and women were doing the same. The silence was uncanny. They looked uneasily through the gaping hole in the roof to the sky. It was several minutes before anyone spoke. Then there was a low chatter, here and there a sharp burst of laughter as individuals realised they were still alive and the factory was not burned down entirely.

As they were returning from the Control Centre, Pieter Vann touched Roland's arm. 'It's stopped, Roland. The factory still stands. Your tool is safe. Come!' He half pulled Roland, passing other men, now talking and gesturing with some animation, and a girl in a tin hat who was spraying the smoking residue of a small fire with a ridiculously small stirrup pump.

They walked through the factory past clusters of stunned and quietened firemen up the now twisted metal steps and through a window, to their watching post, which was still, remarkably, intact. Roland rubbed his blackened eyes to see more clearly before him this city, his modern city, now a smoking ruin with a flickering crown of dancing fire. The sky was red, the scattered lowering clouds touched with purple. The heat of the factory was burning his feet, the heat of the burned and burning city was wafting towards him.

He clutched at Pieter Vann's hand, one part of his abstracted mind noting how small and rough were these hands, hands he had never touched before.

'They've done it, Pieter. They've done it. Bastards.'

'And look! Look!' The little man's voice was hoarse with sorrow. He pointed through the swirl of smoke towards the Cathedral in the middle distance. Its spire was still there but the roof was burning steadily. Near to it, the spire of Holy Trinity, still intact, kept it forlorn company.

'They say they bombed everything. Factories to be sure. Hospitals, shelters...' muttered Pieter Vann.

Roland put a hand to his face. 'Lizza and Rebecca. No, they'll be all right. That shelter's deep. They'll be safe. I'm sure of it. Won't they, Pieter?' But Pieter couldn't hear him. He was crying, great ugly sobs racking his broad body. Then, as Roland watched, he fell to his knees and on to the ground, shuddering, his eyes staring.

'Come on, come on, Pieter. At least we're here!' But there was no response. So, humping the Dutchman on to his shoulders, Roland struggled to return the way they had come. He carried him through the burning shops towards the central shelter, past other people who were stunned or crying or staring straight ahead of them in disbelieving relief. A first-aid worker helped Pieter down from Roland's back and settled him on a stretcher beside a member of the rescue squad who had an ominous space under the blanket where his left foot should be. She pulled a blanket up over Pieter Vann and stroked the hair out of his wide, staring and terrified eyes.

The gentleness of her gesture made Roland slump on to a bench in tears. Another young woman in uniform was in front of him, holding out a mug. 'Tea, love?' He felt the softness of her hand as he took the hot mug, and thought of Lizza, longing with every sinew to be with her. He would go. Soon.

'I want to see my wife. To check...'

'You can go now. Any time.'

She was young, this girl, no more than eighteen. He frowned. 'Is it all over? I didn't hear the all-clear.'

She smiled grimly. 'We got it by note. There's no electricity.' She shook her head. 'No electricity, no gas, no water. No nothing, mate. They got us good and proper this time.'

He gulped down the strong sweet tea. 'I've got to go. My wife and my daughter...'

She took the cup. 'Good luck, mate!'

He took out his notebook from his inside pocket. Beside November 14 he put: *'Great raid. My estimation three hundred planes, continuous drop.'* He closed his eyes to estimate the tonnage but his brain, normally so obedient, would not work. *'Incendiaries all night lighting and relighting the target. Flying bombs. Land-mines. There must be thousands of dead.'*

141

He glanced at the comatose figure of Pieter Vann and clipped his pen to his top pocket. 'I've got to get to my wife and daughter,' he said dully.

The girl gave him a little push. 'Well, go, will you, and good luck.'

She stood watching as he stumped out, his step quickening with every yard, and then went back to her tea-urn.

The message about the all-clear had rippled through the factory and Roland King was only one of hundreds of weary fire-fighters racing home to check on homes and family who could very well be dead.

His tired brain now allowed him to panic. The wall of the bike shed had been blown off and his was one of the few bikes still in one piece. He wheeled it through the heaps of debris in the factory yard. Outside it was impossible even to wheel it, so he lifted it on his back and walked. There were more barriers in the road, some caused by bomb damage, others man-made barriers to keep walkers away from unexploded bombs. He made his way around a hole in the road with a car in it. There was blood on the door but no passengers. He passed buses which were turned sideways at bizarre angles. He passed policemen, soldiers and rescue workers digging steadily at piles of rubble. He passed a woman crying quietly in the doorway of a bombed house. He passed a woman being led along by a small child of about six years. The child's face was calm but the mother was emitting loud inhuman shrieks. Her coat flapped open and she was naked underneath.

In some places the overhead wires were down. In a place where they were still intact, he saw a fur coat hanging over them, flapping in the wind like a scarecrow. On one corner a man in army uniform was sitting in the gutter, his head in his hands. On another, more people were digging steadily at debris. On another, there were two soldiers whose tidy uniform and clean faces told you they had just entered the city. They had machine-guns strapped to their backs. At one point he stood back against a wall to allow passage to a platoon of soldiers—all young, clean-faced, all fully armed—marching steadily towards the centre.

The way finally cleared. He clattered his bike on to the road and started to pedal like fury, steering around potholes and on to pavements to maintain some kind of speed.

There was a crater the size of a double decker where the entrance to the big shelter had been. Wheeling his bike carefully around it, he buttonholed one of the policemen who were clustered beside it.

The policeman shook his head. 'Sorry, mate. No one left here. Most got out and the rest have gone...' He nodded to a receding ambulance. '...hospital or mortuary.'

He shut his eyes. 'Dear God. Anything, anything. You can have anything if they are safe. I promise I'll go to church every Sunday, do anything...' Then, clear as a bell, he heard

Lizza's voice. 'No, Rollie, not for me. You know better than that.'

He whipped around but the scene was just as it had been before. No Lizza. Then, throwing his bike to one side, he started running towards his house. A journey which would normally have taken him five minutes took him twenty. The back parts of the house were flattened, open to the sky. At the front, the white lace fluttered from a front window bereft of glass. Some of Lizza's pretty things were untouched. He looked around. Her pretty china ladies were missing. They must be among the debris. Incredibly, his garage was still standing. Through the splintered wood he could see his car, intact.

Something caught his eye on the ground. He picked up Rebecca's fireman doll. She'd had it when he left them outside the shelter. They must be here at the house. They had to be. He started to pull at a great spar of wood, then looked around in despair.

He ran to three different recovery squads, who repulsed him, saying they were too busy to help. But the last sent two soldiers with him, saying they would come when they could. He started to pull away at the stones. 'Steady, boy, steady!' said the older soldier. They insisted he work very slowly, moving the stones one by one. They came to a place where two spars from the roof had left a void, and there in the space below was Rebecca, lying peacefully and untouched, her eyes closed. Thrilling with relief, he grabbed her. But she was inert, her skin too cool. One soldier gently pulled at his back. 'I think she's gone, mate. Here. Give her to me.'

Roland clutched her to him even closer. Then a woman in some kind of uniform was standing beside him. She removed Rebecca from his clasp and lay her on a blanket in a part of the garden where the grass was clear. She pulled another blanket, quite rough and grey, up over the child's face. The storm inside him quietened when he could not see his daughter's face.

'Keep her safe,' he said urgently to the woman. 'Keep her safe.'

The soldier touched Roland's arm. 'Now, mate, the other one might be all right.'

'Three. There's my wife and nephew and my friend.'

Alex suddenly loomed up beside him.

'You're here!' Roland looked behind him. 'Where's Lizza...and...'

Alex shook his head, folding his mouth tight, his face grey and old. 'We never went into the shelter, Roland. Rebecca cried. So they came back to the house. I went off to find Josie and the others. Now Josie's ma and little Anne-Marie's been shot by them bastards, in the road. We found them there this morning, being lifted on to a truck. Josie won't leave her...' The boy's strained voice ceased as his panicky, wandering eye came to rest on the body on the lawn covered by the grey blanket. '...Who's that?' he said.

Roland did not answer. Alex went over, knelt down and pulled back the blanket. He looked up at Roland, tears standing in his eyes. 'Our Lizza?' he said.

145

Roland nodded at the wrecked house where the soldiers, and now two more men from the rescue squad, were delicately picking off stones and bricks. The two of them joined the digging. Several times Roland had to restrain Alex, who became impatient with the caution and started to tear away recklessly at the stones, always muttering, 'Me Gram'll kill us. She'll kill me for leaving our Lizza like this.' In his head images of Maeve Callaghan, the side of her face torn with a bullet wound, slopped around, mixed up with the calm face of little Rebecca, equally dead. 'Me Gram'll kill us.'

'Stop it!' yelled Roland finally, pulling him off and looking him hard in the eye. 'You'll kill her yourself at this rate. Do it gently, like they say! Here, help me with this window. And stay quiet. We're listening for them.'

Very carefully they lifted off the bay window, now bereft of its coloured glass and clear of the chimney stones which had been weighing it down. They worked towards the stairwell. Roland worked in silence, his black-rimmed eyes now narrow and hard with concentration.

The rescue squad man signalled them all to stop, then said quietly to Roland, 'Call, son. If she's there she should hear you now.'

Roland stood up straight, rubbed his eyes and shouted. 'Lizza! Lizza! Where in heaven are you?'

He called again.

Then they heard a voice, very faint. 'Rollie! Rollie! Here! We're here! But Rebecca...is she there? Is she outside?'

CHAPTER 10

Lizza and Krystof yelled and shouted in response to Roland. But after hearing his first shout they could hear no more voices, no matter how hard they called. Lizza felt as though they were shouting into a void. Soon, though, light began to filter into their restricted space. The heavy dust in the cellar started to whirl up in the beams of light, and the planks of the staircase above them started to shudder.

Krystof put up his arms over Lizza's head to hold the timbers fast. Blinking against the gritty dust, Lizza could just make out the tendons standing out on the inside of his wrists. She placed her hands so they were between his on the timber and pushed hard. She could feel the wood trembling like a living thing.

'Don't push,' said Krystof urgently. 'The baby. Remember your baby. I'll keep it off.'

She slackened her pressure and put her hands on top of his. Her palms itched with the feel of the coarse hair on the back of his hands. Power was flowing between them as she added her will to his, to prevent their rescuers being their executioners.

Then at last she could hear the voices again: Roland and Alex calling to her to hold on, hold on, they would be there soon. There was a great creaking and a crash and Krystof slumped beside her as a joist fell on his head.

'Come on, Krystof, they're nearly here,' she said. 'Come on!' She put her hand on the beam and pushed and could see daylight. Then it was all over. The weight of the timbers was being lifted from her hands. Roland and a man in uniform were carefully removing wood and plaster from her legs, and the cellar door off the foot that had hurt so much.

Roland pulled her up, half lifting her from the ground. 'Krystof, get Krystof,' she muttered. 'Something hit him.'

Then she stood much straighter on her one good foot. 'Rebecca? Did you get Rebecca?'

His hands fell away. 'Lizza...I... We...' He turned away from her and leaned his head against a wall.

Tears in his eyes, it was Alex who took her arm and led her, limping, through the debris. 'She didn't make it, Lizz. She's not hurt, marked, like. But she didn't make it. The rescue man said it was the blast. Not a mark on her. Just tossed up like a doll.'

He brought her to where Rebecca was lying, on the clear space of lawn. She kneeled and turned back the grey blanket and touched the cold, perfect face with one finger, pushing some stray hair behind the little ear. Then she pulled the body to her and looked up at the sky and around her, where the morning was made dusk by the black smoke and soot which seemed to be everywhere.

She laughed shrilly up into Alex's face. 'He wants me to be grateful now, you know.

148

Grateful that I had her for two years before He took her, so much more than the other two. He wants me to be grateful now.' She held Rebecca even closer and her tears fell into the auburn curls which she had combed round her finger that morning, into glossy little sausage curls.

Krystof was unconscious when they pulled him out. The rescue squad man put a hip flask to his lips and forced him to drink, and he came round. The bump on his head was the size of an egg, but apart from that he seemed well enough.

'You all right, mate?' The tired face of the rescuer looked down at him, pleased that, after so many dead, this was a live one.

Krystof rubbed his temple and nodded.

The man offered Krystof a cigarette, which he took gratefully. 'Right. We'll love yer and leave yer now. The lad and Mr King here'll watch out for the lady and you. We've got a dozen more to tackle like this. Dead or alive, God only knows.' He took a deep breath, brushed down his jacket, straightened up and marched onwards for the next one. He had worked eleven hours straight, helping to rescue twelve people so far that night. And lifted out seventeen bodies and parts of bodies. And he didn't know whether or not his own family were alive or dead.

Krystof sat up straight and looked round, taking in the rigid figure of Roland beside the wall and Lizza, clutching a little bundle in a grey blanket. Painfully he got to his feet and, leaning on Alex, went across to Roland.

149

He put a hand on his shoulder. 'How are you, my boy?'

The face that turned to him was blank, quite clear of feeling. Roland shook his head. 'I can't think, Krystof. I am so tired. They've got the factory. I can't think what to say to her. Our little girl dead now. Caught in the blast. And...'

They both looked at Lizza with her sad burden. 'Go to her, Roland!'

Roland shook his head and turned his face back to the wall.

Krystof went and knelt down beside Lizza, who was rocking Rebecca's body in her arms. He looked up at Alex, who shrugged helplessly. 'Come across to Roland, Lizza,' said Krystof. 'He needs you.'

She folded her lips and did not lift her gaze from Rebecca's face. 'I don't want him,' she said.

An explosion ripped the following silence and their heads turned as a great swirl of dust filled the street. Out of the dust, wheeling a rickety pram with a rickety wheel, walked Josie Callaghan. Her little brother Liam was sitting inside, wrapped in a filthy blanket still stiff with sticky blood. In his hand he clutched a single high-heeled shoe, scuffed with mud. His mouth was open wide and he was crying almost silently.

Alex went and put a hand on Josie's arm. Lizza heaved herself to her feet, took Rebecca's body across, the blanket trailing, and carefully placed her in Roland's arms. 'Take care of her, Rollie. She wants nothing lying on the ground.'

Then she went across and put an arm round Josie.

'Mammy's dead, Mrs King. And the baby,' said Josie in a dry voice. 'I didn't know what to do. You were the only one I could think of.' She looked across at Roland. 'And is that little Rebecca, too?'

Now her own sobs joined Liam's silent howling.

Lizza shook her by the shoulders and from somewhere deep inside found a smile for the girl. 'Don't cry, Josie. You have to keep going for Liam's sake.' She pushed Josie into Alex's grasp and leaned into the pram and heaved the heavy toddler into her arms, pulling his legs around her hips. The child's mouth closed and his howls were reduced to hiccups.

Still holding the boy, she walked over to Roland. 'That evil man, that Hitler, he killed my Rebecca, didn't he, Rollie? And Maeve Callaghan and Anne-Marie! And God killed the twins before. There's no mercy any more, is there, Rollie? No mercy.'

Roland sat down hard on the broken wall and bent his head low over the dead figure of his daughter. 'No, Lizza, there's no mercy.'

'So we can't rely on either of them. For good or evil, evil or good. All we have is ourselves. Just ourselves.'

Krystof was beside her. 'That's the spirit, Lizza. That's the spirit,' he said softly. He turned to Roland. 'Get on your feet, my friend.

151

We have to take care of your daughter, find somewhere for her to rest peacefully. And we have to find some place for your family here to shelter. Are there centres? There were in London. Then we have to get to the factory, if there's anything left of it. Stand up, Roland! We need your aeroplanes more than ever now.'

Alex, standing with the frozen figure of Josie, breathed out hard. 'Yes. The factory,' he said. 'There'll be clearing up to do. I'm coming with yer.' He looked up at the sky, now black with fire-smoke but free from planes. 'There'll be no more mercy from us either, you bastards.'

Lizza hid her face in Liam's soft neck. She rocked him to and fro and his whimpers stopped altogether. Josie put her face to the sky, still glowing with fire, streaked with swirling black smoke, and started screaming.

The voice emerging in its miraculous way from the polished cabinet was measured and careful. '...When dawn broke next morning, it was drizzling and there was a mist over the town. Men and women began to crawl out of their shelters to look for their friends and survey the ruins of the city. They could hardly recognise it. It was impossible to see where the central streets we knew so well had been. That Friday morning we were surprised when we heard that a building had not been hit. It seemed hopeless with so much of our homes, shops, places of work and so much of our lovely city in ruins...'

Beatrice leaned over and turned off the wireless. She looked at her mother rocking

152

away violently on the wooden rocker by the fire. 'We'll find out soon, Ma.'

Her mother placed a tight-closed fist on the three days' newspapers piled up on her knee. 'It says many killed. Many killed, lass.'

'It's a big city, Ma. More'n a hundred thousand people, there'd be a lot—most really—not killed.' She was desperate herself; her own voice, reassuring her mother, sounded hollow in her own ears.

The pace of the rocking increased. 'I sometimes wonder what I've done to deserve all this. My man first, then my son behind wire, probably dead, and now my little lad, probably blown to pieces...'

Beatrice took a breath. 'Alex is my little lad, Ma. And if he is lost—and I don't believe he is—it's my loss first.'

The rocking stopped.

Beatrice went on. 'You haven't mentioned Lizza, Ma. She's closer to you in blood than Alex. And I would think, more precious, because she was born from love, not rape.'

Her mother lashed out. 'Stop that, it's dirty talk!'

'Aren't you worried about Lizza, and Rebecca and Roland?'

The rocking started again. 'Lizza'll look after herself. Always has.'

Beatrice laughed shrilly. 'Ma, how d'you think she'll look after herself with tons of high explosive raining down on her?'

Her mother looked at her. 'Our Lizza doesn't need me. Never has since she went away to work

153

when she was fourteen. Independent. That's what she is.'

'You sent her away. She didn't run away.'

'Yes. 'Cause she was independent, don't yer see?'

Beatrice stood up. 'You mean she didn't kow-tow to you like we did? Better out of the way?'

Her mother shrugged. Beatrice was right in her way. Lizza, the middle one, had always been defiant in that quiet, intelligent way which was so hard to deal with, much harder than open defiance, which could be dealt with by a good hard clip round the ear. Or the belt if need be. But Lizza would argue in that determined voice, defeat you with words. It had lost her her one and only domestic place, where she was sacked for quoting Shakespeare at the lady of the house. So, unlike the other girls who were much more biddable, she had to go away to get work. And Alice knew, of all of them, Lizza would survive even the harsh environment of the mills. She was a survivor, Lizza.

'But what about the men? Our Bernard did plenty kow-towing and now he's doing it to that wife of his. But Jonnie didn't, and neither does Alex...'

'Men're different,' said Alice Bremner.

'You just don't know the heartache you've caused that girl, do you? No idea.' Saying the words she had swallowed back for years was a heady experience. She felt like smiling.

Alice shrugged. 'I've told you, she can look after herself, the men...where are you going?'

'Out for a walk.'

Alice waited for the door to close behind her daughter and stood up to poke the fire. Her eye flickered to the picture of Tom in his soldier's uniform. 'I know he's to come to you, this boy. You want him there. I can feel it.'

When Beatrice came back twenty minutes later she was smiling broadly. She had two letters in her hands. 'I caught the postman. One from each of them, Ma, so they're both all right.'

Alice held her hand out. Beatrice looked at them both, sighed, and gave her mother the one in Alex's handwriting.

Lizza's letter was on soiled white paper. The handwriting was uncharacteristically shaky.

17.11.40

Dear Ma and Beatrice,

I've tried to send a telegram. I've tried to telephone the minister so he could tell you, but it is impossible. As a final effort, Roland's taking these letters to work to give to one of the drivers to post in Leicester. The factory was very badly damaged but they are working night and day to get it back in production. The roof's already repaired.

The raid on the fourteenth has left this city a city of the dead, among whom is Rebecca, our little daughter. She was unharmed. There was no mark or bruise on her. She still had on that nice blouse you made her, Beatrice. A bit muddy. But her skirt was in shreds. You know, the one where you embroidered the tuck? That

155

was a pity. Such a nice skirt. But she wasn't marked, not a mark on her. Not a hair out of place. There was this great blast which brought most of the house down. It kind of killed her and sucked her away somehow. So she wasn't bruised or damaged or anything. There is a problem over the funeral. Too many to bury. They say there will be a mass grave. But that would be too much for her, I know it. I don't know how I can stand this. But there is the new baby and he is kicking away. And my neighbour was killed with her baby and I have her little boy and her young daughter to take care of. We are in their house as ours is damaged. We have no gas or electric light, no water, no milk or bread at the moment. They say mobile vans are going round with bread and water but not round here so far. Loudspeakers are going round telling the homeless where to meet to be taken out of the city. At least we're not homeless. I can't write more.

Always your affectionate Lizza

Alex's letter was scrawled in his schoolboy hand

...just to let you know I'm all right as are Lizza and Roland. Lizza says she will tell you about little Rebecca. We are now in the house of the Callaghans, where the mother was killed in a line of people getting out of the city. Machine-gunned from a plane. The daughter, Josie, is a brave kid, and Lizza's keeping us all together, I can't think how, as she is heartbroken over

Rebecca. That's plain for anyone to see. Roland is never here, always at the factory, rebuilding. I've been there myself helping, but not the hours that he does. There's all sorts of schemes to get production under way. We have a lodger here, a Polish worker whose hostel was blasted to bits. He's a good bloke. The real point of this letter is to say that I am definitely joining up as soon as they let me. There is no question that you are safer up in the air than down here on the ground. I've learned that anyway. There was no danger of that, anyway, on this raid. As far as I can tell none of our fighter planes was up there, anyway, in the big raid. Roland says not and he makes big charts of all these things. Where were they? Can't think where they were, it was such a big show. London probably.
Love Alex

Alice Bremner stood up and peered into the mirror over the high mantelpiece. Her own image dissolved and the face that stared back at her was that of the fourteen-year-old Lizza, her eyes masking fear with boldness and defiance, and a borrowed hat tipped saucily on her wild curls. The girl needed that boldness to go off that day to the mills in Bradford at her age, and survive.

'Now's the time to be brave again, lass,' she whispered. 'God bless.'

'What's that, Mam?' Beatrice's face appeared beside hers in the mirror.

Alice folded her mouth tight and turned away. 'Nowt,' she said.

Beatrice went to a drawer, pulled out a thin lined pad and a pencil and put it on the scrubbed kitchen table. 'There!'

'What's that?'

'Write to her. Write to them! Tell them to come home. It's safe, much safer here.'

Alice shrugged. 'There was a bomb here, last week, over near the coast.'

Beatrice laughed hysterically. 'Did you listen to the wireless? Did you read the paper? Do you know what they've just gone through? You write and ask them.'

Beatrice took her mother's arm. Alice looked down at the hand. They never touched. Probably the last time Alice had touched her daughter was when she cut her hair when she was so ill after Alex was born. The time before that was when Beatrice was a little child herself.

Beatrice shook her. 'You write, Mam. And tell them to come home. Leave Roland to do whatever he has to do there and come here.'

'She says she has those others with her now...and this house is too small...'

'They're children, Ma, those others. Like those children at Carhoe Orphanage you always want to bring home. It's safer here. There were six of us in this house when we were little. We all fitted in.' She pushed her mother into the hard kitchen chair. 'Write, will you? Tell them to come home.'

Slowly, Alice picked up the pen and started to write.

CHAPTER 11

In the week following the raid, the people camping out in the damaged Callaghan house numbly worked themselves into a routine, at the centre of which was survival.

Only the downstairs of the house was habitable. The blast which had killed Rebecca and flattened Lizza's house had stripped the roof tiles off the Callaghan house. On the first day Alex had liberated a four-wheeled barrow from a deserted garden shed and dragged Josie off round the streets to find tarpaulins. He had heard that soldiers had tarpaulins which could be thrown over roofs to make the houses habitable.

The streets still smelt of smoke and gas and cordite, and soon the stink of sewage from broken pipes seemed to be behind and underneath everything. The pavements were busy with firemen still putting out the remaining fires. Soldiers were sweeping away glass, helping rescue workers, who were still moving masonry with a surgeon's care. Anxious relatives were still insisting that they had heard tappings, or they knew that the bodies of their loved ones were still inside the rows of collapsed houses. In streets which were still standing, furniture vans were being loaded with the lifetime possessions of people who had decided, finally, that they had had enough.

After half an hour's prowling, Alex and Josie did come upon a truck full of tarpaulins manned by a crew of soldiers. They were supplying the tarpaulins to some building workers in civvies, who were tackling the job of making half-destroyed houses habitable. Alex told the soldiers he was tackling the same job himself ten streets away, so could he please have one? After some consultation between the soldiers, a tarpaulin was handed over.

On their way back, Alex and Josie were stopped on the road by two more soldiers, a corporal and a private, standing on a corner with fixed bayonets.

'And where might you two be going?' The Corporal had a Scottish accent. He raised his fixed bayonet across their path.

'What's it to you?' said Josie belligerently.

'Och, we've got a cocky one here, Private Campbell.'

'It's a tarpaulin,' said Alex, more intimidated than he would like to have admitted. 'For our roof; it was blown off.'

The private used his bayonet to poke at the tarpaulin.

Josie put a hand on the barrow. 'Leave it alone. There's nothing there.'

He scowled at her. 'No saying you might not be looters. Stopped three of those blighters this morning, is that not true, Corporal? One of them had a silver tea service. Another feller had two wirelesses.'

'No tea set here,' said Josie.

The soldiers stared at them, unmoving.

'What's this?' said Josie. 'Sure, it's no better than bloody Nazi Germany? The Germans bomb us out and kill us and here is you carrying on like bloody Nazis.'

The Corporal stepped right in front of her. 'Irish, are ye?' he growled. 'Och, the Irish have nothing to tell us! Claim they're not spitting in anyone's yard but'll open the back gate for dirty Germans all the same.'

She leapt upon him then and he started to push at her, none too gently, with the stock of his rifle. Alex finally got between them and pulled her off. 'I'm English. She's English,' he said through gritted teeth. 'And her ma, who was Irish, and her little sister, who's English, was shot dead in the road on Thursday night by a Nazi plane. Just what is it you want from us?'

The Corporal scowled from one of them to the other, then took a step back. 'Pass,' he said.

They moved the length of one street and Josie looked up at Alex. 'Let's do it,' she said.

'What?'

'Some looting.'

'Don't talk rubbish.'

'Let's at least go to Beaconsfield to see it's still there. And if it is, we can loot the rose window and take it back with us.'

The house was still there; the rose window was still intact. They wandered around the upstairs room, unwilling to return to the realities of the broken streets. Finally Josie turned him to face her. 'Let's do it.'

'What this time?'

161

'What married people do.'

'What? It's eleven o'clock in the morning.'

She laughed and brought her face up to his and kissed him. She stroked her hands down the sleeves of his Burberry then unbuttoned it. Then she was pulling him by the belt to the bed. 'Have you done it before? The whole thing?'

He was brick red. 'No...'

'Have you seen anyone do it?'

'No. I only ever lived with women on their own. And Lizza and Roland don't seem to look at each other... What about you? Have you done...seen it?'

'Oh, I ain't done it. I've seen it all right, many a time. But it ain't too pretty the way *he* does it to her. He tried it with me once but she stopped him. He gave her a great beating that night...'

'Who?'

'My dad, with my mammy.' She eyed him soberly. 'But all that don't matter no more, now she's dead. And he's God knows where, getting killed I hope. And we all might be dead tomorrow.' She sighed. 'I always thought there might be a nice way... Now there might not be time. We could all be dead tomorrow.'

'Defeatist talk!' He kissed her then. On her wet eyes, and on her cheeks. On her stringy hair and on her thin shoulders over her blouse. She guided his hand to her breast and he could feel her nipples tickling his palm.

'Can I see?' he said humbly.

She unbuttoned her dress and pulled the top down round her waist and then her thin arms were above her head as she pulled off her vest.

162

He touched the crinkling flesh of the deep raspberry nipples with the tip of his finger. 'I didn't know you could have them so small,' he said wonderingly.

'Now that's a foolish thing to say.' She lifted her hand to the back of his head. 'Would you like to kiss them?'

Then her hands were in his hair and his lips were kissing her left nipple, his tongue was teasing the puckered flesh, and even, daringly, he caught it gently between his teeth. She gave a roaring laugh of delight. 'Now the other! Now the other!' she instructed.

He felt he could detonate better than any bomb. He pulled her to the bed and lay her down and kissed her face and breasts again, twisting himself like a contortionist to take off his coat and his jacket as he did so.

'Do you know what to do?' She was breathing heavily now. She guided his hand beneath her skirt and to her knickers. He pulled away at them and got them over her greyish socks. 'Look now. Do you see where you're going?'

Her stomach was slender. He touched the fine baby-like hair. 'Feel!' she said. 'I do sometimes. It's nice.' He stroked his finger towards the cleft and felt a delicate, pulsing mound of flesh. Her hand was on his. Her finger over his. 'Like this,' she said.

She tensed as both their fingers went in.

'Does it hurt?' he mumbled, his lips feeling too thick. He pulled both their hands away.

'Just the littlest bit.'

163

He groaned, pressing his legs together, in agony now.

'But can I go there?'

'If you're a good boy.'

The air was suddenly full of the smell of his grandmother's kitchen when she put raw dough to prove. 'Now kiss me properly,' she said.

Then he was kissing her mouth, pulling desperately at his own waistband, terrified of the humiliation that the explosion would happen too soon. She shouted a little as he entered her and he tried to pause but he couldn't. Then she said, 'Keep going! Keep going!' and started chanting swear words. He tried to keep the thrusting going but could only last a few minutes before he finally came, filling the space they had made with their fingers with his own liquids, making them finally one.

When they rolled away from each other they lay quiet for several minutes. Then she shivered.

'Did it hurt?' he whispered.

'Yes.'

'Was it nice?'

'Some bits.' She was whispering too, as though there were some things you could only say in whispers. 'But you were so big I thought there was no room for you. That hurt.'

'They say it doesn't hurt all the time.'

'How do you know?'

'There was this lad at school. He told me. He read it in a book they had in their house. He promised to lend it to me but never did.' He paused. 'Why d'you swear like that?'

'Didn't I tell you? I do that when I stand on my hands. Then nothing matters. Nothing counts.' She sat up and said in her normal voice. 'Sure it's time we were away now, Alex. Lizza'll be battling with the leaks for the want of that tarpaulin.'

He stood up and buttoned his shirt and pulled up his pants. She put on her vest and blouse and pulled on her knickers. She looked down. 'There's blood,' she said.

He looked around the room. 'It don't matter. We'll not be back here again. We have to get on with things.'

She nodded slowly. 'Right,' she said. 'We'll take the rose window. It'll go under the tarpaulin.'

They never did return to the house. That night there was no raid. But the following night there was a raid, much smaller than that on the fourteenth. But in that raid the street in which Beaconsfield stood was demolished by a high-explosive bomb.

In those first days the smallest thing took the greatest effort on everyone's part. Lizza cooked on the open fire, fuelled at first by what was left of the coal, then by scrap wood scavenged by Alex and Josie from the bomb sites. There was no water, so they had to catch rainwater in buckets and dishes, and raid water butts to supplement the unreliable supplies from the water waggons. At least they could get food, some specially off-ration in the emergency.

They had to drag mattresses downstairs to

sleep on, so there was no privacy. If this offended Roland's fastidious soul it wasn't obvious. He stayed as many hours as he could at the factory. He was rarely in the house, but when he was he was silent. He had spoken little to Lizza since the night of the Blitz.

Krystof was very quiet too. His hostel had been demolished, and he was pressed to stay by Roland. He treated Lizza with immaculate courtesy, but met her gaze very little. Their unity on the night of the Blitz might just have been a passing dream woven from the confusion.

Lizza herself was preoccupied; every minute of the day, limping round the house, she looked behind her for Rebecca, her soul aching for the sight of the small head, the sound of the chuckling voice. The presence of Liam was healing in its own way. The little boy was cheerful enough during the day but wouldn't let Lizza out of his sight. He screamed at night. He slept beside Josie but at midnight he would start screaming and would only be pacified by being taken to Lizza's side of the mattress she shared with Josie, to sleep in the crook of her arm. Later she would stir in her troubled sleep and pull him to her, muttering Rebecca's name.

The only life in the house was in the air between Alex and Josie, who were rarely out of each other's sight and who seemed to survive the days on a series of private jokes. They ran around procuring wood and water, queued for food and wandered through the streets of the

166

besieged city picking up scraps of news to carry home to the others.

Roland had instructed Alex to stay at the house, and 'see to things there'. He and Krystof were working at the factory from dawn till well after dusk, making their contribution to the repair work. They shared a mattress inside the front door, so as not to disturb the others, who had to go to bed with the fading of the natural light.

Lizza's greatest practical problem was where to bury Rebecca by herself, in her own private space. Waylaid in a midnight whispered conversation, Roland merely talked about the mass grave where all the victims would be buried. He shrugged when Lizza protested, mentioning the emergency, the pressure on resources, and she beat his unresisting body, shouting that it was their daughter they were talking about, not some anonymous victim of the mass bombing: Rebecca with her bright hair with its sausage curls, her white skin and her cheeky round eyes.

Then Liam started to cry and she went to comfort him.

Lizza finally decided that she did not want Rebecca buried in Coventry at all. On the fifth day she received a short pencilled note from her mother. '...*It's time you and those bairns were away from there. There's room and safety here for you.*' It was a cold, polite note that inevitably fuelled her perpetual anger with her mother. Couldn't she have written in urgent terms, saying she wanted her, needed her there?

Later that morning, queuing for bread with Liam straddling her hip, she took her turn next to a turbaned beefy woman who was complaining about the shortages in a loud voice. She recognised the accent and touched the woman's arm. 'You must come where I come from. South Durham?'

'Aye, pet, how'd'yer guess? Dinnat say me voice is givin' us away again. An' I just had this man from the wireless ask me to read the news!' She roared at this, her shoulders and her fat upper arms shaking. 'An' you? C'n hardly tell from your talk.'

'I've been away a long while.'

'A long while? Why, man, I've been down here fifteen year an' me daughter ses I'm still thicker than a Co-op loaf. Ha! Let's see what they'll make of her up there now, like, with her Coventry twang.'

'You're going back up home?'

'First thing in the mornin', pet. Waggon's packed up. We're sleepin' on floors tonight.'

'Where d'you come from?'

'Rulton, a village north-west of Priorton, south of Durham City.'

'You pass through Bracks Hill?'

'Bracks Hill? The place with the clock? Know nowhere better, pet!'

Lizza's mind focused on a possibility, a solution to a problem which had been sitting in her head somewhere since she had been rescued from the wreck of her house and Roland had put Rebecca in her arms. 'If I brought you something could you drop it off

168

there? At Bracks Hill?' she said.

'I don't know.' The woman was hesitant. 'What it is?'

'A—a box. Only a box.' She opened her arms wide. 'Just about this big.'

'Oh, well, nee harm I suppose,' said the woman. 'Ye'll have to bring it round tonight, pet. Like I said, we're off first thing. Bring it round. We live in Bleach Avenue. Can't miss us. The van's outside... Hey missis, dinnat run off like that, yer'll lose yer place in the queue!'

Lizza left the screaming Liam with Josie, emptied the Callaghan pram and walked it to the crematorium. It didn't take her long to persuade the man to let her have Rebecca, in her neat unvarnished box. He had more bodies than he could cope with anyway.

When she explained to Alex what he had to do, he objected at first. The last thing he wanted to do was return to Bracks Hill. 'But I can't let her go on her own, can I, Alex? Your...Beatrice and your Gram'll know what to do. The minister and all that. They can let their God take care of her. I won't have her here with all those...other poor people. She's one, not a mass. And I have to be here, for Liam and Josie, and Roland. Please, Alex!'

He looked at Josie, who shrugged her thin shoulders.

'The kid needs to be in her own land,' said Josie. 'Ain't it the only thing you can do?'

169

'I'm coming back!' said Alex.

'Come back!' said Lizza. 'But do this for me.'

Alex's arms ached, and the sweat stood on his brow, as he carried the box in his arms from the main road, round the corner of the back lane, then down towards his grandmother's back gate. He had not thought that little Rebecca would weigh so heavy. He passed an old man with a garden fork over one shoulder and a sackful of potatoes over another. The old man stopped, dropped his burdens and removed his battered cap, holding it over his heart.

Women standing at the gates of their back yards glanced in sympathy and curiosity at the boy with his painful burden. One of them came out and held up her flapping washing so that Alex could duck through. 'Poor bairn,' she murmured.

There was a patter of feet behind him.

'Alex!' It was Beatrice. Her gaze dropped to the box. 'It's the bairn!'

He nodded, breathing heavily. 'Our Lizza wanted her to come home. I brought her on a waggon with some folks from Rulton.'

Beatrice took one end of the coffin and they walked along together with Rebecca between them. She helped him manoeuvre it through the gate. Carefully, they placed it on the top of the brick boiler which was in the corner of the yard.

Beatrice shook her head, her lips trembling.

170

'Poor little thing.' She called out to her mother.

Alice Bremner stood in the back door and stared at the white-wood unvarnished box. She put her hands together and closed her eyes. *Suffer little children to come unto me.*

Then she glared at Alex. 'Well, then, lad! Bring the bairn inside! Are ye gunna leave her there all day, like?' she said. 'She can go in the front room. Then you can run for the minister.'

'Aw, Gram, don't I get a cup of tea first? I've come a long way, you know. Slept in a waggon last night.' (The fat woman had sworn like a trooper when she realised what she had committed herself to carrying, and made him stay close by it for the whole journey. He had cocked an eye at her and told her he wanted to do that anyway.)

Now, carefully, he took one end of the little coffin, and Beatrice the other.

'You're black as clarts, Alex. Don't they have any water down there?' Alice scowled at him. 'Well, bring her in, bring her in! She can go on the front-room table.'

'Water? Down there? Well, no, seeing as you ask. Not since the big raid. Taps're dry,' he grumbled, wincing at the movement inside the box as they tipped it slightly to get it through the narrow entrance to the scullery.

She stood to one side to let them through the kitchen with their burden. 'Well, I suppose the bairn's in no hurry. You can get a wash and a cup of tea and *then* run get the minister.'

Behind him, she was smiling faintly.

CHAPTER 12

Pieter Vann had still not returned to work after five days so, at the end of another heavy day sorting debris, Roland and Krystof went in search of him. They started at the two hospitals, which were clearing their own bomb damage as well as dealing with patients. At the Gulson, a nurse checked a list and said that a Mr Vann had been sent off to Kenilworth, out of the way of the bombs. She checked the list again. '...but there's no note of injury here. He might just have gone home.' She gave them a Cheylesmore address.

They tracked over to Cheylesmore, which had had its share of damage. They needed the help of the pencil-thin light of Krystof's torch as they picked their way in the pitch dark through rubble, around potholes, avoiding streets closed off because of unexploded bombs. Pieter Vann's house, much larger than Roland had expected, was untouched. The neat garden, its glossy evergreens on duty beside the front door, was clear of debris.

It took five minutes of knocking before the door finally opened and a grey-faced Pieter Vann hustled them into the house quickly to restore the black-out. 'Ah! Friends! I was sleeping. Come in!'

The echoing hall was in darkness. They

fumbled their way after Pieter through to a small kitchen which was lit by an oil lamp. Pieter cleared away a book and the detritus of supper and they sat down round the narrow table.

Roland looked up at him. 'You're looking better, Mr Vann!'

Pieter Vann smiled grimly. 'For a time in my mind I am back with my family, in my childhood. I come to myself in the hospital in Kenilworth. Then that is bombed too. I look around and decide that I am much better than the poor broken people around me, so I walked back here just yesterday afternoon. I look for my landlady but a neighbour informs me the poor woman was in a shelter that had a direct hit. At the crematorium hundreds of people are looking for their relatives. There is much anger, a riot almost. I come away.' He looked round. 'The dear lady must have known. Back here on the kitchen table I find an envelope with a will, saying the house is for me. Perhaps I will own it for a day, a week, and it too will be bombed.' He shook his head, leaned down into a cupboard and brought out a bottle of beer and three thick glasses. 'We will drink to this kind woman. I have no water to make you tea in the English way, but this is the last of six bottles of beer my landlady got for me. With it we will drink to staying and you will tell me about the works. And your family, Mr King? Are they well? And you, Krystof?...'

Roland's eyes stayed on his glass. It was Krystof who spoke.

'My hostel was bombed, so I stay with the

Kings for these days.' He eyed Roland. 'But the Kings also were bombed out, Mr Vann. And the little girl was killed. They stay now in a neighbour's house, itself half bombed...'

'They're getting a new temporary roof on the works, Mr Vann,' interrupted Roland. 'Some of the production line is back in place...'

Pieter Vann shook his head. 'I'm sorry about your little girl, Mr King. It must be very hard for you, your wife.' He glanced around. 'You could stay here...'

Roland shook his head. 'It'll not be necessary. Lizza'll be going back North when I can get her a train ticket. She won't want to, but I'll make her.'

They drank the beer in strained silence, then Roland and Krystof got up to go. They shook hands with Pieter Vann.

'Good to know you're not harmed, Mr Vann.'

The other man smiled. 'It seems you are my friends, coming here to make sure I am well. I would be pleased if you would call me Pieter.'

Roland smiled. 'Good to know you're not harmed, Pieter.'

Pieter Vann bowed. 'I will be at the works tomorrow. There is a good deal to do.'

On their way back through the dense blackness of the streets, the two men did not speak. Roland's heart was sinking at the thought of Lizza's grim distraction and the chaotic household. Krystof was frowning into the darkness, dealing with the thoughts which had been with him again since the night of the big Blitz: thoughts of the train crash that had killed his two sons on their way to the boat. The faces of the two boys kept rising before him—one dark and bright-eyed, the other with that shock of fair hair just like his mother. His notebook was filling with drawings of them. But he worked hard to stop himself thinking of Wanda, his wife. The thought of her, in the place where she must be now, was too hard to bear.

At the Callaghan house, they found Lizza still up at the kitchen table, reading by the light of a candle.

'Where's Alex?' whispered Roland, taking off his coat and clattering his tin hat on to the table.

She told him about sending Alex with Rebecca. He sat very still for a moment, resisting feeling anything. Then he nodded. 'Your mother will see to it properly. Pieter Vann went up to the big crematorium to find his landlady. He said there was a riot. You did right, Lizz.' He paused. 'And now you should go North yourself.'

She shook her head. 'No. I'm staying here with you. I don't belong up there. Never have. That house. My mother.'

'It's safe, so much safer. You have to go. There's the new baby...'

'No.'

'You're going. I'll write to Amos Silkin. He'll find you somewhere to stay.' Roland still corresponded with Amos Silkin, a solicitor who had kept a fatherly eye on him when he had been at school in the North. He stood up.

'I'm not going,' she said, and ducked her head back down over her book.

'Good night then,' he said coldly, then marched through to the other room where he fell down on the mattress and went instantly to sleep.

'Well,' said Krystof awkwardly, 'I will say good night.'

She looked up at him resentfully. 'You're running away too? Am I such an ogre?'

He took off his coat, pulled out a chair and sat on it. 'It is hard for me, Lizza. My sons are not here. My wife is imprisoned. The world explodes around me time after time. I am in a strange land, living in a stranger's house.'

She looked at him. 'You and I are not strangers,' she said, holding his gaze till he dropped it.

He reached for his rucksack and pulled out the folder. He slipped out a single sheet and gave it to her. She held it so the light of the candle flickered on to it. Rebecca looked back out at her from the paper. She had a merry glint in her eye and her lips turned in her own sweet smile. She was clutching her doll, the knitted fireman.

'I drew it, remembering that night,' said Krystof. 'I just have to close my eyes and she is there in front of me. My boys too. I see their faces. I draw them too.'

Lizza put the paper on the table, placed her face flat beside it and wept.

She felt Krystof's hand on her hair. 'I cannot stay here, Lizza. All this is too much. Pieter

176

Vann has a big house and no people. I will stay with him.' Then the middle door closed behind him and she was alone.

She was at the table all night, first weeping, then sleeping. Roland found her there the next morning and all he could feel was irritation. 'For goodness' sake, Lizza, go in there and get some proper sleep!'

She looked up at him and wondered just who he was.

She did sleep for most of the day, lying on the mattress, submitting to wave upon wave of numbing exhaustion. Josie went off with Liam, saying she would check out a place where they were supposed to be giving away clothes. 'Sure, you can't go round in me mammy's clothes any longer, Mrs King. They don't fit you and they make you look like a gypsy, which you ain't.' She said it easily, with no resentment, no remorse.

Lizza reached up and took Josie's skinny hand in hers. 'How're you feeling, Josie?'

'Me? Well, Alex is a big miss...'

'I was thinking about your mam and that day with the Ouija board. Those words. Fire. Castle. Child. The Dead. I've seen all that in drawings Krystof has done.'

Josie pressed the hand that held hers, unsure of what to say.

'You must miss them, Josie, your mam and little Anne-Marie?'

Josie pulled her hand away and changed Liam to the other hip. 'Sometimes I just forget'm, like the only thing that matters is here and now.

Sometimes I ache, thinking Mammy won't know my own children. Mostly I forget,' she said abruptly, and whirled out of the door.

That night Roland came home early from work without Krystof. He insisted that she come out of the house with him to walk down the street along the avenue, past the blasted trees and the broken pavements.

He looked at their feet as they walked. 'You have to go home, Lizza. Your mother has invited you. I know you don't want to. You know I care about you. I always have, since I first saw you on the railway station, you being hustled off to work and me being taken back to school yet again. I always will care for you, no matter what you do, no matter what I do. But this thing, the war, is putting its black hand on us, just as sure as if I were out there in North Africa fighting in the army. We are such bad friends now.'

'There's no need to be like that. We need...'

'What we need doesn't matter, Lizza. Our needs aren't important. You know what I'm like. I can only think of one thing at a time. Just now, all I can think of is what's there at work. What I can do for the war. That is all I can think of. I'm sorry.' He stood beside a drunken electricity pylon, whose lines trailed down to the ground like a drunken maiden's train.

He reached out and pulled her to him. He put his hand to her stomach, where the baby was even now taking its languorous stretches. 'He has to be taken care of.'

'He? It was always *she...*'

'It's *he*, I am certain of that now. I know you

ache because his little sisters went too soon. I can feel it and it makes me afraid of you. For you. But he won't go too soon. We have to see to that, Lizza, you and me. And one way is for us to be apart. Just for a time, till all this is over...'

She looked up at him and shook her head. 'He'll be all right. But if we part now, we...'

'We have to. Otherwise I can't tolerate all this.'

'You! You! It is always about you! There's something wrong with us, Roland, war or no war. We're different people now.'

'No. It's not that. The times are strange. When things get back to normal, you and I'll be...'

She shook her head. 'Roland. We've had three children who are dead. To you they might be your stick-men on one of your charts. Our nice house is smashed to smithereens but you don't care. We only have the clothes we stand up in. You're stupid if you think we can get back to normal from that, that we'll ever be the same as we were. We're not the same. Can you not get it into your thick skull that we are not the same? These things change us and there's no going back.'

He put his hand on her arm and she shook it off. She ran around the corner and bumped into Krystof who held her elbows to steady her. 'Lizza! I have come for my things. Pieter Vann is happy for me to go to his house.' She relaxed against him and Roland came round the corner. 'Ah, Roland. I was saying to Lizza that I will

179

go to Pieter Vann's. It is a big gloomy house for him to be on his own.'

Lizza disentangled herself from Krystof and, without looking behind her, walked steadily back to the Callaghan house. As she did so she was greeted by the bloodcurdling wail of the air-raid siren as it ripped the air. Wearily, she set off to run and grab Josie and Liam.

Rebecca's funeral was a simple affair: a short service in the chapel followed by a burial at Carr Hill Cemetery. Alice Bremner was dignified in the dark grey coat she always wore for chapel and a black hat with the trimming removed. Beatrice went to the Store to use her last coupons for a dark blazer and black tie for Alex. She wore her old grey tweed coat and Alex thought how old she looked, compared with Lizza, who was really only three years her junior. They had thought that they would be the only ones there, but many of the women from the street put their best coats over their pinnies and came to pay their respects.

So many people came back to the house that Beatrice had to run along to Jacob Smith, whom she knew would sell her some of his illegal home-cured ham, for a price. In the house there was sympathetic talk about a child dying in a war, which should be men's business. 'Poor bairn. Mind you, Beatrice says it was blast. She never felt a thing. Not a mark on her. Some of them were blown to a thousand pieces.'

'Never felt a thing!' The words were echoed time and again in the house, as though the speakers were comforting themselves, warding off the worst of their own fears.

They asked Alex about the Blitz, which he was only too pleased to describe in gory detail. 'They say there's more than a thousand people died.'

'More than a thousand!'

'More than a thousand!'

'Our turn next! You watch!'

The day after the funeral, when his grandmother was out taking her turn to polish the brasses in the chapel, Alex went off to Newcastle to sign on for the RAF.

It took two days for Roland to get the travel warrants for Lizza and Josie and Liam. The day he had them, he brought Krystof home with him. 'I'm being sent to help set up a new development unit near works in Glasgow. I had thought I might join the section in the North East. But you can still go there, to be safe. Think of those two Callaghan children. It'll make them safe too. I had to tell the office they were ours, to get the warrants.'

Liam was streaming with cold. Josie was mooching around missing Alex. Lizza was dirty and exhausted. Her hands were never properly clean. Her nails, formerly a source of pride, were broken and black. She nodded and let him win. 'Yes. We'll all go.'

Josie, even dirtier, was staring at her. 'What's he talking about?'

'For us to go to my...where I came from. You

181

and me and Liam can go there,' said Lizza. 'We'll be safer there.'

Roland nodded, satisfied.

Josie's lip came out. 'There's the funeral. Mammy and Anne-Marie.'

The crematorium to which Maeve and Anne-Marie had been taken had been bombed in its turn. There was nothing left of them. They would be, it was *said*, interred in the mass grave. Lizza understood the implicit deception but had said nothing of this to Josie. 'Roland's got the warrants for us, Josie. He said you were our children. We have to go.'

'Krystof will go to the funeral, Josie. He'll take care of your mother and Anne-Marie,' said Roland quietly. 'I've been to the army here and they'll get the information to your father somehow.'

'I will take care of them for you, Josie, your mother and sister. Their spirit will live on.' Krystof put a hand on her shoulder. 'Do not worry.'

Lizza closed her eyes, overcome by a wave of nausea. An image of the little coffin holding the scrap of flesh that was her daughter floated before her. *Her* spirit and those of her little sisters would only live on if there was a God. And she knew even more now that there wasn't a God. They wouldn't live on. None of them.

She opened her eyes and on their periphery she could see the stiff figure of Krystof Sobieski, standing slightly to attention. And this will be the last time I see you, too, she thought.

I won't have the problem now of avoiding your eyes; of remembering those hours in the dark. And your prayers to a God that doesn't exist. And the tight clasp of your hand. No longer.

II

Roses

Quite over-canopied by luscious woodbine,
With sweet musk-roses, and with eglantine;
There sleeps Titania some time of the night,
Lulled in these flowers with dances and
   delight...
   Shakespeare, *A Midsummer Night's Dream*

CHAPTER 13

In the dim light of the railway carriage, Min Roebuck felt a heavy hand on her knee. A hoarse voice lipped itself into her ear.

'So how long do you think we'll be stuck here, love?'

As she squeezed herself further into the corner, her hat (a smart toque in plum-coloured velour) tipped into her lap. She jammed it back on her head, destroying the smooth line of her black hair. Then she lifted the soldier's hand from her knee and threw it back in the direction of the voice. 'I don't know how long we will be stuck here. You heard the guard. "An obstruction on the line." '

The soldier sniggered, and from the darkness opposite his mate said something about him being all right, there, Duffy, mate.

The compartment was packed with tired people, bags, cases and packages. Above Min's head, in the luggage rack, were two children whose feet, clad unseasonably in sandals, were dangling in front of her. Her own feet, in her smart maroon suede shoes, were squashed to one side by the bulky rucksacks belonging to the soldier and his mate, who was sitting opposite her.

She had been stuck in the seat for two hours. Any attempt to get to the toilet would have been laughable; apparently her bladder, like her fancier clothes, had to be put aside for the duration. She was starving; she had consumed her carefully packed lunch in its dainty napkin hours ago. The journey, which she had estimated would take ten hours, had taken sixteen hours already.

In the darkness, the hand crept back on her knee and squeezed hard. The voice of the soldier called Duffy crept hoarsely out of the gloom. 'Nice scent that, miss. Ashes of Roses is it?'

She unwedged her foot from its place under the rucksack, lifted it slightly to the right, and jammed the high heel right down the khaki leg, on to the toe of the thick boot.

'Christ!' It was his turn to pull away. 'I've bin stood on by a python.'

'Yer'd better lay off, Duffy, and get some kip,' came his comrade's voice from the darkness. 'Python ain't willin' to do its bit for the war effort, you can't help it.'

'Lay off, Duffy,' echoed Min. 'Next time it'll bite.'

A little snigger went around the crowded compartment and this time he did leave her alone. She lifted the blind and peered out into the dark of a night made total by black-out regulations. Apart from a slight change in density where the embankment rose, the view was absolutely black: no glow of streetlights, no gloss of windows, no bright stacked lights of industrial premises; even the gleam of water and canal deliberately dulled with soot. All the pre-war signals that normally helped you to locate yourself were gone now. The world outside the train was entirely impenetrable.

Apart from knowing that she was north rather than south of the Wash, Min Roebuck had no idea where she was. There were no signs or names on any of the dozens of stations her trains had chugged through that day. She might have been in China for all she knew. She found herself smiling, thinking of the rumours that were put about, now and then, about enemy aliens arriving at night under the cloak of darkness and doing evil deeds: rumours which seemed to have multiplied since the end of September, when Hitler appeared to have abandoned his plan for a direct military invasion. Now, they were saying, what he couldn't do in mass he would do in stealth. *Drip by drip, one by one.* But, thought Min, how on earth would an enemy find his way around in this pitch-black world without notices or signs? Probably they would stumble into the nearest police station to ask the way.

She closed her eyes, then opened them quickly as, shuddering, the train strained and clanked to a start. The darkness of the carriage lightened up a bit. A murmur of relief passed around the compartment, then stilled. Outside, in addition to the lumbering noise of the train, they could hear the crump of explosions.

The soldier sitting beside her tensed. 'Blast it!'

'We're best on the move, Duffy,' muttered his friend reassuringly. 'Give Jerry a moving target.'

The explosions continued as the train moved more smoothly now, the wheels clicking with a steady rhythm, moving at the regulation thirty miles an hour.

Min became concerned about Duffy's rigidity. Putting her face to his, she saw that his eyes were closed, his skin was a bluish white. 'I think he's fainted.'

His friend leaned across and loosened the collar of his battledress.

'Is he all right?' she whispered.

'He will be,' said the soldier. 'He's been in hospital. Off on home leave now.'

'What's wrong with him?'

'He was wounded at Dunkirk. Bombed where he stood.'

The soldier beside her took a deep strangled breath and opened his eyes. They were blue. For the first time she noticed how young he was. Younger than her. No more than twenty.

'Are you all right?' she said.

He smiled and sat up. 'I'm fine, Miss Python. Musta been them spam and powdered-egg sandwiches they gave me in the hospital mess.'

She nodded and sat away from him, not wanting to encourage his earlier attentions, despite her sympathy at his wounded-hero status. The train's whistle went as it chugged into a tunnel and they were in deeper darkness.

Duffy didn't put his hand on her knee this time, but he did speak. 'Not in the Forces yourself, then, Miss Python?'

'No. I'm a teacher.'

'Never had teachers like you when I was at school,' said Duffy's friend, leering across.

'Cushy job,' said Duffy.

She put her chin up. 'Not so cushy. I've been bombed out twice.'

'In London?'

'No. Hitler's not just interested in London, you know! On Tyneside. And then in Cumbria. Our school on Tyneside was bombed. So we evacuated across to Cumbria and the bombers came there. Some of our children were killed.'

'Hard luck, that,' said Duffy's friend.

'Well, Miss Python, I'm almost moved to say sorry for making a pass,' said Duffy. 'But I'd be lying. I have to keep up my score.'

'Score?' She started to smile.

'Stuck there in hospital strung up like a chicken ready for the oven, I vowed when—if—I got out I'd make a pass at every girl I met till I reached a hundred.'

'What then?'

'Then, if He wanted me He could have me.'

Min laughed. 'That's like the children I teach, holding their breath to count a hundred, then making a wish.'

'It helps us to be a kid at heart. All you want is someone to wake up and tell you it was all just some dream. Or nightmare.' The voice was strained again.

'OK, Duffy, steady on.' His friend lifted up the blind. 'Where are we now?'

Duffy leaned past Min to move the blind on their side. 'We must be somewhere in the

191

Midlands now. For all I know we're riding round and round my own village in this *tootoo.*'

As if in response the train slowed. Duffy lifted the blind properly. 'Ha! Come on,' he said urgently. 'This *is* me. It *is* my place. See that ironwork rose under where the clock would have been? I used to hang by my ankles on that when I was a kid.'

The train lurched and clanked to a stop and then there was a great flurry as they hoisted their rucksacks on their backs. The children in the racks turned back their heels and the people in the compartment had to duck as the two soldiers swung around. Duffy eyed Min, then saluted her. 'Another time, another place, Miss Python,' he said.

His friend clouted him on his shaven bristly neck. 'Come on, Duffy. You're not in the pictures now. Come on!'

Min leaned out of the window. The station itself was only small, but in the distance she could see a much bigger town glittering with flares of fire and sparked by tracer bullets.

'Is there space in here?' Min turned round. A young woman wearing a tight headscarf and with a grimy face was looking at her with angry eyes. She had a case in one hand and a bulky string bag in the other and a sinewy looking youngster was clinging to her neck. Beside her was a scraggy girl of fourteen or so wearing a tightly belted wool coat that was too big for her. Behind her were more eager travellers looking for seats.

Min sat down quickly. 'Yes. Yes.' She

192

smoothed her hair back neatly under her hat and sat back. The woman sat down in Duffy's place, and the stringy girl squeezed in opposite, where Duffy's friend had been. She lifted the child on to her knee. The woman tucked her case on its end in front of her own knees, took off her scarf and shook out a mass of dark auburn bob-cut hair. Min wondered about the relationships. The girl was too old to be a daughter. A sister? But there was no resemblance, none at all.

The little group brought a smoky, musty smell into the compartment. Min waited till they were settled, then asked the woman, 'What place is that, where the bombs are falling?'

'Coventry.' The woman smiled ruefully. 'Well, it used to be.'

'There's a raid on now?'

'Well, a bit of a one. We had much worse last week. Not much left to go at now, after the big raid...'

'Coventry!' Min whistled. 'How on earth did I get here?'

'Where're you coming from, then?'

'Liverpool. I've changed trains three times, been left in sidings, been dive-bombed, shot at, and goodness knows what else! And I'm going in the opposite direction to what I thought I was! Where did they tell you this one was headed?'

'York.'

'Phew! At least we're going, north.'

'Where are you aiming for, like?'

'Tyneside.'

'Do you come from Liverpool?'

Min lowered her voice even more. 'No. I belong to Tyneside. My father's a harbour pilot. Working out of Liverpool now. He wanted some of his kit so he got me a warrant to take it across for him. I'm on my way back.' She wondered why she was telling all this to this stranger—forbidden things in these days. Walls have ears and all that. She shook her head. This journey had been just too long.

'You're right out of your way here, then.'

'It's my fourth train.'

'Did you say it was Tyneside you were from?'

'That's right.'

'Couldn't tell that from your voice.'

Min laughed heartily. 'I tell you what! Between my Pa and the training college, good old Tyneside didn't get a chance. Are you from Coventry?'

'No, all over really. Started out in South Durham.'

'Can't tell that either.'

'My young brother used to tantalise me when I went home, for losing the accent. Said I had a twang.'

'That's the future. Citizens of England. Of Europe. Not one small patch.'

Lizza laughed and sat back. She had classified this woman as a superior type, with her elegant clothes, her pale skin and make-up which looked deceptively natural. But there was something about her which made Lizza feel very comfortable, made her want to smile.

'Coventry?' Min was saying, her eyes narrowing. 'According to my Dad, that raid on the fourteenth was the worst ever. Worse on the night than any of the London raids.'

Lizza glanced cautiously around the packed compartment. 'It was bad, very bad. My house went. And these two lost their family.' She nodded across at Liam and Josie, who had her head back against the plush headrest, her eyes closed.

'I thought they were your family.'

'No. Well I suppose they are, now.' Lizza looked the smart woman in the eye. 'You might say I inherited them. Their mother was my neighbour. I've no children left. I lost them. Rebecca my daughter. And the twins.' Her voice was dry, beaten very thin with the desire not to show feeling.

'Me too!' Min touched Lizza's hand. 'Me too. I lost my children.'

'You?' Lizza glanced at Min's beautifully manicured, ringless hand.

'I'm a teacher. We took our children out of Tyneside across to Cumbria, away from the bombs. Then Jerry dropped a loose one on his way back from a raid. On Glasgow, I think.' She sat back in her seat. 'I lost nine of them. I taught them their left from their right, to read and to draw, then I lost them.'

'No! I'm so sorry. That bloody Jerry!' As the rhythms of the wheels on the tracks ticked into her, Lizza felt herself relax for the first time in many days. The train was gathering speed,

195

as was permitted outside of the air-raid zone; she could hear the rain slashing away at the windows. It was hissing and chugging its way north, away from her treasured city, back to her own land, *the land of her own possession.* Now where did that come from? Yes. Her mother had quoted it to her once when she had first gone away. 'Never forget this, Lizza, the land of your own possession.' Some phrase from her beloved Bible, most likely.

'What took you to Coventry?' asked Min.

'My husband's an aero-engineer. He's still there.'

'Did you meet him there?'

'I worked in Bradford when I first left home. In the mills. Roland was doing his apprenticeship then. Then I went back to Durham, to Sedgefield, a big hospital, for my training. And he followed.'

'You're a nurse?'

Lizza felt herself responding to the intense quality of the woman's gaze. 'I was a mental nurse. I trained as a mental nurse.' She laughed as she sensed the withdrawal of the woman beside her. 'It's not like that, you know. Not like that at all.'

Min stayed silent, her mind processing childhood nightmares. She remembered a slight, pale-faced person who chattered all the time, laughed a lot, and would occasionally clasp her so tight that the maid had to get the milkman to help to unclasp her. There was a visit to a building, turreted like a great castle on a hill. She felt the iron clasp there again. This time

196

it was nurses in starched uniforms who had to free her. On her teacher-training course she had learned about inherited abilities, and disabilities. She often wondered if she would end up like that, with nurses in uniform pulling at her tense fingers.

'I nursed old ladies,' Lizza was saying. 'Some were more mad than bad. Some had been in there since they were thirteen. They'd got pregnant and that was seen as a sign of insanity. Or smashed the house up one day, when their ma'd given them one too many tasks to do. Or had gone berserk, having been beaten and worse by their fathers and brothers. As sane as you or me, inside the place, but being there made them act strange outside. So when they got out they acted strange, stopped eating, kicked the baby or stole something, they soon came back. These women could remember things that you and I have forgotten. From before they could speak. One old woman would tell you, every Monday, how she had been born, from her mother's first labour pains till she got out in the world. They said she was raving. Hallucinating. But what if it were true? How do we know it's not? I don't know whether she really could remember. The details were right. But it was the images, the pictures she painted, that were so convincing.'

Min nodded, her eyes bright with interest, her own nightmares forgotten.

'One woman thought she was Queen Victoria. She was a lamb to deal with, if you called her Your Majesty. And she had a little friend, Emma, whom she thought was her daughter.

Emma was forty if she were a day, but small-statured with some growth problem, I think. And very slow in the mind. But the Queen washed her and dressed her. She brushed her hair a hundred times a day and put ribbons in it. Woe betide anyone who mistreated Emma, I can tell you!' Lizza laughed. It was a long time since she had talked about the hospital, reminded herself of her other self, with her crisp uniform and her cap.

Min shook her head, smiling. 'Must've been hard getting used to all that.'

'All of it was hard. At one time I thought I'd be a teacher...anyway because of my education, or lack of it, it was only the mental hospitals that would take me for training. But I was pleased in the end. You're right. It was hard. It was all hard. We used to come out of night shift straight into lectures. And we did lots of night shift.'

Josie's eyes were open now, and she was listening avidly. 'I didn't know you did that, Mrs King! Sure, you musta seen some funny things with all them loonies.'

Lizza shook her head. 'Not loonies, Josie. I've seen a lot of what you would call raving. But these folks were mostly confused or strange-acting. The ones that were worse than that, you could always work out reasons why. We know so much more about it all now. It's there in the new text books. There were a few that were more bad than mad. But you get those outside hospitals as well. There's one stomping and raving across there in Germany at this minute.'

The mutter of agreement round the compartment made her realise that she had an audience of more than two.

'I was in a place like that once,' said Min, her face going pink. 'It was a big gloomy place, like a medieval castle.'

'A "castle, precipice-encurled", like in Browning?' Lizza smiled at the slight surprise in the other woman's eyes.

'Not quite. Although it might have seemed so, to some of the folks in there. But it did have long echoing corridors, stone steps, and the occasional shriek here and there. Ghostly! Ghastly!'

Lizza laughed. 'Well, even the ghastly things could be funny. On night shift the most junior nurse had to go down and get the dinner boxes for the nurses. Well, we called them "dinner boxes", but it was midnight when we ate the food, of course. Once, I was coming back up these stone stairs with the dinner boxes when I heard something on the steps above me. There, eyes glittering, was a rat on a step two from the top. I froze where I was. But then I had to go on. I was more scared of Sister than I was of any old rat. I crept up the stairs on the opposite side, forcing myself to pretend that I hadn't seen it.'

There were shudders and appreciative nods around the compartment. Min chuckled. 'My tutors at college were like that.'

'Like the rat?' Lizza's brow raised.

'No! Like the Sister. Dragons in lisle stockings,' she said feelingly. 'Don't get me wrong. There were some brilliant women there. More dedicated than nuns, certainly more useful. Just hard and strong. I saw later they'd to be. Their sweethearts killed in the Great War, making their own way. Some as eccentric as your Queenly patient. Protected by the college like she was protected by the hospital.'

In the silence that followed Lizza could sense them all waiting for more. She smiled. 'There were some funny ones too. One sister who was always on day shift used to get on the nerves of this particular patient. There was a fish tank just inside the ward door and every day when she came in, the first thing this sister did before she took her cloak off was to feed the fishes. She used to talk to them, call them her "little darlings". The nurses didn't like it but the patients hated it. They were so jealous of those fishes. One patient, Mary Cantor, used to meet me when I came on nights with a whole wail of complaints about this day sister and her obsession with the fishes. "The woman's mad!" Mary Cantor would say, clinging tightly to my arm. "Mad as a hatter!"

'One night when I came in, the fish tank was empty and Mary Cantor was nowhere to be seen. I finally tracked her down to the bathroom, a big echoey place. "I see the fishes are gone, Mary," I says, my voice booming back at me from the walls.

'She took my arm, made me face the corner and brought her face really close to mine. "You'll see'm no more, nurse. And neither will that mad woman."

' "What happened to them, Mary?" '

'She looked behind her and behind me and whispered, "I showed her, the mad bugger, I put them between two slices of bread and et'm!" '

A shout of laughter went round the carriage and, red-faced, Lizza put her hand to her lips. 'I'm sorry. I shouldn't have sworn, but...'

'Don't worry,' said Min, wiping her eyes. 'You tell a story so well.'

Josie spoke. 'Alex says Lizza writes good stories in her letters.'

'Alex?'

'My young brother,' Lizza's smile faded as she remembered. 'He went on ahead with...he went on ahead.'

'And you're Lizza? And these are...'

'Josie and Liam.'

Liam lifted his head when he heard his name. He looked directly at Lizza. 'I wanna do a big Number Two,' he said mournfully.

Lizza looked helplessly at the crowded compartment and the packed corridor outside. Min stood up, leaned over, picked him up and handed him to the person nearest the door. 'Pass him down the corridor and ask the last person to put him on the toilet!' she instructed, in a teacherly tone which brooked no argument.

Lizza smiled gratefully at her. 'Thank you for that.'

Min smiled. 'I wish someone could do that with me but I'm a bit too much on the large side!'

As Liam was returned hand over hand, with a sailor's hat on his head and clutching a

201

bag of sweets, a chorus of 'Praise the Lord and pass the ammunition' bubbled up the corridor and continued in the compartment. Liam joined in with 'La-las' from his place back on Josie's knee.

Lizza, drained now of the desire to talk, was happy to sit back and listen to the trickle of songs which followed. 'One of these days', 'The last time I saw Paris', 'By the Light of the Silvery Moon'. When they reached 'Bless 'em All', she was fast asleep. She dreamed that Beatrice was standing at a window with Rebecca in her arms, urging the child to, 'Wave! Wave at your mammy!' But Rebecca put her head on Beatrice's shoulder and refused.

She awoke as the rhythm of the train changed as it slowed down and prepared to stop. Josie was shaking her. 'It's us, Mrs King. It's us! Didn't we have to change at York?'

CHAPTER 14

'Move along there!' The guard, an officious man, too young for his old-fashioned bristling moustaches, poked Lizza in the back. She turned and glared at him. 'I've a child here if you don't mind, and fifty people in front of me.'

'Attagirl!' shouted Min, struggling along the platform beside her. 'See if you can get to the buffet. The board says the next train to

Darlington, on to Newcastle, is in an hour and a half.'

The platform was crowded with people, most of them men and women in uniform of one kind or another. A pall of smoke weighed down on the station: residual steam from the hissing engines sitting on top of the heavier cigarette smoke. When she reached the buffet Lizza's heart failed as she stood in the doorway looking at the crowded tables, occupied by people who looked as though they were camped out there for the duration.

'Wait here!' Min marched across to a small table by the wall, occupied by two RAF officers, complete with pilot's wings. They were less military but also somehow less dishevelled than the other uniformed occupants of the buffet.

'I wondered if you would be so kind as to give a seat to my friend by the door,' she said. 'She is just here from Coventry and has had a wretched journey.'

They sat tight. The older boy, with drooping curly hair and a white scarf, smiled at her. 'Love to, sweetheart. But we've had a long journey ourselves and it took us more than an hour to get this table,' he said lazily. She judged his accent to be Australian, or New Zealand.

She looked from one to the other. 'My mistake...' She turned to Lizza, who was now beside her. 'Afraid these...gentlemen...don't feel able to do the honourable thing, Lizza, in spite of your...condition.'

The men exchanged glances.

'Are you fliers?' said Lizza, eyeing each of them keenly.

They laughed at the superfluous question, being used to their uniform declaring them the heroes of the times, representatives of 'the few' who, by their valour, had saved Britain from the Hun.

'Fighter pilots?'

They nodded, and sat back, waiting for the appreciation.

'Well,' she said stubbornly, 'we couldn't half have done with a few of you over Coventry on the fourteenth of November. Then just maybe my daughter would be alive now, as would the sister and mother of these two children. And I'd have a house and a life.'

The curly-haired boy went red, pushed his chair back, and stood up, and the other followed suit.

'I'm sorry for your loss, ma'am. Truly. If I personally could have done anything...' He flicked his hair out of his eyes and stormed away, followed by his comrade.

Josie whistled.

Shaking slightly, Lizza sat in the man's seat with the sleepy Liam on her knee, while Josie hitched her bottom on to a narrow window-sill and leaned up against the black-out blinds.

Min sat on the other chair and smiled across at her. 'Bravo!'

'I meant it,' said Lizza.

Josie whistled again. 'Sure, I'd want you on my side in any war, Mrs King.'

Min gave Josie a ten-shilling note. 'Go and

see if you can get us a sandwich, something to drink, Josie. I'm starving, I don't know about you.' She sat watching Josie struggle to the counter then turned to Lizza. 'You're all right now?'

'How did you know?'

'Know what?'

'That I was expecting?'

Min clapped her hands. 'You are? How wonderful! I just made it up, to make them move their fat complacent bottoms.'

'I'm not so sure about wonderful.'

'It is! It is! Such a hopeful thing in all this carnage. What do you want? A boy or a girl?'

Lizza, slumped back in her seat now, shrugged wearily. 'At first I thought it was a girl. Then somehow both Roland and I started calling him a boy. Can't think why anyone would want a boy, to kill or be killed in the next war.'

Min looked at her, then fiddled in her neat suitcase and brought out a green beret and a green silk Paisley scarf. She pushed them towards Lizza, with her handbag on top of them. 'You're all in. Give me that child and go and wash and freshen up,' she ordered. 'Put on this scarf and hat to brighten yourself up. And there's some powder in the bag. Have a dab.'

Mesmerised, Lizza did as she was told.

In the lady's room she stripped down to her brassière and skirt and washed her face, neck and arms thoroughly. She splashed water on her hair to bring back the curl. Then she opened the elegant suede bag, pulled out a heavy compact figured with gold dragons, and dabbed powder not just on her nose, but on her neck and shoulders. She found a small Pond's lipstick and outlined her lips. As she pushed the lipstick back into the bag, her fingers brushed against a soft leather purse. After a moment's hesitation she clicked the purse open with one hand and put her fingertips against the wodge of white five-pound notes. She realised she didn't even know the girl's name. How old must she be? Anywhere between twenty-three and thirty. Hard to tell. Funny thing, going round handing her purse to strangers.

She fished out a brush and stood before the oval mirror to brush her hair, smoothing out tangles that had been there since she had been buried under the house with Krystof Sobieski. A hundred strokes. Her mother had always said a hundred strokes. Drops of water stood out among the curls like glass beads. Suddenly she was looking forward to being in the house at Bracks Hill, to the tin bath before the fire, to Beatrice rubbing her hair with the liquefied soap she made specially into a shampoo. To be clean again: that was a simple enough desire.

When she returned, the little table was laden with thick cups of tea and a plate of sandwiches, some of which were being wolfed down by Josie and Liam, who was sitting quite comfortably on Min's knee.

Josie whistled, spitting crumbs of bread as Lizza came towards them wearing the beret on her curls and the green Paisley scarf round her neck. 'That's more like it, Mrs King!' She turned to Min. 'You should'a seen her before,

before the bombing, miss. Sure, she had the prettiest things!'

'Josie!' warned Lizza. She turned to Min. 'That's a beautiful compact.'

'That? One of a dozen or so my doting pa's brought me, given by his friends coming ashore from the Far East.' Reaching round Liam she fished in the bag. 'Here, you have it! Don't shake your head, take it! You must have lost all your things. I've got a dozen others just the same, still in their wrappings.' She pushed it into Lizza's hand and put her other hand over it. 'Take it!'

Lizza nodded and slipped it into the string bag which held her things. 'We don't even know your name. You gave me your bag and you don't even know me.'

'I do. You told me all about yourself on the train.'

Lizza frowned. 'Did I? Well, I don't know anything about you. Not even your name.'

'My name is Min Roebuck.'

'Min? That's a funny name,' said Josie.

Min laughed, flicked an eye round the room and leaned forward. 'Well, I wouldn't tell everyone, but I've this great-aunt who's German, called Minna. Pa's uncle married her after the Great War. We both have the same name, Miranda, from Shakespeare's...'

'*Tempest*,' finished Lizza.

Min raised an appreciative eyebrow. 'Well, my name's Min Roebuck. I come from North Shields. My pa's in the Merchant Navy and has been the doting parent since

207

my mother...died...when I was twelve.'

She frowned. After that event, she and her father had been everything to each other. After that event he had taken her fully to his heart and, on two memorable and painful occasions which neither of them mentioned now, to his bed.

'I'm sorry about your mother,' said Lizza, wondering what life would have been like without her own mother.

The following silence was broken by Josie. 'I bet you went to a posh school,' she said shrewdly.

'I went away to St Bridget's School for Girls which was like a first-order prison, and the St Hild's Training College in Durham which was not quite so bad. I've been teaching now for five years, but haven't had the adventures that you've had, Lizza. Unless you count catching nits three times and impetigo once! I love those children but sometimes I can't stand them. And what else about me? I like nice clothes and I like drawing and looking at pictures. That's about it.'

Josie slurped her tea. 'You're not like any teacher in my school, Miss Roebuck. They all have tree-trunk legs and moustaches. The women teachers that is. And they wouldn't come near enough to a real child to catch the nits!'

'Josie!' warned Lizza, biting back a smile.

'Why d'yer not get married then?' pursued Josie. 'Like I say, yer not bad looking for a teacher. Like one of those film-stars from the silent pictures, with that hair.'

Min laughed, removing her hat and shaking back her cap of short black hair. 'I haven't been married because I like my job too much. I couldn't continue if I got married and none of the sailors or shopkeepers or shipyard workers I've met seemed worth it. Not one who measures up to my pa, who's six foot tall, looks like a film-star himself and knows how to treat a lady!' She replaced her hat and pulled the kiss-curl forward on the left-hand side.

'Same with me,' said Lizza with feeling. 'Not the father thing. I never knew mine, except for a tiny memory in the First War. But nursing's the same as teaching. I had to stop nursing when I got married. Couldn't finish my training.'

'Couldn't you wait?'

Lizza shrugged. 'It felt very urgent at the time.' She met the other woman's eyes, and knew that she knew what she meant.

Min nodded. 'Well, if I met a man that moved mountains for me, I'm not sure I wouldn't succumb. But I haven't so far.'

Josie looked from one to the other, then smacked Liam's hand which was reaching for another sandwich and made him cry. Min stroked his head and soothed him, as Lizza scowled at Josie.

'And teaching them, I don't miss having children,' she laughed. 'At least I can send them home at the end of the day.'

They talked on with the ease of old friends until the train came. Moving again through the double doors of the buffet Lizza wondered just how late it would be before she got to Bracks Hill.

They were first into the compartment. Min handed Liam over to Josie and swept the crumbs off her coat and settled down beside Lizza again. She closed her eyes. 'It's nice to be going back North, don't you think. I always feel better the further north I get!'

Lizza hesitated. 'No,' she said soberly, 'I don't feel like that at all.'

Min opened one eye. 'You don't like it? Going home?'

'It's not home to me. Not since I was fourteen. The further north we get, the more my heart sinks. It gets blacker and dirtier, more mean...'

'No! No! Lizza! It's a wonderful land. It opens out to you. Yes there are the pits and the factories, but a few miles from them and you are at the sea. And that is wild, beautiful and free! Or a few miles another way and you are up in the deep countryside at Blanchland or Wolsingham. Beautiful. And not mean. The people are full-hearted, funny, original...'

There was a little silence, then Lizza laughed. 'I can see it depends on who you are. I'd think you're the kind of person who'd see a gold coin in a midden.'

'What's a midden?' said Josie.

Min and Lizza laughed together at this. 'Now there's someone who's never lived in your wonderful land, Min!'

The even rhythms of the train as it steamed north soon entered Lizza's system and she slept, waking up with her head on Min's shoulder when the train finally stopped.

'Darlington, it's Darlington. Your stop, Lizza!' Min was shaking her. Then there was a rush of activity as they and many others piled off the train. In three minutes Lizza was on the platform, with Liam in her arms and her case and string bag by her side and the train slowly pulling out of the station. She felt as exhausted and miserable as she had in all the last week.

'Lizza!' Min was at the window holding out a piece of paper which was fluttering in the slight movement of the train. 'Here! Keep in touch!'

Josie raced after the train and caught the piece of paper as Min dropped it. She brought it back to Lizza and put it before her eyes. It was a North Shields address.

Lizza smiled slightly. 'Wave, Liam,' she urged. 'Wave at Min!'

They watched the train go out of sight and Lizza said, 'Put that paper inside the compact, Josie. It'll be safe there.'

The station, like York, was thronged with pale people in and out of uniform, waiting for yet more trains. Lizza waylaid a porter and was assured that there was definitely no train to Bracks Hill until the milk train at four-thirty the next morning. Like automatons, she and Josie found a space on the floor in the corner of the waiting room, lay down and tried to rest.

Josie and Liam, with their heads on the carrier bag, went straight back to sleep. Lying beside them Lizza thought first about Rebecca, seeing her again as she was in the café flirting with the old ladies. Then she turned her head restlessly to find a more comfortable position on the wooden floor, wondering just what kind of a welcome, if any, was waiting for her at Bracks Hill.

CHAPTER 15

Roland had seen Lizza off into the van with barely disguised relief. The Callaghan house might be empty and cold now, but he could concentrate wholeheartedly on work without having to deal with the anger he felt at Lizza and the guilt he felt about being angry.

He was working for most of a day shoulder to shoulder with Krystof, sorting good steel from bad in the wrecked factory, when Krystof mentioned the loss of his own wife and children.

'With the boys it was too quick. I put them on the train. One minute they were in this world, the next minute they were not. One minute I was feeling relief because they were out of the...what word do I use...menace? terror? of that situation; the next minute I had lost them to God's not so infinite mercy. One minute we have a family, the next all we have is each other. Then one day I return from the university where I teach and she is gone. Taken because she is Jewish. I am left because I am not.'

Roland shook his head. 'A terrible thing for you.'

'The worst,' he said simply. 'My family, then

212

my country. The load is infinite. I thought I would not want to live, but as each thing happened it was as though my determination to stay on was distilled, became greater. But I will tell you, my friend, that even placed as I was, in these events, it seems that there is a degree of balance, some logic.'

'That's hard to see.'

'The boys' quick death they had in the train was a blessing compared with what I saw later in my own country and in the slave factory in Germany. Their death was simply a spark, simply extinguished. The other...no, I cannot tell you.' He paused. 'My wife, I am told, is still alive. And me? Well, I have lost my country, but I am here in my grandmother's country, whose language at least is familiar. And, having shared with you the danger and pain of the loss of your own beautiful daughter, I feel myself among friends. We have a bond not to be broken. Or is that too...sentimental for your sturdy English...'

'No, no. I was glad you were there with them that night...' Roland coughed and stopped to light a cigarette, stretching his back. 'She's so full of grief for Rebecca, like she was for the twins. And I'm nowhere in it. She's so much grief in her there is no space for mine. She's so full of their loss there's no room for me. I cannot grieve for Rebecca...' He took the cigarette from his case and lit it. 'This bloody war.'

'At least she is out of it now, Elizabeth.'

'She'll be safe enough up there; Hitler won't invade England now, I'm sure of it. Please God he'll get swamped in the Russian snows.' He laughed grimly. 'It'll be no panic for her. Lizza's mother and herself they are always at odds...'

'At odds?' said Krystof.

'They don't get on. They are bad friends.'

'Is there no other place she could stay up there? No other person who could find her space? Can't you do something?'

'There's one person. I was thinking of him. But how can I contact him in the middle of this chaos? It's complicated to explain in letters.'

'Has he an office? Can you telephone him?'

'Telephone? The telephone lines are still down.'

'Not so. Pieter Vann told me the main office had a single line back in place now. Wait.' He loped off through the factory, now being patiently restored to order and production by the dozens of workers who had reported in.

In ten minutes he was back. 'You are to go to that office at seven-fifteen. Oh. And Pieter said you were to talk to him. Something about the new set-up near Glasgow...'

The corridor was deserted when, at seven-fifteen on the dot, they turned up at the office. The light was on, but the office was empty. Krystof stood near the door. 'Go in there and do it,' he said urgently. 'I'll whistle if anyone comes.'

Roland smiled faintly at him. 'Oh, it's not quite official permission. I forgot you're used to this cloak and dagger stuff, Krystof.'

'Survival, my friend. Survival. Now, I'll whistle four notes for danger near, two notes

214

for danger even closer.'

The solicitor's letters with their elaborate letterhead had been burnt in the bombing, so Roland blessed his total recall for numbers as he dialled Amos Silkin's number. He grunted with relief when he heard the lawyer's rich, port-laden voice at the other end.

'Mr Silkin? This is Roland King.'

'Ah, hello, dear boy! How are you?'

'It's been hard down here. We've had some difficulties. We were bombed out and our daughter Rebecca was killed.' Roland heard this cool statement as though it were said by a voice other than his own.

There was a long pause at the other end. 'Hmm. I am indeed very sorry about that. And yet you are obviously in one piece. That is something in this war. I was just today talking to Mrs Silkin about your father.' He paused again. 'Is there news?'

'I've no news one way or another about him. All I know is he's still missing. This is another matter,' he said hurriedly, hearing Krystof's four-note whistle on the corridor.

'Yes! Anything, dear boy.'

'This might seem a superficial problem compared with much else that is happening, sir. You know my wife is from Bracks Hill? Well, she's just evacuated there today with two children—evacuees from the bombing. She's at her mother's house. But that's a pit house with little room. And Lizza has always had problems with her mother...'

There was yet another silence at the other

end. Roland could imagine the old boy taking a pull on his battered old pipe.

Amos Silkin cleared his throat. 'I have the solution. It has a pleasing symmetry. Can you somehow transmit her to the following address?'

It was nine o'clock by the time Lizza, Josie and Liam were walking down the backs, to get to her mother's house in Bracks Hill. With the aid of another wash and brush up at Darlington station, and still wearing Min Roebuck's beret and scarf, Lizza felt able to return the stares and the greetings as she made her way past women shaking out their kitchen mats, or taking out ashes to the middens across the back lane.

Mrs Gosden, whose daughter she'd been at school with, greeted her with easy familiarity. 'I wus sorry for yer loss, pet. I wus at the funeral. Poor bairn, I bet yer missin' her. Bad times, these. That bliddy Hitler, time they sorted him out.' Her sharp glance moved to Josie and then Liam, who was clinging to both their hands. 'An' brought some evacuees have yer?'

Josie moved restlessly from foot to foot.

'They lost their mother in the bombing. I thought it would be safer here.'

'Ah dinnet knaa about safer, pet. Did you hear about the bomb that dropped on Carhoe Co-op?'

Lizza started to walk on, but Mrs Gosden kept walking alongside, so she had to ask about Betty, the woman's daughter.

'Our Betty? Why, she's four of her own

216

now, Lizza.' Mrs Gosden said "fower" in the old-fashioned way. Lizza felt her heart sinking with every word coming from the mouth of this woman. 'Ah tek the bairns for her. But she's doin' her bit! Let nobody say! Workin' at the munitions factory in Aycliffe. Lasses from all over the county gan there to work now. Trains runnin' from as far as Blackhall. Yer wanta get yersel' there pet. Earn a bob or two. Our Mary's never been as well off. Doesn't know hersel' now. Yer wanta get yersel' ower there. With your brains you'd be a white-coat in no time.'

Lizza stopped at her mother's gate and smiled wearily at the woman. 'Tell Betty I was asking after her, Mrs Gosden!'

Josie looked with bright curiosity at the narrow green gate, the brick-tiled yard leading to the kitchen door, the gleaming panes and snowy lace at the kitchen window. The curtains twitched, then the door opened and a tall woman came rushing out. She had her hair up in an old-fashioned plaited bun, but there was no doubting her resemblance to Lizza King.

Josie wrested Liam from Lizza's arms.

'Beatrice.' Lizza's voice trembled.

The tall woman embraced Lizza and put her face against hers. 'Thank God you're home, Lizza, out of all that,' she said quietly. 'We're all so sorry about the bairn, pet.'

Lizza looked around. 'What about...'

'They gave Rebecca a nice service, Lizza. The whole street was there. Ma chose the hymns and the minister took the text *Suffer little children...*

217

She's gone to the better place, Lizza,' she said simply.

Lizza put one hand over her eyes. Beatrice hugged her hard till the tears had stopped. Then she put her hand in her apron pocket and pulled out a white embroidered handkerchief. 'Here! You'd better blow,' she said. 'Or the whole street'll be awash.'

When they went into the kitchen Alice Bremner was standing with her back to the fireplace. She nodded at Lizza. 'Good to see you safe, lass,' she said briefly. Her gaze moved to Liam, holding Josie's hand. 'An' you've brought us company I see.'

'This is Josie and Liam, Mam. Refugees like me.'

'Well the tea's mashing here, so you'd all better sit down while our Beatrice pours you one.' She smiled for the first time, at Liam. 'An' I'll get that bairn some milk and biscuits. He looks all in. Come on, pet, we'll find you one of Gram's special biscuits out the back.' She held out her hand and led the compliant Liam through the narrow scullery door.

Numbly resentful, as she always was in her mother's presence, Lizza sat down and looked around at the familiar glitter of the kitchen, a haven of warmth and order, of appetising smells and immaculate routine. Beatrice poured tea for her and Josie. Lizza noted that she used the best cups and saucers: those kept for visitors.

Josie looked hard at Lizza, willing her to ask the question. Lizza took a sip of tea, then asked, 'So where's our Alex? Is he out somewhere?'

Beatrice shrugged. 'He's not here. He went off after the funeral. Mam went mad, like. He went off to sign up for the RAF, he said. Durham, Newcastle, I'm not sure, further afield. Not sure that you can get in that easy. But he'd have to register soon, anyway. I haven't seen him since he went off.' Her gaze was on her sister. She didn't notice the tension in the scruffy, stick-like girl slumped in her chair.

Alice Bremner came back in carrying Liam on one hip. She set him on a chair at the table and placed an oat biscuit on a plate in front of him. 'There, son,' she said.

Lizza looked at her. 'Our Beatrice said the minister gave a good service, Mam, for Rebecca.' She paused. 'It's only a week since it happened, but it seems like a year.'

Alice Bremner nodded. 'You can go down after, talk to the minister, an' he'll take you down to the cemetery.'

'No,' said Lizza. 'I won't be doing that.'

Alice looked at her sharply, started to say something and stopped.

There was a thunderous knocking on the back door. Beatrice lifted the curtain and caught her breath. 'Oh!'

Lizza peered after her. It was a boy in uniform holding a bike steady with one hand.

'Jonnie!' Her mother's voice whispered behind her. Lizza's blood froze. Beatrice went to the door and returned, silently handing Lizza the flimsy envelope.

Lizza stared at it blankly. Roland now. Somehow Roland had got it. It was the bombs.

The bombs they heard from the train.

Liam started to whimper. Alice put a firm hand on his shoulder.

'Shall I open it?' said Beatrice, taking it from Lizza's nerveless fingers. She opened it, read it, and her mouth broke into a smile. 'Here!' she thrust it back at her sister.

There were few words. 'DON'T WORRY STOP HAVE FOUND HOUSE STOP WAIT STOP ROLAND.'

She handed it to her mother, who smiled faintly in her turn. 'Well, at least it's not trouble,' she said. 'Now if you take off your clothes I'll get the boiler on. I could smell yon bairn from the bottom of the yard.' She went off to fill the yard boiler, happy at the pattern of tasks now presented to her.

Lizza's face burned. Always when she got into this house she was reduced to the level of a twelve-year-old girl, awkward and resentful, perpetually upstaged by a much more powerful actor.

Josie stood up. 'Can I go to the lav?'

Beatrice smiled. 'It's across the back, pet. Straight opposite our back gate. The one with the white steps.'

When Josie had left the room Lizza said, 'She was looking out for Alex.'

'Alex?'

'They got up quite a friendship when Alex was down there.'

Beatrice smiled.

Josie walked across the back lane and opened the door above the snow-white step. She backed out instantly, came back into the house and looked accusingly at Lizza, her eyes wide and her nose slightly wrinkled. 'It's a wooden hole! There's ashes and...there's no chain!'

Lizza and Beatrice laughed.

'Well, it's that or nowt, pet!' said Beatrice. 'Didn't our Lizz tell you we were behind the times here?'

'You'll have to use it, Josie. It's all there is...' said Lizza.

Josie's hand was on her mouth. 'I'm gunna be sick.'

'Use the drain outside,' advised Beatrice calmly. 'We do have water drains, even if we don't have water closets!'

Listening to Josie retch outside, Lizza smiled at Beatrice and relaxed against the back of her chair. She would wait. She would wait for Roland's message. For that 'something' he had promised to think about, before she set out for the North.

She had to wait till nine o'clock that night, when the 'something' turned up in the form of a man with a tarpaulin-covered truck. 'I bin deliverin' to the factory at Priorton. I'm to take you here to this house on the paper. Somat about evacuees.' The workman thrust at her a scruffy bit of paper with an address scribbled on it: Campion House, Rollason Terrace, Priorton. 'Your bloke says to tell yer he's all right and he hopes you are all right.'

Collecting his dried clothes from the clothes horse by the fire, they dressed Liam, who had been trailing around in one of Alex's old shirts.

221

Beatrice insisted that Lizza and Josie keep the clothes she had dug out for them, so they thrust their own washed stuff, still warm from the fire, into the one suitcase.

Alice Bremner watched all this flurry with a steady eye. 'You should leave the bairn here. No saying where you'll end up. He'll be safer here.'

Lizza swept Liam up into her arms. 'He goes where we go. He'll come with me and his sister. He's been disturbed enough already.' Beatrice watched this with interest, wondering not for the first time how different her life would have been, had she insisted on keeping Alex for her own, rather than let her mother sweep him up for herself.

They climbed into the front of the waggon and the driver set it to nose its way slowly in the black-out towards Priorton. The only vehicles they passed on the road were three army waggons and a single-decker bus, all moving with caution, guided by the regulation narrow envelope of light directed on to the road below them.

On the hill up into Priorton they drew up beside a man in a cap and a white scarf who was walking a diminutive Jack Russell terrier on a lead. 'Tell us where Rollason Terrace is, mate?'

The man looked up suspiciously at the driver who talked with such a sharp accent. Lizza leaned across. 'We want Rollason Terrace. Is it near the centre?'

Hearing her voice, the man relaxed. 'It's just

behind the High Street, flower. Off Northway. By three big trees. You can't miss it.'

The driver grumbled and wound down the window. 'Back of beyond, up here. Come from more than twenty miles away and they think you're a spy.'

In the pitch black they drove slowly along Rollason Terrace, whose big houses loomed behind high privet, now unprotected by their iron railings which had been sheered off at the low wall and carried away in a waggon for the war effort.

In the end Lizza had to climb out of the waggon to read the house-names, which were cut into the stone gateposts. Campion House was the sixth one along. She signalled the driver to stop.

They pulled up at a house which seemed bigger and gloomier than the others. The driver dumped their case on the pavement and drove off, saying he would set off back south and pull up and sleep on the way.

'Look at this,' said Josie. 'Talk about a haunted castle!'

They marched up the short wide pathway to the door. Lizza knocked, but there was no reply. She tried the handle, and the door opened slowly. They went through a little vestibule into a hall with a fine staircase which was lit by a tiny electric light high in the ceiling. The hall was as big as her mother's front room.

Lizza led the way past the staircase towards a faint light at the back, and into the kitchen. Although it was empty, a fire was flickering in the fireplace, a kettle of water was steaming on the iron hob, and a brown teapot and a big meat pie stood on the steel shelf above the oven.

'It's like the three bears,' said Josie.

Lizza laughed. 'And which of us is Goldilocks?'

Josie poked her finger in the pie and licked it. 'Potatoes! Why, this is nearly as good as Mammy's.'

Lizza shouted 'Halloo' several times, but nobody came.

Within five minutes they were sitting round the table, sharing out the pie and drinking the tea. Lizza was pouring her second cup when she froze. Thumps and bangs were coming through the ceiling from the room overhead. Josie's hand went to her mouth.

A little door in the corner of the kitchen opened and down the last steps of a narrow staircase stepped a wizened old woman, not much taller than Liam, brandishing a thick stick. Her pink scalp shone through her white hair and she was wearing a long cream nightdress covered by a man's old-fashioned tweed coat.

She smiled widely, showing four or five teeth in a stretch of pink gum. 'Wha', hinney, ah thowt yer'd niver get here. That feller Amos Silkin, that lawyer, said you's'd be here by tea-time. But, like I says to meself, lawyers are never in a hurry.'

Lizza smiled. Roland had mentioned Amos Silkin. She stood up and took one step towards the old woman. 'Who are you? Is this Mr Silkin's house?'

'Bessie Harraton's the name, lass. And this is me own house ye're in.' She laughed uproariously at Lizza's look of disbelief. 'An' thereby hangs a tale! But that'll wait.' She plonked herself down in the high chair by the fire. 'The tatie pie. Does it suit? Ah manidged ter get a bit extra lard from the butcher. Telt'im I'd got important warworkers comin' for the orniments factory.'

Lizza smiled.

Later, having been installed by Bessie in her own bedroom, Lizza padded along the corridor to the smaller one, where Josie was to share a bed with Liam. Liam was in bed, fast asleep. Josie was doing a handstand on a blank wall beside the vast wardrobe.

Lizza laughed down at her. 'What're you doing now, Josie?'

'Seeing how many bloody swear words I can say.' The narrow, earnest face, upside down, looked up at her. 'How the hell did we get here, Mrs King? And where the hell is Alex? And who the bloody buggering hell is Bessie Harraton?'

CHAPTER 16

Next morning when Lizza woke up it took some seconds for her to remember where she was. Bessie Harraton had put her in the largest bedroom, whose substantial stone-mullioned windows faced across towards the Prior's Woods and, in the distance, the Priory itself. On the horizon far to the left she could see one of the many pitheads which dug their feet into the land all around Priorton.

She fingered the vast quilt, whose curls and whorls of tiny handstitching followed the lumpy contours of the old bed. She lay back on pillowslips and sheets which were soft and old, snow-white with faded blue hand embroidery.

The previous night, showing her the bedroom, Bessie had put a hand on the quilt and traced a single whorl with a thick fingernail. 'Should be comfortable here, hinney. The old feller allus said this was a comfortable bed.' For a second her bright eye dimmed. 'An' there's the bell.' She nodded at a slightly frayed cord hanging from an ornate ceiling rose just over the bed. 'Just ring it an' ah'll be here. Ah'm just down the landin' on that back corridor.'

Lizza frowned. 'I can't do that, Miss Harraton. I can't ring a bell.'

'Cahl us Bessie, hinney. Naebody cahls us that other. Except mebbe Mr Silkin and ah canna for the life of us get him to cahl us me own name. An' ah let him get away with it, seein' as 'e was so good over the business of the house.' She paused. 'An' you might some day need to ring the bell... Don't worry about me, miss, ah'm used ter it. Worked in this house seventy years, fusst Mrs Barraclough, then 'er son Mr Barraclough who was clerk then manager of the big bank in the 'igh Street.' She nodded towards Lizza's stomach.

'Could come a day, miss, when yer might need the bell.'

Lizza had reddened at that. 'What...?'

Bessie cackled. 'What does an old spinster know about that? Why hinney there's been dozens of girls through here, helpin', through the years. In all kind of conditions.'

'Thank you, Bessie,' said Lizza, now unutterably weary. 'This looks so comfortable. I'll be in danger of sleeping for a week.'

Bessie had grinned then. 'Ye canna dae that. Breakfast's at half past seven sharp. Dinner at twelve and tea at a quarter to six. In the dining room. Tell those bairns ah want hands washed, please. An' I'll need yer ration books to get the Priorton shops marked in. That's not sayin' the pantry's empty, mind you. Bin well stocked up from since before the war.' She sniffed. 'Not that ah've ever 'eld wi' that *hoardin'*, like. Ah listen to the wireless, you know! Got me own set in the kitchen. Old Barraclough, that is the son of old Mrs Barraclough, used to come in on a night an' listen to it.' She coughed. 'But the pantry 'ere 'ad always been stocked up, see? Bottles and tins an' that. Mrs Barraclough insisted on it, 'ad them counted in a book, the tins and bottles. She always said you needed stocks in. Never knew what would happen. This war's not different than the last one, hinney. Nor the South African war, come to that.' She had cackled then. 'Ah'll just go in and see to them bairns. They'll mucky the sheets tonight, by the look of them. But ah'll get the gas boiler on in the morning and they can have a good

227

sleep, an'll be as right as rain in no time.'

During the next day Bessie, refusing all offers of help, let Lizza know that she ran Campion House, which she now owned, just as she had when old Mr Barraclough was alive. She still turned out rooms daily and weekly in the traditional Campion House order; still swept and polished the step three times a week; still shopped at Priorton Co-operative Society on Tuesdays and Thursdays, and the market on Saturdays; still slept in the tiny corner bedroom which she had shared with the other maid when, aged ten, she came into the house as scullery maid in 1880.

Later that day Bessie carried an empty tray into the tall gloomy dining room. Lizza, Josie and Liam had just finished their tea of boiled ham and the luxury of an egg each, followed by currant scones and queen cakes. Bessie started to gather up the plates, putting out a hand to smack Lizza's hand when she made as though to help.

'An egg each was a good treat, Bessie,' said Lizza, sitting back.

'Feller who used to garden here's in the army now. 'e kept 'is hens here. Now 'is wife looks to the garden and watches the hens.' She grunted with satisfaction. 'No problem about eggs if yer keep yer mouth shut.'

Josie watched the old woman with interest. 'Mrs King says you've been in this house all your life, Miss...er...Bessie.'

She smiled her gap-toothed smile. 'How old d'yer think I am, hinney? Or you, miss?' She turned to Lizza and put her head on one side in query, like a little bird.

They both examined her closely. Josie thought she must be about two hundred years old. Lizza thought that in some ways she might have been a seventeen-year-old: bird-like and quick. She had met old women like that in the asylum, who had lived narrow, superficially tranquil, lives in a kind of fossilised virginal state, before they had shattered in contact with some hard person or fact of life.

'Seventy?' she chanced.

Bessie laughed. 'Eighty!'

'Never!' said Josie politely.

'See?' said the old woman victoriously. 'It's the good life that does it! Good food, hard work and...' Her face contorted slightly in a wink. She leaned, putting her face almost too close to Lizza's, 'No temptations.'

She carried on stacking the detritus of the high tea on to the large wooden tray. 'Ah been in this house, in that little bedroom, for seventy years. Ah shared it wi' Florry Cator then, who was called the maid. Old Mrs Barraclough ran yer with a rod of iron in those days. She'd get a stick at yer like a schoolteacher when you got wrong.'

'She beat you with a stick?' said Josie.

The old shoulders lifted in a shrug. 'Only when yer did wrong. At first, she left money around, just so's yer'd pinch it. Then yer'd get the stick. She'd catch you taking food meant for the house, an' yer'd get the stick. An' yer'd burn the bread, an' yer'd get the stick. She'd find dust on the dining-room skirting-board...'

'It ain't right. I'd'a hit her back!' asserted Josie.

'Well, hinney, ah tried that once. That's when Florry Cator held me down while I got a proper beatin'. Then ah was on bread an' water for a week, an' a month's money stopped. Such as it was.'

'What?'

Bessie cackled. 'They had to, see? Ah was a proper bad'n. An' I 'ad ter tek it or it was the *wuckouse.*'

'*Wuckouse?*' said Josie.

'Workhouse,' said Lizza. 'A place for paupers. Didn't your family complain, Bessie?'

She yelped with amusement. 'Me family? Ah'd no family in a hundred miles. They wus all on the road. I'd bin 'ere at Campion House wi' me father who wus 'elpin' build it, with young Mr Barraclough, that ended up as old Barraclough, overminding the building. Me da wus on the roof. I used to help him, carry things and that. In me tenth year I was. He travelled round workin' on the buildin'; mostly roofs. There wus just 'im and me, like. Well, anyway, he wus up on this roof, an' 'e fell off, an' wus dead in three hours. Anyway, the ol' feller, only mebbe a lad of twenty then, he made his old ma take me in. So she 'ad a free 'and with me like. Cane an' all.' She looked into Josie's angry eyes. 'It stopped like, when ah was mebbe your age, pet,' she said reassuringly.

Josie grinned. 'Did you sort her out then?'

'No. Ah wus perfeck by then. Not a foot

wrong. Any part of the house, not a speck o' dust. The bread made three times a week, not a black crust, dinners on the table to the second, fruit bottled, curtains stitched, clothes mended...'

'Slavery.'

Bessie shook her head. 'A home, pet, that's what it was.'

'And it's yours now?' said Lizza, her curiosity getting the better of her.

Bessie cackled. 'That's got yer! It got a few in this town when it 'appened, when the old lad died! It got me, ter tell yer the truth. But the old feller's lawyer, that Silkin, he made sure it was all right, that nobody could say the old feller's gone off his head.'

'He left it to you?'

'Well, hinney, by then, ah was the only family he had. In the end, ah was washing and dressing him like he were me own bairn. An' Mr Silkin was in and out all those years. He could see what ah did.' There was both love and grim satisfaction in her words. She shoved the last plates together noisily. 'Well, this doesn't get the baby a bonnet, does it? Ah'll sort this now, an' then, if you like, you can come in me kitchen an' listen to me wireless. Mr Silkin says ah was to look after you cos you'd bin through it. That's what he said, "bin through it".'

Bessie Harraton's kitchen was entirely different from the rest of the house. It was almost unbearably hot from a huge fire in an iron range, although Bessie did much of her cooking on the more modern gas cooker in the scullery.

A large table was pushed against a settle, which stood by the wall. On this table was Bessie's night work. It might be some pillowslips to darn, some sheets to turn, a tray-cloth to embroider. On Friday and Saturday nights it was a great quilt on which she worked for her own pleasure, stitching the turns and the whorls as it took her fancy.

Beside the fire stood a small easy chair, covered with leatherette, where she always sat to read the *Northern Echo* after she had had her tea, marking off with a stubby pencil those known to her in the *Deaths* and *In Memoriam* columns.

On the other side of the fire was a Windsor chair with a bright neat cushion on the seat. Against its back lay a green cushion which still held the deep-creased dent made by old Mr Barraclough when he came to listen to *Garrison Theatre* or some other programme on Bessie's wireless.

'We wus listening to an episode of *The Four Feathers* when he wus took really bad that last time,' she told Lizza.

On the walls, on the shelves, on every available surface glittered trinkets and colourful gewgaws, bright and cheap, picked up by Bessie for pennies from market stalls and travellers, right down the years. Campion House itself was kept in true gloomy Victorian style, as it had been in the days of old Mrs Barraclough. But the Campion House kitchen was Bessie's territory and she decorated it like a jackdaw trims her nest, making it her very own, affirming in her choice and spread of

232

possessions her unremembered gypsy ancestry.

Within a few days Lizza, Josie and Liam were bound into Bessie's routine. Josie and Liam loved to be in Bessie's kitchen and would stay until shooed out by Bessie, who liked her own company for a good part of the day. Then, while it was light, they would go down into the long garden where they discovered the joys of climbing large trees together.

The kitchen was always too hot for Lizza and she spent her time in the room Bessie called Mr Barraclough's study, although there was only one large book-case in there, filled with law books, glossy with Bessie's regular polishing. There were two soft chairs to sit on and a desk under the window. Bessie always kept a low fire in the cast-iron fireplace.

On the third day, when Lizza had had two good sleeps and had explored all the nooks and crannies of the house, and had her fill of the close-printed and boring books on the history of mathematics, she went in search of Bessie. 'Is there anything I could write on, Bessie? Paper?'

'You need some letter paper?'

'That'd do. But it's not for letters.'

Bessie scowled at her. 'Can't see the benefit of writing things. A lot of squiggles on the page.'

'I just wanted to write some things down about when I was a nurse. This woman suggested I might.'

Rosie sniffed and vanished. She came back with a heavy leather-bound book and opened it. Some pages had been torn out. There were red ledger-lines down to the right of the pages but the surface of the paper was smooth and thick. 'Will this do?'

Lizza fingered the torn edges of the pages. 'Lovely paper, Bessie. What was it?'

Bessie blinked at her like a small owl. 'He called it his wager book. Keen on the races, was the old feller.' She grinned her gap-toothed grin. 'Took me to the races once, York.'

'Who tore the pages out?'

'Ah did that mesel'. Old Mrs Barraclough wouldn't've liked it. For the bets still to be there, on the page, for all to see. So ah burned the pages.' She thrust a hand in her pocket and pulled out a heavy fountain pen. 'Ah sorted this out for yeh. Old feller used it all the time, till he couldn't pick it up between his fingers. Called it the "dratted newfangled thing" but he loved to use it.'

Lizza weighed it in her hand. 'It's nice.'

Bessie beamed. 'Ah bought it him mesel', for a Christmas present, like. After the South African war, when he came back. Just between the two of us. You write with it, hinney. You write about when you were a nurse. Ink in the desk drawer.' Her gaze dropped to Lizza's stomach. 'Is things all right, hinney?'

Lizza coloured. 'Yes, yes. Fine.'

'Is the bairn kicking?'

'Yes, yes.' Lizza fiddled with the lid of the fountain pen.

'Well, I'll leave yer to get writin' then. Tea a quarter to six sharp, mind.' She left a slight smell of mint and carbolic soap in the air as she darted from the room.

Josie came in half an hour later. 'Liam's in the kitchen sink being washed down by Bessie,' she reported. 'He fell into some mud at the bottom of the garden. Out of a tree. There was a big puddle because of all this rain. He started crying for Mummy so I took him to Bessie an' she gave him some crystallised plum an' put him in the sink. Soon shut him up.'

'How did he come to fall out of a tree?'

Josie smiled. 'I ain't sure how it happened, Mrs King.' She leaned over Lizza's shoulder. Lizza could smell Bessie's smell of carbolic and mint. Maybe they all smelled of it now. 'What's this then? Sure, you look like some clerking lady with that big book before you.'

'I'm going to write about when I was nursing, like that Min Roebuck said.'

'What for?'

'I don't know what for. For something to do. Bessie won't let me help here. Perhaps I'm doing it to remember what it was like then, when I wasn't much older than you. When I was sure of things, of who I was...I don't know.'

'Do you think about them, Mrs King? Rebecca and the twins?'

Lizza put the pen down. 'I think about Rebecca all the time. I feel she's just behind my left elbow. The twins less now.'

'I think about my mammy and Anne-Marie a lot. I have this ache and I think I'm gunna turn round and they'll be there.'

Lizza nodded. 'Me too.'

'An' suddenly this afternoon, when Liam was

235

falling out of the tree, I thought of Daddy. I wonder where he is now?'

Lizza looked at her. 'Roland got in touch with the army, you know. He will get to know.' She stared at Josie, knowing in her heart how, on top of all this, she was pleased not to have to face Theo Callaghan. He was the last person she wanted to bring into her mind. 'You'll hear from him soon, Josie.'

'No. I don't care whether he knows or not. Mammy hated him.'

Lizza put her hand over Josie's small rough one. 'He's your father, Josie. They must have loved each other once. He has to know about her and little Anne-Marie.'

'He'll come here,' said Josie with certainty.

Lizza looked round the stuffy little room with its antimacassars, its tassels and velvet. There could be no greater contrast with her neat, pretty room in Coventry where Theo Callaghan had jumped on her and tried to use her like some animal. 'To be honest, Josie, I don't want him here,' she said.

'No more do I,' said Josie urgently. 'With luck he won't find us. Sure he can never have loved her, the way he treated her, never...' She paused. 'When can we go back to Bracks Hill?'

'Why do you want to go there?'

'I thought you'd want to go. Your mammy's there. Your sister.'

Lizza smiled slightly and filled the fountain pen from the bottle. She knew full well what the attraction of Bracks Hill was for Josie. 'Go and see what Liam's up to, Josie. Bessie's got plenty

236

to do in this house without playing mother.'

And Lizza was left with an echo in her mind of Maeve Callaghan's voice, the night Theo received his call-up papers. *'I'll hand him over to Jerry. No fate is bad enough. They can have the old bugger.'* Well, it was Maeve and Anne-Marie that Jerry had taken. And it was they who'd had the worst of fates. She hoped with all her heart that the army had better things to do than let Theo Callaghan know just where they were.

Then she started to write a story about this nurse who met an old woman in the mental home where she worked; how the old woman told the nurse the story of her childhood when her father, a gypsy, had left her in the care of the family for whom he was working. The child was easy to conjure up, in this room, in this house.

Alex walked back into the Bracks Hill house as though he had been away for just an hour rather than several days.

His grandmother took his jacket from him and pushed him to the seat closest to the fire, saying his face was dirty, she would get him water to wash. Beatrice uncharacteristically touched his shoulder. 'I thought you were off to join up.'

He grinned and called into the scullery, 'Our Beatrice wants rid of us, Gram!'

'Don't talk soft,' said Alice Bremner. 'No one wants rid of you. What happened?'

'Nah. I was talking to these fellers in Newcastle. Say it takes a year to get trained to be a pilot. You have training and exams and tests and things. The war'll be over by the time I get up there.'

'You'll pass all the tests. Never had an exam you didn't pass,' said Beatrice.

'Well, I'm just thinking. See action faster in one of the other services.'

Alice pushed a thick sandwich into his hand. 'Maybe you should think of the Air Force, if there's that much education in it.'

He grinned up at her from the chair where he was sprawled. His mouth full, he talked through the thick paste sandwich. 'Gotcher, Gram! You think I should go with them 'cause it'll be over by the time I get my training too!' He looked round.

'Lizza's here, and those two children of her neighbour who died,' said Beatrice.

Alex grinned and looked round. 'Where is she? Our Lizza?' He did not mention Josie.

'She came,' said Beatrice. 'But Roland got her fixed up with some lodgings, I think. Up at Priorton.'

'She always lands on her feet, that one,' said Alice grimly.

Alex looked at his Gram, scowling. 'You can't say that. Her house was wrecked. Rebecca died. The kid died.'

Beatrice whitened and Mrs Bremner's worn hand went over her eyes for a moment.

'But where is she?'

'They,' said Beatrice watching him carefully. 'There was a girl with her, Josie, and a little boy, Liam.'

'Yes.' His mind was in some kind of turmoil

238

about Josie. He wanted her and wanted to forget about her at the same time.

'They're both there at Priorton?' said Alex.

'So far as I can tell. Our Lizza seems to have taken them on.'

The boy stood up and looked into his grandmother's eyes with conscious charm. 'By, Gram, I forgot how nice your bread was. Did I tell yer our Lizza never bakes?'

Mrs Bremner sniffed. 'Too busy working. Savin' the lives of old women. Never learnt.'

Beatrice looked sharply at her mother. 'Never had the chance, you mean. You and me and our Renee did it all here. And she was away from here at fourteen, always in other folks' houses.' She leaned over and wrested the sandwich from Alex's hand. 'You eat like a pig,' she said crossly. 'And you can't say anything about Lizza. She took you in.'

He shrugged and rescued his sandwich. 'I knew Lizza wouldn't stay here. Likes to be her own boss. She's a queer'n, Lizza.'

Beatrice looked at her son, thinking how she'd kept her distance from him; allowed her mother to commandeer him. She thought that there were things about him that she disliked: a coldness and a tendency to use people and things as they suited him. For the first time in years she allowed herself to think of his father, and the possibility that in some part of Alex's being he might be like his father: self-interested to the exclusion of humanity in any other person. What if he did to some girl what his father had done to her? She reached out, took him by the shirt and shook him hard. 'That's me sister you talk about, lad, your aunt. She took you in down there, she...'

He removed her hands from his shirt. 'Like me Gram says, Lizza can take care of herself, Beatrice. Don't yer know yer own sister?'

Mrs Bremner put a bowl of water on the table and stood back watching, arms folded while he had a wash. Her concentration was so complete that she did not notice her daughter gather her coat from the back of the door and quietly leave the house.

CHAPTER 17

On the first Saturday after their arrival Liam followed Bessie to the shops and the market. She turned and glared at him in annoyance; asking him where his sister was, criticising Josie loudly for letting him stray. But she let him come, making him hold on to the handle of her string bag. She had her reward: during the long waits in queues she had a good topic of conversation about her evacuees and how Mr Silkin had persuaded her to do this special war work for these poor victims of the Coventry bombing. She also aroused sympathy in shopkeepers with the tale of Liam's poor orphaned status. This, on more than one occasion, led them to allow her extra quantities, which were not hers by right.

It was nearly noon when she got to the

butcher's queue and found herself standing beside Enid Cator. Enid was Headmistress of St Bennet's Primary School. Her grandmother, Florry, had been Bessie's first housemaid, the one who had held her down while Mrs Barraclough beat her. Bessie had known Enid's mother from the day she was born and had minded Enid herself when she was a child. The child Enid was squat and not too prepossessing and the victim of many cruel taunts from the boys at school. But she stuck in at school and those who had mocked her spent the late twenties and thirties on the dole, while step by step she worked her way up the Infant School ladder until, at the very young age of forty, she was made headteacher. She had a passionate unrequited spirit, which slaked itself by focusing on the children in her care, and the more generalised wider world of children. She was on the management committee of Carhoe Orphanage and fought many a dogged battle on behalf of those motherless children.

She squinted down through her tiny glasses and smiled at Liam, and shuddered on hearing of the dreadful time the child had had in the bombing. He put his head on one side and stared up at her steadily. 'And now he's billeted with you! Can you cope, Bessie?'

'Ah kin cope with owt's gets heaped on me. Owld Barraclough allus said ah wus his tower o' strength. An' anyway it's three extra ration books, dis tha knaa?' Bessie smiled up at her cunningly. 'There's nowt ah canna get now.'

Enid laughed and shook her close-cropped

241

head. 'Bessie! You're incorrigible. Well, anyway, why don't you get his sister to bring him in to school? He's very young but there's a nursery class now, and I'm certain we can find a place for him.'

Bessie smiled to herself as she collected her extra sausages. That was the little bairn taken care of. Now the big lass: she would surely be taken on at the factory. Then she could make herself a bit of money and forget about the bad things that had happened to her. She would get on to her. Money there for the taking. The war wasn't all bad. It gave you chances.

Back at Campion House, after scolding Josie about letting her little brother stray, she started on about the factory. 'Lots of the lasses work there, hinney, earn good money. Ah heard it in the queue at the baker's. Yer dinnat want ter end up like me, skivvying after other folks all your life.'

Josie giggled. 'Sure, I wouldn't mind endin' up like you, Bessie. Can you by any chance stand on your head?'

Bessie snorted. 'Course ah can—only stopped deein' it when I was seventy, when the old feller cum on us, showin' me drawers. He put a stop to it. Said it wasn't'—she twisted her lips in cruel mimicry—'seemly.'

Josie grinned, then lowered her voice and looked round the empty kitchen. 'Did you swear when you did it, too?'

Bessie smiled with delight. 'You know about that? Well I never!'

Josie leaned across and rubbed a larger hole in the steamed surface of the window. The bus wheezed and creaked to a stop on Carlton Ridge, beside the Post Office. 'See Liam, there! There's another one. That's four in three miles.' She put her nose to the surface and peered through at the swirling wheel and the straining cables of Carlton Pithead. 'Aren't they amazing things, Mrs King? Like some great flytrap? Those wheels and ropes hauling men and coals from the bowels of the earth.'

Lizza put her face beside her and saw the dark winter landscape: the huddle of houses that was Carlton village and above it, Carlton Pit etched against the winter sky, almost floating on a raft of fog. Close by, climbing the gantry, trudged miners, head down, going in for the two o'clock shift. 'They're just big dirty pits, Josie.'

'Aw, Mrs King. Just look at it, swirling away there. They're not just that. They say it's really hot down there under the earth. Hotter than hell.' She relished the excuse to swear in an upright position.

'Who say?'

'Me dad used to bring two fellers home from the pub to play cards. He said miners were born gamblers, cos they wagered their lives every day in the pit. Those fellers were always talking about the pit; loved it like a wife.'

'But it beats them; they don't beat it.' The words came to Lizza unbidden.

Josie sat back on the wooden seat and put her hand over her mouth.

'Sorry, Josie, I shouldn't have said that.'

'No, Mrs King, it's not that. I felt sick, this old bus is swaying so much.'

'I know about pits, Josie. My brothers went down the pit. Bernard's in Cornwall now, still digging the black stuff. He loves it, like them men you talk about. Once you get him started he won't stop. But Jonnie hated it, couldn't wait to get out and get into the army.'

'And he's a prisoner now?'

Lizza nodded. 'We hope so. Officially he's missing. Perhaps even Jonnie would give his eye teeth to be walking over the gantry at this minute, rather than sitting under the nose of a German rifle.' She moved the subject slightly. 'Was there a pit at Coventry? Didn't know that.'

'Well, there's one at least. These fellers worked there.'

She hadn't known that. Hadn't associated pits with that fast, modern city. Lizza frowned, still staring out at the countryside as the bus moved along. This was what her mother had called the land of her own possession. Small fields and hedges, with the land rising to hills in the distance; little villages clustered round large pits; the proud fronts of nineteenth-century chapels and less frequent older spires of churches.

This was the land she thought she had escaped from; where people were always looking deep into holes in the ground, always looking backwards to past times, past pain, great triumphs. She wondered if you really lived beyond a time of great pain. Would she herself be fossilised in the moment when the

244

blast flattened her house and took her daughter, just as her mother had been fossilised in the years of the First War, when her great love had been squashed like a fly in the trenches, leaving the rest of her life a painful waiting time: waiting to rejoin him. Lizza shook her head. She didn't even have that sense of afterlife as consolation. Gone is gone. 'We have to look forward, Josie,' she said.

'What was that, Mrs King?'

'I said it's no good wallowing in the past, waiting to wake up from a bad dream. We have to move forward.'

Josie nodded her head wisely. 'That's what I always say, Mrs King. Do you think Alex'll be back at Bracks Hill yet?'

Lizza laughed, ruffled Josie's newly washed hair hanging now in soft black curls, and sat back to endure the rest of the bumping journey. She thought about a story she could write in the big ledger, about a young miner who hated the thought, then the reality of the pit, volunteered for the army—no, she would make it the navy, all that freedom, sea and sky would contrast with the depths of the earth—and was drowned at sea on his first voyage.

Her mother and Beatrice were sitting reading when they arrived: her mother was poring over a colourful religious tract bought from a traveller; Beatrice had a copy of *People's Friend* just under the large Bible which was opened on the kitchen table. She leapt up to greet them, delight mixing with relief on her face. 'Lizza. I thought you'd forgotten about us.'

'Never. Just took us a bit to settle down, that's all.' Lizza dropped her gas mask then peeled off her gloves and put them over the mantelrail. 'It's cold out there,' she said, holding out her hands to the hot fire.

'Do they have no coal, then, at your billet?' said her mother, speaking for the first time.

'Oh, our landlady Bessie seems to have plenty of coal. Her butcher's brother-in-law is a pitman who seems to have more than he needs.'

'The houses are always hot here,' volunteered Josie, looking around eagerly. 'Never bin in such hot houses.'

'If we can't be warm with millions of tons of coal beneath our feet, then there's sommat wrong,' asserted Beatrice. She glanced at the graceful mahogany clock on the back wall. 'Now then, all sit down. It's nearly tea-time so I might as well set it out.'

As she went through to the scullery she called round the partition up the stairs, 'Alex! Our Lizza's here.'

There was a thumping as he belted down the steep stairs. He whirled into the small kitchen, kissed Lizza on the cheek, whirled Josie round in circles, then grasped Liam and held him up by his feet till he squealed.

Beatrice brought in a tray and started to set the table.

Alice looked on this exhibition of excessive emotion with disapproval. 'I know you go up after dinner to read those ungodly aeroplane books, but at least have some respect for the

Lord's Day when you come into the presence of other people.'

He put Liam the right way up and grinned at her. 'Just pleased to see our Lizza, Gram. The last time I saw her she was in a halo of flames.'

Lizza smiled at him. 'I thought you'd gone off to be a scourge of the skies.'

'I came home to have a think about it. Training so long for the Air Force, it'll all be over before I get to grips with them. They told me if you got on you might even have to go to America to train. Thought I might try the army. But I've been sitting up there deciding it can only be the RAF...'

'If they'll have you; they're very choosy, you know...' cut in Beatrice.

'Oh, they'll have me all right,' said Alex, winking at Josie. 'They'll know *A-one* when they see it!'

'The trouble is,' said Lizza gloomily, 'he's probably right, and that'll do nothing to knock him back.'

He got hold of her shoulders. 'Just think, though, Lizza. Me up there, shooting down Huns. Bombing their factories...'

'They all die,' said Alice. 'The boys all die.' The air stilled as they looked at her.

'Mother!' said Beatrice.

'I read it in the paper. All those lads in the Battle of Britain. Scores...hundreds of them. Die. Might as well put yourself on a bullseye on a shooting range. No son of mine, if you go off doing that stupid thing.'

Beatrice spoke up. 'He is no son of yours, Ma.' She looked at Alex. 'Are you really set on it, Alex?'

He looked at her steadily, the humour gone from his eyes, and nodded slowly.

'Then I think you have the right to go and do your bit.'

Alice's rage filled the air in the kitchen like a thick mist, but she said nothing. Glancing at her, Alex dragged Josie from the chair. 'Come on, little'n. I'll show you the delights of Bracks Hill. You aren't half in for a treat!'

'Alex, your gas masks! Your tea!' Beatrice called to their retreating backs. She shrugged. 'They're hardly likely to need their gas masks here. Now we'll have to wait tea till they get back.'

'It's Chapel at six and we'll have to go, tea or no tea,' said Alice. She looked at her daughters. 'You'll be coming?'

'No. Ma.' Lizza shook her head.

'I'll stay with Lizza,' said Beatrice with unusual firmness.

Liam started to whimper. 'Wan' play out with Josie.'

Beatrice dug in the back of the fireside cupboard and found him a wooden car and a box of bricks in faded colours of red, blue and green. 'Here, Liam, these were our Alex's. You can play with them in the front room on the lino. He used to like to do that.'

He chattered to her as she rolled up the front-room carpet and set him down to play.

She came back and picked up her tract, Alice

sniffed. 'RAF? The lad's never been the same since he went to that Godforsaken place...' She sniffed.

Lizza said, 'Do you mean Coventry?'

Alice Bremner watched her calmly. 'Yes I do.'

'Well, how would you know what Coventry was like? You never went, did you?' She turned to Beatrice who was coming through the middle door. 'When you came to help me,' she said, pausing deliberately, 'when my children died, you came, Beatrice, because Ma wouldn't—couldn't come. Did you think Coventry was a Godforsaken place?'

Beatrice shook her head. 'No.'

'What was it, then?'

'It was bright, busy, everything was fast. Lots of cars, motorbikes, bicycles...'

'Godless,' put in Alice decisively.

'Godless? There's a Cathedral and two great churches, Mother.'

'Popery,' said Alice triumphantly.

'Mother...'

Beatrice put a hand on Lizza's shoulder and she relaxed. 'Well, you might be right now, Mother,' she said. 'The town's flattened, the Cathedral's in ashes and a thousand people killed, including, if you're interested, your own granddaughter, so there can't be a God, there or anywhere.'

'It's the sin of man,' said Alice confidently, 'going to war at all for some foreign quarrel. They should know better after last time.'

Now Lizza leapt to her feet properly. 'Know

249

better! Know better! The madman Hitler is evil;
has to be stopped. Do you know, they have great
villages set up specially for prisoners, where
they're starved and beaten to death? Roland
works with people who have family that it's
happening to. That they take people from their
homes and kill them if they're Jewish? They take
people from their homes and make them slaves
in factories.'

'Jews,' said her mother, sniffing.

Lizza leapt on her mother, taking her by the
shoulders and shaking her, ' "*If ye cut me, do I
not also bleed? If ye cut me...*" '

Alice glanced at Beatrice, who dragged at
Lizza, trying to pull her off. Then she had to
unclasp her fingers one by one as Lizza still
raged on. 'You sit here in this little backwater
like God Almighty yourself, Mother, safe from
harm to all intents and purposes. And you
pontificate about whole groups of people who
you know nothing of. You sit here barely
moving from this street, in no danger, giving
nothing...'

Beatrice finally got herself between them.

Alice looked up into her younger daughter's
eyes. 'We share things, lass. I too've given
of my substance,' she said. 'I've given my
brothers and my man, my son and now...'
She threw a sideways glance at Beatrice. '...my
grandson.' She dropped her eye to her tract
again.

Beatrice pulled Lizza into the scullery. 'You
can't blame her, Lizz, for what she doesn't
know, what she hasn't seen. None of us. Half

the time even I don't know what you're talking about.'

'We have to imagine, Bea, check things up, make them connect. She might be ignorant but she'll pass judgement on plenty things she hasn't seen. Like the whole of the Church of England though she's only ever been in chapels. Like every Jewish person who ever walked the earth, though she's never met one. Like a whole town where she's never even set foot...'

Beatrice shook her gently by the shoulders. 'Sometimes I envy her her certainty, Lizza. Sometimes I envy you yours,' she said quietly.

The door opened and Alice walked calmly between them into the tiny pantry. 'I'll get a biscuit to take through for the bairn, we're not to have our teas till later. No telling how late our Alex'll be, once he's out.'

They followed her through to the kitchen and then through the open front-room door they could hear her soft talk to the child and his chirruping reply.

Lizza grinned at her sister. 'I wonder if she'd be so cosy with Liam if she knew he was a Catholic?'

The side door to the chapel was open and Alex and Josie let themselves in. They could hear muttering in the adjacent room, but Alex pulled Josie across the highly polished floor and up a shining staircase, through a low door and up a much narrower staircase. They clambered into a dusty space beneath the sloping roof which was banded by beams.

'Like the inside of a boat,' whispered Josie, very impressed.

'Not quite like Beaconsfield,' said Alex in her ear. He was happy that, while Beaconsfield had been her territory, this was his. He was in charge here.

'How d'you find this place?'

'A lad whose dad helped to build the chapel showed me when I was ten. I've been coming ever since. Here. Look!'

He dragged her over to kneel on the floor and pulled a sack away to reveal a square aperture in the floor. Beneath them lay the whole spread of the chapel. There were lights at the front and the back of the plain, shining interior; the gallery like a great, glittering wheel over the rows of seats below.

They could see the bald head of the minister moving in the dim space below, the rustle as he made the hymn books perfectly straight in the pews. They could hear the creaks and squeaks as Florrie Jewitt settled her bulk on the organ stool, and her muttering to Sid, her nephew, whose turn it was to work the bellows.

Josie giggled. 'Sure, this is a great place, Alex.'

'As good as Beaconsfield?' he whispered, his lips near her cheeks.

Below them the main lights went on, and, like little ants, the people started coming in, in ones and twos, and in whole family clusters, down the central aisles. He pointed out people he knew. The postwoman and the milkman, his old infant-school teacher, and boys and girls who had lived in the same street as him with their mothers, and in some cases their fathers.

'A lot less men now, one way or another,' he said. 'Lor' there's me Gram in her best hat. No Beatrice. Now she'll be in trouble.' He moved so his body was alongside hers. 'Is it better than Beaconsfield?' he whispered.

'That all depends.' She pressed her back towards him in response to his pressure. Below them, Florrie was striking up the chords for 'Praise my soul, the King of Heaven'. And Alice Bremner was smoothing the fragile page of the hymn book, pleased to be out of the house, out of the way of her vexing daughters.

Alex started to kiss Josie's neck, turning her towards him. She laughed up at him in gloom. 'Sure, it's a different boy you are here, Alex,' she whispered.

He nipped at her cheek with his teeth. 'My territory,' he said. 'Anyway, Jose, I'm off tomorrow to defend you, to get them for what they did to your ma and Anne-Marie. And our Rebecca. It's different now. It feels different.' He kissed her lips hard, his mouth closed. 'Do you want to? Might be the only, the last time.'

'Here?'

'No better place.'

The organ below swelled on the line *well our feeble frame he knows* and he could hear his grandmother's fine voice rising to the echo.

'Not here, Alex, over there in the corner!' whispered Josie.

'Why not here? They can't see us. We're

253

seventy feet in the air. A dot on their horizon.'

She was crawling now to a corner deep under the eaves. 'Sure, it's hot in here. Everywhere in this blessed country is hot. Under the earth. In the houses. And now in their blessed church.' She crossed herself. She muttered, 'We'll have to take our clothes off.'

'All of them?' he said, grinning in the dark, happy now to let her take charge.

'All of them.'

Below them, the minister was climbing the high pulpit, armed with his long sermon on the just war, of which, though he said it himself, he was very proud.

'So it's near Glasgow?' said Roland, frowning.

Krystof, Roland and Pieter were making their way back to Pieter Vann's house, after their eighth consecutive shift at work. Pieter had persuaded Roland to move in with him and Krystof, rather than return each night to the cold empty Callaghan house.

He had waited till the end of the day to broach the subject of the relocation of the development facility to a safer place.

'They've found a spot near Glasgow,' said Pieter. 'They'll link it to one of the shadow factories near there. There was some suggestion that it was located on one of the islands, but we won't know those details till we travel up there. I've offered this house to the billeting people while I'm away.'

'Glasgow's as risky as Coventry, surely?'

Pieter shrugged. 'Wherever it is, now, it will

254

be well away from any city, I should think.'

'I'd hoped the section was going to the plant in the North-East. My wife's expecting me there.'

'That was one option. But it is Glasgow, as we thought. And we go tomorrow.'

'Straight away?'

'Instant moves is policy, you know, Roland. A matter of security.'

Roland turned to the Pole. 'Krystof? Did you know? Are you coming?'

Krystof glanced sideways at him. 'Yes, I did know. No, I'm not coming. They say I can have some leave. I have to go into hospital for some examinations—just to check that I've fully recovered from my long walk. Then they have a new commission for some industrial drawing for me. I had hoped to join the Polish Army in Scotland. But that will have to wait.'

The hand-shattering, back-numbing work of clearing the bomb damage was nearly complete. The factory was beginning to return to some kind of order. The improvised roofing was in place and the debris had been cleared out to the factory yard. The worst problem was a machine which had been welded to the wall by the heat of the fire. One section of one line was working now, and there were hopes of achieving fifty per cent of production within the month.

So the move was to be Glasgow, not the North-East as he had hoped. Roland sighed. In one way he saw himself as a soldier in the front line of this war, as crucial to the war effort as any of the men who piloted their planes over

255

France and Germany. This being the case, he had to take orders like this and not quail. At least he was still alive. At least he didn't have to carry a gun, or press the buttons that dropped the bombs.

Sometimes he worried about this fact, that he was happy to be in a reserved profession and not to have to kill, and not risk his life deliberately. On the other hand, his tools helped to make the bombers more efficient in their killing task. Sometimes he thought he had the instincts but not the courage of the conscientious objectors who were so reviled in the papers.

Later, as Krystof concocted a spicy potato soup, he asked Roland casually about Lizza. 'Your wife, is she happy being away from the chaos here?'

'I'm not sure about happy.' Roland plucked a letter from his inside pocket. 'The billet my father's friend Amos Silkin found for her sounds good.' He drew the letter towards the oil lamp which was still the only light in the house.

This is the biggest house I have ever been in, Roland, apart from the hospital. The food's good, as Bessie Harraton (that's the woman's name) has more contacts in this town than any black marketeer. Somebody's brother's uncle has always just killed a pig or taken delivery of extra cheese or—Heaven, this—stumbled in the dark over a box of oranges. But you should hear her going on about the Black Market, and what she would do to those perpetrators, those traitors to the country's good. She's always listening to

256

those talks on the wireless about how we should go on, but goes her own sweet way anyway. Sometimes, if it weren't for the wireless and the black-out, and all the soldiers who flush into Priorton from Killock Camp on Saturday nights, you wouldn't think there was a war on. I've read over that bit of my letter again. In fact, all that just shows there's a war on, doesn't it? But what I mean is there isn't the tension, the harassed feeling there was in Coventry with everyone jumpy about the raids or the thought of one. Oh, and there's a big garden with apple trees and a vegetable plot here which young Liam loves. The garden's looked after by this woman who is the wife of the man who was the gardener who's now fighting in Egypt. There are hens so we have eggs galore. As it has been rainy and windy here Liam is always cold and covered with mud, but he loves it. How Rebecca would have loved it. I think of her most of the time, but it is hard to realise it is only a week or so since I lost her. It feels like years. This Bessie Harraton, who runs the house, is an ancient spinster who is half gorgon and half fairy-godmother. She rules us with a rod of iron. Liam and Josie love her, even if they only understand half she says. She's eighty but has the strength of mind and body of a woman half that age. I'm allowed to do very little, as she is very fussy about my condition, which leaves time hanging on my hands. So I'm reading even more than usual and have started to write some things in a ledger Bessie found for me. I went home, but it was fairly disastrous, as

I started to argue with my mother about Hitler and the Jews...

Roland glanced at Pieter. 'She chatters on...' His voice petered out, aware that there was a hunger for more than food in the room; that he was reading his own letter to two men who would never now get a letter from their loved ones. 'She goes on,' he repeated lamely.

Krystof ladled the soup on to three thick plates. 'One can hear her voice in the words. She writes? What does she write? Stories, poems?'

Roland shrugged. 'I can't say. She has her secrets, has Lizza. She was always a keen reader. And she writes letters. But this proper kind of writing is a new one on me.'

'You must miss her,' said Pieter.

Roland looked into Pieter's sympathetic face. 'It might seem a bit obvious, but I miss my daughter more because I know she isn't there at all. Before, even if I didn't see her, I knew she was there in the house, playing her games with Lizza. I always thought of her and Lizza as a pair. My family. I didn't get much chance to play with her, to see her. But she was there inside my head. But that's the only place she is, now. Inside my head. And in Lizza's. I know Lizza's there and am pleased she's safe, but in some ways not having to see her at the end of the day makes things easier.' He frowned at the thought of his own treachery. 'But it's easier now to get on with work, without worrying...where did you say this factory in Scotland was, Pieter?'

Pieter bent his head over the serious business of eating, shovelling food to mouth in one easy movement. 'In the West, fifteen miles from Glasgow in the hills. And they want us there by the end of the week to help set up the section.'

'In the hills? Fifteen miles from Glasgow?'

'Well, that's what they say. Could be anywhere. They say anything to protect us from our own tongues. We'll not know exactly where until we get to the Glasgow depot.'

Krystof had been eating silently through all the talk. Roland thought how much he liked him. In the short time they had worked together he had come to trust him, to depend on the quiet wit of some of his comments and respect his quizzical foreigner's perception of what was going on around him. But still there was something about him which was hard to access... He jumped as the wail of a siren pierced the companionable silence in the room. Krystof flung his spoon down on the table with a crash, swearing violently in Polish. That was it, thought Roland, standing up to put his nose through the black-out curtain. That was it. There was violence, passion in the man: one, two, three levels below the mild courtly surface: feeling that was well reined in. 'They're there,' he said. 'I can hear them.'

He returned to the table. 'Good soup, Krystof,' he said, picking up his spoon.

Pieter and Krystof picked up their spoons and carefully and deliberately, in defiance of Hitler, went on with their supper. It was a short raid, and mercifully not in their district. But the three men did not go to the shelter.

The next day the three friends parted at the factory gates as Roland and Pieter set off at noon with a loaded truck, to follow two other loaded trucks to Scotland. Roland shook Krystof's hand heartily. 'You'll keep in touch, Krystof? And if you get to that part of the world, see Lizza and the Callaghans, see how they are for me? I was sure I'd get leave to see them, but it's hurry hurry hurry and don't I know there's a war on. No question of leave.'

As the truck bumped on its way he turned to Pieter. 'Some people have all the luck,' he said, only half joking, resentful of the privilege of Krystof's leave.

The gears ground together as Pieter changed them with his podgy, capable hand. 'Did he not tell you?' he said. 'I am not certain how much of a secret it really is. They...some ministry...have told him to go off for a month to draw. They gave him a commission. Another set of drawings they want for their archive.' His voice trailed off and he gave less details than he knew, haunted by the imperative for discretion that came at them from the hoardings, from the papers, from the wireless.

It was more than a day before they caught a glimpse of their destination, from a ferry boat that rocked perilously in crashing November seas. The island sat on a veil of mist and seemed to exude vapour from the peaks that rose in the far distance. The rain was swirling towards them in horizontal sweeps, biting into their cheeks like spears of ice.

'A factory here?' Pieter shouted into his ear.

'It'll be some boffin's folly,' Roland shouted back as the wind screamed again.

'What?' shouted Pieter.

Roland shook his head and the wind caught his trilby, sending it skimming through the air. It danced on the foam for a second and sank.

As they drove the truck off the ferry, a boy of about twelve leapt on to the running board and thrust his sodden head through the window. 'Ye two're to come with me, yon two with Jamie. An' the back lads with Angus.' His friends had run on to the other trucks. 'Ah'm tae take ye to Bell House, they're tae take the others tae Mrs Robertson's. Billets.'

Roland closed his eyes with thanks at their deliverance, and kept them closed until the truck jerked to a stop. They were beside a long house which looked over a small harbour. As he rubbed his eyes he saw that the harbour opened not to the sea but to a wide bounded sweep of Loch, trimmed sharply on the other side by mountains. The surface of the Loch milled and moved about with sullen energy, but the waves here were minuscule, compared with those they had just ploughed through, on the ferry.

Then light was streaming at them from an opening door, and Roland instinctively looked up to the sky and wondered how hot they were here, in the wilds, on the black-out regulations.

In the doorway stood a tall woman muffled in a man's greatcoat and scarves round her

261

head and her face. 'Come in and welcome,' she said in an unwelcoming tone, shutting the door behind them and staring coldly at the stream of muddy rain that was dripping from their boots on to the immaculate stone flag floor. 'Your bedroom's on the first floor. The bathroom's next door and the boiler is full of water as you...obviously...need a bath. There is only enough for one, so you will have to share water. There's a fire in the bedroom and a tray with a flask of coffee and sandwiches, and whisky with which you may wish to warm yourselves. Now if you will excuse me I must go to bed myself as I am crucified with migraine.'

And she was gone.

Too weary to comment on this cavalier welcome, they trudged upstairs, found the bedroom, and devoured the coffee and fine beef sandwiches. Roland unpacked his rucksack while Pieter had his bath, then dived into Pieter's water and sat there sipping half a tumblerful of whisky as he soaked. The chilling water brought him back to the present and he jumped out, rubbed himself vigorously on a thick towel and wrapped it around himself. He went back to the bedroom to find Pieter in one bed, snoring away, fast asleep. He threw himself on to the other bed, and he too was asleep in sixty seconds.

The next morning the pale light streaming through a crack in the curtains woke him, and he pulled on his one clean set of clothes, quietly made his way downstairs and let himself out of the front door. He looked at his watch, raised his brows at the lateness of the hour, then looked around.

The storm had stopped and the day was pale and still. Before him the loch was smooth as glass, reflecting in absolute symmetry the mountains and woodlands on the opposite side. Roland held his breath, feeling that if he breathed hard or coughed, the picture would disintegrate and he would see again the canyons of dereliction he had left behind in Coventry.

'You are admiring my view?' said a smooth, well-modulated voice behind him.

He swung around, and this time he did catch his breath. In the doorway, leaning with folded arms against the door jamb, stood the most beautiful woman he had ever seen. She was slender and must have been about six feet tall in her bare feet. Her skin was brown, almost olive, and her dark hair, parted in the middle, was plaited to one side and tied with green ribbon.

'H-hello,' he stuttered.

She held out a large, capable hand and grasped his. 'I am Mara Laine, and this is my house you and your friend are invading.'

When Alex and Josie came back from the chapel Lizza was waiting at the back gate talking to Beatrice, the anger of her talk with her mother still bubbling out of her. Beatrice was saying to take no notice of her, she didn't think of what she was saying. She turned to scold them. 'You're late. At this rate these'll miss their bus.'

263

Josie caught Lizza's arm urgently. 'I was saying, Mrs King, I can't see why Alex can't come on to Priorton with us. I'm certain Bessie'll find him a space.'

Coolly, Alex took a step away from her and stood beside Beatrice. Cheering up now, Lizza said yes, there was indeed lots of room at Campion House. And Bessie would welcome him as long as he brought his ration book.

Alex shook his head slowly. 'I'll be away any day now, Lizza,' he said. 'It's not worth it.'

After tonight, up there in the chapel loft, looking down on the congregation like a pilot would on the people on the ground, he knew he was dying to go. Nothing would stop him. Nothing was going to stop him, now, not his young age, nor Josie's entrancing little body, nor his grandmother's silent powerful restraint.

Josie dropped back into the shadow of the wall and watched as he walked down the yard into the house, his shoulders swinging slightly in the manner of the pilots he had seen in the films. She was silent in the blacked-out bus all the way home, but Lizza, with Liam asleep on her knee and her thoughts still back at the house in Bracks Hill, failed to notice.

Bessie opened the door to Lizza and smiled widely. 'Ah've put yer visitor in the sitting room. Like ah telt yer a'fore, we allus has a nice fire in there on a Sunduh. Did ah tell yer a friend of the butcher's works in the coal yard?'

Lizza raced to the sitting-room door and turned the knob, her heart quickening.

CHAPTER 18

The person's face was masked by the wings of the chair, so Lizza saw the feet first, stretched out towards the fire. They were shod in highly polished black leather shoes, with a red leather trim cut into the instep; then into view came a long sweep of well-modelled silk-clad leg up to the hem of a short skirt in sooty green tweed.

'Hello,' said Lizza hesitantly, surprised as she finally recognised the unlooked-for face of Min Roebuck, the woman from the train.

Min grinned at her mischievously, then stood up, holding out her hand. Embarrassed, Lizza gripped the small, shapely hand in hers. She couldn't remember the last time she had shaken another person's hand so formally. The action had always seemed so odd to her, voluntarily to hold the hand of a stranger.

'How did you know where to...?'

Min grinned. 'I followed Liam and his sister on Friday. She came to collect him from the nursery class at the school where I'm working. I recognised them. So I followed them.'

'You're at school here? You followed them?' Lizza sat down in a high overstuffed chair and stretched her own legs to the fire.

Min sank back into her chair, wondering just what she had done, renewing her acquaintance with this rag-bag of a family. It wasn't the first time in her life she had acted on a wild impulse, but this was a weird one. It was a strange stroke of fate which had led her to this town. The vicar ministering to her own bombed school on Tyneside noticed her exhausted state and had mentioned to her Head an urgent vacancy in a diocesan school in Priorton. Would Miss Roebuck be interested to fill the position?

Recognising the name of the town, she had jumped at the chance. She told herself that it was reaction against the bombing and the loss of her pupils; that a chance to be up in the country would be a relief.

But when she saw the sharp, thin girl collecting her little brother from the school yard, she knew there were other reasons. She could not explain even to herself why she followed them rather than greeted them, and waited till Sunday afternoon to put on her best suit and her best shoes and come visiting.

'To tell you the truth I don't know why I've come,' she said now, her ease more apparent than real. 'You and your little family've been on my mind since I met you on the train. It's this war, I think. I felt it in my bones that we'd meet again. To tell you the truth, I felt you could be my friend. So I made it happen.'

Lizza blushed, uncomfortable at the directness of this woman.

Min looked around the room. 'You've found yourself a comfortable spot. Though I must say I found your woman a little...bizarre.'

'She's not my...'

At that moment Bessie clattered in with a

tea-tray. Lizza got up to help but subsided when she was glared at.

Bessie clashed the cups and saucers and the silver tea-service on the hexagonal table beside Min. 'Ah've butterfly cakes ah'll get yer,' she growled, throwing a glance at Lizza, then stumped out.

Min watched the door close behind her. 'As I said, bizarre.'

Lizza roused herself. 'She's not my woman, Miss Roebuck...Min. Her name's Miss Bessie Harraton and she's very much her own woman. This is very much her own house and we are very much her own visitors, on her kindness and charity.'

'Oops!' Min raised a thick, arched brow. 'It's not very often I put my foot in it.'

'But how would you know when you did? You go on and on and don't always notice...' said Lizza.

Min hooted with laughter. 'I knew it! I knew I liked you.' She leaned sideways towards the table. 'Now do you think the benevolent dragon would mind if I pour? This teacher I'm lodging with doesn't believe in tea. Believe! I'm thinking of painting myself an icon entirely made of tea-leaves. I discover that I do believe in tea-leaves.'

Bessie banged in again with a small plate on which were four cakes, the tops cut and squashed on top of ersatz cream in the form of butterflies.

'Thank you, Bessie,' said Lizza. 'This is Miss Roebuck who's just come to teach in Liam's

267

little school. St Bennets.'

'Yeh'll known Enid Cator, then?' Bessie folded her arms under her bust and looked steadily at the newcomer.

'The Headmistress? I've just met her.' Min found Miss Cator stern and impenetrable, totally proof against the Roebuck charm.

'Ah knew Enid's grandma, nobody better. Ah worked with her grandma before even her ma were born. An' Enid, like, she's sat in my kitchen since she was in nappies. A real clever lassie. Scholarships and thet, with a little help from old Barraclough. Clever lass. Mind yer, her ma had a real problem gettin' that lass dry. She was wettin' her knickers till she was seven. Naw. Ah tell a lie. Till she was ten years old.'

Lizza put her hand to her mouth to cover a smile. Min's brows were up in her carefully carved fringe. 'St Bennet's is a very good school.'

'It would be. Neither she nor her ma nor her grandma ever did things by halves. It wus her ma trained me here as maid of all wuk. Hard, she wus. Very hard.'

Lizza stood up and Min followed suit. 'Sit and have some tea with us, Bessie.'

The old woman looked around the room and sniffed. 'Ah niver sat down in this room ever an' I'm not likely tuh start now.' She started to leave, then turned, her hand on the door knob. 'Ah'm in me kitchen mixin' me Christmas cake wi' them bairns. It'll gan in the coal oven owernight. Carrots! It 'as to 'ave carrots in. That 'Itler 'as sommat to answer for. Anyway, no doubt yer'll want to cum in and listen to the news on my wireless at nine o'clock. It said on the six o'clock that we wus to have extra sugar an' tea for Christmas. Ah'll believe that when ah see it. An' there'll be nee bananas soon, they say. Bananas! Ah haven't seen a banana for weeks.'

The door clicked behind her.

'Well!' said Min. 'How...'

'She's been in this house since she was ten as a maid. And the owner left it to her in his will.'

'Couldn't have left it to a nicer person,' said Min, and Lizza laughed.

Min handed her a cake. 'You look a different person than the one I met on the train, Lizza. Ten years younger,' she said frankly.

Lizza shrugged. 'Surprising what a good bath can do.' She bit into the cake and discovered the cream was not ersatz. 'Now, if you're supposed to be my friend, you'd better tell me all about yourself. Bessie's bound to ask.'

'Yes, ma'am.' Min gave her a crisp naval salute. 'Well, here goes! I've lived at home on Tyneside most of my life with my father. He's a river pilot. I'm on my own now, though. He transferred a year ago across to the Mersey. My mother was dragged off to the loony bin when I was three and I've been queen of the roost since then. She died when I was twelve. My mother's cousin Daphne runs the house, but has done as I say since I was five. I was dry by then, by the way! No wet knickers.'

Lizza laughed.

'I suppose the fashionable description of what I was—am, maybe—is a Free Spirit. When I was little I was left for hours on my own in that house on the harbour. I played up there, weaving my own world where I was queen, and when the others—my father and Daphne—came, they had to join in my dream. I always know what I want. And I decided I wanted you for a friend. That's why I came here.' The intensity of her gaze again defeated Lizza, making her eye drop to her empty cup.

'What else? I can draw and paint. And I like to look smart. I make my own clothes, having demanded to be taught by a tailor when I was twelve. Daphne's dressmaker had made a mess of a dress and I wasn't having any of that.

'I can copy any design in any magazine you can present to me. I can make skirts out of coats and trousers; women's jackets out of men's. Blouses out of shirts. I make all my father's shirts and underclothes from American stuff he gets off ships. So even the bloody rationing doesn't defeat me.' She put her hand to her mouth. 'Pardon my French. Sailor's talk,' she said unapologetically.

'Talking about sailors, I've met lots of those who would put a ring on my finger or through my nose, I'm not sure which. And teachers. And lawyers. But none of them ever, could ever, measure up to my father.' Her cheeks were suddenly pink. 'He's very special. Here...' She rummaged in her snakeskin handbag and handed a cardboard-framed photograph to Lizza.

Staring out at her, posed rather consciously in

270

some kind of naval uniform, stood a fair man in his early fifties. Scrawled across the bottom was, *'To my only sweetheart. A.R.'*

She handed the photograph back. 'He's very handsome. You're not like him.' She laughed. 'I don't mean you're not...you're very...but you're different.'

'Well, thank you if that was a compliment. And he's even more handsome in the flesh. He alway says I'm the double of my mother in every way.'

'I suppose that's why you're close.'

She laughed. 'I suppose so. Although if I go loony when I'm thirty I won't be so pleased. I had a little do after the bombing, raving about the place; that frightened the pants off me.'

Lizza settled back even more comfortably in her chair, enjoying the performance. 'What about school? What's that like?'

'Well, it's different here at St Bennet's. The Tyneside school I worked in, before it was bombed, was high, built of red brick. You know the kind. Large windows and sills high enough to deny seductive glimpses of the busy world outside. Tyneside's come to life again these days, with all these warships they're building now. We could see the gantries from the school yard, through the narrow end of Sea Street. They're building ships at a great pace now. The place is singing with work again. The children I teach...taught...sometimes I love them because they look at me with the eyes of angels. Sometimes I hate them because they're dirty and snotty and lousy, liars and cheats.'

271

'But they're poor...' said Lizza.

'Lizza! The affluence of those families ebbs and flows with the Tyne tide. Boots and jackets come and go in and out of "Uncle's" with a rhythm which matches the comings and goings of the ships.'

'It must be very hard, teaching there.'

'It is. But it's more complicated than that. I had my first lesson in just how complicated it was soon after I had got out, with some relief, of St Hild's Training College. I was very keen to teach the poor children, to bring the light of reason into their dark lives.

'A Wednesday I think it was, just as I was leaving school. This big taxi cab nearly knocked me down, roaring to a stop before me. Dermot McBain, the biggest rascal in my class, elbowed me to one side. "Pardon, miss."'

' "Dad!"' he shouted. He had a little sister on each hand, whom he lifted, one by one, into the arms of a brown-faced man in a bright silk scarf who was sitting there in the taxi with his arms open wide.

'I can still see the bare soles of their feet, as the man beamed at me over their heads and signalled the taxi-driver to drive on. He'd just come ashore with a pocketful of money of course, and they were off for big treats.'

Lizza shook her head. 'What about the other children?'

'Well, for one thing they're all colours and creeds. Their dads and grandads, even great-grandads, were sailors who came into the town from Africa and Arabia.'

272

'I bet they like you, the kids. No teachers in my school like you when I was little.'

Min cast her eyes down, smiling. 'That's what one of those RAF boys said on the train. I think the children take to me because I'm different. I'm a generation younger than the other teachers. They all have buns, and smell of cabbage mixed with eau-de-Cologne. It's very useful: the children sit still just to watch me.' This was said without vanity. 'Sometimes that backfires on me, though. They'll stare and stare and finally glaze over and not hear a word I say.'

They were just laughing at this when Josie crashed through the door. 'Bessie said I was to come to tell you that it's nearly time for the news and she has fresh tea brewing and you're to put the fireguard round the fire before you come.'

Min grinned at her. 'And how are you, Josie?'

Josie cocked her head to one side. 'Well enough, miss. Sure, I must have eaten something that disagrees with me lately, for the old tummy's upset. But apart from that, pretty sparky.'

'Won't you be going to school, like Liam, Josie?'

'Me? I've finished school now. Bessie says there's a chance I'll get in the munitions factory here, and earn meself a barrel of money.'

'They say they're hard places to work, Josie.'

'No matter. My da used to say that money sweetens labour.'

Lizza was silent, her mind going back to the

formal little letter she had just sent to Theo Callaghan, communicating her sympathy on the loss of his wife and baby daughter, and stating that his other two children were lodged with her and he wasn't to worry, that she would keep them safe. She had sent it to his former office, hoping that it wouldn't reach him for a good time if at all. The letter salved her conscience, but she hadn't told Josie what she had done.

The smell of baking spice met them as they opened the kitchen door. Bessie was at the big stone sink just finishing washing up the mixing bowls. Liam was sitting up on the draining board wiping the spoons with a cloth. She dried the last bowl and took the cloth, wiped his hands then hers, and lifted him down. She sat on her little seat by the fire, folded her hands together and waited for the news signal.

The bubble of humour created by Min's stories died in Lizza as she listened to the news, to the grave voice of the announcer speaking of the bombing of Southampton and Bristol, and the resignation of the American Ambassador Mr Kennedy.

'Ah think them Americkys'll come in with us now,' declared Bessie.

The announcer's voice was lifting now as he told of the sinking of a dangerous U-boat by *HMS Forfar*, making Josie cheer and Min clap her hands.

Min had remained standing, and when the news finished she pulled on her gloves. 'Oh, Lizza, I'm starting an art class in the town,

274

in the old church hall. You could come and help me.'

Lizza smiled slightly. 'I can't draw.'

'She writes stories,' put in Josie.

Min smiled. 'Well, then, you can sharpen the pencils, Lizza. I'll go now, or Miss Hewlett'll think I've run back to the Tyne for lack of tea.'

'Thank you, Bessie Harraton, for the welcome.' She leaned down and kissed the old woman on the head.

Bessie wriggled away. 'Dinnet fuss, man!' she squeaked.

Min proceeded to kiss Liam on the head, Josie on the cheek, and Lizza on both cheeks, and in a second, without asking permission, she had vanished through the back door.

'Should'a waited to be shown out proper, out the front,' grumbled Bessie. 'She disn't knaa how to dee things right. Too much slop.'

Josie nodded her head vigorously, her mouth full of a little cake Bessie called 'triers', which she made from the Christmas cake mixture.

Lizza smiled, then went to lock and bolt the door behind her visitor, rubbing the sticky place on her cheek where the lipstick had touched.

'Will she come again?' said Josie.

'Oh, I think so,' said Lizza. 'I'm certain she'll be back.'

'If you were old Barraclough,' said Bessie, 'you'd be putting money on it.'

Walking steadily back into the crowded hut, Alex Bremner put the pile of clothes on the

275

rough cot and started to put the smaller items in the cabinet which was squashed between his bed and the next one. He had arrived late. Around him, young men of his age and older were sitting and lying around chattering, reading and playing cards.

They had watched in silence as he entered the room, then returned to their conversation, the loudest of which was about the comparative warlike talents of the Italians and Greeks, coming down strongly on the side of the Greeks who were busy just now routing the Italians in Albania.

The chunky boy in the next cot to Alex did not join in. Hands linked behind his head, he lay and watched Alex's every move. 'Rum do, this,' he said finally. 'All this waiting around. Now I see it was you we were waiting for,' he drawled in a stiff-jawed fashion, his voice a bit like Roland's.

The chatter in the room stilled.

Alex shrugged. Steadily, he started to change into his working gear. 'Couldn't help bein' late. Me train got stopped by a faulty engine.'

The blond boy grinned. 'A Geordie? We've a Geordie comrade here, chaps. Bolshevik, I bet my boots! Is that not so, Geordie?'

A murmured comment flashed round the room.

'Me name's Alex Bremner, not Geordie. An' I'm no Bolshevik.' Alex squatted to tie the boots, pulling at the long laces.

'Tell us about your pits, Geordie,' called a skinny boy opposite. 'Is it true they eat men

276

whole down under the earth?'

'Me name's Alex Bremner,' he said grimly, 'an' I've never been in a pit, although me uncles have. I was in school, then I was in Coventry, then I was here.'

The blond boy whistled. 'Coventry? Were you there for the bombing. Did you see the big raid?'

'Yes,' he said. 'The RAF were conspicuous by their absence there.'

'So it seems,' said the blond boy. 'They were preoccupied elsewhere.'

'So it seems,' said Alex.

The boy stood up, came over and proffered his hand, which Alex shook heartily.

'Jack Stubbs,' the boy said. 'Straight from school, too. What're you after? I'm going on to Spitfires. Fighters, the only thing.'

Alex envied the sheer brass of this boy, no older than himself. 'I don't know. Whatever they offer me.'

'Come on, man! What do you want?'

'Bomber,' asserted Alex. 'I want to blow their land and people into the sky, just as they've blown mine.'

Jack Stubbs sat on Alex's bed. 'No, you don't want bombers, Geordie, heavy lumbering carthorse things! You want fighters! The deadly wasps, the guardians of the skies.'

Alex sat beside him, fastening his tie. 'I tell you what, Jack Stubbs, if I get the chance, after training, I'll do exactly what I came here to do: fly bombers over them and blow them to smithereens. Give them a dose of their own medicine. And I'll tell you one thing for certain. If you call me Geordie once more I'll bust your nose to smithereens without no bomber to help me.'

Jack Stubbs put a hand on his shoulder, 'There now, Geo...Alex, no need to scowl. Maybe you'll get to fly this big new Yank bomber we've got. Heard of it?'

Alex shook his head.

'Well, my uncle, who's a bit prone to exaggeration but who's in the know, seems to think it can fly right to Russia and back. Brilliant for reconnaissance.'

Alex laughed. 'Maybe I'll just do that, Jack Stubbs, just to make you eat that sarky smile some day.'

'Well, Alex. It seems you know your own way. But, my boy, I'll give you one piece of advice which'll help you on your way in this cut-throat military world. Given to me by my mother's cousin, who's a squadron-leader.' He lit a cigarette.

'What's that?'

'Don't let them have your socks. Don't send your socks to the laundry. They come back like cardboard and crucify your feet when we're doing our squarebashing.'

'What do you do with them? Wash them yourself?'

'Well, never having washed a sock in my life, old chap, I send them home and the dear old nanny does them for me.' He pushed across a battered packet of Gold Flake. 'Here. Do you smoke?'

278

In the days following Min Roebuck's visit, Josie seemed to lose her sparkle. Bessie was dosing her with some messy white pudding-stuff for her stomach upset and Josie was snapping at Liam, and not answering when Lizza asked her simple questions.

She was not even cheered when Lizza produced a letter from Alex, describing his first days of training and saying there was a chance of him having a couple of days off before Christmas, before they started the training proper—*'whatever that means'*.

Josie scowled and threw herself into a chair.

Lizza threw the letter down on the table. 'Really, Josie, perhaps Bessie's right, perhaps you would probably be much better working at the factory than moping around the house getting under everyone's feet.'

Josie stared at the fire. 'Sure, I can't see the difference in what you think. You're not me own mother. I've no mother. Didn't I see her flattened with the bullet? We're all on our own here and it's no point in pretending otherwise...'

Lizza looked at her, brought down herself by Josie's moroseness. Then she ran out of the room, across the echoing hall, up the stairs and to her bedroom, crying painfully as she went. She sat on the bed trying to make the sheer longing for Rebecca subside from her body. She put out her arms to try and rehearse again the feeling as her little daughter leapt up into them. This time last month she had done just that. But for the first time the feeling refused to come. She thought of how it must be not just that you lose them, but you lose the memory of their presence, the feeling of them in your arms.

And where was Roland? No word from him, just as there had been no real word lately when he was by her side. He should know she needed him in her mourning for Rebecca. He should know. But he had forgotten about her: beside the war she had no importance at all. He no more knew her at a distance than he had close to.

She stood up and started scrabbling in her case. Read. She must find something to read. Her hand brought out *Gone With the Wind*. Roland had bought it for her just before the big raid. It was still wrapped loosely in its wrapper. She had been reading it on the night before the raid, because the film was to be shown at the Rex the following week. Roland knew she liked to read books before she saw the films. Of course the film was never shown, as the Rex was bombed with the rest of Corporation Street on that night. There had been some jokes about that. 'The Rex was certainly *Gone With the Wind...* '

She opened the book, and a piece of paper fluttered out. It was the drawing of Rebecca, done by Krystof Sobieski. The little face glowed out at her. She thought of Min Roebuck. She knew about drawing. She would like this picture. Clutching the drawing of Rebecca, her mind went to Krystof. She could picture his intense, graceful face perfectly: the funny dark hair with its auburn patches; the straight brows; the veiled eyes; the black smudge on his cheek and the egg-like bump which was the only mark on him after their night sheltering from the bombs.

She blinked and tried to think of Roland, but the image would not come. And it was Krystof Sobieski who walked beside her, who lay beside her in her dream that night.

CHAPTER 19

When they arrived on the island, Roland, Pieter Vann and the other crews set about assembling the workshop in a warehouse on a quay, on the inner reaches of the sea loch. They recruited the help of five retired fishermen of varying degrees of fitness. After three days, the fishermen vanished for a night and half a day, returning with vague explanations about some fishing trip.

Pieter Vann became exasperated and started to shout at them about loyalty and the war.

'There is no need to alarm yersel', sir,' said Archie Robertson, the oldest of the four, in his soft voice. 'We're back noo.'

'But we've lost a day. You must see that's important. Even yesterday we lost planes over Germany.'

Archie glanced up and down the deserted jetty, and up into the empty skies, and smiled.

'We need the fish for oor families,' he said, then exchanged glances and soft rapid words in Gaelic with the other old men, who smiled.

This enraged Pieter even further so that Roland had to pull him away and sit him on an upturned packing case. 'Calm down, Pieter. They've been fishing. What's the matter with you?'

Pieter shook his head, breathing heavily. 'We—you and me, Roland—have worked without ceasing all these weeks since the factory was bombed.'

Roland put a hand on his shoulder. 'Perhaps it's time we went fishing, before we explode ourselves.'

'If we don't believe in all of it, every last bit, if we don't work without ceasing,' said Pieter soberly, 'we might as well hand it all over to those Nazis. It is a matter of the heart and the mind, not just these little things we do.'

The next day the work came to a full stop anyway, when supplies which had to come by boat were delayed because of gales. So even Pieter and Roland were forced to take it easy.

In the five days they had stayed in her house, they had seen nothing of their landlady, who was in bed each morning when they got up and in bed when they finally arrived home, leaving bread and very basic food for them for supper.

Even so, Roland could sense her presence in the house: the faintest drift of perfume and cigarette smoke; a new arrangement of stones, driftwood and dried flowers in the hall; a single

282

cup and plate, washed and dried, on the table beside their set places.

On the day their materials ran out, they finished at four o'clock, and although dusk was well under way and they had to battle against the wind and rain, they could pick their way back down to the house without using their pencil torches.

The fire was blazing in the kitchen when they let themselves in. Mara Laine was sitting at the table poring over a book, a cup in one hand and smoke rising lazily from the cigarette in the other. She stood up and backed towards the inner door as they came in.

Roland put out his hand. 'Don't run away.' He peered towards the book. *'Island Flora.* Are you interested in plants?'

She shrugged and sat back down at the table. 'I'm interested in the islands. I try to identify plants I find as I walk. Sometimes it's stones or rock-formations. Tree-clumps. I keep a record. Not much to find at this time of year.' She lifted a notebook from a pile on the corner of the table and turned the pages. They were neatly divided in half by a ruled line. In each half-page was a plant, tree or rock, immaculately drawn from two angles, and labelled with a paragraph of sloping writing. On the bottom of each page were dates and symbols. On the back page was a summary with more symbols in columns. 'I check them season by season, year by year. I note the numbers, the ebb and flow of growth.'

Pieter busied himself with the kettle. Roland

283

took off his mackintosh and put it on a peg by the fire where it steamed gently. 'I do something the same myself, but with me it's aircraft,' he said eagerly. 'I've graphs and drawings of every one I've seen since the outbreak of war, German and English.'

She raised a dark brow.

'No! It is interesting!' He found himself determined to convince her. 'Why do we make out lists and notations? To understand, to get some control.'

She laughed. 'Well, my lists help me to understand. But control? I don't think so.'

'You do! You know when things get less, when they die, if they're under threat. You can do something about it. At least you have the record. I...I'll show you.' He went off, bouncing up the stairs to find his notebooks.

Mara exchanged a glance with Pieter, who shrugged. 'He can be very enthusiastic, Roland. Me, I don't know what differences his graphs and lists make. Perhaps a degree of understanding, an illusion of control where no control is possible in this or any other war.'

Roland and Mara spent the evening together comparing notebooks and the next two days tramping the storm-ridden island checking trees and stones against Mara Laine's careful notations. Despite the chill and the soakings, Roland could not remember when he had enjoyed himself so much. 'If ever I did,' he said to himself in bed the second night, wincing at his disloyalty to Lizza. 'If ever...'

Alex marched along the back street, his knapsack bouncing on his back, relishing the stares and whistles that greeted him on each corner. When he entered the house, his grandmother barely looked up from her knitting although Beatrice ran to get water for tea.

'Buck-shee two-day leave, Gram,' he said to the side of his grandmother's face. 'Can't have Christmas, but we're between two bouts of training, so they say two days now.' He put out his hand, to stop her hand moving over the knitting needles. 'I came to see you.'

She nodded, her eyes on the khaki wool.

'Not even a smile for the prodigal grandson, Gram?'

She looked up and allowed the faintest of smiles to pass over her face. 'Are they feedin' yer there?'

'Nah. Never enough. Lads has ter buy more at the NAAFI. I promised Jack Stubbs I'd take him some of your cherry cake. He'll like that. Neither his ma nor his grandma never made him nowt.'

'He was an orphan?' she said, interested.

'Nah. His ma and pa was in India and he was at school in the term and in holidays at the mercy of school cooks and masters' wives that sound more like coal-face workers.'

'Poor bairn.'

Alex hooted. 'He's six foot and fifteen stone. Not so poor either.' He watched as Beatrice poured out tea. 'And how's Beatrice?'

She smiled. 'Ah can see how you are. Cockier than ever.'

He took the cup from her. 'Keeps me head above water, Beatrice, me head above water.'

Alice folded up her knitting. 'She's been called to go in the factory.'

'That right Bea?'

Beatrice shrugged. 'Got a letter. Certain age, no dependants. They're calling for them all. It's the armaments factory in Nelton.'

'She wants nothing going there,' Alice grunted. 'You hear them talk about it at the store. Them lasses are harlots, all of them.'

'I'm surprised at yer, Gram,' said Alex, 'you always say you never listen to the rubbish they talk down there.'

'Young Josie Callaghan works down there,' said Beatrice. 'If she can, I suppose I can.' But her tone was uncertain. The thought of the factory was new and frightening.

Alex hadn't thought of Josie in weeks. Now suddenly he was dying to see her, to tell her about Jack Stubbs and the other lads and what it was like to be upside-down in an aeroplane, even when you were only a passenger. He would not tell her about the squarebashing and the bull, the passing humiliations laid on to show you your place. He had just about forgotten all that himself. There were better tales to tell.

Josie had loved the factory from the first day: the droves of what seemed like thousands of girls linking arms as they walked in the dark mornings along from the Nelton railway halt to the factory; the loud talk and laughter; the sweet, faintly threatening smell in the factory itself; the sense of urgency and power exuding from the boxes of gleaming bullets which were just one product of their operation.

On her first day she was grabbed by two turbaned girls on her way into the factory. One was tall and thin, the other much smaller and round-faced.

'Why, pet, what it is to see a new face, and young. Ye canna be old enough to go to this hell-hole, pet,' said the tall one, hanging on to her arm on one side.

'What're you called, pet?' said the other, grabbing the other arm. 'This big galoot is Esme Right 'n' I'm Mary Osgood.'

She tried to pull herself out of their clasp but failed. 'Me name's Josie Callaghan, and sure I'm old enough to work. Left school ages ago.'

'My!' said Esme Right. 'We've got us a live one here, Mary. And Irish at that. A fine Irish rose, though she looks like she needs feedin' up a bit. Josie? No, Rosie. We'll call you that.'

'I ain't called Rosie,' said Josie stubbornly. 'Me name's Josie, an' you'll call me that or nothing.'

Mary Osgood pulled her round and put her face close to hers and tweaked one of her black curls. 'We'll have to work on you, pet. That hair needs a cut or sommat. You'll have to tie it back—dangerous flying about like that. The whitecoats'll have yer for it.'

They were inside the echoing entrance to the factory. Mary pulled her towards the toilets and Esme followed. Once inside, Esme held on to Josie while Mary felt in the pockets of her slacks and produced a brown thing that proved to be a cut-off stocking top, and a comb. 'Here!' She put the greasy brush through Josie's hair until it was smooth, then pulled on the stocking top in a tight band round her head, then between them, she and Esme tucked Josie's hair up into it.

'Here!' They pulled her in front of the one cracked mirror. Josie put a hand up to her head. 'Feels like a bloody sausage,' she said. Then she looked in the mirror and turned her head from side to side. 'Makes me look older.'

'That's all to the good,' said Esme. 'Can't have schoolkids takin' our wages off us, can we, Josie?'

Josie shook her head laughing and linked the other two as they walked out of the toilets up through the factory into the changing room before they went on to their line.

It didn't take many days for Josie to become accustomed to the strict strip and search before she went on to the line, the smell of sulphur in her lungs, and the monotonous routine of filling shell-cases. By dinner-time she was as eager as the others to get dressed again and go outside into the cold damp air to go to the canteen and have her dinner and a smoke, a habit which Esme and Mary encouraged. She worked between the two girls, who kept her going with their coarse jokes when she was almost nodding off with exhaustion towards the end of the shift.

On the first Friday Josie was trudging back to the train when Esme caught up with her. 'Where to tonight, Josie?'

Josie shook her head. 'Back to Priorton, dinner, then me bed. In that order. I'm buggered.' Swearing while upright had become easy during the week.

Esme caught hold of her arm. 'That's no good, Rosie, working your guts out and not havin' a bit of play.'

'There's a dance at Priorton but I can't do it, dance I mean.'

'Come to Darlington with me. Old Mary's off with her boyfriend Harold who's on leave. I work in the Duke's buffet in Darlington on a Friday night. It's a laugh. Lots of soldiers from Killock in there. A man plays the piano. Come on!'

'I'm in me work clothes.'

'I've two changes there. You can have some of mine.'

By nine o'clock on that Friday night Liam had shouted for Josie and finally cried himself to sleep when she didn't come. Having settled him down, Lizza sat with Bessie in the kitchen listening to some report on the news, about spies being caught somewhere in the South. Bessie was doing some smocking, little steel glasses on the end of her nose. She reached across to turn off the radio.

'Is the bairn all right?'

'Yes, he's just dropped asleep. He was asking for Josie.' Lizza's brow furrowed. 'She's really late. The factory won't be working this late, surely. Not on a Friday.'

'She'll have got on with somebody. You know how some young'ns do.'

Lizza laughed. 'You're very tolerant, Bessie, for someone who...'

Bessie cackled. 'Who's hardly bin out o' this house all her life, who's niver had a ring on her finger, nor children?'

Lizza laughed and nodded.

'Well, hinney, I watch and listen.' She lifted her hand from her stitching and touched her sparse silver hair. 'An' in there I see things, know things that I might o' done in some other life, so I know what to do in this one.'

'You mean you have a good imagination?'

'That's what some people call it, hinney. Ah'll give yer an instance. Now listen carefully. That bairn, that girl who's late from work now, she has more in common with yer than yer know yerself. It's a thing ah'd a' given me eye teeth for, if I'd had any eye teeth left to give.' She snipped at some embroidery thread with over-large scissors. 'But there's another thing about her...' Her voice faded.

Lizza frowned. 'What on earth does that mean?'

'Just think on. You'll realise.' Bessie refused to be drawn and asked Lizza to read her a bit from the paper about that butter dealer who was caught selling a pound of butter by a Ministry spy. Bessie had read it herself, but it made her laugh when she heard it again.

It was a quarter to eleven when Josie got in, dressed in strange clothes and with traces of lipstick on her mouth. Lizza tried to ask her where she had been but she only replied, grinning, 'Not very far, Mrs King. Not very far at all. Sure there's no need to worry about me at all.' And Lizza could not get another word out of her.

She had had a wonderful time, clearing the glasses for Esme, and being swept into a spontaneous waltz by a young soldier who had been hanging over the piano-player. She had drunk beer herself for the first time and earned three and sevenpence in tips. She firmly resolved to do it again.

On Saturday they had, unusually, been asked to go into work, but they finished by lunch-time. Esme talked Josie into going to the dance at Killock Camp with her that night. Swinging through the factory gates arm in arm with Mary and Esme, she couldn't contain her broad grin when she saw Alex, looking very dashing in his uniform at the factory gates.

'What's happened to you? You're getting fat and bonny,' he grinned, kissing her on the cheek.

'How d'you know where to come?'

'I went over our Lizza's and she told me.'

As they sat together in the rattling train she plied him with questions about the RAF, smug at the knowledge that Esme and Mary were sitting behind her, consumed with admiration and curiosity.

Esme tapped her on the shoulder. 'Aren't ye comin' to the dance with us tonight then?' she said, rolling her eyes towards Alex.

Josie shook her head. 'Not tonight, Esme.'

Esme grinned. 'I don't blame yer, pet.'

'What dance was that?' asked Alex as he

291

jumped off the train with her.

'There's a dance at an army camp not far from here. There's buses, but Esme and Mary go in a taxi. They were gunna take me.'

'Yer want nothing going to army dances,' he said darkly, and she punched his arm and said he could mind his own business.

Outside Campion House he stopped, pulled her into the deep shadow of the porch and kissed her hard. Then he stood back and sighed. 'I've been saving that up for weeks,' he lied. Then he wrinkled his nose. 'You smell nice.'

' "Evening in Paris". Me friend Esme gave me a go of hers. She says all men fall for it. You like it?'

'Yes, but I don't like this.' He started to pull at the roll round her head, dislodging lumps of hair.

She smacked his hand away. 'Leave it! It's smart. It makes me look more...me own age, not some kid.'

He caught the hand. 'But that's what you are, Josie, some kid.' His body started to push against hers and they kissed again. And again. He groaned.

'Excuse me!' A bright clear voice cut the darkness behind them.

Josie pulled away, pushing the handfuls of hair back into the stocking-top band. 'Oh. Miss Roebuck. We didn't see you there.'

'So I notice. I was just wanting to see Mrs King. I want to drag her to the pictures. *Night Train to Munich* is on at the Old Savoy. That wonderful Anton Walbrook.'

Then there was a hubbub in the hall as Lizza, Liam and Bessie came out to meet them. Bessie took Min into the sitting room, where the usual fire was blazing. Liam followed, his thumb in his mouth, fascinated to see a teacher in his own house.

Josie and Alex spent the afternoon parading Priorton High Street and had tea in the Co-op. In the evening they went to the Savoy themselves to see the wonderful Anton Walbrook. Alex put his arm round her in the darkness and clasped her hand tightly on his thigh.

They kissed on the doorstep again. 'What we need is a room to go to,' muttered Alex, slipping one hand inside her thick coat.

She kissed him on the nose. 'No Beaconsfields here, mate. No bomb sites, no deserted houses, no crying babies.' She paused. 'I was wondering...'

He was busy pulling all her hair out of the band so it was in its familiar tangle. 'What?'

'What happened to our rose window.'

'Rose window?' He had forgotten about that even in this short time. So much had happened. All that stuff seemed so silly and childish to him now, compared with the exploits he and Jack Stubbs talked about. He wondered if Jack invented as much as he did. 'Oh, that? I imagine it was smashed to smithereens like everything else in Lizza's house,' he said carelessly.

Josie smacked his hands away from her, pushed her hair back roughly into its band and rang the doorbell before he could stop her. They were greeted by Lizza who, remembering

Josie's escapade last night, turned down Alex's request to stay. 'Your Gram and our Beatrice'll want to see you. You can have some tea and biscuits in the kitchen, then get away home.'

He grinned at her, not too unhappy at her refusal. 'Our Beatrice is in a spin cause they say she has to work in a factory or join one of the women's forces. She is sticking her heels in and trying to refuse. I reckon she's scared. Never been out of the house hardly all her life.'

Josie pricked up her ears. 'No need to be scared. You tell her she can come with me. I know about it now.'

Alex and Lizza exchanged glances and laughed. 'Come on then, Miss Knowitall Josie Callaghan,' said Alex. 'Are you gonna make me a cup of tea before I go or not?'

He had his cup of tea and went soon after, saying he didn't know when he would get back. Josie waved at him carelessly enough, but when she came in she marched upstairs with a face like thunder.

In the sitting room Min was kneeling down, poking away at the fire to make a better glow. She grinned up at Lizza. 'Two things. What about the pictures again next Saturday? And this class—I'm going to start it off on Wednesday, I thought you might like to come. To sharpen the pencils, like we said.'

'I don't mind about the pictures,' said Lizza. 'I enjoyed your beloved Anton Walbrook today. I need a change from this house, even if Bessie Harraton is a sweet old duck. But I don't know about the class. I don't know anything about art or artists.' She paused. 'I've something I'd like to show you.' She vanished and came back five minutes later with Krystof's drawing of Rebecca. 'This is my daughter. The one who...I lost in Coventry. This was drawn by an artist. But I don't know him too well. Hardly at all. But he was there that night. And he drew this then, that night. It seems a year ago, ten years, not a few weeks. This war's stretching time like elastic.' Her voice was desolate.

Min took the picture gently from her, smoothing the edges with her polished fingers. 'She's a lovely child, Lizza. Looks bright and sparky.'

'She was lovely. She would've had you eating out of her hand. She charmed everyone...'

Min put her arms around her and rocked to and fro, feeling rather than hearing Lizza's shuddering sobs.

Alex decided not to bother about the bus, and to walk back to Bracks Hill. This world back home seemed so small now that he felt he could encompass it with a stride. He marched along jauntily, enjoying the rough push of the uniform against his neck. The evening was fine, the cold night air giving a crisp edge to what had been a damp day.

It had been good to see Lizza looking so bouncy; must be something good about that queer old woman's house. Or maybe it was being away from Roland. Those two had been jumpy together even before the bombing. Then Josie. She had given him a warm welcome. But she had changed a lot. Seemed much more—he searched in his mind for the word—*woman-y*. She was not the cocky self-confident tomboy who had led him such a dance through the streets of Coventry and played those games in the house called Beaconsfield. He had liked that. But she was different now. Just a kid. That's all she was, really, just a kid.

He thought back to a conversation at the camp, in the huts after lights-out. The fellows had all been whacked after a day's squarebashing and some of them were flat out, dead to the world. At first, the rest of them talked of how they couldn't wait to get past this basic training and on to the serious flying stuff. Then about our fellows now at last getting their planes over Germany to do some damage. There was some talk about the particular qualities of the Spitfire. Then they had started talking about their girlfriends. Jack Stubbs had a WAAF at Catterick and a model in London. Or so he said. Another bloke had a girl who was a secretary back in Canada, who was a wizard horsewoman. When they asked Alex about his girlfriend he said he had none, but had just finished with this leggy nurse in Coventry because she was too keen. They talked of the get-togethers and the dances and the times they would have when they came out of training.

Like it or not, Josie couldn't fit into that. She was just a kid.

He put his shoulders back and peered at the stars in the clear sky; the moon was nearly on the horizon, big and brightly clear. Bomber's moon. The thought had no sooner lodged itself in his head when he heard the uneven deadly wail of air-raid sirens, from Priorton behind him, and the village of Carlton ahead of him. He looked up at the clear sky, his ears pricking out the familiar distinctive low roar of an invisible German bomber. For a second he froze where he was on the dark pathway. Then an image came to his mind of the shocking, sprawled and bloody state of Maeve Callaghan and Anne-Marie as they were loaded with little dignity into the back of an army lorry.

He plunged deep into a prickly hedge for cover. Then, using his elbows, he edged forward so that he could see through the hedge into the field next to the road. At its centre, standing out clear in the moonlight, stood a big burly man, shading his eyes and looking to the sky.

'Get down! Take cover, idiot,' shrieked Alex hearing the ever nearer drone of the plane. The man stood very still, transfixed by the sound.

Alex wrestled himself free of the hedge and raced towards the man. As he did so, a resonating boom filled his ears and he was thrown to the ground with great force and the world was reduced to a furry blackness.

After what seemed only a minute he had to try desperately to summon the energy to open his eyes, to reduce the blackness. He finally managed to do so as the mouth of a tin bottle was pressed to his lips. He opened one eye, finally recovering complete consciousness in the presence of two hefty Land Girls, one of whom was pressing him to drink from her bottle.

'That's better, pet,' said the smaller girl. 'Ah thowt yeh were a goner too.'

'That man?' he said. 'What happened to him?'

'Blawn to Kingdom Come, poor feller.' The bigger girl helped him to his feet. 'Nowt left bar a shoe and his cap. Come on, pet, we'll tek yer down the farmhouse. Yeh've got blood on yer face an' ye were oot twenny minutes at least...'

He shook her free. 'No. I gotta get home. Who was the feller, then? The one that copped it?'

'John Armitage, he's the farmer, our boss.' She exchanged glances with the smaller girl. 'We were sent to look for him when the bomb dropped. His missis is havin' a fit back there.'

'Horrible feller, like,' said the smaller girl, 'but you wouldn't wish that on anyone, even on him.'

An hour later, standing outside his grandmother's house, Alex started to shake. He could hardly open the door. Once inside, he stood trembling in the scullery until Beatrice came to see what was up. She took one glance at him and pushed him through the kitchen and on to the hard sofa in the front room. Alice followed them, muttering about the blood on his face.

'It's just from the hedge. I was hidden in a hedge and got scratched getting out...'

He told them about the plane.

'We heard it,' said Alice. 'The sirens went.'

'Well. This bomb dropped on this feller where

he stood, right in the middle of this field.'

'Poor feller,' said Beatrice. 'To happen like that, all at once. Did they say who he was? What's this?' She unclasped a man's cap from his hand.

'It's his cap, the man. John Armitage. A farmer. The woman said that was his name.' He lay his head back and so missed the way Beatrice closed her eyes and swayed a little.

'Here, give way.' Alice, bowl in hand, towel over shoulder, was elbowing her daughter out of the way. 'Here, son,' she said tenderly, 'we'll get that face washed and the muck off those hands and you'll be right as rain.'

'Gram!' he said wearily. 'I'm not six.'

'You still need to get washed so you can see if you're damaged anywhere,' she said calmly.

Beatrice left them to it and slipped into the kitchen. She looked at the cap and smiled slightly. She knew John Armitage. She knew all about him. She knew how he jumped at you from behind and ripped away your skirts and petticoats. She knew how he yelled at you that you were a whore and not fit to walk the decent earth. She knew how he could force himself into you like the reddest and hottest of burning pokers, telling you all the while you must be punished. *Must-be-punished.* She held her hand up high then dropped the cap on to the hot coals. Then she took the long poker and forced the cap deep into the heart of the fire, watching the flames flare as they met the human grease round the rim.

When the cap had burnt and the smoke and

flames had died down, all that was there was flaky ash, which she stirred and spread over all the fire.

She would never tell Alex, of course, that he had witnessed the death of his own father, the man who raped her eighteen years ago. He had no need to know that. No need at all.

She sat down on her mother's chair and started to rock backwards and forwards, silently blessing the German pilot who had loosed off his last bomb on the empty countryside, on his way back home from his raid further north. Those Germans weren't all bad. There was at least one good one, blessed with excellent aim.

CHAPTER 20

Mara Laine started to delay her own supper and join Roland and Pieter Vann to eat. The supper was now hot, although economically prepared: thick potato soup with hard, one-day-old bread; fish stew; mutton casserole. She presided at the heavy kitchen table calmly, quietly responding to questions but asking none.

Roland started to look forward each day to that supper, to wish for a shorter working day. Unlike Pieter, he welcomed the fact that their own working time seemed to reduce to island rhythms. The work at the unit always stopped at dusk, so getting rid of the need to light the job, a light which would have needed elaborate

300

black-out arrangements.

It was Pieter, sensing another refugee, who prevailed upon Mara to talk about her own life. She did so without emotion, as though she were talking about someone else.

It seemed that Colonel Laine, in France at the end of the Great War, had discovered her as a child, half dead in a French brothel, mistreated by both the women and their clients. She looked Pieter in the eye. 'So you will see why I wasn't pleased when the billeting officer said I was to have two workmen—strangers—billeted on me. I think it was thought something of a joke. They are kind people, but sometimes they play their jokes on me, as I am an outsider here.'

The Colonel had taken her to an hotel away from the war zone, and paid for her protection. After the war he had returned to France with his old nanny, to escort her back to England, where she and the nanny took up residence in a small house in Pimlico, London. In this house she learned to read and write in both French and English, with tutors supplied by the Colonel. Seven years later, when his wife had died and when she herself was twenty, he had married her.

Roland searched her face, looking for emotion as she talked of her husband, but there was none. Reading his thoughts, she turned to him. 'The Colonel was kind; but for him I would have been dead. He was also very demanding.' She left it at that.

'And how did you come to be on the island?' asked Pieter.

'Two years ago, with another war threatening, the Colonel, believing he had fought the war to end all wars, suffered great *ennui*. Before my eyes he became very old and tired and his thoughts turned to this island, the home of his boyhood. He was born and spent his young years in this very house.'

'So you came back?'

'We came back and in six months he was dead. He is buried in the graveyard on the headland where the loch meets the sea.' She lit another cigarette. 'He made me promise I would stay here to watch him. I go there most days on my walks.'

'But...' protested Roland. She turned the full glare of her dark eyes on him and his protest subsided.

The following Sunday, while Pieter stayed in bed, she permitted Roland to join her for her long walk around the headland. The wind, which was stirring up the loch, blew his thin raincoat against him and burnt his uncovered ears with its icy blast. They battled forward until it seemed that every step was making only an inch's progress. She pulled at his arm and he turned sideways after her. In three minutes they were in the shelter of a stone wall. She tugged away a board on the ground and uncovered a hole. She knelt and slipped through it and he followed her. They dropped into a dry chamber which had a narrow seawards window blocked with thick glass.

He removed his cap and shook his head to get the sound of the storm from his ears. Then he looked round. 'This is quite a...' He was shouting. It was unnecessary here. He modified his voice, '...retreat.'

She took the heavy scarf from her head and shook out her hair. 'It is always windy on the headland, and in a storm it is impossible. I need a retreat, some days. I have always needed it but have never found it till I came to this island.'

'What is this place?'

'Well, the ruined wall above is the remains of a farm that was cleared of its workers by the landlord many years ago.'

'But this?'

She looked around the cave-like space. 'I think this is much much older. Ancient. A prehistoric fort, according to an old friend of the Colonel's, who used to visit. An archaeologist. She said it was a defence against the sea and the marauders who sailed on it. She and I used to sit here for hours and she would paint a picture with words of what it would be like in those times. We used to sit here.' She took his hand and pulled him towards a crude bench fashioned from sea-bleached wood, and sat him down, placing herself beside him.

He leaned back against the stone and soaked in the very age of it. Then he felt her arm through his, her hard slender hand creeping down towards his hand. His eyes flew open. Her other hand was on his face, turning it towards her. When they kissed it was as though all his senses rushed to the surface of his skin, turning the storm chill to desert heat.

Then they made love, making their way to

each other through sticky layers of clothing. He felt her small, unsupported breasts. Her nipples were prickling up under the layers of damp wool. He cupped her round buttock inside the corduroy. She unbuckled his leather belt and her hands were on his bare waist, pulling him to her, pushing downwards to free his throbbing penis from its cloth constraints.

Then they made love, half sitting, half standing as they were. His explosion came first but she clung him to her until she too burned, then relaxed with her own release. After a few moments her breathing became even and she moved to one side, pulled up her slacks and adjusted her jumpers. Then she laughed. 'That's how we deal with marauders from across the sea.'

'What?' His head, down with embarrassment as he fiddled with the buckle of his belt, shot up. 'Always?'

She leaned against the ancient wall, still smiling. 'You are my first marauder.' She paused and the smile faded. 'You are the first one, the first man, for whom I was willing.'

'But your husband?'

She shrugged. 'He liked that I was unwilling. A soldier, remember? Love as conquest?'

'But you stay here. You visit his grave every day!'

She shrugged again. 'There is the war. I have nowhere else. And I am grateful to the old dear.' Her voice hardened. 'It is too late to go there today. We must get back.'

He tried to hold her hand as they battled their

way back, but she pushed him away. But later that night he stayed awake till Pieter dropped to sleep. Then he crept to her room, a long space under the eaves, with deep windows on two sides. A driftwood fire was blazing in the narrow hearth. She was sitting up in bed with a plaid round her shoulders, reading by the light of a small oil lamp.

He stood just inside the door looking at her.

She raised the hand with the book in it, smiling slightly. 'Sit here beside me, Roland,' she said. The plaid slipped off one shoulder and one breast and he saw she was naked underneath. 'I wish you to tell me things.'

The bed creaked as he sat on the edge of it. He reached for her hand. 'What things?'

'About your wife and your family.'

'We have no family. Our little girl was killed in the bombing.'

Her hand turned and tightened on his. 'You must be very sad. Your wife, too.'

He wished he could go now, and that this had not started. He coughed. 'My wife's taking it very hard. It's hard for everyone. We'll have a new little one in March. Perhaps...'

'What is she like, your wife?'

He squirmed. 'I can't talk like this.'

She threw his hand away from her and pulled the plaid up to her neck. When she spoke, her scornful words were like chipped ice. 'You come here to my room in the middle of the night expecting me to give myself, expecting to give the whole of yourself, and you will not tell me the simplest part of your life. Leave me now.'

At that moment he wanted her as he had wanted nothing or no one in the whole of his life. He grabbed at her hand, fought her silently for it, and finally held it again, quiescent in his. 'I can't go,' he said simply.

'Then you must tell me. What is she like, your wife? Is she beautiful? Clever?'

'Beautiful? No. She's striking in a sturdy sort of way. Red hair.' With every word he felt the betrayer. 'And she is clever. Sometimes I tell her she thinks too much, feels too much. Too much of a dreamer. She used to nurse mad old women. Loved them. She was very good at it, I think.'

'She sounds interesting. I would like her. Do you love her?'

He blushed. 'Seems I always loved her. I met her when she was fourteen.'

She nodded. 'And you must have been a babe, too.'

Now it was his turn to pull his hand away. 'I can't do this,' he said.

She touched his cheek. 'It is all right, dear friend. Inquisition over.' Then she swung her feet out of bed. 'The fire needs attention. I will place more wood and you may remove your clothes.' The plaid dropped off her as she walked across the room. From the back, her figure was narrow and boyish, but when she kneeled forward to place the driftwood her small breasts dropped to two fine points edged by the fireglow, and there was no mistaking her sex.

He started to struggle with his pyjama cord, pleased to ease his clothes away from his painful erection. She turned to face him and very slowly undid her thick plait and brought her hair down round her shoulders and it flowed to her narrow waist. She kept her eyes on his. 'Do you like this room? You can see down the loch in two directions from the windows.'

'It's nice. Very big.'

Her eyes swept down him. She laughed. 'It was the Colonel's nursery and he insisted we make it into our bedroom.' Her hair shimmered in the firelight as she leant down and picked up a fine cane which rested against the hearth. 'His nanny's cane stayed up here. He liked to administer punishment. And sometimes to receive it. To be treated like a very naughty boy. The nanny was still doing it when I first met him.' She sighed. 'It was very wearing. Very childish.'

Very carefully she placed the cane on top of the blazing wood, and held it till it started to burn. 'Very childish,' she repeated. 'There will be no more of that, ever.'

He moved towards her, took her in his arms, pushed the hair from her face and kissed her eyes, then her cheeks, then her lips. She pulled away from him and, as tall as he was, looked him in the eye. 'Now we will make love like grown-ups, Roland, in this war of no tomorrows. Like we did this afternoon but much, much more slowly.'

The next night, when Roland got in from work, there were two letters waiting for him. He felt a twinge of guilt, then a kind of anger against

307

Lizza, as he read her cheery one-page letter telling him the varied news from Priorton. The other was from the Ministry, enclosing travel warrants and permission, seeing as the work on the island had slowed down, for four day's leave, long requested.

Roland caught the dusk ferry to the mainland. He needed an early start the next day, on what he knew would be a long train journey. The journey in the dirty, crowded train allowed him to think hard about the new, blood-heating presence of Mara Laine in his life. Somehow, the journey across the turbulent water back to the mainland and then on through the grim streets of Glasgow had been like waking up again to real life. By the time he was waiting for his connection at Newcastle station, the island, the gracious house and its intriguing owner, and the ancient fort, were all locked at the back of his mind like a parcelled dream.

Now, he started to look forward to seeing Lizza. Her letters sounded very cheerful: the old woman with whom she was staying sounded quite a card and that rapscallion Josie Callaghan was at least working. And then there was this woman Lizza had met on the train. A teacher. Good friend for Lizza; they could talk about Lizza's interminable books.

It was seven o'clock at night by the time he was knocking on the door of Campion House. The old woman called Bessie, once her suspicious enquiry discovered who he was, welcomed him with open arms. 'Eh, lad, she'll be that sorry she missed yer,' she said, taking his coat. 'She's just out at the pictures wi' that schoolteacher friend of 'ers. Now come on through. It's nearly time for the news. I've got this meat 'n' tatie pie on the slab that'll warm up nice for yeh. More tatie than meat this week. That butcher's gettin' sticky. Ah bet ye'r starvin', lad. Them trains is no better'n middens, thet say. Not a crumb of food, not a drop of watter. Not that ah've bin on one meself. I heard this woman say it in the store when ah wus waitin' fur me butter ration. Did yer see that feller got fined for sellin' a pound o' butter? Forty shillin's. This other feller was spyin' on 'im an' he got caught. Serves him right, I say. Feller should be more careful. What do yer say?'

But Roland, his head against the back of the rocking chair, was fast asleep, his mouth open. When Josie came bursting into the kitchen from the sitting room, Bessie put her finger to her lips. Josie had been sitting glumly all evening, feeling slightly sick and pretending she wasn't waiting for Alex to come.

Bessie followed her into the scullery. 'It's Mrs King's husband,' she whispered.

'Yes. I know that. Ain't I seen him before? In Coventry? He was mostly asleep, then.'

'Did you think it was yon lad?'

Josie shrugged. 'Nah. I wanted a cup of cocoa before I get off to bed.'

Lizza had had a good night at the pictures with Min, watching James Cagney act tough in *The Roaring Twenties*. As they walked Min kept up the pressure on Lizza to come to her art class. 'You'd enjoy it. It would give you a change.'

Lizza was still laughing her refusal when she left Min at the bus-stop waiting for the last Number 1. Her cheeks were glowing when she came into the kitchen. She leapt towards Roland with delight. 'You're here? Why didn't you let me know? You should have sent a wire!'

He shook himself awake from a dream where he had been back on the island. 'Telegram? I'd no idea just when I'd get here; there's no relying on the trains.' He struggled from her grasp to jump up and hug her in his turn. 'Lizza! You look wonderful.'

'Good northern air!' she said.

'I never thought I'd hear you say such a thing.' He stood away from her and looked her up and down. 'And how's the baby?'

She raised her brows. 'Haven't thought much of him to be honest. He has a kick in the morning and at tea-time, and that's about that.'

'Now,' interrupted Bessie from behind them. 'Now ye're awake, Mr King, will yeh have me meat an' tatie pie or not? It's keepin' warm over water in the coal oven. Or'—she looked up to the ceiling—'will youse two want to be on yer own?'

'Bessie!' scolded Lizza, red-faced. 'Of course he'll have something to eat.' She whizzed around the kitchen, getting in Bessie's way, then sat beside Roland as he ate, asking him questions about work and how he was and what he had been doing.

Roland basked in all this attention. Then, restored by his supper, he jumped to his feet. 'Would it be possible to have a bath? I'm filthy from the train and couldn't sleep on any bed in this state.'

Bessie folded her hands over her stomach. 'Mrs King'll show you how to work the boiler an' there's plenty of soap. Ah'll put you a fresh bar out on me way to bed. Ah got this whole lot in 1938. Just in case, like.'

Lizza showed him the bedroom and where to leave his things and went to fiddle with the boiler in the manner approved by Bessie. By the time he was in the bathroom, wearing just his shirt, the water was gushing in and the bath was half full. Seeing him like this, Lizza was suddenly shy. She sidestepped his arms. 'I'll go and turn down the bed,' she said. 'Don't be long.'

She was sitting up in bed when he came in, polished clean with Bessie's thick towels, his blond hair wet and combed neatly to one side.

'Roland! You don't look a day over seventeen!' She opened her arms.

He came over and sat on the bed and took her in his arms. 'I missed you,' he whispered.

'What?'

'I missed you,' he said.

'What?'

'I missed you!' He bellowed.

In the small room along the corridor, Bessie turned in her narrow cot and smiled with satisfaction.

311

The next day Lizza went with Roland to Amos Silkin's office, where he greeted Roland like a long-lost son and acknowledged Lizza, whom he had never met before, with great cordiality.

She thanked him for finding them such a good billet. He put a hand up. 'Think nothing of it, my dear. It was inevitable the old dear would have had to share the house in some way, in these times. I have a protective brief with regard to her, handed to me from my old friend Mr Barraclough. The two of them were devoted to each other. I was pleased to find someone whom I knew would be congenial and civilised. One hears such tales about evacuees.'

Seeing Lizza's gaze harden, he changed tack. 'And you're working in Scotland, dear boy? Now where would that be? I know Scotland very well.'

'I can't say where,' said Roland.

'Ah, I forget the nature of your work, dear boy. Weapons to rid us of this monstrous Hun who is gnawing at our heels again.' Mr Silkin had been a staff officer in the Great War.

'Well...' Roland shrugged.

Then the lawyer coughed and his demeanour changed, his face darkened. 'It is fortuitous that you came, dear boy. I fear I've the worst of news for you.'

'My father...' said Roland. Lizza grasped his hand.

'I fear so. At first it looked like good news. His ship was torpedoed and after some days he and others were picked up from an open boat

312

by a following convoy.'

Roland frowned. 'He was saved?'

'Well. The ship did come ashore at Liverpool. He disembarked safely enough, hungry and wet but safe.'

'The bombing,' said Roland dully.

'I fear so. The night-time raid. It wiped out the small hotel where he and the other survivors were staying. They tried to find you but couldn't. My name was in his papers, so they notified me.'

'Bastards!' Roland leapt to his feet.

Mr Silkin glanced uneasily at Lizza. 'I know you must feel angry about this, my boy. May I offer you my very deepest condolences, m'dear boy.' He put his hands on Roland's shoulders and looked into his eyes. 'Your father was the best of friends to me, and the bravest of men for his country. Do him the honour of taking this terrible blow with courage.' His hands dropped to his sides and he stepped back, embarrassed at showing even this much emotion.

Lizza stood up and hugged Roland. 'I'm so sorry, Rollie. I'm so sorry.' His body was stiff.

Mr Silkin was behind his desk. 'As you know, Roland, your father's legal affairs are in my hands and I have the will...'

Roland shook his head. 'Not now! Not now! Tomorrow. I'll come back tomorrow.' He shook off Lizza's clasp and left the office. The etched glass in the door rattled as he slammed it.

Lizza looked at Mr Silkin.

'Go to him, dear girl. But get him back in here tomorrow. I must see him.'

She had to run to keep up with Roland and he ignored all her attempts to say something. When they got back to Campion House he leapt straight upstairs, and when she got to the bedroom it was locked. She beat hard on the door but he ignored her. Josie came out of the bedroom where she was playing with Liam. 'What's up?'

'It's Roland. He's had bad news about his father. He's taking it so badly.'

Later, sitting alone at the desk in the study, she wrote in the big ledger:

His wife could not understand his grief for a father who was never near, whom he never saw, when she knew his grief for his own children, three of whom were dead, was nothing like as great.

The bedroom door was still locked at bedtime and she climbed into bed with Josie, who hugged her in wordless comfort. The next morning, when she came downstairs, he was in the hall, already dressed for travel with his rucksack beside him.

'Where are you going?' she said coldly.

'Back to work.'

'But you have three days. I was hoping you'd stretch it to Christmas.'

'The work won't wait. The sooner we get the bastards the sooner all this is finished.'

'But another day won't make a difference, Roland.'

'It will to me.'

She caught his arm. 'I don't recognise you, Roland. Your own children died and you weren't like this. Rebecca died...'

He shook off her arm. 'That was different.'

She stood like stone before him. 'Mr Silkin wants to see you this morning. He said so,' she said, her voice rasping with the control she was imposing on it.

He reached in a pocket and handed her a letter. 'Give him that. Gives him permission to tell you everything.'

She recognised the Campion House paper which she herself had borrowed from Bessie to write to him. She backed away.

'I have to go, Lizza,' he said, his voice softening just a bit.

She put up her chin. 'Don't let me keep you waiting.' She turned her head away, and when she turned it back he was gone.

Bessie's voice came from behind her and a small hand patted her back. 'Ah 'ad to len' him the paper. He 'ad to 'ave paper, he says, wild-eyed. Dinnet fret, hinney. They're hard times these, for all of them. For all of us, for that matter.'

Then Lizza was crying on Bessie's shoulder, the old woman clutching her awkwardly round the waist. When the storm was over, Bessie pulled away with some relief. 'Now if you get yerself sat down in that study, hinney, I'll get yer a wee glass o' rum I've put away. Old Barraclough was fond of a drop of rum. Then breakfast! Me an' that Liam has made some canny oatcakes for breakfast. That'll set yer up

315

for the day. Ye dinnet want ter see old Silkin on an empty stomach, ah can tell yer that.'

Minutes later, sitting very still in the study with the rum swilling around in the heavy glass, Lizza realised that buried in her anger towards Roland was the fact that she hadn't had the chance to ask Roland about Krystof Sobieski. And the question of Krystof was still burrowing away somewhere at the back of her mind after these long weeks in the North.

Later that day she learned from a grave Amos Silkin that Captain King had left the whole of his property and money to Roland. Mr Silkin estimated that, with the house in Southampton and the cottage in West Wales, the value would be in the region of sixty-five thousand pounds. He smiled slightly. 'A great fortune my dear, for a man who works with his hands.'

Lizza walked home slowly, trying to absorb the fact that Roland was now richer than anyone she had ever spoken to, except for the son of one of her old patients, who was content to have his mother in a public ward although he was said to be a millionaire.

Beatrice handed Alex two pairs of socks, neatly turned in on themselves. 'Your Gram made you these.'

He balanced them on his palms. 'Right colour. Didn't know you could get the right colour here.' They were in his little bedroom under the eaves; Alex was packing his clothes on his narrow iron bed. They could hear Alice moving around in the next bedroom which she and Beatrice shared. Alex's bedroom was kept for him, linen changed every week.

'There's this woman in High Wood who has wool for all the services. She gives it out. Don't know where she gets it from.'

He tucked the socks deep into his bag. 'Me Gram's hardly spoke to me at all, this leave.'

Bea looked at the wall and lowered her voice. 'She's funny. Has you mixed up with our Jonnie and me da.'

He pulled the string, then pulled the buckles tight on the bag. He coughed, keeping his eye on his busy hands. 'She...you...never said nowt about me own da. In the hut they ask and I say he was a miner, killed in the pit.'

'Ye're not far wrong there, pet.'

'He died before you could get married?'

'That's it.'

'What was his name?'

'I can't tell you that.'

Now he looked her in the eye. 'Why?'

'It'd be difficult for his family. They never knew. He never knew.'

His mouth hardened. 'I'll find out. On my next leave I'll find out. Look up the *Echo* eighteen years ago.'

'Suit yourself. But the name Bremner's done well by you so far.' Amazingly now, her voice started to tremble, and he came round the bed and put a hand on her shoulder.

'You've done great, you and me Gram, Beatrice. I couldn't have wished for a better ma, nor grandma for that matter. But a man needs to know who he is, before he...does what

317

I'll do before next year's out.'

She closed her eyes and let his hand lie there. Then she took a step back out of his reach. 'You are who you are, Alex. Who you've grown to be in this house. You're the light in our eyes, the spring in our step.' She turned at the door. 'Now get yourself finished. There's a leek pie in the oven, last of me best leeks. You're to have early dinner. Ma wants you going off with a full stomach. And she's made you a cherry cake and a fruit cake to go back with, though where she got the fruit, God only knows.'

As he pulled on his jacket and stripped his bed, he wondered if he should have gone back to Priorton to see Josie. He shook his head. That was finished. She was only a kid. No girlfriend for a fully fledged, even a half-fledged, airman.

Downstairs, Beatrice found her mother putting the cakes in a tin, carefully folded first in brown paper then newspaper. She grunted over the task. 'Yer want nothing telling that bairn lies. Lying's sinful. More so with your own.'

Beatrice slumped in the rocker. 'There's tellin' lies and there's livin' lies, Mother. It's a lie, you stoppin' me tellin' you what happened those years ago; you makin' on it was my sin when a brute who I'd never seen before overcame me, and brutalised me. You pretendin' there was no rape, only sin. An' somehow my sin as well as his. An' then you pretendin' he was yours not mine. Another child for your possession. Another lie.'

'Lass...' Her mother's eye went beyond her.

318

'There y'are, lad. I thought yer'd never be down. The mornin'll be gone afore you get yourself away. Yer cakes're in the tin. Sit here and get your dinner.'

He slipped the tin into a side pocket in the bag. 'No time for dinner, Gram. Need to get away.' His tone was steady but he avoided looking at Beatrice.

He swung the bag on his shoulder. 'I'll get off, then. Ta-ra Gram, Ta-ra Beatrice.' Now he had a wide smile that didn't reach his eyes. 'Ta-ra.' And he was gone.

Alice turned to poke the fire and Beatrice woke up from her trance and followed him down the back lane, shouting, 'Alex! Alex! You forgot your gas mask.'

He stopped, put down his bag, and turned to face her.

She handed him the gas mask. 'You're who you are, Alex Bremner. Your own self. There is, never has been, any blame on you.'

He stared at her for a second. 'Many a time I wanted to call you Mam, you know. Many a time.' He shook his head. 'But it would'a been too big a thing to do an' I'm not that big, thinkin' o' meself all the time.'

She reached out and gave him a timid kiss on the cheek. 'You mind yourself, up there.'

'The quicker I'm up there in the sky, the quicker it's over,' he said, more his old cocky self. He heaved his bag back on to his shoulder and smiled at her. 'Ta-ra, Mam.'

'Ta-ra, son.'

The next day Beatrice turned up at Campion

319

House to tell Lizza that Alex had gone. 'Ma's going mad. On and on again about losing her last man, that he's about to join me da. The trouble is, this time I feel she's right. I feel we won't see him again. I had to get out.'

They both swung round at a cry from behind them.

'He never came back! He never came back!' Josie was wailing, her eyes wide and red-rimmed. Bessie was standing, eyes bright with interest, beside her. 'I want him. I want my mammy...'

Beatrice shook her head. 'I forgot about the bairn.'

Josie stopped shouting. 'I'm not a bairn. Aren't I working? Earning a wage?'

Beatrice turned back to Lizza. 'If Ma's not raving about those men, she's in a dark shell and will not speak at all. I'm sick of it, Lizza,' she said simply. 'I've had enough. It's time for me now.'

'You've come—I nearly said run!—away?'

'Looks like it. I have to go to work in the factory anyway.' She looked round the spacious hall then glanced down at Bessie. 'If I worked I could pay rent. Would there be room here?'

'Have yer brought yer ration book, hinney?'

Beatrice nodded. 'And I've savings for a few weeks' rent even before I start work.'

Josie's tears dried on her face as a new idea came into her head. 'You can come with me, Beatrice. I'll take care of you. Don't I know the ropes now?'

Beatrice smiled. 'Ta. An' I promise I won't

320

call you a bairn again.'

'Huh!' said Josie gloomily, 'That's to be seen.'

'But Ma'll be alone...' Lizza's brain was racing.

'Apart from Alex and our Jonnie, she's been alone since Da died. I don't know that we count, Lizza. Girls.'

'I know I don't, Bea. Never have.' Her voice was bitter. 'But you. She depends on you.'

'Depends on nobody but herself. Only thinks of me that I brought her Alex on a plate, so to speak.'

'But...'

'You see to her if you like. I've done my bit.' She drew very close to Lizza, 'He's dead, Lizza,' she whispered.

'Who?'

'That two-rooted ram that made me...where Alex came from, he's dead. You had five hundred pilots in their planes over you down in Coventry, Lizza. And I was sorry for you and quite rightly I cursed them. They took away your little Rebecca.' She paused. 'But I've had just one pilot in the sky over me. One blessed Jerry pilot. He dropped a bomb right on that man. He was standing there, right in the middle of his field. Only a cap and a shoe left. And I burnt the cap. I bless that pilot, Lizza. He took the shadow from me. Now I've got to get on with things.'

'Beatrice...'

'Leave it, Lizza. I've got to get on with things now. At last there's things to look forward to. At last.'

321

CHAPTER 21

Min Roebuck's art classes were to be held in the draughty hall of St Bennet's church. The vicar had suggested she leave it till after Christmas, but she insisted there was time for a couple of classes before then. On the first night, Matt Clayton, St Bennet's verger, helped Min to set the room up. They pulled the dusty old curtains over the high window to secure the black-out, dragged out the hefty folding tables, now surplus to the requirements of the senior school, and placed them in a horseshoe in the draughty hall. Matt had also found three old blackboard easels which could be used as painting easels.

At first she thought it would have to be all drawing, as, although she had a box of charcoal from her own stores, paint in any quantity was hard to get hold of.

'Paint?' Matt scratched his head. 'Why, if ah were you, miss, ah'd git up there in them lofts at Saint Bennet's seniors. Ah was caretaker there after the last war. New headteacher back from the war had this permanent sore head, and didn't gan for this drawing lark, nor the teacher that did all that. Called him a pansy-buttercup. He told me to get shot of the paint double quick to stop the feller in his tracks. So ah put the tins up there with all the other junk. The feller left the next week.'

Min got permission to scour the dusty lofts of St Bennet's senior school, and among the junk found another blackboard easel and twelve unlabelled tins of a familiar shape and size, although very dull with age. Sitting on the filthy floor with her torch in her mouth, using her nail scissors, she had levered open the tins one by one. The familiar tangy smell invaded her nose, and the dull red of Vermilion powder paint shone back at her in the torchlight. She opened the others. Three tins Cobalt Blue. Three tins Yellow Ochre. Three tins Chrome Green. Three Ivory Black. That was it. She scrabbled around, but there was no White. She sat back. It was impossible without White. They would just have to draw, use charcoal, pen and ink. She put out her hand to steady herself as she stood up and clutched at a cardboard box which, when she moved it, gave a familiar rattle.

'That's it!' she said to herself. 'That'll do the trick.'

Now, as she mixed her colours for the night's work, she looked with satisfaction at the dish of white paint concocted from ground-down blackboard chalk and flour-paste. Matt was sitting very comfortably at the table by the door, cutting rolls of wallpaper into large rectangles with Min's sewing scissors. She wished Lizza King had decided to come. She was good company, Lizza, had a funny, appealing mind...

The door opened and a sharp breath of winter air cut into the fug created by Matt Clayton's temperamental stove in the middle of the wall opposite.

People started to trickle in. A young, thick-set man in a cap, two men in army uniform, a stout, middle-aged lady in an old-fashioned cloche hat, two serious-looking young women with bobbed hair wearing identical red lipstick, and a boy with thick black hair and round, owl-like glasses.

They sat in rustling silence as Min pinned a large sheet of the wallpaper to the blackboard she had set up at the centre of the open end of the horseshoe. She turned to face them. The rustling stilled and every face looked at her expectantly. She smiled radiantly from one face to the other, willing them one by one to be with her, to be on her side. She had used this successful ploy from her first day of teaching, having picked it up from one of her tutors at St Hild's Training College. The students used to call this woman the Hypnotist, laughing at her while they fell for her. But while Min was laughing with them she noted it as a technique which never failed.

It had never failed her, either, with any group of people she taught: from the juniors whom she normally worked with, right through to seniors whom she occasionally taught and adults with whom she had always pursued her own personal interest in painting and drawing. Now, one by one, she attempted to draw this group under her spell.

They looked at her eagerly.

'Thank you for coming,' she said. 'I didn't know how many would be here—it's the middle of the term and the notices went out so late.

But now we're here could we say who we are? Let's start with me. I'm Min Roebuck. I'm from Tyneside and I've come here to teach in St Bennet's junior school...'

The girls were sisters, Janet and Pauline Fenwick, and they worked in the Home and Colonial. They couldn't draw but came here because their mother wouldn't let them go to the dance at the Gaunt Valley Hotel or get the bus to the Killock Camp dance. The thick-set man growled that he was called Michael Stratton and he worked at Priorton Old Pit; the boy was James Otter and was at the grammar school. The soldiers were Sidney Allerman and Anthony Burton and said they couldn't draw, but had come here because they couldn't dance either and at the dance at the Gaunt Valley Hotel it was the blokes who could who got the girls. Anthony Burton winked at the Fenwick girls and they both giggled. The woman in the cloche hat said she was Mrs Constantine and she had always been fond of drawing.

The door flew wide open and the wind lifted papers from the tables. A man was standing there in an unfamiliar pale uniform blinking in the light.

'Shut that door,' growled Matt, still adding to his mountain of cut paper. 'You'll have the warden after us.'

The man shut it and Min smiled directly at him as he turned. 'Welcome. Can you find a place?' She was looking into blue eyes under a soft grey military cap of some kind. 'We haven't yet started.'

He brought his heels together very lightly, dipped his head and then found a place beside Janet Fenwick. He took off the soft grey cap and placed it neatly beside the paper, still curling slightly from its long imprisonment on the roll.

For no reason at all Min's face burned and she had to take a breath before, looking around all the faces again, she proceeded. She could not bring herself to go through the rigmarole about who and why with the latecomer. 'Now my problem is, I'm new here, and I don't know any of you and you don't know me. If we've got to work together we have to know each other. And what we are about here is images rather than words. So what I would like us to do is take ten minutes and use the charcoal to draw something which will tell the rest of us something about you, or perhaps what you think about things.'

A stunned silence settled on the group. She had lost them at a stroke. 'Anything,' she added. 'No matter how simple or straightforward.'

Janet Fenwick put up her hand. 'Like we work at the Home and Colonial. There's nothing there...'

'Yes there is,' said Min eagerly. 'Think of the shelves with the rows of tins, the bins of flour and sugar. The patterns, the colours.'

There was a loud laugh at that.

'Don't you know there's a war on?' sneered Pauline Fenwick. An uneasy silence ensued.

The latecomer put up a finger. 'It's possible to show what we are doing in the war.' His accent was alien. 'What about the queues outside your

326

shop? The line of people? That would be a good picture.'

The girls exchanged glances and shrugged.

'We could do the black-out,' said James Otter. 'That'd be easy enough. Just cover the page with black.'

There was a shout of laughter at that and the tension eased. 'Well,' Min said, turning her back to them, 'I'll start mine.'

Without thinking about it, she started to line out the parallel lines of a railway with hills rising in the distance. For a second the only sound was the scrape of her stubby charcoal on the paper. Then she could hear the rustling of other papers, the scrape of other charcoals, and she relaxed. Then she concentrated on her drawing, blocking in the horizon, the sea in the distance and finally the toy-like train chuffing its way along the parallel lines.

When she turned round, everyone's head was down over their papers. She walked round the horseshoe on tiptoe. The two girls were executing almost identical pictures of people in a queue: neat wooden people with round heads, differentiated by headgear and clothes; the boy was drawing two very accurate Spitfires fighting a Messerschmitt caught in a mesh of headlights; Michael Stratton was swiftly completing a very accomplished drawing of the winding gear of a pit, his crouching body the very image of concentration; the woman in the cloche hat was drawing flowers which just might resemble the iris in a vase.

The soldiers were tackling scenes from life in

the camp. Sidney was drawing stick figures in a queue beside a table which had huge tubs of what must be food. Anthony was drawing a child's-eye view of a hut, the rows of beds and men making a tight pattern.

When she finally came to the latecomer she almost fell over with shock. In the bottom left-hand corner of his sheet, growing under his confident, decisive hand, was the figure of a woman in a cow-like shawl. In the background he had already blocked in buildings in flames and in the top right-hand corner, in pure black, was the menacing figure, elbows out, of a man with a machine-gun.

She was trembling slightly as she went to the front, resisting the desire to pull down her own worthless effort from the blackboard. Michael Stratton was infinitely more skilful than she was; the latecoming foreigner was drawing with even greater power and accomplishment than Michael Stratton.

She took a breath and turned round, smiling brightly. 'Now, I think we've all done enough for a start. I can tell there is a lot of talent here. There's more than one person here who should be standing teaching this class instead of me. Shall we tell each other what inspired our drawing, and shall we consider what the use of paint, colour, might do to transform these ideas?'

Although she looked on with vivid interest as each person talked about his or her picture, she was most impatient for the latecomer to tell his story.

James Otter said he had drawn the Messerschmitt from a 109 he had seen exhibited at the covered market. 'You could see the bullet-holes. The propeller was all buckled.' And if they wanted to see a Spitfire there was one being shown at the Town Hall next week for the Spitfire Fund.

Michael Stratton was terse. 'Ah see this every time ah go on shift. Ah have done since I was twelve when ah started. At first it was a manacle, an instrument of torture. Then one day ah'd just come off foreshift an' ah looked back up the gantry. It was one of them wet autumn afternoons. Grey sky. Black earth. But in that minute, as I looked back, the sun broke through the clouds an' picked out the gantry and the wheel like a fine web. That was when I stopped drawing flowers and rocks and started drawing the pit.' A murmur of appreciation passed round the group. Michael coughed. 'This paper's nee good, like, missis. Me charcoal's broke through it twice and it'll take up the paint like blotting paper.'

'Well, it'll have to do for tonight,' said Min brightly. 'We'll have to think of an alternative for another night.'

Mrs Constantine put up a tentative hand. 'My husband's a cabinet maker. He has offcuts of wood we might use. If it were oil, that is...' her voice faded away uncertainly.

'That's a brilliant idea, Mrs Constantine. I've mixed watercolour tonight but perhaps we'll be able to mix the powder with oil another night. That'll go on board. I've seen that done before.

329

If we can get some oil, that is,' Min laughed. She turned to the newcomer. At last it was his turn. 'Now...' She laughed too radiantly, embarrassing herself. 'We don't even know your name, Mr...'

'Sobieski,' said the man. 'Krystof Sobieski. I am in the Polish Army temporarily at Killock Camp while I recover from an illness which recurs from when I was imprisoned in Germany. Then I am to do some work at the arms factory near here.'

Josie took a great fancy for Beatrice who, having brought her ration book and her two weeks' rent, was now in residence at Campion House. She was sleeping in a bedroom nearly as small as Bessie's, off the back corridor. It had been used as a box room, but Josie and Beatrice had helped Bessie move the boxes and trunks so that they made a kind of wall, leaving room for a narrow bed which she and Beatrice humped down from the attic.

Lizza was surprised to find herself less than happy about Beatrice's move. In analysing her surprise, she recognised her own selfishness. She had always felt resentful at being pushed out and left out of the house in Bracks Hill, but Beatrice's presence in that house had always absolved her of any personal responsibility for her mother. Now she found herself wondering how her mother was coping on her own. Concern for her mother's well-being was a novel emotion, unlike the barely controlled anger she usually felt towards her.

Beatrice was enjoying herself. She got on well with Bessie: living with her mother had trained her to help without getting under anyone's feet. She and Josie were very relaxed with each other. She told Josie she thought that coming north had done her good. She was growing up, not the scraggy urchin she had been when she first arrived. She was rounding up nicely now on Bessie's good northern cooking. Josie in turn teased Beatrice about her old-fashioned manner and style, a teasing which amused but did not faze her.

Lizza and Josie decided, on Beatrice's first Saturday, to take her to visit the Spitfire exhibition, in the Town Hall part of the War Weapons Week. The girls on Josie's line at the factory had raised a good sum with a raffle and an impromptu concert in the canteen. Their contribution would be on the board at the Town Hall and Josie wanted to see it. Alex was still on her mind; she was curious about the Spitfire which he had gone on so much about.

The exhibition was crowded with people eager to see the Spitfire which had crashed on British soil. Josie read out the carefully written note on a card propped up on the buckled wing: ' *"The Spitfire had been used in the Battle of Britain and was instrumental in 3½ kills..."* And what in the world would be half a kill?' She broke into her own reading.

A boy in round spectacles, standing drawing close by, looked up. 'Anyone knows that,' he said scornfully. 'Half a kill is where they witness

331

severe damage to the target plane although it may fly on.'

She grinned at him. 'Ta for that. Now... *"The pilot of this craft bailed out over England and was bruised on landing but was in action in another aircraft the following day."* Now there's courage for you.' She peered over the boy's shoulder. 'Sure you ain't half a bad drawer.'

He glared at her. 'Now what does that mean? Am I good or am I bad.'

She winked at him. 'You know you're good, all right.'

He went dark red and put his head down over his pad.

'Josie!' Lizza was calling to her to come and listen to a man who was going to show them exactly what their funds would buy.

It was when they were coming out of the exhibition that Josie mentioned Min.

'That Miss Roebuck was a bit of a flash in the pan, wasn't she, Mrs King? At first she was never off the doorstep. Now she hasn't been round for days.'

'Who's that?' said Beatrice.

'This woman I met on the train back here. She's a teacher. We've been to the pictures a couple of times. And asked me to join her art class even though I can't draw. So I said no.'

'Maybe she's huffed,' said Beatrice. 'Talking about the pictures, I see David Niven's on here in something called *Raffles*. What about going to that?'

Josie linked her arm. 'Sure, that's a very good idea.'

Beatrice laughed. 'I asked the engine driver not the oil-rag. Lizza?'

'What? Oh yes. The pictures.' Lizza had noticed Min's cooling off and had had a twinge of disappointment. Perhaps she was only interested to be friends till she made other, more suitable friends in the town. Lizza felt dull and grey at this thought. 'Yes, Beatrice. Course we can see the picture. We can go tonight if Bessie minds Liam.'

Krystof pulled Min's hand through his arm and shone his torch on the pavement to show the way down the street which, though dark, was full of shadowy figures lighting their own way home from the pictures.

He smiled down at her. 'You enjoy the film?' he said.

She could see his breath on the air. 'He's very dashing, I suppose. But the real things happening around us these days seem to make the fact more heroic and more terrible than anything on the pictures.'

He laughed. 'Yes, the pilots every day in the skies. The army in the desert.'

'And you and your countrymen walking through Europe to get here to turn round and fight again. Fighting and escaping.' In the days she had known him, she had winkled part of his story from him.

Apart from the two art-class evenings he had attended they had been out together three times. Once to supper in the Gaunt Valley Hotel. That was hardly a romantic meal: soup, macaroni and veal, sponge and custard. She had paid, as it was her invitation: five shillings for the two of them. Once they had gone to a dance at the Gaunt Valley Hotel, where they had rubbed shoulders with soldiers from Killock Camp who were there to flash their khaki at the local girls. And this time tonight to the pictures to see David Niven in *Raffles*. She had not been able to concentrate on David Niven, being far too aware of the man beside her. There was a buzz in the air between them. Her hand slipped into his in the dark and when he squeezed it hard she knew that he felt the buzz, too.

They turned down the narrow side street where she lived and stopped beside the tall door of her lodgings, secure in its shadow. He switched off his torch. With that tiny light gone, they were in total darkness. Her hands felt their way to his shoulders and she put her face up for his kiss. His lips grazed her cheeks and brow and only finally came to her lips. At first the kiss was gentle and unemphatic. But her hands were on his neck in his hair pulling at it, then pulling him to her. The kiss became deeper and more urgent.

She broke away and they were both trembling. 'I...I...must go,' he said, thickly, turning away.

She pulled him back. 'Wait! Wait!' She used her key to open the door behind her and was briefly tangled in the black-out curtain. She re-emerged and grasped his hand. 'Come in,' she whispered. 'Miss Connaught my landlady's out. Playing whist with the woman next door. Sometimes not back till eleven o'clock.'

He allowed himself to be pulled up two flights of stairs and into a bedroom which smelled of mothballs. When she lit the gas mantle he saw the room was large, heavily and rather grandly furnished, with a bed, a wardrobe, a large battered desk and two easy chairs.

'The room is very nice,' he said politely.

She took off her hat and coat, put them in the tall wardrobe. 'Now yours.' She held out her arms and he gave her his greatcoat which she put in the wardrobe beside hers. Then she poured two small sherries from the bottle on a tray on the desk. She handed him his glass, sat on the desk, crossed her legs and held out her glass to him. 'Mr Sobieski! Hero of Poland. Your health!' she said, then drank off the contents of her glass.

He put his head on one side. 'You're very direct,' he said, smiling slightly.

'I'm a sailor's daughter. Brought up to be direct.' She tossed her head so that the gleaming cap of hair lifted in the gaslight. 'And life's short. You'll be gone by tomorrow or the next day.'

He walked across and put the glass of sherry back on the table. 'I do not like your sherry,' he said. 'It makes me think of the church and High Mass.' He put his hands on her thighs and ran them lightly up towards her waist, then gently upwards over her breasts until they were on her shoulders and his left thumb was on her throat, stroking up and down, up and down. She shivered.

335

His lips were on her ear. 'You're sure...?'

He could feel her nod, see her heavy breath in the cold air of the bedroom. Then he kissed her hard and in one movement swept her into his arms and carried her across to the great lumpy bed.

She lay back and grinned at him as he struggled to regain his breath. 'You're not in condition for romantic gestures, you know,' she giggled.

Then he grasped her and kissed her till she thought she would have no breath, till she thought the two of them were totally welded through their lips. She broke off, gasping. 'The light! Turn out the light,' she whispered.

He stood back and shook his head, his hands going to the glittering buttons of his battledress. 'No,' he said. 'I like to see.'

Later, when they were lying inside the tented arch of blankets, stroking each other after the first storm and slowly quickening with desire for the second, the front door slammed and almost simultaneously there was an enormous crash from the wardrobe across the room and they both froze.

There was a noise on the staircase and a knocking at the bedroom door. 'Miss Roebuck, Miss Roebuck, what was that? Are you all right?'

Min leapt out of bed and turned down the gas, then pulled on a silk wrap her father had bought her and went to open the door a crack.

'It is all right, Miss Connaught. It's just the

336

rail in the wardrobe which seems to have fallen. I will soon put it right.'

'Are you sure? I can help you do it, Miss Roebuck.' Miss Connaught gave a slight push to the door but Min stood firm.

'I can manage. Good night, Miss Connaught!' She stood like a statue for a few minutes and there was perfect silence in the room. Then she turned. 'I think Miss Connaught harbours secret desires for me,' she murmured.

A fierce whisper came from the bed. 'Come here!'

'No!' she whispered back. 'My clothes! I must put the rail back!' She started to lift up her precious clothes from the heap and he came across and started to help her, stroking them into neat piles on the tumbled bed.

She came to his greatcoat. 'This is what caused the trouble,' she said fiercely, putting it over the back of one of the chairs.

He put one hand on his forehead. '*Mea culpa!*' he whispered back, grinning, then kissed her left breast.

She wriggled away to slot the rail back into place and he brought all the clothes back to her, item by item. One by one she shook them out carefully and returned them to their regular place. He came across with the last blouse and he put it to his face. 'You have lovely clothes. This smells of you, not of this strange room,' he said.

'The perfume is from Paris, like this robe.' She ran a finger along the tasselled tie and sat leaning back on the bed.

'You have an admirer?'

She was chilled by the cool disinterest in his tone.

'My father. He's a navy pilot. Before the war he would put an order with his friends and they would bring him things.' She was cross with herself, at her defensive tone.

He laughed and came to kiss her on the nose. 'If I were your father I too would bring you things; spice from India; icons from Russia; perfume from Paris. You would be my princess.' Then he was on his knees before her, his hands busy loosening the tassels, his lips back to her breasts.

'The bed! The bed!' she said. 'Krystof! My feet are freezing here on the linoleum.'

'We will warm each other,' he said, pulling her to the cold floor. 'I will warm you.'

III

Blossom

And 'tis my faith that every flower
Enjoys the earth it breathes
    Wordsworth, *Lines Written in Early Spring*

III

CHAPTER 22

Beatrice felt all fingers and thumbs trying to keep up with the swift fingers of Josie and Esme. The job was piling up behind her and Josie was waiting impatiently to complete her stage in the process. Then Josie came round and joined her on her bench. 'Hutch up,' she ordered. 'I'll do a few to stop this log-jam.'

The girls they worked with were polite enough with Beatrice but she could tell they were holding themselves back when she was around. They would put their hand dramatically to their mouths to stop a swearword bubbling out, and mutter comments in low voices so that she couldn't hear.

At the end of the first day, Beatrice was so shattered with the physical efforts that as soon as she got in she went to bed and cried, thinking she should go home to Bracks Hill and volunteer for the Land Army. Working in the fields just could not be as hard, as bone-shatteringly wearying as working at a factory bench. Her respect for Josie and her swift-fingered friends had increased a hundredfold in a day.

She was awoken from a deep sleep by Josie shaking her. 'Come on, Beatrice! Bessie's keeping your tea hot. And I've got a surprise for you.' She allowed herself to be led downstairs

341

and obediently sat at the mountain of corned-beef hash, finding herself increasingly hungry as she did so. She looked up to find them all looking at her: Bessie, hunched and feather-edged like the wise old bird she was; Lizza with anxious solicitation, and Josie with the light of anticipation in her eye.

Beatrice put down her fork. 'Now,' she said. 'What was this surprise?'

'Here!' With a magician's flourish Josie brought a gleaming pair of scissors out of her apron pocket. 'Proper hairdressers' scissors. Bessie had them to cut the old man's hair.'

Beatrice put her hand to her head. 'No!'

'Yes!' said Josie firmly. 'When did you last have your hair cut?'

'I don't know.'

'It would be when you had Alex, when you were ill,' said Lizza. 'Ma cut it.' She was pushing the table to one side, to clear a space by the fire.

'In 1923,' said Beatrice. She had haemorrhaged on and off for four days after the birth and been quite ill. Her mother had cut off her hair when she was in bed.

'Eighteen years. Me mammy used to say it wasn't like Samson in the Bible. A big head of hair's got to take a woman's strength away. That's why the men like it. So this'll do you good. Good!' She spread pages from the *Northern Echo* over the floor, and placed a kitchen chair on top of it. 'Sit!'

Obediently, Beatrice sat, putting a tentative hand to her tightly braided hair.

'Let me do it.' Tenderly, Lizza took down the braids, putting the hairpins in a saucer on the table. She put her fingers through the tight plaits, separating the strands so that Beatrice's hair cascaded in tight brown silk waves over her shoulders to her knees. 'It seems such a pity,' she said.

Josie put her to one side. 'No it isn't. This hair was grown years ago. It's not Beatrice now. She's today.' The scissors in her hand glittered in the firelight.

Beatrice caught hold of the hand and looked Josie in the eye. Then she let go. 'Go on then. Why not?'

The hair whispered its way down to the floor in great lumps and she could feel an unfamiliar draught on her neck. She shook her head, bobbing it from side to side.

'Here! Keep still!' Josie ordered. 'I'm not finished yet.' She took a long time, snipping and snipping, and Beatrice felt sure she must be quite bald.

'There, enough for you to push into a snood, but short enough for you to put in curlers,' said Josie. 'You can look now.'

She looked into the small oval mirror over the fireplace and a total stranger looked out. The stranger had a long fringe over well-marked brows and fine dark eyes. The straight-cut sides of the hair brought out the strong cheekbones. The shorter hair fluffed out over her ears and just reached her chin. The hair at the back fluttered out and up, crackling with electricity. Her neck looked white and bare.

She was smiling when she turned round and they all clapped. Even Liam clapped. He was not sure what had happened but generally liked to clap his hands.

'Beatrice, that's wonderful,' said Lizza smiling with delight.

'Yeh look ten year younger, hinney,' chirped Bessie. 'More'n that even.'

Beatrice looked at Josie. 'Thank you,' she said.

Smiling slightly, Josie shrugged. 'Didn't I want to stop those cows at work asking if you're me grandma?'

The next day at the factory the work seemed somehow easier and the girls, after remarking vociferously on her transformation, included her in their shouted comments and stopped worrying about whether or not she could hear them swearing. Esme linked her on the way to the canteen and told her it was time she got herself a feller before the time ran out.

Lizza was trying to write a story in the big ledger, based on the time her father came home from leave from the First World War. She could remember her mother holding his slimy army fatigues with wooden tongs over boiling water, and the lice dropping into the water with soft plops. And their laughter. It echoed in her ears now, combining heartiness and intimacy. She blinked. Her mother would have been her age. Just a little older. Early thirties. Now that was a thought. A young mother. Full of passion.

And another scene, when, the sun behind

344

sparking off his auburn hair, her father had squatted on his haunches—could she say 'hunkers' in a written story?—he had squatted on his hunkers and urged her to toddle on home while he stayed at the corner with his mates. She had to make her way slowly, as in each chubby hand she was balancing a large green apple.

She started.

It was difficult to see them through the clouds of steam. They were laughing and jousting over a pile of clothes. A jacket dropped to the ground close to her and she could see the louse walking tip-toe through the folds of khaki...

She worked without stopping for two hours, her thoughts speeding up as she wrote. She was so engrossed that she jumped when she felt a light hand on her shoulder.

'Sorry, Lizza,' groaned Min. 'Bessie let me in. I walked home with Liam and the old witch has him now in her lair eating oatcakes. She said you'd been scratching away for hours.'

Lizza sat back in her chair and smiled her welcome.

'What's that?' Min leaned over the ledger but Lizza closed it quickly. 'The magnum opus?'

Lizza frowned.

'Sorry, "The great work." '

'I wouldn't call it that. It's a story from when I was very young. From the last war.'

Min sat down, peeled off her gloves and stretched out her feet before the flickering fire. 'A *story*!'

'What does that mean?' said Lizza sharply.

Min held up her hands. 'Nothing! Nothing! Just that you're full of surprises. Can I read it?'

'What? So you can mark it out of ten?'

'No. That's not what I mean. We are prickly this afternoon, aren't we? I just want to read it, Lizza, as a friend who's interested in what her friend is up to. Like I would show you a picture I've drawn.'

Lizza laughed. 'Prickly? Maybe I'm spending too much time on my own here with Bessie and the children.'

'Children? That Josie's no child, I can tell you.'

'No child? Of course she is.'

'No she isn't. I could tell, when I was working with senior girls, when they went from child to woman.'

Lizza coloured. 'You mean, when they start with...their Friend?'

'Is that what you call it? I call it the Curse and think it well named. No, I don't mean that. I mean when they get...experience. You can tell.'

'Josie? You must be joking. I know she's working at the factory now and there's tales about those girls...'

'No. I don't mean now. I knew when I saw her on the train.'

Lizza laughed out loud at this. 'You're mad!' she said affectionately. 'Now,' she said, dismissing that topic, 'to what do I owe this pleasure? I haven't seen you since your classes started. I thought I'd huffed you saying I wouldn't sharpen your pencils.'

Min leapt to her feet and grabbed Lizza and kissed her hard on both cheeks. 'You couldn't—as you say—huff me! I'll be on your shoulder, telling you my troubles, in twenty years' time. They'll be wheeling me in my wheelchair to see you when I'm a croaky old maid. I knew it on the train. You watch!'

Lizza touched one of her cheeks where Min's lips had touched it, her amazement at Min's gesture tinged with satisfaction at her words. 'Well, then,' she said just a bit stiffly, 'what do you want?'

'To talk to you.'

The silence lasted too many seconds.

Lizza sighed. 'So how is the art class going?'

'I thought you'd never ask. It's wonderful. We're painting oil on wood now. There's a boy there who's very promising, and a miner who's the best draughtsman I've seen in or out of college. Energy, power, promise. It's all there. I've lent him my books of Impressionist prints and he's in heaven.' She paused.

'And...' said Lizza.

'And there is this man. Lizza, I swear to you I've never been in love. No one could love me like my father, who showed me how to love and be loved. Puny men have come and gone, but...'

'But this one's different.'

'Lizza! You don't know how different. Lizza...'

There was a crash at the study door as Liam

347

pushed it open for Bessie, who was carrying a laden tea-tray. 'Ah thowt yeh lasses'd a' bin ready for some tea.' She clashed it on the desk beside the ledger. Lizza noted there were three cups on it. She stood up. 'You sit here, Bessie.'

Bessie sniffed. 'Ah telt yer ah never sit down in this room. But ah will have a cup.' She picked up one of the cups with its faded blue Spode pattern. 'Ah've had many a cup of tea in here standing up, like. With the old man.' Her mouth puckered out into a secret smile. 'He used ter ask us—beg us—ter sit down wi' him, like. But ah telt 'im. Ah niver sit down in 'ere. Niver!'

Lizza handed a cup to Min, whose eyes were brimming with undisguised amusement. Min turned to the old woman. 'You're really the reason I came this afternoon, Bessie.'

The old woman put her head on one side.

'I wondered if you'd like some more lodgers?'

'More?'

'No, Min,' said Lizza quickly. 'All this is too much for Bessie anyway.'

Bessie shot her a glance. 'Mind your own business, missie.' She looked back at Min. 'Ration book?'

Min nodded.

'Proper rent?'

Min nodded again.

'How many?'

'Two. One's an artist and needs a lot of light to work by. One's me. The old teacher I'm lodging with camps herself outside my door

348

every hour of the day and night and she's getting on my nerves.'

'I can put you with Lizza an' then there's an attic room... Needs clearin' out like.'

'I'll help clear it,' said Min eagerly.

Bessie nodded slowly. 'Two rents, two ration books.'

'Bessie!' warned Lizza. 'Mr Silkin will...'

Bessie shot her a look.

Lizza tried to think of a way to tell Min that this was all too much for Bessie, that she was an old woman. 'Min, I don't think...'

Bessie talked through her. 'There's May Lynn off Princess Street. She'd give us a hand, for a bit off the ration.' She looked at Min. 'Yes. Ah'll dee it. Dependin' on who they are. Who did you say the other was?'

'Well, one of the people in my class. He's a good artist, he...'

'He!' Bessie cackled. 'Mind, no hanky-panky. Ah dinnet want no hanky-panky. It'd send us to an early grave dyin' of envy!'

Their laughter was interrupted by Josie, coming in bright-cheeked and glowing with the crisp winter day.

'Beatrice's collapsed on the bed again,' she announced. 'Can't take the pace. Don't know what hard work is, these women who stay at home. And the women at work liked her hair. And ain't I got three orders for haircuts now?' As the girl whirled through the room Lizza looked at her more closely. Yes, she had filled out. Yes, her eyes were bright, and her hair, now up in its precocious roll, was glossy. And she looked almost pretty.

Lizza looked across at Min, who raised her brows questioningly.

'I have to go. I can get across and pack my things,' said Min. 'My class starts at six. I can move in here after that, Bessie, if that's all right with you. Nine o'clock. And I'll bring the artist round to see you after the class. Will that do, Bessie?'

'Proper whirlwind you are. Not like a teacher at all.' Bessie cackled. 'Why aye, hinney. The more the merrier.' She was literally rubbing her arthritic old hands at the thought of more ration books and more money.

In a minute Min had pulled on her gloves and clashed out of the door. The others made their way to the kitchen to prepare for the tea. Peeling carrots in the scullery, Lizza wondered just what was so special about this miner who could paint. She wouldn't have long to wait to find out, would she, if Min was bringing him round after the class?

Krystof was very restrained in the class, not showing by a single glance what had gone on between him and the teacher. Min's longing for a meaningful glance, a special tone of voice, went unrewarded.

He and Michael Stratton now worked side by side. They spoke very little but occasionally a consultation about light and shade, the use of certain painting techniques, would occur, eavesdropped on with great interest by the rest of the group.

Krystof had persuaded Michael to use one of the large easels, the better to understand the impact of light on his painting. Michael was doing a large study of a mining gallery: men, stone and paint used to powerful architectural effect. He could only work on it in the church hall, as there was no room for such a big study in the little pit house he shared with two brothers and his father.

Krystof was working on a detailed large drawing of Priorton Market Place with the Priory gates on one side and on the other the medieval market cross. To the left, in the distance, was the silhouette of an eastern town, complete with minarets. To the right the sky was criss-crossed with light, and in the beam he had drawn a Nazi bomber: a Messerschmitt caught like a fly in amber. James Otter kept coming up to him to make sure he was getting the details of the aeroplane correct.

The evening seemed interminable to Min, and she was pleased that Krystof did not need asking to stay back with her and Matt, to help haul away the tables and to stow Michael's painting in a safe place.

While Matt Clayton was locking the back areas she looked at Krystof. 'You were telling me you were looking for lodgings in the town for when you work at the factory. Somewhere you could paint?'

He nodded, not quite sure of what was coming.

'Well, I've found you somewhere. A big attic

in this enormous house where my friend stays. Nice people.'

He shrugged. 'I do need somewhere.'

'They have space for me, so I can get away from old Ma Connaught.'

He frowned. 'Min, I don't think we should...'

She laughed heartily. 'Don't worry. It is perfectly respectable. You needed a room and I needed to get away from Connaught before I go potty. Just a coincidence. Honestly. I've said we'd go there after the class tonight. I'm moving in. You can take a look. I've organised a taxi for me at nine o'clock so we need to get a move on here.' Min averted her eyes, busying herself stowing away the tins of paint and removing her brown overall. She wanted to say that she loved him, wanted him with her, but she knew very well that he did not love her. After that first night in Connaught's bed she had asked him about his wife. He had frowned then, looked older. 'They came for her. I arranged for her to get away,' he said. 'But she did not arrive at the meeting place. I heard she had been on a transport East. But I am not sure.' His tone had been cold, measured, distancing, and she knew she had done the wrong thing in asking him at all.

He shrugged now, his lack of enthusiasm for her scheme only too evident. But he went with her to Connaught's house where her taxi—in reality an ancient man with a pony and trap, drafted in for war service during petrol rationing—was waiting. Krystof picked up Min's luggage which was already in the hall and she shoved her pile of post into her pocket.

Swept along unwillingly by her enthusiasm, Krystof wondered just what he was letting himself in for, at this house where she was taking him.

CHAPTER 23

The minute the nine o'clock news was finished Bessie turned off the wireless and settled down again with her fine needle and her meandering hand on her quilt. 'He's after them Russians now, that old Hitler. Well, they saw off old Boneyparte so they'll see off him.'

Lizza and Bessie were alone in the hot kitchen. Beatrice and Josie had gone to bed, tired out, at nine o'clock.

Lizza looked up from her book in surprise. 'You know about Napoleon, Bessie?'

Bessie shot a look at her. 'What d'yah think ah am, daft?'

'Sorry, I...'

Bessie grinned. 'Old Barraclough had this old man come, years back, whose granda—mebbe great-granda—had fought as a lad in the Battle o' Waterloo. The two of 'm used to fight all the battles on me dinin' table. I'd play war with him about the scratches. Then he'd go in the huff. Allus more wuk for me though.'

'You watched them play these games?'

'They used to drag us in, an' say, Bessie, what

353

next, what'd 'appen next? They had bets on it. Bets on me. More often than not ah wus right. That old Boney wus a cunning feller. Mistake ter turn east though. Old Barraclough said, a mistake ter turn east. He wus right there. Now this feller's meckin' same mistake. This Hitler.'

'I hope you're right, Bessie.' Lizza picked up her book.

Bessie pointed at her with the fine needle. 'Ah know about it all anyway from the book.'

Lizza put down her book.

'What book's that, Bessie?'

'The one about Prince Andrew and Pierre, about them Rostovs and Bolkonsis.'

'*War and Peace*? You read *War and Peace*?'

'Me read? Dinnet be soft. Ah've telt ye. Ah canna be bothered to read, except the *Echo* every day. He read it to us, sittin' there where you're sittin' now. While ah wus on with me quilts, or mekkin' his shirts or sommat.'

'He read *War and Peace* to you?'

'Yes, an' the others. He 'ad a lovely voice when he read to yer. An' he had a lot of time for them Russians, had old Barraclough. He read us other ones, the ones about when the feller was in the army, an' when he and his marrahs wus fightin' us, at Sebastopol. An' one about the woman's ran off from her husband, Anna, Anna...'

'Karenina,' said Lizza.

'How do you know about it?' Bessie peered at her suspiciously.

'I've read them too.'

Bessie's eye dropped to the book in Lizza's hand. 'What's that one, like?'

'It's by Daphne du Maurier.'

'Another foreigner?'

'No. She's English.'

'What's it about?'

'It's about this woman who comes to this big house as the second wife of this man. And it's haunted by his first wife, called Rebecca.' Lizza paused. 'Same name as my daughter.'

Bessie jabbed her needle at the padded fabric. 'The bairn as got killed? Hard on yer, Mrs King, that little lass still bein' at yer skirts, an' two more hangin' on her skirts too. I seen 'er. Nice curls she 'as. An' I seen the others, the babbies. They do 'aunt yer, the dead. That old Barraclough niver leaves me. Niver! Dinnet worry though; the little lassies is just watchin' till their brother gets 'ere. Then they'll gerraway.'

Lizza stared at her. She knew Bessie never went near church or chapel. 'Where to, Bessie? Heaven? Is that what you believe in?'

Bessie lifted her bony shoulders. 'Things. Everything is part of another. The trees, the land, livin' folks, dead folks. But the livin' call on to the dead, cling on to 'em. They canna let 'em gan to the land. Like Peter and Matthew an' them. They couldn't let that Jesus gan to the land; he even had to show 'imself. Not a shade nor a shadow but 'is livin' self. An' only then would they let 'im go. Strong stuff. Powerful fellers, that Peter an' Matthew an' them. That old Barraclough stays here cos 'e's waitin' for me to gan with'm. Bin together so long 'e disn't wanna gan on 'is own.' She cackled. 'But 'e'll 'ave to wait on. Ah'm not gannin' yet.'

Lizza found herself smiling at this. Then she sobered at another thought. 'There must be millions of shadows, with this war, Bessie. The land couldn't take them. In Coventry they say a thousand people died in a night. The land's not large enough.'

Bessie chuckled. 'The land's fathoms deep, hinney. As deep as the thoughts in yer 'ead. As many fathoms as the stars in number, as wide as the skies. Every soul down there creates a new land, new flowers, new trees, a new sky for the new generations. Even war canna defeat the land. New flowers rise. Even old Hitler'll not stop that, poison the land as 'e may.'

Lizza sat back trying to absorb this, wondering where in that pattern lay her own rejected God, the God her mother talked to every day.

Bessie put her head on one side. 'Tell yer what, Mrs King, that story sounds all right, the one about the second wife.' She looked at Lizza expectantly. 'What 'appens? In the story, like?'

Lizza grinned at her, resisting the desire to hug her. 'Would you like me to read it to you, Bessie?'

Bessie grinned, her thin lips stretched over the hard gum. 'Lovely,' she said. 'But yer'll have to start at the beginnin' again.'

Obediently, Lizza turned back to the beginning and started to read. Bessie bent her head over her tiny stitches, finally content.

At ten o'clock the chime of the hall clock clashed with the jingle of the doorbell as it

356

bounced on its board in the kitchen. Lizza put the book on the table with some relief and rubbed her eyes. Reading aloud was so much more tiring than reading in your own head. 'I'll go, Bessie.'

She opened the door to see Min, surrounded by cases and packages. Behind her in the darkness stood a tall, shadowy figure. Lizza fussed with the black-out curtain. 'If you bring all that stuff into the porch, Min, then I can shut the door to keep the light in.' She picked up a case and turned to dump it in the shadowy porch. As she turned to pick up another a quiet voice came to her out of the darkness and said, 'Lizza?'

Her heart did a somersault and she hurriedly put on the porch light.

'Krystof!'

He was standing in the beam of light, holding three hat boxes and a wooden travel case, smiling at her in polite greeting.

She pulled back and smiled politely. 'What're you doing in Priorton, Krystof?' She turned to Min. 'So this is your...'

'Artist!' said Min brightly. 'Goodness. How do you know each other? No! That can wait. Let's get into the house and get the light out. I can see a little man lurking down the path with a tin hat on.' She bustled them into the hall and clattered the porch door shut behind them.

Krystof nodded slightly at Lizza. 'You look well, Lizza. Blooming. It suits you, being away from the bombs.'

Lizza, fiery red, put her hands down into the pockets of her smock. She knew very well the baby was showing now. She swallowed, to keep her voice normal. She turned to Min. 'Krystof worked with Roland in Coventry.'

'Lizza was kind enough to give me her hospitality, Min.' He turned to Lizza. 'I'm at Killock Camp, just recovering from an illness to the chest. On Monday I go to the factory to do more drawings for the government.'

'But,' said Lizza, 'why here? Why not in Scotland like Roland?'

He shrugged. 'There's no production up there yet. The factory's here. They wanted the documentation on this factory.'

Min looked very carefully from one to the other. 'Now!' she said. 'All you need to do is turn on that charm for Bessie, Krystof, and she'll let you have this big room at the top of the house.'

He raised his brow. 'Turn on?' he said.

She laughed, took his arm and hustled him down the back passage. In the kitchen Krystof clicked his heels and bowed low over the old woman's hand.

Bessie put her head on one side and peered up at him. 'Pierre? Did the schoolteacher say yer name wus Pierre?'

'No, madame. My name is Krystof, Krystof Sobieski.'

'Russki? She didn't tell us you were a Russian.'

'I am delighted to tell you I am not a Russian, madame. I am Polish. The Russians are my enemy and the enemy of my family. I have fought against the Russians in my time.'

'Well,' said Bessie, with just the faintest echo of his accent. 'The *Russians*'re the enemy of that old Hitler. So where does that leave you?'

'Bessie,' Min butted in. 'Mr Sobieski is our ally. He's here to do some work for our government at the factory. And he needs a billet. You said about the attic...'

Bessie put down the needle and stood up. 'I'll show yer,' she said. She opened a drawer, took out a heavy torch then went across to the narrow door that opened on to the back staircase. 'You lasses stay here. Nee room for neebody on those back landin's.'

Watching Krystof vanish, Lizza turned to Min. 'So he's your artist. I thought it was the pitman.'

'No. *He's* tucked up nicely at home with his *da* and *oor Tom* and *oor Marky*.'

'That's rude, that.'

'What?'

'Imitating the way folks talk. Do you do it with my words behind my back?'

'Sorree! See, I need to be around you, Lizza, so you can teach me to mind my manners! Anyway, how do you know the glorious Krystof Sobieski? You could have knocked me down with a feather when he said your name.'

'Like he said, Roland brought him home. He was at the house the night of the big raid. He drew the picture of Rebecca.'

Min slapped her forehead. 'The drawing! You know, I've been watching him drawing and thinking his work reminded me of someone, and now I know he reminded me of himself.'

'Look,' said Lizza, not wanting to talk about Krystof, 'let's get all your stuff out of the hall and into the bedroom or Bessie'll be lecturing us about her tiles.'

They were on their second trip when Bessie and Krystof came down the stairs. Krystof was wiping dust and cobwebs from his grey uniform.

He beamed at Min. 'Wonderful,' he said. 'There are half-windows on two walls and two gigantic skylights.'

'Good,' she said, pleased to see him showing his first glimmer of enthusiasm for the idea. She turned to Bessie. 'What do you think, Bessie?'

Bessie squeezed her eyes and looked up at him. 'Ah dinnet see why not. One thing though, lad. Niver, when you're under this roof, niver say a word against the Russians. D'ye hear? Old Barraclough'd be against that.'

He bowed his head. 'Never, Mrs...Bessie.'

'An' ye can get here as soon as ye like termorrer. Don't forget yer ration book. Like I showed yer up there, there's everything to move.'

He turned to Min and Lizza. 'I must go. If I run I will get the camp bus outside the Gaunt Hotel at eleven...'

He was interrupted by a thundering knock on the door which made them all swing round. Lizza ran to open it. Outside, lit eerily by their own torches, stood a warden and a policeman, the latter angrily asking about the showing of lights. 'Mr Gresham here said there were lights showing at this house earlier and I myself saw signalling from the roof of the house.'

Min laughed and he glared at her. 'It is no laughing matter, Miss,' he said.

Krystof spoke up. 'It was merely Miss Bessie showing me her attic. I am to come here to stay.'

The policeman's torch swung round to take him in, travelling up and down his alien uniform, his ears ringing with the alien accent. 'And who might you be, sir?'

'My name is Krystof Sobieski. I am at present at Killock Camp.' He fished out his identity card before it was asked for.

The policeman shone the light on it, then he stood up straight and the warden moved just behind his right shoulder. 'I'll have to ask you to come with me to the station to verify this.'

'You can't...' said Lizza fiercely.

Krystof turned and squeezed her hand. 'I will go Lizza and it will all come clear. I have a government telephone number. And the number of Killock Camp. They can telephone and all will be clear. It is not safe to be a foreigner on this island at the moment. One has to be very careful.' He moved to stand beside the warden.

The policeman looked at Lizza. 'And whatever happens in the case of this gentleman, the householder here will be summonsed for showing a light.'

'Me?' squeaked Bessie. 'In the court? Will I be in the *Echo*?'

'Yes, missis. If you're the householder.'

The three women watched silently as the two men marched Krystof away. Bessie led the other two back into the house, muttering away about being in the paper. They couldn't work out whether she was pleased or annoyed about her anticipated fame.

Min moved to the mirror to remove her hat, then picked up her outdoor coat from a bench in the hall. As she did so the sheaf of letters fell out of her coat. A yellow telegram, lighter than the rest, fluttered free and floated on to the black and white tiles.

'Eeh, what...' said Bessie. She lowered herself on to her arthritic knees and picked it up. She put it carefully into Min's hand. 'There y'are, pet.'

Throwing down her coat, Min opened it and held it up under the dim hall light. The date was three days old. It had been addressed first to the Tyneside address. 'REGRET INFORM FATHER CAPTAIN CHARLES HUGO ROEBUCK MISSING FEARED DEAD. TORPEDO RAID ON SHIP. LETTER FOLLOWING'. They felt rather than heard her whisper the words as she read it, and Lizza caught it as it fluttered to the ground.

Min was shrieking. 'No, no.' She caught Lizza by the shoulders and shook her hard. 'No. It's not possible. There's a mistake. He was a pilot in the harbour. He'd no business being out at sea.' She laughed shrilly. 'No. That's it. It's not him. It's a mistake.'

Then a small voice came down to them from above. 'Is there a bomb?'

They looked up. Josie was standing bleary-eyed at the turn of the stairs, Liam on her hip. Beatrice was coming down behind her.

The phrase echoed in Lizza's mind and chilled her into action. She wriggled, twisting herself free from Min's grip, which was so tight that she could feel the bruises growing. 'Go back to bed, Josie. Miss Roebuck's had bad news. Just go back to bed.'

Bessie put a hand on Lizza's arm. 'Tek her up to bed, hinney. Ah'll bring you some cocoa. The old feller used to swear by my cocoa.'

Lizza shepherded Min up the stairs, made her take off her clothes and put on the sheer pink nightdress which was on the top of the things in her case.

She was leading her to the high bed when Min turned and gripped her again, wide-eyed. 'He can't be dead, Lizza, can he? The children are dead, the children I took to Cumbria to be safe. But they died. And my father, he was safe too, wasn't he? Just there in the harbour. Not on the high seas. He can't be dead.'

Lizza peeled the small hands from her shoulders and held them in hers. 'It said *feared* dead, Min. They're not certain. Come on. Jump into bed and I'll tuck you in.'

Min sat up obediently as she tucked her in. Lizza was just putting on her own nightdress when Bessie clanked in balancing a small tray with two large white china cups and a silver flask.

'The cocoa's to pour. Ah sorted out 'is flask.'
The creaky old voice was full of affection.
'Yeh'd better get inter bed too, hinney, or
yeh'll get yer death. Me, ah'm gunna get ter
bed mesel'. Ah've gotta full day termorrer an' I
need ter gan round ter May Lynn ter tell her.
An' we'll need ter gan the poliss ter see they
an't locked away yon Russian feller...' She was
still talking as the door clicked behind her.

As Lizza poured the cocoa from the flask, the
smell of whisky in the steam tickled her nose.
No wonder old Barraclough had liked it. She
pressed Min's hand round the white cup and
ordered, 'Drink!' guiding her so that she took
a good gulp of the warm liquid.

She poured her own, put the light out and
balanced her cup in her hand as she manoeuvred
herself into bed beside Min. She sipped her
cocoa and felt it go instantly to her head. Bessie
must have measured the whisky half and half.

Min's voice came to her out of the darkness.
'He is dead, you know.'

'You don't know that, Min. It said missing.'

'He's gone. I can't feel him anywhere.'

'You don't know that.'

'I loved him. Did you love your father,
Lizza?'

'I didn't know him. I only knew my mother.
I've little memories of my father. Something
about apples. And the way, when he held your
hand in his, it was so big he had to put his little
finger up your sleeve to accommodate it.'

'Yes! Yes! Me too. And when you cried he
would wipe your tears. And when you washed

your hair he would rub your head with a towel, hard, till your ears rang. And your hands, when you were cold, he would rub them till they tingled with heat.' Min paused to sip the last of the cocoa. 'He would buckle your shoes and plait your hair.' Min laughed. 'The plaits would all be wispy and the girls at school would laugh at you. But you didn't care.' Lizza could hear her gulp the cocoa. 'Is there more of this, Lizza?'

Lizza felt for the flask and drained it into Min's cup.

The dreamy voice went on. 'And when they came to drag your screaming mother to the loony bin he would take you in his arms and hold you. And when the night was cold and you feared the dark he would come and warm you, hold you, show you you were not alone...' Her voice hardened. 'How could any man match up to that?'

Lizza was not sure of what she was hearing. The hot whisky was confusing her. 'No one? Not Krystof?' she said, trying to get on to safer ground.

'Not Krystof... No. Not even Krystof.' Min, her speech slowing down, relaxed against the pillow. 'One part of the way it was with my father, Lizza, with Captain Charles Hugo Roebuck, was the sheer focus on me, the unquestioning adoration. Maybe I do love Krystof a bit, but for him I am just interesting, a *jollee girl* as he calls me. He loves someone else,' she said authoritatively. Lizza could feel her wriggle. 'I thought it was his wife, but...'

365

'His wife?'

Min drained her cup, thrust it at Lizza and shuffled down in the bed. Lizza put the cups on the side table, shuffled down facing the edge of the bed and keeping herself clear of Min. She settled down to try to sleep, wondering why she had not thought about Krystof being married before.

She could feel Min wriggle over and put her head on her shoulder, an arm round her waist, tucking herself into Lizza as though they were a pair of apostrophes. Lizza relaxed. This was how she and Beatrice had slept many years ago in the tight confines of the house at Bracks Hill.

Inside her, the baby started the late-night acrobatics which were his custom when she stretched out to sleep.

'What's that? Is that the baby?' Min's half-curled fist shot away from Lizza's stomach.

'He's always restless at this time of night.'

'Ugh.'

'It's wonderful. A living being, with so much dying... Oh, I'm sorry, Min.'

The tentative hand came back on her stomach. 'No, you're right. It's wonderful.'

The baby did another somersault.

'There, he's performing for me, Lizza. It's a sign. You must call him Charles Hugo. For my father.'

'Min, I...'

'Promise!' The voice in her ear was steely now.

'All right, Min. If it'll make you feel better.'

Min relaxed, snuggling her face into Lizza's

366

back and drifting off in a whisky-aided sleep.

Even though Lizza was happy enough at the comradeship of this sleeping arrangement, she stayed awake. Her mind, moving away from the problem of Min, allowed itself to return to the point earlier in the evening where Josie had stood at the top of the stairs and asked if 'it' were a bomb; just as Rebecca had stood, bright-eyed and very much alive, asking the same question, the night Lizza smashed the ornaments, after Theo Callaghan had tried to rape her. Rebecca, whom Bessie could see tugging at Lizza's skirts, her little sisters beside her.

Alice Bremner was arranging three newspaper clippings, a piece of paper and a card on the scrubbed kitchen table. One was a cutting from 1918 headlined 'BRACKS HILL HERO' describing Tom's heroism on the day he died. The other cutting was from a June's *Echo:* a list of names of those missing, believed killed, at Dunkirk. Near the bottom of the list, marked with a pencil, was the name of John Bremner. Alongside that she placed a card with a German stamp. On it, scribbled in pencil, were the words, *'Dear Ma, just to say I'm alive and taken prisoner. Do not worry about me. I am well. Love Jonnie.'* That was all.

Alongside that she put a short note from Alex. *'Just to say I have arrived back safely, Gram. More training tomorrow. Lads liked your cherry cake. Keep your chin up. Love Alex.'*

She raised her eyes to the photo on the wall.

'That's it, isn't it, Tom. Lad's lives on bits of paper and cardboard. All of you gone now...'

The sneck on the kitchen door clicked and she didn't have time to move the papers before Lizza was there in the room peering over her shoulder. 'You've heard from Jonnie, Ma! Wonderful.' She put her hand on a shoulder which was wrenched away. She sat down beside her mother. 'What's the matter, Ma. Was there other news?'

Alice shrugged. 'There's nothing. Bits of paper. They're all dead.' She pulled them together in one hand and flung them into the back of the fire. The dry newspaper flared up instantly but the card took longer to burn and Lizza managed to retrieve it with the long black fire tongs.

She blew on it to cool the charred edges, then said sharply. 'You'd no right to do that. That's news of our brother and Beatrice's son.'

'They're mine...'

'Ma. You're never happy unless you're at the centre, unless you own everybody around you.' She looked up at the picture on the wall. 'Even me da you keep here with your constant talk. You won't even let him go after all these years.'

Her mother stared hard at her hands, closed into fists on the table. Lizza looked at her and her resolve crumbled. 'I'm sorry, Ma, but you shouldn't have burned them. Our Bea and Renee, our Bernard, they...'

Her mother interrupted her. 'You were never biddable like the others, Lizza. Short of a good hiding, they said round here, and they were

right. You've no right to come round here
undoing what I've done. No right to come
round here 'ticing our Beatrice away from her
own home, making my lad mad to join up...'

Then Lizza was shaking her mother by the
shoulders. 'You never never listen to anyone
else, see anyone else's point of view. Never-
never-never.' Then the shoulders seemed very
fragile under her hands and she stood away
from her mother, shaking. 'I came to tell you
our Beatrice is all right, if you were interested.
She has a job at the factory and seems all right.
And I came to get news of Alex and Jonnie to
take back to her. Well, I've got that, though it's
a bit charred round the edges. So I'll go.'

As she walked along the back lane a woman
at one of the back gates nodded at her. 'Is it
trouble, pet?'

Lizza took out her hankie and blotted the
wash of tears from her face. She shook her head.
'Ma has news that our Jonnie's been captured.
Not dead like they thought.'

'Well, pet, that's something,' said the woman.
'That's something.'

CHAPTER 24

At first only the dinner-time breaks made
Beatrice's hard-working life bearable at the
factory. Between twelve and one, outside a bit
when the sun was shining, or in the leaky cold

369

canteen when it was wet and cold, there was fun to be had. The meals were good, reflecting the recognition of the crucial work the girls were doing; they were better than some girls got at home, and were eaten with relish. After eating, cluster by cluster, the women would retreat into their own pastimes.

Some groups of women sat knitting, knee to knee, their tongues clattering a hundred to the dozen in tune with the needles. Beatrice had her back to such a group on her first lunch-time and her ears burned at the openness, the frankness with which the women turned from topics like what was on at the pictures and managing on the ration and making anything at all of Christmas this year, to frank stories of their youthful pursuit of men. 'I chased him till he caught me!' was one phrase which generated appreciative laughter.

One day there were fierce arguments about contraception and—amazing to Beatrice—the options available to a woman, the most radical of which was some kind of purgative in *his* night-time tea. One woman was teased unmercifully because she was so loyal to her soldier husband that she wouldn't go to the dances at the Gaunt Valley Hotel and Killock Camp, or even down to Darlington for a drink.

'Me mother'd kill us,' she said in final defence.

'Still tethered to yer mammy like a little maa-lamb,' hooted her friend, a tall woman whose massy hair, dyed deep orange like that of many of the girls who worked with explosives, was continually tumbling from her turban, a tendency which earned her reprimands from the assiduous white-coats worried about lice as well as general safety. 'What you need is a bliddy good night out.'

That day some of the younger girls were dancing in pairs to a wind-up gramophone in a corner, trying out a new foxtrot. Beatrice watched, as Josie was swept around the cleared corner space with some style, in the arms of Mary Osgood.

Esme came up to her. 'What about you, Beatrice?'

She shook her head. 'I wouldn't know how, pet.'

'Hawa-y man, have a go. Young Josie never had an idea at first. It's easy. You just follow the sound. Hawa-ay. Yeh let Josie cut yer hair. Now let me teach yer the foxtrot.' She pulled Beatrice from her chair. 'Haway. I'll take man. Show yer how.'

After two steps, Beatrice, nearly twice as tall as her partner, stepped on Esme's toes and nearly bowled her over. Then, as the rhythms in the music lodged themselves into her mind, her feet started to accommodate the repeated movements and she was away, allowing Esme's small firm hand to steer her, in sweeping arcs, around the cleared space. By the time the record came to a stop they were the only ones dancing and, as Esme finished with a flourishing bow, the crowd of girls gave them a round of applause.

Josie came close to Beatrice and grinned

at her. 'Now that's something to tell Mrs King about, ain't it, Beatrice?' She turned to Esme. 'Mrs King, Beatrice's sister, she's a lovely dancer. Used to dance all the time with Mr King in Coventry. They won cups.'

The next morning Josie and Esme, both very nimble-fingered, were sent over to work in the shop where the explosives were handled, and Beatrice was left to work with Mary, who was less chatty than Esme, but still a good companion. Within a week, the work seemed more congenial, and Beatrice began to look forward every day to work. Thoughts of her mother crossed her mind several times a day but she pushed the thought aside and got on with her new routines as doggedly as she had got on with those in the Bracks Hill house in the days after Alex had been born.

Alex Bremner was aware of the fact that he had to learn how to drink beer without disclosing that he was a newcomer to the craft. He had signed the pledge when he was ten, with a dozen other children, at a Chapel mission meeting, and had not yet had any reason to break the pledge.

But in this company, with the lads from the hut, that shallow commitment fizzled like a damp squib. The last thing he wanted was to mark himself out as even more different from the others. On their first night out, he copied the nonchalant way Jack Stubbs ordered the beer in the Green Tree, a pub frequented by each new cycle of trainees and avoided by

372

the instructors. He noted that after two beers Jack became more loquacious and confiding, even sentimental, and he decided he would not descend into banality at the same speed. He soon learned that the decision was not in his hands; his own judgement fled after the second beer, too. At this point he felt wise and lordly, not just in charge of his own world but of the world around him. He felt quite confident that he could hold his beer like any man. But this confidence put him one pint ahead of Jack, then two pints ahead. So it was Jack who ended up carrying Alex back to the camp piggyback fashion.

As Jack tipped him on to the bed Alex mumbled, 'Sorry old lad, not used to it. No beer before... Never drank...signed the pledge.'

Jack pulled off his boots. 'Ha! What? An alcoholic virgin! And a virgin in another way, shouldn't wonder.'

'No, no,' protested Alex. 'Josie'n me... wonderful...Josie...do you know she used to do handstands an' swear...' He passed out.

Jack heaved him out of his battledress, pulled off his trousers and threw a blanket over him before he sat down heavily on his own bed. 'What you need most, friend, is a bloody good night's sleep.' And he fell back himself, fully clothed, and started snoring.

The next day, after he had ejaculated the total contents of his stomach into the toilet, Alex went up in a training craft with his instructor, who proceeded to show him how to do a slow roll. Then, as the plane started to tip, he felt himself thrown dangerously free in the cockpit, at which point he thought he would be thrown from the aircraft and smash to the ground in a second. In that second, as he was bounced painfully round his cockpit space, he saw his grandmother wringing her hands, Beatrice raising her eyebrows in gentle sarcasm and Josie grinning at him. In that moment also he wondered again about the rose window, which he and Josie had looted from the house called Beaconsfield. How he wished it was still there and not smashed to smithereens. Then he could hear his instructor, who was yelling at him, and he could feel the hard pull at the steering column. At last they were right way up and he was back in the seat.

The voice hollered down the tube. 'Bremner! Of all the idiots. You forgot to do up your ruddy straps!'

As they circled before landing, Alex wondered what kind of rocket he would get from his fierce instructor when they were on terra firma. He climbed out first, then stood fingering his helmet waiting for him to climb down. The thin, weathered face of his instructor loomed too close to him, then split into a sly nicotine-stained grin. 'I can't see you forgetting your straps again, Bremner, not in a million years. Can you?'

And no more was said. Alex didn't even tell Jack Stubbs. But, hung over or not, he never forgot his straps again.

At the tea-table, the last Friday before Christmas, Josie mentioned the dancing, and how wonderful a dancer Beatrice was.

Lizza looked up in surprise. 'Didn't know you could dance, Bea.'

Beatrice shrugged. 'Neither did I.'

'Wasn't I telling her how you and Mr King used to go to the dance in Coventry? Danced to big bands, not just the gramophone.'

Lizza munched on the last piece of what was, unknown to her, black-market ham. 'Mmm. Every Saturday until the work stepped up at the factory.'

'Was Roland a good dancer?' asked Min with interest.

'He *is* a good dancer,' corrected Lizza. 'Doesn't get much chance to, nowadays. Treading water on that loch. But he used to love it.'

Bessie, standing pouring Krystof's tea, said, 'I like a bit dance meself.' She cackled as heads shot up in surprise. 'There, that's got yer!'

'Did you go dancing, Miss Bessie?' asked Krystof, who would never call her just by her Christian name.

'No, I didn't *go* dancing. I *stayed* dancing. Here. Old Barraclough used to love the waltz. An' when he got too old for all that silly courtin' in the town, he teached me how to waltz, an' we danced here oursel's. When 'is legs got bad, ah used to dance fer 'im on me own.' She grinned into Lizza's wide eyes. 'Well, hinney, there wus a lot of long winters, a lot of long winter evenings, in the end. The records are still there, in the left-hand cupboard in the dresser in the sittin' room.' She looked at Krystof. 'An'

375

the windy-up gramophone's up where you are somewhere. In the attic.'

Min clapped her hands. 'Bessie. That's a wonderful idea. Krystof, go and get it. Bessie, would you like to dance tonight?'

'I dinna see why not. Mind, I don't wanter miss the news.'

Lizza and Beatrice washed up, while Josie let Liam help her roll back Bessie's precious carpet in the sitting room. Krystof went in search of the gramophone and Min read out the titles of the records to Bessie.

First, Beatrice danced an exhibition dance with Josie, to loud applause, making Beatrice, hair wild and springing from her snood, her face pink with the effort, look almost pretty. Then they all danced: Lizza and Beatrice, Min and Krystof, and Josie with Liam, while Bessie looked on tapping her cane. Min changed the record and Krystof took Bessie's cane from her, clicked his heels and insisted she danced with him. He handled her as though she were made of china and she danced like a woman half her age.

Min joined in, dancing with Beatrice, and Josie whirled around with Liam on her hip, leaving Lizza on the sidelines, smiling from one to the other. The music was still beating on when Bessie stopped. 'Hey, lad, I've no puff left. Yeh'll have ter sit us down.'

He returned her stick to her and sat her in the small chair in the bay window. He turned round and bowed in a courtly fashion to Lizza. 'And Mrs King. Will you permit?'

She moved stiffly, unwillingly, into his arms and he set off around the room. Despite her ungainly size she moved easily to the remembered rhythm, and finally relaxed with his arm around her, his warm dry hand grasping hers, his face so close to hers that she could see the fine lines running down his cheek, the flaring curve of his mouth.

The others stopped to watch them as they whirled round.

The music swam out of her mind and thoughts swam in, unbidden. His arm: his arm had last been around her in that tomb which had once been her dear house; when hell was hammering at its door; when Rebecca, though she did not know it, had just died. Still only weeks ago and the world had been whirling just as the room did in this dance.

The music stopped and they stood looking at each other for a second, his eyes boring hard into hers, and her mouth straining, and failing, to form some kind of thank you. The others put their hands together in a patter of applause and she looked around blushing and nodding. 'I'm so tired,' she said. Then she fled.

She walked very steadily upstairs, undressed with deliberate care, lay on the coverlet and closed her eyes, the despair running through her, her body aching, aching for Rebecca. After a few minutes a small fat hand touched her face. She stayed very still, her eyes closed. Bessie was right about Rebecca being there. She was a wise old bird.

The hand stroked her tearless cheek. 'Lizza

sad,' a little voice growled. Her eyes flew open to meet the round, anxious eyes of Liam Callaghan who was straining up to reach her on the high bed. He put his head on one side. 'Liam sad.'

She reached down, pulled him up and held him to her. Then, her tears did start to flow as she used the hem of her nightie to wipe his away.

Half an hour later, they were still curled together asleep when Josie and Beatrice came in search of Liam. 'Come on, Liam,' said Josie crossly, pulling him up and plonking his sleeping head on her shoulder. 'Don't you be bothering Mrs King when she's poorly.'

'Oh, he's no bother, Josie.' She smiled drowsily. 'He's no bother at all.'

Beatrice rolled her over and tucked her under the covers. She lay back, her eyes closed. She heard the door click as they left the room. Then, above the ticking of the round bedroom clock, she could hear the creak of floorboards and the murmur of voices from the attic above her as Krystof and Min had their customary evening cocoa together.

Well, that was what Min claimed it was, and conversation about art. The whole household knew about this and the whole household accepted the cocoa explanation. But Lizza knew that Bessie knew what was really happening: she was probably no stranger to creaking floorboards or creaking beds.

She rolled over and, despite herself, started thinking too intensely about making love with Roland when she was this pregnant with the twins. What fun it had been. How different things were then. Now she was aching, aching for that again, so she stroked her hands over her belly and down her thighs to relieve her ache. But the face before her as she kneaded away was that of the man she had danced with in Bessie's sitting room, not that of her husband so many hundreds of miles away.

When Min came in an hour later, she was sitting up wide awake, writing in the big ledger.

'I'm sorry, Lizza, did I wake you?' Her concern was genuine. Her hair was up in spikes and there was no make-up left on her face.

'No. I've been asleep, then awake. It gets uncomfortable.'

'What are you writing?'

'A kind of story about what Bessie's life must have been like, in this house, all those years.'

'Mmm.' With practised hand, Min was undoing her back suspenders. 'Did you hear that bit about dancing? They must have had quite a time, those two, behind these closed doors.'

Over the book, Lizza watched as Min stripped to the skin in her uninhibited fashion and slipped a very plain bias-cut silk nightie over her head. 'Your clothes, Min! How you dress like that on coupons, I don't know.'

Min ran her hands down the silk and turned to and fro to catch the effect of the lamplight on the silk. She laughed. 'This? Out of the coffers, like much of the stuff I wear. The loony mother had it made from Chinese silk in 1920. Never wore it. I took off all the frills and lowered the

379

neck. Pa likes...liked it.' She folded her lip but did not cry.

'It's beautiful, Min,' said Lizza simply.

Min sat beside her on the bed and put a hand on hers. 'You looked beautiful yourself there tonight, Lizz, whirling around the floor...'

'Like a great elephant,' said Lizza.

'No. No. Like some graceful ship just tipping the top of the waves.' She picked up the hand she was holding and kissed it. 'I said so to Krystof and he agreed, then said some Polish word which, when I beat him, he translated as feather on the foam. I think he was making it up. We spend half our time talking about you,' she added gloomily.

'Don't be silly,' said Lizza, picking up her book.

'We do.' She knelt up and put her hands on Lizza's shoulders. 'In fact I got so mad at him I told him he could send you a kiss. This one.' She put her soft mouth to Lizza's and pressed it hard. 'And then there were the others.' She kissed Lizza's brow and both cheeks and her lips slipped to her throat.

Lizza pushed her away. 'Stop fooling, Min, and get to sleep. I want to finish this paragraph.'

She dipped her fiery face closer to the book and Min slipped down in the bed beside her. It was ten minutes before she got up to turn down the lamp. She swung back into bed and snuggled down pulling the quilt under her chin. As Min tucked herself in behind her in all her usual position she whispered, 'Not fooling, Lizza, dear. Not at all.'

Roland was sitting at the kitchen table in the house on the loch, writing to Lizza, saying how, much as he would love to, he would just not manage to get home for the holiday. He could truly write that the work was now getting under way and that they had Ministry wallahs coming just after Christmas to inspect the progress.

Pieter, at the opposite side of the table reading the paper, looked up at him, beaming. 'Here it is, what we heard on the wireless. There is news here, Roland. Good news. Our navy, the Dutch Navy, is escaped to Hull. They brought it over, lock stock and barrel.' He bent closer ' "*Cruisers, destroyers, torpedo boats, minesweepers and submarines. And also passenger vessels, cargo ships, pilot cutters and trawlers*"—the lot, Roland. And here read this. "*One cargo boat brought across fifteen hundred German prisoners. When the Luftwaffe flew over, the captain opened up the hatches, but gave a Jew a machine-gun to forestall escape attempts.*" Well, now. Can you think of that, Roland?'

Roland grinned across at him. 'Wonderful. Hull overrun by Dutchmen. Think of the clatter of all those clogs. You should go and see them. There'll be someone you know...'

Pieter shook his head slowly. 'No, I have doubts about that. Great doubts. But to hear my own language spoken, to make a Christmas toast to my own country...' His voice lightened. 'There might be news, word-of-mouth...'

'Go,' urged Roland. 'Take your Christmas leave. I'll hold the fort here.'

381

'But your wife...'

'She is there safe with her family.' He hesitated. 'I...I'm saving leave for when she has the baby in March.'

Pieter put his pipe in his mouth and lit it. 'Yes. I think I must. I might come across something...'

Roland could not resist exchanging glances with Mara Laine, sitting opposite him at the same table. Her head was dipped now over her notebook, the tip of her tongue just showing, labelling her completed autumn drawings in fancy Gothic lettering.

Lizza changed her shopping from one arm to the other, and transferred Liam to the opposite side. She had insisted on doing the Saturday shopping for Bessie, who was busy making mince pies with her friend May Lynn. Lizza had let Liam come with her for this first trip; for the second, which involved more queuing, she would have to leave Liam in Bessie's care, or with Min. She smiled at that thought. She had left Min yawning like a languorous cat, muttering about the wonder of Saturdays when one could have a lie-in.

Liam squealed suddenly as he was snatched from her grasp up into the arms of a man in uniform. It took her a second to recognise Theo Callaghan in his army uniform. 'Well, Mrs King, I can see you're taking good care of Liam here. He's as fat as butter, clean as ice.'

'Mr Callaghan!' she said, still keeping up her pace. 'You found us.'

'Well, yes, Mrs King. I did appreciate your somewhat belated effort to let me know the sad news. I was so put about to hear about my dear wife and child, and so glad to see you'd took on the others. I was cast down by the news about Maeve, truly.' From the tone of his voice, he might have been talking about a dead rabbit. 'Kindness itself, as I said to my sergeant, Mrs King, is kindness itself. So accommodating. And he insisted, insisted that I take leave to check on the safety of my dear children.' He lifted the whimpering Liam up on his shoulders and jiggled him as he walked.

She kept him at the gate of Campion House. 'Well, Liam is well, as you see.'

He examined the big house carefully. 'Good billet you've got here,' he said. 'Josie here with you, too?'

'Yes,' she said. 'But she's at work. Weekend overtime. At the armaments factory.'

'Ah,' he said. 'Doing her bit is she?'

'She seems to enjoy it.'

He lifted the handle of the gate. 'I'll just come in and wait.'

She stepped in front of him. 'No. It's the house of a very old lady and she wouldn't be happy.'

For a second he pushed against her, then he relaxed. 'That's all right, Mrs King. I'll seek Josie at her work. She can find me somewhere to lay my weary head. She knows which side her bread's buttered on.' He started to walk away, with Liam still on his shoulders. Liam twisted around and started to shriek for Lizza.

Lizza ran and held on to Theo's arm. 'Leave the boy, Mr Callaghan. Leave the boy.'

He looked down at the hand as though it were a snake, then laughed. He put his arms up and lifted the boy from his shoulders and thrust him into her arms. 'There now, Liam, go to your auntie.' He slapped the boy sharply on the cheek, saying, 'Now you behave yourself or it's a good hiding you'll get from me.'

The boy roared and Lizza clutched him to her. 'Leave him, leave us alone,' she said fiercely. 'There's nothing for you here.'

He saluted her in a mock military salute. 'Oh yes there is, Mrs Lizza King. Oh yes there is! You just wait and see.'

CHAPTER 25

It was Josie and Esme's custom to talk all through the day at their workbench. That Saturday, they had discussed in detail, yet again, exactly what it was like in the big Blitz in Coventry; then, how Tyneside was a prime target because of the ships. 'You can see the big lights they throw up against the German planes. Right from our back door,' said Esme. 'Twenty-odd miles it is.'

'It was straight overhead for us, they shot at us from their planes,' said Josie, winning that point as usual.

Ignoring her, Esme then swept on, in her

seamless fashion, to the subject of the bloody Germans going into Russia and how her uncle had gone to Russia in the thirties on a fraternal visit to their miners. Then she moved to the problems of stockings in the winter when a bit of gravy browning and black pencil wouldn't do. Purple legs didn't go with gravy browning. Good thing slacks were all the fashion. Then the tale about her cousin (son to the man who had been to Moscow), who was fighting in the desert, and the woman in her street who was fined for showing a light although it was widely known that it was an issue of grudge between her and the warden who had a fancy for her, and was also the cousin of her husband who was also fighting in the desert. 'She wouldn't allow him across her threshold. She kneed him where it most hurt the one time he tried.'

Then there were the Greeks and them being such good fighters because they had fought in the old times. 'When I was in St Bennet's we did this book on the Trojan Wars. They was fighting then, too. Do you know that feller, like?' Her fingers still busy with the delicate job of loading the bullets with the help of tweezers, she nodded at Krystof, who was propped up at the end of the line, drawing on a large block which he held at an angle against his hip.

Josie nodded. 'He lodges in the same house. He's Polish. Walked here from Poland.'

'What? Walking on water? Who does he bloody think he is? Jesus?'

'Shut up, Esme. You know what I mean.'

'What's his name?'

'Krystof.' Josie stopped working, wriggled her shoulders and shook her hands. 'Blimey, I think I'll seize up in a minute.'

'Gerron, Josie,' instructed Esme. 'We've got this tally to keep up. You'll have the white-coat on to us any second. Hey, you! Krystof!' She called across. 'Who was it give you permission to draw us, like?'

He smiled back and kept drawing.

'Hey! Give us a look,' she persisted.

Krystof stood up straight, came across and turned his board towards them. They saw themselves there at their bench, their fingers moving in a blur over their task. Esme's mouth was open and Josie's head was cocked to listen to her, the sweep of her hair in its roll making a halo around a face which was fuller now, since she had been in Priorton.

'Y'bugger,' said Esme, her fingers still busy. 'We could be lookin' in the mirror. Ye're bliddy clever, I'll give yer that.'

He tucked his drawing board under his arm, clicked his heels and bowed. 'Thank you, miss,' he said, smiling slightly. Mrs Montague, a small woman replete with the power of recently acquired white-coat status, her red beret perched jauntily on her head, was striding determinedly towards them. 'You are very good subjects, miss,' said Krystof. 'Now I must go elsewhere before the schoolmistress reprimands me.'

'Reprimands.' Esme rolled the word round her tongue. 'Bliddy *reprimands*!'

By the time Mrs Montague got to them, they had their heads down over their tasks, mouths stiff with repressed giggles. They felt, rather than watched, her leave them. Esme said, 'He's a clever feller, that Pole. All right too, even though he's old.'

'What do you mean, all right?'

'I mean, why, not good-looking, but...well, a bit like Leslie Howard, except for that darker hair. Kind of film-starrish. You know.'

'Sure you've some funny ideas, Esme. He's an old man. Mind you...'

Esme's head went up, her fingers still for once. 'Mind you, what?'

'There's a woman who lodges with us, a schoolteacher who...'

The tit-bit was forestalled by Mrs Montague calling to them in her loud chirrup from ten yards away to shut their clatter and get on with the job. Didn't they know there was a war on?

Later, Josie turned down Esme's offer of a night out at the Killock dance and waited just inside the factory gates for Beatrice. She liked going home with Beatrice: sitting on the train with her, linking her arm on the final walk home, in the women's way she had recently learned. Beatrice was quiet and listened with grave respect to Josie's views on the world in general and factory life in particular.

As the last people got out of their carriage and the train chugged the short distance down to Priorton, she turned to Beatrice. 'Can I ask you a question, Bea?'

Bea was stretching her weary legs before her. 'Yes, pet. Anything.'

'And will you cross your heart and tell nobody?'

Beatrice smiled, and crossed her heart over her old grey coat.

'You know your monthlies?'

Beatrice had heard much coded talk about the vagaries of the menstrual cycle in the factory canteen, but still she blushed. 'Yes, pet,' she said bravely.

'Can you run over, can it be more than a month?'

'I don't know really, pet. I've never heard *talk* of it at all, till I started at the factory. I've gone longer meself sometimes. When I had Alex, of course. And then again when I was poorly once with measles. And just when there was a lot of bother in the house when our Jonnie went off and was hurt at Dunkirk. Why?'

'I just realised this morning, the last time I had it, the blood, was well before the big Blitz, maybe two months ago now. I remember standing on my hands, then, and talking to little Rebecca who was killed. So I must be maybe three, four weeks over.'

Beatrice chilled, remembering the weeks when she had been three, then four, then five, then six weeks over, her mother keeping as careful count as she did. Menstruation was neither mentioned nor visible in the crowded house, after the first basic provision by her mother of snowy strips of cloth which were washed and dried overnight like shameful ghosts. So only her mother had known that the monthly rituals had not been performed and only the pair of them knew that

388

Beatrice was pregnant as a result of the attack, which was also never mentioned. The creeping fear in her soul could not be shared.

She had no notion, then, about how she could have got out of this dilemma. She had learned of that possibility after Alex was born, from a sneering woman who had mocked her predicament. 'Ye dinnet know there's ways to stop it?...'

Pulling herself back to the present, she asked Josie, 'Could there be a reason?'

'A reason?' Josie frowned.

'A woman stops getting her monthlies when... when she's going to have a baby, but that wouldn't apply as you're not...you've never...'

She paused, seeing the bright red flush on Josie's cheeks. 'What is it, Josie? No, not you. Could it be that?'

Josie looked at her, wide-eyed with this new terror, and Beatrice found herself looking again at the plumper, rounded, more grown-up girl, no longer a child.

'It is possible, isn't it, Josie?'

Josie's eyes were on the wooden floor of the compartment. She nodded.

'Was it...did someone attack you?'

Josie shook her head then lifted her gaze to Beatrice. 'I wanted it. I liked it,' she said simply.

Then it dawned on Beatrice. 'Alex. It was Alex.'

Josie looked at her.

Beatrice put her fingers over her eyes, then through them looked at Josie. 'That was how

389

he...I had him like this. You knew that?' Her voice hard.

Josie nodded, her face now white with strain. 'But it was not like this, not at all.' Beatrice relented, her voice softer now. 'You wanted to do it, Josie, you said. I was forced by a man I'd not seen two minutes before and've never seen since. A cruel man, now dead thank the merciful Lord.'

The train was grinding to a halt now, and it was a relief to busy themselves getting off at their stop. Josie, back straight, marched on ahead and Beatrice had to run to catch up with her.

She linked the girl's arm and slowed her down. 'Now, Josie, let's think about it. Do you love him?'

Josie shrugged. 'I don't know. We were just playing games together. It was fun. An' it wasn't like my mammy an' daddy, cause he just did it to her and mostly beat her, so she didn't love him. An' not like Mr and Mrs King who could be, well, quite soppy sometimes when we first knew them. Early days. You know? Not like recently. So I don't know about me an' Alex. We were just playing games.' It was the plaintive cry of a child. 'An he's forgot me, now he's up in those planes, so it's no good. An' I can hardly remember what he looks like, sometimes.'

Beatrice stopped and pulled her round to face her. 'Do you want to have a baby, Josie?'

'No-o,' she wailed.

Beatrice walked on. 'There's this woman. You can get something to make it...to make it go

390

away. Would you like that?'

'I don't want any baby,' Josie repeated dully. 'Yes, yes, Bea. Anything.'

'Well then, that's it. We'll do that. I'll go through to Bracks Hill after tea. And get it for you. Don't you worry.' She was decisive, certain of what must be done.

Josie hugged Bea's arm to her. 'Thanks, Bea.'

'No one...should have to endure it, Josie, I know.'

It was when they were five hundred yards from Campion House that she noticed the man. She caught him with the corner of her eye as she crossed the road. Then, glancing back, she noted he crossed the road, too. 'There's a soldier following us, Josie. Keep walking.'

Josie glanced back, then stopped, pulling Beatrice to a halt. 'It's me daddy,' she said.

To Beatrice's surprise there was no delight in her voice, no effusive greeting.

The man drew nearer. His uniform was rumpled, as though he had slept in it, and there was a bristly shadow on his face. He smiled. 'Josie, it is you. I was watching for me little girl at the station and what have we here? A young woman no less.' He took her by the shoulders and she squirmed away from his lips. He looked across at Beatrice. 'And is this your friend?'

'Daddy, this is Beatrice. She's Mrs King's sister.'

He kept tight hold of Josie's upper arm. 'Mrs King? I hope you have a softer heart than your sister, missis. Now there's a hard woman. You just ask her for a night's billet and she shuts the door in your face. Not a jot of pity for a poor feller who's lost his wife and daughter, not a jot.'

'She's not like that, Daddy. She helped me and Liam, helps everybody.'

'Above herself.' He was talking through gritted teeth. 'Thinks she's the bee's knees.'

Josie was wriggling hard to get away from him. 'Daddy! Leave go!'

Beatrice stepped up and wrenched his hand away to free Josie. He grabbed Beatrice's shoulders and brought her close to him. She could smell beer on his breath, see the hair in his nostrils. 'Don't you dream of stepping between a man and his daughter, missis.'

She looked at him as calmly as she could. 'You were hurting the child.' Through the corner of her eye she could see Josie backing away.

He chortled and dropped his hands. 'Child? Have you seen her? Changed from child to woman in a month. Well, maybe she's woman enough to look after her daddy.'

Josie started to run and he set off after her, bringing her down easily in a rugby tackle. She shrieked as she hit the ground and Beatrice was again clawing at him to get him away. He turned to face her; this time his face had lost its jocular sneer and was full of hatred. 'Get off us, you bloody...woman.'

They fought silently, and he tripped her, and she was on the ground and he was kicking her. Josie hauled herself to her feet and pulled him away from Beatrice. A phrase of Esme's was throbbing in her head. About kneeing the man where it counts. She brought her knee up hard between her father's legs. He screamed, dropping his hands away from her as he doubled up on the ground.

Josie helped Beatrice to her feet. 'Run, run!' she said urgently, and, holding hands, they ran the last hundred yards to Campion House.

Lizza heard their story and ran out into the darkening street, but there was no sign of Theo Callaghan or anyone else.

Lizza dressed Josie's scraped and scratched face and left her in the kitchen with a very angry Bessie. Upstairs she found Beatrice changing out of her muddy work clothes and examining her bruised ribs.

'He's a bad man,' said Lizza. As she watched, Beatrice climbed into her one better blouse and skirt. 'What's this? Where are you going?'

'I'm going to Bracks Hill.'

Lizza frowned. 'To see Ma? If so, I'll come with you. I want to talk to her about Christmas Day. She can't be on her own then.'

'No. Not to see her. Come if you like but I'm going to see someone else... You'll have to know, being her guardian, like...' She sighed, and reluctantly shared Josie's secret with Lizza.

Lizza sat very quiet, taking it in. 'You're sure she wants it? That?'

'Lizza! She's fifteen. Alex'll be goodness knows where soon, please God still alive but hopeless, selfish, ambitious.'

'It might not work. I knew nurses who tried it and just got a belly-ache for their pains.'

'She wants to end it, Lizz.'

'I'm coming with you then. I'll ask this woman questions.'

Beatrice looked pointedly at Lizza's heavily pregnant condition. 'You'll give her the willies; she'll think you want it, in your advanced state.'

'I'll come with you anyway and see Ma,' said Lizza stubbornly. 'Don't think you can stop me.'

'Suit yourself.' Beatrice looked into the ornate little mirror which hung above her fireplace and combed her hair, wondering if her mother would recognise her; if the changes inside showed on the outside as much as she thought they did. 'It's time I went to see her meself. But not a word to her about our errand. She'll have us in hellfire before she'd let us do something like that.'

Listening to the almost complacent tone of satisfaction in her sister's voice, Lizza suddenly thought that, of all of them, Beatrice was probably the most changed by this war.

CHAPTER 26

Min had had a good Saturday. She got up late and had a bath in the afternoon, after persuading Bessie that people didn't catch pneumonia from bathing before sunset. She fastened her Chinese kimono modestly, combed sugar-water through her hair and put it in curlers. Then she went downstairs and knelt, ducking her head towards the sitting-room fire while it dried. Liam wandered in and stood beside her, his thumb in his mouth.

She smiled. 'Hello, Liam.'

His eyes stared hard at her. 'Saying prayers,' he said.

She laughed and got to her feet. 'Would you like a story?'

He nodded. She climbed up on a stool to reach a high shelf where she had spotted some battered children's books. She selected *Fairy Tales of the Brothers Grimm* and settled down in a chair to read it to him. ' "A great King had a daughter who was very beautiful, but so proud and haughty and conceited that none of the princes who came to ask for her in marriage were good enough for her, and she only made sport of them"...what is it, Liam?'

He was tugging at her heavy sleeve. 'King George?' he said.

'No, this one's called King Grisly Beard.'

'Your daddy?'

She fingered the silk collar of her gown. 'No, but my daddy has a beard, Liam. Dark and very curly, all round here.' She pinched the side of his soft cheek. 'He had one. He's not here now.'

A frown creased Liam's smooth brow. 'My daddy came. Not here now.'

'No, it's not the same...' She picked up the book. 'Do you want to hear the rest?'

He climbed under her arm now, on to her knee, and settled down to hear the rest of the story. When she was finished she took him into the kitchen and sat him beside Bessie, who was sitting on a chair at the table, peeling carrots into an enamel bowl.

Assailed by passing unfamiliar guilt, Min asked if she could help.

'No, hinney, you get yourself a bit of a lie down. Can't be gettin' much sleep these days.' Bessie's tone was casual, but the corner of her mouth trembled with a smile. 'I'll watch the bairn till his sister comes.' She took Liam on to her knee and gave him a peeled carrot. 'Or Mrs King.'

Min leaned against the doorpost. 'I have to say, Bessie, you're a woman of the world.'

Bessie grinned. 'When yer old yer see there's but one life of this kind put on yer. An' two folks givin' comfort an' no harm to anyone else don't seem so bad. But I'll tell yer sommat, lass. The feller, nice as he is, is not for you nor none of his kind.'

Min frowned, disappointed. 'You mean foreign, Polish?'

'No. None of that. What yer tek us for?' Then she turned her attention to Liam and it was as though Min wasn't there.

Back up in her bedroom Min brushed out her hair till it crackled and stood out from her face in a frizzy halo. Then she very carefully marked her plucked eyebrows and drew a single smudged line under her eyes with a soft lead pencil and put on her reddest lipstick. Then,

396

very quietly, she made her way up the steep back stairs to the attic where Krystof lived and painted.

The glow from the skylight allowed her to move through the roof-space without kicking anything over. The long room was furnished with an odd collection of furniture: the three-quarter iron bed, which, as she knew well, creaked like mad; the curlicued hall stand for his clothes; a chair pulled up to a small table on which stood one of the three oil lamps (the gas supply did not reach up here); the other two lamps were placed strategically on a long table with jars and brushes, and careful stacks of completed drawings, unused drawing paper and newspaper; then there were the two table-easels constructed cunningly from reversed kitchen chairs.

She lit the lamps and started to go through the sheaf of completed drawings. They were mostly of people in the house, the finest being a series of studies of Bessie in her various moods, bringing out her ancient quality, her gipsy demeanour. The last arresting image was the same face, the same character but fifty or sixty years younger, with abundant hair and a high-necked Victorian blouse.

Min shuddered and turned to the next sheet. These were more expected studies of the women at the factory, very modern turbaned figures in clusters and groups. There was one of the shoals of women streaming towards the railway station on their way home from work. She recognised drawings of Beatrice and Josie. There were no images of machinery or production lines: all such drawings stayed at work.

'And has the teacher marked the work out of ten?' a quiet voice said behind her.

She whirled round. 'Krystof, sorry, I came up here because I thought I heard you...'

He looked at his heavy watch. 'Mm. I got an early train. There was nothing to finish and the manager said I should come away.' He smiled slightly. 'He is uncomfortable. Does not know what to make of me.' He walked across and returned the drawings to their neat piles while she stood there like a naughty schoolgirl. 'Now if you will excuse me I have to change my clothes.'

As she moved beside him he took her by the shoulders and kissed her on the brow. 'You look beautiful today, Min, like a Rossetti lady.'

Then he held the door for her to leave.

She went straight to the bathroom and sloshed cold water over her hair then dried the straightening locks, muttering, 'Never, never, never again. Never again will I gaud myself up for some man.'

Lizza let herself into the house at Bracks Hill, and made her way through the darkened kitchen towards the middle door. The house was resonating with the wheezing sound of the harmonium, overlaid by her mother's lovely throaty contralto.

'...and through the howling wilderness
My way pursue

'The goodly land I see
With peace and plenty blessed;
A land of sacred liberty
And endless rest
Where milk and honey flow
And oil and wine abound
And trees of life for ever grow
With mercy crowned...'

The sneck rattled as Lizza lifted it, and the music stopped. Her mother looked up at her in the lamplight.

'Go on, Ma. That's a lovely hymn.' She had wanted to say, 'Go on, Ma, your voice sounds lovely.' But she didn't.

Alice pulled down the lid and shrugged. 'You'd hear plenty of those if you went to Chapel like you should. It'd do you a bit of good.'

'If I went to Chapel it would be a lie. A mockery. And I learned in Chapel that God will not be mocked.'

Alice stood up. 'You think too much. Always did.' Her glance went beyond Lizza. 'You're on your own?'

'Our Beatrice came with me, but she's gone off to see someone...'

'Who would she go and see?' said Alice shortly, ushering her back into the hot kitchen, away from the cool front room and its music.

'Some girl she knew from school.'

'Our Beatrice never visits people she knew from school.'

'Well she is now,' said Lizza. 'Now can I sit down or will you keep me standing here?'

'This is yer home. You don't need telling to sit down.'

Lizza looked around. It was true. She had spent half her life away from here and in her heart this place was still 'home'. So, whatever her mother had done to her, whatever the differences they had had since she was small, her mother had created something which would live on in her, and in all of them as home. This feeling for home and what he was defending must have held value for her father Tom in his four years in the trenches, and perhaps had value for Jonnie now behind whichever barbed wire held him. And now Alex intoxicating himself in the wide skies, he needed something to tether him to the earth and this was it.

'Have you heard from Alex?' she said.

'I had a card,' said Alice, pushing it to her across the table. 'Beatrice might like to have it. Says it looks like the training'll take some time. Talks of Canada.' She gave a quiet smile and looked Lizza in the eye. 'The longer the better, in my view.'

Lizza smiled in return, understanding her meaning, her heart leaping as she acknowledged the revolution of her mother speaking to her as an equal. She did not comment on it, as she knew that if she did the moment would splinter, like spun glass battered by a hammer.

'What will you do on Wednesday, Ma?' she said casually. Christmas Day had been on her mind.

'Well, there's Chapel,' her mother said calmly.

Lizza took a risk. 'I want you to come to Priorton, to have your Christmas dinner.'

'Christmas dinner? I'll miss Chapel.' She paused, glancing at the photo on the wall. 'I did think that mebbe you and our Beatrice would come here. Those children too.'

Lizza shook her head. 'There're others, Ma: Bessie, whose house it is, is nearly eighty, I reckon. And Min and Krystof, the other lodgers.'

Alice sniffed. 'Strangers,' was all she said.

Lizza threw up her hands. She wanted to shout at her mother, who had left her floundering among strangers since she was fourteen. She folded her mouth on the words. But those same words, unspoken, seemed to hang in the air between them.

Her mother put her head on one side, the faintest of smiles on her lips. 'We'll see,' she said. 'We'll see.'

Lizza's heart leapt.

Then, as always, action replaced and postponed intimacy, as her mother busied herself with teapot and cups. She sat herself in the chair opposite Lizza. And, taking refuge in concrete fact, she said, 'And yon lad, will he be here for Christmas Day?' She had never called Roland by his name.

'No. This work unit he's involved with, on the island, he has to stay to, kind of, mind it. It would take a day at least to get down here and a day back.' She paused. 'It wouldn't be worth it.'

When she had got his letter she had retreated to her bedroom in Campion House to sound out her own feeling in response to it. In her heart she could find neither anger nor pique. The only feeling she could identify was relief. Then, sitting up in bed, she had written something about it in Mr Barraclough's big ledger, about this woman whose love for her husband had died as the bombs crashed round her, destroying her house and killing her child.

Alice was looking at her.

'The war keeps him there, Ma,' she said. 'At least he's safe. He might be in North Africa. Or some German prison.' She glanced across into the fire. 'One of Bessie's lodgers has been in a German camp.'

Her mother was instantly interested. 'Was he fighting them? At Dunkirk?'

'No. He's Polish. He was marched across Germany to work in an armaments factory. One time he was pulled out of the factory with ten other lads and they made to shoot them. Then they let them go back.'

Anyone else would have asked how he had got here, this Pole who had worked as a slave for the Germans.

'Is he Jewish?'

'No. I think his wife may have been. He doesn't say.'

'There's a new helper to the minister at the chapel,' said Alice. 'An old feller who's training to preach cause the other lad was called up. He said they...the Jews...know the whole of the Old Testament. It's their Bible.' She paused. 'He was preaching last week about the camps they take the Jewish people to. And other people. You've never heard such things. He said they knew the whole of the Old Testament. The Jews. And they would say the Psalms like we do.'

Lizza swallowed her frustration at her mother taking any new thing and pressing it through the colander of the Chapel before she would accept it into her own mind.

Then the cold outside air hit them with a flourish, the back door clattered, and Beatrice invaded the kitchen, rubbing her hands and holding them towards the roaring fire.

At first Beatrice and Alice were circumspect with each other and talked polite banalities. Alice was careful not to remark on her elder daughter's sharper manner and the radical change in appearance which her short hair had wrought; Beatrice was careful not to ask how her mother was managing on her own. She read out Alex's card and they agreed that the longer the training, the less active service he would see. Alice told her mother that her schoolfriend was out; she had wanted to tell her she had a message for her, from her cousin who worked with her at the factory, who had come across from Hartlepool. There was no recrimination from Alice at her daughter leaving her; there was no justification from Beatrice. The whole subject was ignored.

Later, as they walked to the bus stop, Lizza asked Beatrice about the potion. 'I've got it in my pocket,' said Beatrice. On the blacked-out bus they opened the screw of newspaper and peered at the rustling screw of leaves it contained.

'I'm not sure she should do this, Beatrice. It's a terrible thing to do, to take a life.'

'Lizz. Alex means more to me than anyone, even you; even me mother. But if this saves that bairn Josie spending a lifetime in the wrong, and saves her baby the pain of this bitter life, then...'

Lizza remained silent then, thinking that even the vagaries of her own life had been hard sometimes, but at least they were the consequence of living it. She had been luckier than Beatrice, whose numb endurance of a life only ever had secondary meaning: second to her mother, second to Alex, second to Lizza herself. She squeezed Beatrice's arm to her side, trying to show her warmth without sullying the space between them with inadequate words.

When they got back to the house, everyone except Josie was hovering in the kitchen: Min subdued in a brown cardigan, her hair restored to a simple shining cap, with Liam on her knee fast asleep; Bessie at her quilting; Krystof at the table reading the paper.

Beatrice looked around. 'Where's Josie?'

Min nodded at the door which led to the narrow back staircase. 'She seemed quite ill. Went to bed. She wouldn't let any of us near her. We kept Liam down here.' Lizza raced towards the stairs, followed by Beatrice.

Josie was sitting hunched up on a little chair, her knees tight together and her face white and old. Lizza went to kneel beside her.

'What is it, Josie?'

'Something terrible's happened, Mrs King. Terrible. This horrible pain. Horrible. An' I went to the lav, an' it's all a mess in there an'...Beatrice.' Tears as big as peas were rolling down her face and Beatrice put her arms round her and started to rock her backwards and forwards. 'Never mind, honey, we're here now. Me and Lizza is here now.'

'Let's get you into bed,' said Lizza, her nursing self to the fore.

Josie shook her head. 'I can't get up, I can't,' she wailed.

Beatrice picked her up bodily, as though she were half her age, and cuddled her to her. Lizza noted the huge blot of blood on the chair. 'Hang on to her, Bea,' she said and raced off, returning with newspapers, sheets and towels. She stripped off the bed to its striped ticking and covered it with newspaper and a thick pad of two old sheets. 'Lie her down now and get her clothes off if you can. There must be a nightie here somewhere.'

Min was at the door. 'Can I do anything, Lizza?' she said quietly.

'Yes,' said Lizza. 'You can put a light to that fire and get some heat in here. It's freezing. This child will catch her death of cold. Then you can go to the bathroom and clean that mess there. This child has lost a baby tonight.'

Min put one hand to her throat and then hurried to do exactly as she was told.

Beatrice sat the sobbing Josie on the bed and undressed her as though she were three. Then

405

she covered her nakedness with a nightie and sat there, still rocking her in her arms.

Lizza returned with a steaming bowl of water and flannels and, old practice returning, she washed Josie, rigging up torn towels as protection against further bleeding. Odd how little difference there was between this and giving some old lady a bed-bath after she had had what was called an 'accident'. When she had completed her task, Beatrice lifted Josie again, while Lizza whipped the soiled sheets and newspaper off and remade the bed entirely, complete with hospital corners.

Beatrice tucked Josie into the smooth, tidy bed. 'There, pet, nice and comfy now.'

Josie put her head back on the pillow but clung tight to Beatrice's hand. Beatrice looked at Lizza. 'I'll stay with her till she goes to sleep.'

Keeping her eyes closed, Josie mumbled, 'Liam. Let him come. He'll be worried.'

Min walked slowly down the broad front stairs with Lizza. 'Poor little thing,' she said. 'I had no idea.'

'I think she really only realised herself today, according to Bea. Then her father turned up and knocked her down. That must have done it.'

'Beast,' said Min. 'Anyway, she was lucky to have you here. You were wonderful, Lizza.'

Lizza smiled at her. 'You weren't so bad yourself, for a schoolteacher.'

They moved towards the kitchen. 'What shall we tell them?' said Min.

'Just that she's had some kind of sickness attack that's settled down now, no need for Krystof to know,' said Lizza. 'And I'll tell Bessie when the time is right.'

Min smiled. 'She'll take it. She's a wise old bird that. How she got to be worldly wise like that, stuck here in this house for seventy years, I'll never know.' Her smile faded. 'That father of Josie's, is he here in Priorton?'

'Yes. I saw him when I was with Liam. I sent him away with a flea in his ear. He must have waited for her off the train. He attacked her and Bea.'

'A madman,' said Min.

'No,' said Lizza with feeling. 'He's a bad man, a very bad man.'

By then they were in the kitchen with Bessie and she couldn't explain further.

The next morning Josie was up early on to go to the toilet. Hearing movement in the attic, she crept up into Krystof's studio. The early morning light flowed on to him from the skylight as he worked at one of the easels with his back to her.

Hearing her step he turned and smiled. 'Ah, Josie. Are you better?' He examined her white, drawn face with an artist's concentration.

Josie nodded. 'Much better now.' Beatrice had assured her that Krystof had accepted the fact that she had caught some tummy bug at work. She pointed to his painting, which showed the black silhouette and the shocking red of a city on fire.

'Is this Coventry, then?'

'No, Josie. It is the town where I lived. In Poland.'

'It looks like Coventry. That night.' From the road where her mother and Anne-Marie had been killed, she had looked up and seen the town bathed in blood-red light. The blood seemed to fill the world, like her own blood last night. First the pain, then the lumpy gush of blood.

'I would imagine that all cities on fire look the same, dear child. The fire is all-consuming. It makes all things equal.'

'But things aren't equal are they?' She turned, walked down the narrow stairs and woke Beatrice up, saying they would be late for work.

Beatrice took her hand and squeezed it. 'You're a silly sausage. It's Sunday. Go and get some more sleep. No work today. Go to sleep and think of Christmas.'

CHAPTER 27

On Christmas Eve Bessie and her friend Mary Lynn took charge of Liam, while Lizza went to queue for dates; Bessie had heard that McLintocks had taken a delivery. After that she was instructed to go to the store, where, rumour had it, there were oranges to be had. It was a bitterly cold day which looked as though it would turn to snow, and Bessie had raked out a big green cloak, unworn, saying it had been a present from old Barraclough. She sniffed. 'Far too big. Allus gettin' us things that were no earthly use to us. It'll cover yer better'n that old coat of yours.' She fastened the toggles as though Lizza were a child.

After queuing for nearly an hour at Mc-Lintocks Lizza acquired one small box of dates and then, her heart failing at the sight of the queue at the store, she stepped into the King's Hall Café for a cup of tea and a warm before she joined the queue for oranges.

She sat down beside a steamy window, watching the crowd of women scurrying about in their last attempts to make the second Christmas of the war seem something like Christmas. Making this season special was sensible for dogged reasons of selfish survival; it also had public value as part of one's personal war effort, a way of thumbing one's nose at Hitler. She looked round, thinking of the time when she had taken Josie and Rebecca to the Windmill Café just before the big Blitz. The women here were similar: middle-aged or apparently so, well corseted and, in two cases, wearing hats grand in the pre-war fashion; in two other cases, wearing felt versions of the war-time turban. The woman who had just served her might have been the twin of the waitress at the Windmill: slightly stringy and wearing her uniform with the bleak assurance of an undertaker.

Lizza poured a cup of tea from the silver teapot, and selected one of the two oat biscuits placed with pre-war grandeur on a starched lace doily. She leaned down and plucked from her

409

bag a bookmarked copy of *The Power and the Glory* lent to her by Min. 'You'll like this, Lizz: this fellow struggles with God much the same as you do.'

Lizza didn't see much resemblance between her puny anger and the struggles of a whisky-priest in Mexico. However, in the light of her own creative efforts to set down her thoughts in her own words between the covers of Mr Barraclough's ledger, she relished the quality of this writing.

The chair scraped beside her. 'The joy it is to see a pretty woman with her head buried in a book.'

Lizza's head snapped up as Theo Callaghan sat down beside her. She half stood up, but his hand on her arm pulled her back down again. 'Now you don't want to make a fool of yourself in this respectable place, do you?'

Two turbaned heads were turned in their direction. Lizza sat down. 'I've nothing to say to you, Mr Callaghan,' she said fiercely. 'Nothing.'

He held up his hand and the waitress came. 'Some tea, like my...cousin here, and any kind of sandwich if you have one.' He tucked his cap in his epaulet. He had been shaved, and was slightly cleaner than the last time she had seen him.

'Why're you still here, Mr Callaghan? Do you know that Josie was very ill after you pushed her down the other day?'

He shrugged. 'She's my daughter.'

'That doesn't mean you can do as you like with her.'

410

He looked her in the eye. 'Yes it does.'

'Not when I am anywhere near...' She stopped as the waitress came with more tea and a rather generous plate of paste sandwiches, a tacit acknowledgement of his uniform. He grabbed a sandwich, which he proceeded to wolf down.

'I can't understand you, Mr Callaghan. All you do is make them frightened of you...your mother, Maeve too when they were with us.'

His eyes stared coldly at her over his bulging cheeks and he spoke with his mouth full. 'Nothing wrong with that. It's the way things work. I was frightened of me own da. Now it's their turn.'

'Well, you don't frighten me. So go away.'

'But it's you I want. Here we are, it's nearly Christmas, and I've nowhere to go, nowhere to lay my weary head. So I thought you might like a visitor in that big house of yours, over the festive season.'

'No! It's not my house and anyway it's full,' Lizza shouted out and heads turned round again. She dropped her voice to a fierce whisper. 'Go back to your camp, whatever it is. Your leave must be over now?'

'Leave? It's not a matter of leave, Mrs King. I can't go back to Doncaster. There was this little problem about some of the Quartermaster's stock that went missing. Nothing to do with me of course. But I knew they'd come for me, so I came over the wall.'

A deserter. That explained the dishevelled uniform, the rough appearance. 'Well, you can't come to Campion House. There's no room and

411

you're not wanted. By anyone there.'

He slurped his tea. 'Well, Mrs High-and-Mighty, that ain't the only alternative. I could turn up anyway, just in time for the Christmas pud...' He put up a hand to stop her protest. 'But I needn't, if I had just a bit of money to see me on my way.'

Lizza wavered. 'Money?'

'Well, to get away I gotta have money, see? An' you, livin' in that fine house, must be able to put your hand on something, some money, or something a man could sell.'

'I haven't anything. Just an allowance from my husband. And, as I said, the house is not mine.'

'Mmm. An allowance!' He sneered and chewed back the final sandwich. 'Anyone who has an allowance can find a *mechanism* for an advance on the allowance.' He wiped his mouth with the back of his hand. 'I need fifty pounds to get away: back down to Coventry, or even London. You can lose yourself there and they say there's good pickings there even if you've no bloody ration book.' All the pretence of clerkish gentility which she had associated with him in Coventry had gone.

'You'd go away?' she said.

He put two fingers to his forehead. 'Scout's honour, Mrs King. I'll come to the house with you.'

She pushed her book into her bag and stood up. 'No. I'll see you outside this shop in two hours' time.' She pulled on her big green cloak. He grasped her elbow. 'You be here. I ain't

412

joking. If you don't turn up I'll be round that house like a shot.' He looked down the length of her. 'You're lookin' really well, Mrs King, considering your condition.'

She pulled the cloak around her and stalked off.

'Mrs King!' He was striding after her. All eyes in the café were on them. 'Thank you for my tea. You won't forget to pay, will you, dear cousin?' He was close to her now and he leaned to whisper in her ear, 'Mind you, I still think you need a good seein' to, condition or no condition.'

She had to fumble with her purse. When she finally got outside the café, he was nowhere to be seen. She strode past the dwindled orange queue outside the Store and, coming on the glossy black door which fronted Amos Silkin's office, stopped and went in. The lawyer listened quietly to her stumbling request for an advance on the weekly allowance which he administered for Roland. He put up a hand to stop further explanations about Christmas expenses. 'You've anticipated me, Mrs King. I was about to walk round to Campion House with this.' He pushed a heavy brown envelope across the gleaming desk towards her. 'Roland telephoned this morning, asking me to inform you of his great regret that he cannot get to Priorton to see you in the Yuletide season. And he instructed me to withdraw this from his account for you so that you could buy extra items for yourself and the children for whom you now find yourself responsible. And

413

he apologised that he did not think of it earlier.'

'How did he sound?'

'Much as usual, Mrs King.'

She lifted the flap of the envelope and glimpsed the wad of crisp five-pound notes. 'Goodness!'

'There is one hundred pounds there.'

'That's far too much, Mr Silkin. I don't need it.'

The lawyer waved a hand. 'His father's estate is near to settlement. There are houses, shares in the shipping line he worked for. That is a mere token.'

She tucked it safely in her bag beside *The Power and the Glory.* 'He sounded well, then?'

'In fine fettle. Enthusiastic about the plant up there, which is now into production. And his part in the war effort.' He coughed. 'Of course, he was desolate about not being at home, very sad.' He rubbed his chin. In truth, the boy had not sounded sad at all; just brisk and business-like.

Lizza raced back to the store, where the queue was now down to four, to discover that all that was available was tinned prunes and dried figs. She bought a pound of figs and made three other stops for extra Christmas presents before she made her way home.

She had a cup of tea in the kitchen with Bessie and May Lynn before she finally made her way upstairs to count the money and separate fifty pounds into a small envelope for Theo Callaghan. When she came back down, Bessie

414

was seeing May Lynn off at the back door. A cruel wind was sweeping into the back passage through the door, bringing flakes of snow with it. May Lynn shuddered in her shawl. Lizza lifted the green cloak off the banister knob where she had left it. 'Here, May Lynn, take this. You'll get your death of cold out there.' Bessie nodded approvingly.

'Ah canna dee that, Mrs King. Yeh'll need it yersel'.'

'No. I've to go out later but I can use our Beatrice's big grey one. Go on!'

'Aal right, hinney. Good of yer. Ah'm comin' for me dinner tomorrer so ah'll bring it back.'

Lizza tucked the cloak round her. May Lynn was taller than Bessie so it fitted her quite well. Lizza pulled up the hood and wrapped the old lady's shawl back round her shoulders. 'There you are, May Lynn. Snug as a bug in a rug.'

She was just seeing her off when Krystof came in through the back gate, juggling with packages and his picture folder. Lizza kept the door open for him. 'Thank you Elizabeth...Lizza.'

She smiled. 'You're laden like a donkey!'

'Ah, Christmas! We must say, like Tiny Tim, *"Bless us everyone."* I have presents here for the children, which will be a secret even from you till tomorrow.'

'Presents! How did you manage that?'

'Ways and means. Those ladies in the factory are very creative. I had to put in my orders!' he said mysteriously. 'But it is a great pleasure to give presents to children for the first time in many years.' He put them on the table and turned to her.

'It's important to make a Christmas for children, especially in these dark days.' She smiled at his delight, thinking of the irony of one of those 'children' having had a miscarriage just days before. He smiled down at her, then leaned down and kissed her on one cheek. 'My dear girl, you look no more than a child yourself.'

Her face burned and she bolted upstairs to find Beatrice's coat, trying to cool her mind and calm her heart with the thoughts of her errand to bribe Theo Callaghan.

But he wasn't outside the Kings Café when she arrived. She waited for an hour and ten minutes, thinking that this was some test, that he was lurking somewhere, watching her unseen, playing her like a fisherman plays a fish for pleasure. But finally, she was so cold that she didn't care if he came or not, and she set off to trudge her weary, frozen way home. They were waiting, all watching out for her there, and all expressed their concern, even anger that she should stay out in the cold so long, even if it were on some Christmas errand. She allowed herself to be bullied by Beatrice into a hot bath and a warm unworn man's dressing-gown provided by Bessie from her store of Barraclough goodies.

She rested on the bed until Josie and Liam came for her. Josie looked well now, younger than ever, having bounced back from her ordeal with characteristic animation. Standing beside her, Liam was eyeing Lizza uncertainly. Lizza

416

sat up and opened her arms and he jumped into them.

'They sent us upstairs to get you,' announced Josie. 'Bessie has unlocked the piano in the sitting room for Miss Roebuck to play. Sure, hasn't she bought some new music? And,' she said, her voice dropping, 'Bessie's *sitting down* in there. Can you believe it?'

Lizza laughed and swung her legs over the edge of the bed, hauling Liam with her. 'I have to see this.' She dropped Liam to the floor. 'Lead on MacDuff!'

The evening vanquished Lizza's exhaustion and her niggling fears about Theo Callaghan. Min played her new songs for them: 'Oh Jonny', 'You Are My Sunshine', 'How High the Moon', 'South of the Border' and 'Blueberry Hill', and made them join in the choruses. Bessie, sitting enthroned by the fire with Liam on her knee, la-la'd, conducting to the music with a teaspoon. Lizza sat beside Min on the piano bench, the others clustered round the piano to read the words, clapping themselves heartily at the end of every song.

They ended the evening with two choruses of 'The Holly and the Ivy', mince pies and a glass of port and toasted the King and Mr Churchill, and damned Hitler to the back of the fire. Then Lizza made Liam and Josie hang up their stockings on the high mantelpiece. Josie protested that she was a working girl now, but complied with an appreciative giggle.

Liam was black-eyed with excitement and exhaustion.

'I'll take Liam off up to bed,' said Josie. 'And I reckon I'll hop in myself. I'm buggered.'

'Josie!' said Lizza.

'Oops! Sorry! It's that Esme, she's a very bad influence.'

The rest of them gathered in the kitchen to make up the Christmas stockings. For Liam there was a package of toy soldiers purloined by Bessie from the Barraclough collection; woolly hat and gloves knitted for him by Beatrice; a tin whistle and a red ball from Lizza, topped up by an envelope containing a crisp five-pound note; a tiny alphabet book from Min; two sticks of barley sugar and a large picture book from Krystof; and an orange each, left by May Lynn, who had done her queuing early.

For Josie's stocking, as well as May Lynn's orange, there was an embroidered belt from Beatrice, a pair of her own earrings from Min, a pair of stockings and two fivers in an envelope from Lizza, a little silver Barraclough candlestick from Bessie and some hand-knitted mittens and a silver photo frame from Krystof.

They hung these with some difficulty to either side of the fireplace. Then Krystof brought out a large, bright-eyed teddy bear made from beige blanket material, dressed in a little suit, with red ribbons round his neck. Bessie clapped her hands.

'A lady at the factory was making these for money,' said Krystof, 'so I thought the boy might like it.'

They all trickled off to bed but Lizza returned to the sitting room to survey the scene of the teddy bear and the bulky stockings. She had to bite her lip. Her heart ached for Rebecca. A hand touched her shoulder briefly. 'Are you all right, Lizza?'

She turned round and looked into Krystof's eyes.

'It is hard,' he said, 'but I think, I know, it will get better.'

Then she was in his arms and he was kissing her eyes, her cheeks, her lips. She opened her lips slightly, luxuriating in the shared taste of port and the spicy sweetness of mince pies burning through their softness. Then her arms went round him, her hands into his hair, and he lifted his face away and groaned. Then he lifted her and took her to the couch so recently ruled by Bessie and lay her so that he could kneel beside her and stroke her hair, kiss her. 'My love, lovely girl.'

She pulled him towards her, her hungry body discarding its long-refined barriers. She wanted him as she had wanted nothing, no person, ever before. His lips were on her neck, inside her collar, his hands were stroking the long oval of her body, pausing as he felt the rippling kick of the baby inside her. 'The miracle,' he said.

She took his face and lay it against her stomach to share even more with him, this new life. They were quiet like that for a few moments, then roused by the sound of the sitting-room door clicking shut.

She sat up guiltily and Krystof got to his feet.

'Bessie,' she said, reaching up to turn down

the mantel. 'We must go.'

He stopped her in the darkness beside the door, grasped her hands and kissed her palms. His own hands were shaking. 'I have never felt like this, dear Lizza, never in my life.' Then he placed her hands by her side and she passed.

When she got to the bedroom Min was flitting around in her silk wrap, putting final touches to a pile of presents on her bedside table. Lizza sat down heavily at the dressing table, exhausted beyond measure at the day's events. Min thrust a towel and one of her own wraps into her hand. 'I've run a bath for you, and made loads of bubbles with some of my soapflakes. You look as though you need it. Go on! Go and have a soak and I'll go down and make us some cocoa.'

Lizza luxuriated in her second bath of the evening, playing games with the baby as she always did, patting him slightly on one side of her stomach and watching and feeling his movement as he reacted. 'When you come, Charley,' she whispered, 'I'll tell you about your sister Rebecca, and your other little sisters. And you'll learn about how you kept me going in these months, kept me going through these terrible times.' Then she lay back in the steam and welcomed the return of the sensual feelings she had felt earlier as Krystof kissed her, wondering if he, on the floor above, was thinking of her.

There was a rattle on the door. 'Cocoa, Lizza,' came Min's voice. Lizza dried herself and loosened her hair, which she had pinned up to protect her from the water. Min was sitting on the side of the bed, clasping her cocoa. Lizza picked her cup up and took it to the dressing table, where she sat down rather heavily to brush her hair.

Min looked at her through the mirror. 'You look absolutely beautiful. Here, let me.' She took the brush from Lizza and started to brush her hair in small firm strokes. Lizza put her head back, taking in Min's scent, and relaxed, the hypnotic strokes almost sending her to sleep.

The brushing stopped and Min's hands were on her shoulders. Lizza looked at Min through the mirror. 'That was lovely, Min. Just what the doctor ordered.'

Min kissed the top of her head. 'You're beautiful and I'm here to please.' She stared at Lizza. 'Lizz, you must miss Roland?'

Lizza blushed and shook her head. 'I don't know what it is, Min,' she said soberly. 'But sometimes I can't even get his face into my mind. I don't want to think about that night in Coventry when I lost Rebecca and I don't want to think of him. It's as though he didn't exist, as though now there is just me and little Charley.'

Min smiled slightly to acknowledge her own father's name. 'He could have come, Roland, couldn't he?'

Lizza nodded, 'I'm sure he could have come, if he really wanted.'

They got into bed and, as Min snuggled into her back, she murmured in Lizza's ear, 'My problem is, loving you both, I don't know whether I am jealous of you with him, or him with you.'

It took a few seconds for Lizza to realise that it must have been *Min* who had seen her and Krystof on the couch in the sitting room: Min, not Bessie, had clicked the door shut on them. Min was an odd creature. You'd have thought she would be angry, spitting feathers at her instead of cuddling in. Sometimes she reminded Lizza so much of Rebecca, all that charm, those flirtatious ways. That was an odd thought. Lizza closed her eyes and let the notion pass.

Her mind moved to the problem of the whereabouts of Theo Callaghan. He must be back in camp by now, probably picked up by military policemen. You saw them about enough, their eyes everywhere. Then she turned over on the soft mattress and savoured again the thought of Krystof's lips on her cheek and her throat, and fell into a deep and dreamless sleep.

Christmas Day itself began in a quietly festive fashion. Everyone greeted each other and their presents with delight. Of all the presents which were exchanged, Bessie's gifts were the most poignant, like some personal reiteration of her own history. She had risen before the crack of dawn to put out unwrapped presents, abstracted from the Barraclough bequest, for everyone: the rest of the set of Napoleonic soldiers for Liam; the rest of the hall-marked silver dressing set for Josie; a bright tartan Scottish rug for Beatrice; a silver-backed brush set, unused, for Min;

a beautiful woollen coat for Krystof, in new condition, which fitted him perfectly.

'Ah thowt you had just his build, when the old feller was still straight and upright.' Then she put her hand in her apron pocket and pulled out a blue leather box. 'An' this is for you, hinney.'

Lizza opened it with a click. In the morning light, white from the snow outside, an emerald glinted up at her. It was set in a finely wrought gold mount, with three diamonds on either side. Lizza took a breath. 'Bessie, you mustn't.'

Bessie's little face glowed up at her. 'Dinnet be silly, lass. "A pretty thing for a pretty girl." That's what he always said, silly old coot.'

Lizza still hesitated.

'Gan on, lass, put it on.' Bessie lifted her eye calmly to Krystof. 'Give the lass a hand.'

Lizza had hardly looked at him that morning, but now she had to as he took the box from her, removed the ring and put it on the third finger of her right hand. She took her hand away and turned quickly to show the ring to Beatrice and the others.

Krystof clicked the box shut and looked at Bessie. 'He must have loved you very much, Miss Bessie.'

Bessie put her head on one side. 'Aye, that he did. More'n anything. And that made it all right.'

Lizza was the only one who didn't go to some kind of church that morning: Beatrice persuaded Bessie to go with her to Linnet Street Chapel, Min went to St Bennet's Church of England,

and Krystof, Josie and Liam to St Osbert's Catholic Church.

Krystof looked at her keenly. 'Would you not wish to go to the church even on this Christmas Day?'

Lizza shook her head. 'No,' she said, keeping her glance very neutral as she looked at him, putting the incidents of the previous night behind a barrier at the very back of her mind.

It was good to have the house to herself when they had all gone. After she had basted the turkey and set the big dining table, she sat down in the sitting room and looked at her other presents. Two pairs of silk stockings from Josie and Liam. An enamelled brooch from Beatrice. A green brocade headband and a notebook from Min. And, from Krystof, a small immaculate drawing, mounted and framed, of an elegant street of houses in Cracow: the street where he had been born. With the house empty, she allowed herself to think of last night: of those few healing moments of intimacy which could never be repeated.

Her reverie was interrupted by a thunderous knocking on the front door. She knew with cold certainty just who this was. She raced upstairs to get the envelope, then to the kitchen to get a knife.

He looked darker and wilder than ever, 'The Season's Greetings to you!' Theo Callaghan stood there swaying as she opened the door.

'There you are. Go away, and never come back,' she yelled at him, and threw the envelope on to the snowy ground, holding the knife out with the other hand. 'If you come back I'll put the police on to you, for definite.'

He bent to pick up the envelope and she slammed the door, leaning against it, her hand hurting as she gripped the knife too tightly. He battered at the door a few times, but she heard finally his trudging footsteps on the path.

She was still trembling a little when the others came back, but they were bustling in from the cold and didn't notice. Bessie was fussing on about May Lynn, who had not been at Chapel, and when she and Beatrice had gone round, had not been at her house. 'Ah thowt she might be here, but she isn't. She's gone and done it again.'

'Done what?' said Beatrice.

'She goes walkin' sometimes, for no reason. She was away once for three days.'

'Walking?' said Lizza blankly.

'She's born to travellers, like me, is May Lynn. Itchy feet. She did this two Christmases ago.' She sat down hard on her chair, her eyes filling. 'An' I had a nice present for her, some pillow-cases. Linen, pre-war, too.'

Lizza took Bessie's coat and hung it up. 'Never mind, Bessie. She'll be back soon. And you can have another little Christmas together. Just the two of you.'

Bessie brightened at this and stood up to take charge of the Christmas dinner. Even so it was quite a subdued meal, with Bessie still troubled over May Lynn, Lizza listening for the door in case Theo Callaghan returned, and Min casting

425

meaningful glances at Krystof which were never returned.

But then, just after the King's speech, and the messages from the refugee children on the wireless, there was a knock on the door. Lizza leapt up. 'I'll get it. I'll get it.' She raced to the door, rehearsing phrases of vituperation to spit out at the hateful man. Then she opened the door and nearly fell down with shock.

'I thought I'd come,' said Alice Bremner, 'or goodness knows when these cakes'd get eaten.'

Lizza beamed, and opened the door wide. 'Beatrice, Beatrice,' she called. 'Look who's here. It's Ma.'

The arrival of Mrs Bremner seemed to raise them all to better levels of celebration, as the others caught Lizza and Beatrice's excitement at their mother's presence on what was now their territory. Even so, later on, playing carols for them all to sing, she seemed to make that territory her own, charming Min with the beauty of her singing and tickling Bessie at what she saw as Alice's resemblance to Lizza. 'Ye two are the pot model of each other! Pot model!' she crowed.

Later that afternoon, after her mother had gone, Lizza stared at herself in the hall mirror. There was no way on earth she looked like her mother. No way on earth. But Bessie was a wise old bird. She had spotted something. Lizza smiled faintly at her own reflection. Whatever Bessie's point was, she knew that now she and her mother had turned a page in a book. Things would be different from now on.

CHAPTER 28

Pieter Vann returned from Hull on the afternoon of 3 January and went straight to the plant. Roland greeted him heartily, wishing him a very happy and peaceful 1941. They walked round the installation, congratulating each other that their small production line was now underway after a few hiccups.

Pieter returned to the house that night by the loch to discover changes. He looked on in some bewilderment as Roland kissed Mara openly when they entered the house. Their banter, innocent enough in itself, had an elusive quality of intimacy which was hard to pin down.

Over supper Roland questioned Pieter closely about his visit to Hull: whether he had come across anyone he had known previously.

Pieter shook his head. 'No. No one that I knew. But they told me of the terrible things happening in my country. Deportations and imprisonments are widespread. Innocent people shot as examples.' He laughed shortly. 'Of course, those I met were pleased with themselves, their clever escape, and bringing the ships over to the Allies. And it was good for me to sit and listen to them, to talk and even sing some of our songs. The language a kind of balm to my ears. They laughed at the way I spoke my...our own language, called it

427

John Bull Dutch.'

Roland smiled. 'It must have been hard to drag yourself away, Pieter.'

Pieter shook his head. 'No. In the end it was quite simple. The men there, they had each other and the comradeship of their recent exploit. I was on the outside. In the end I only wished to be back here, getting on with the job.' He cocked an ear towards the kitchen, where Mara Laine was singing as she prepared the evening meal. 'You did not get home to your wife for Christmas?'

Roland coloured. 'We only stopped production for one day. There wasn't time.'

It had been wonderful: he had made his daily routine checks of the plant, but apart from that it had been a secret circle of time for the two of them, the nights luxuriating in the shared bed, the days exploring the shores of the loch, guided by Mara, whose eye was as quick and excitable as that of a child. They had eaten meals and drunk the late Colonel Laine's brandy in firelight and made love yet again beside the flickering flames. Lizza had come to his mind now and then, but in a distant and unreal fashion, like images on a film screen. He reassured himself she was well taken care of, there in the bosom of her family. It had been Mara who had asked about Christmas presents, on the eve of Christmas Eve, leading him to race down to the plant to telephone Amos Silkin about a gift of money.

Pieter Vann was watching him soberly.

Roland moved to safer ground. 'I see we're

giving the Italians a good run for their money in North Africa.'

Pieter nodded and sat down at the table. 'Those Italians have no stomach for it. Singers not fighters.'

'Here we are!' Mara Laine placed a large pottery bowl of steaming stew on the table and started to serve it into bowls. Looking at her, Pieter was struck by the thought that she had shed years in the last week. She must be forty if she was a day, but in this candlelight, with the purple bandeau tying back her heavy hair, she looked half that age.

He dipped the thick bread into the broth. 'Tonight I go to play chess with the man from the ferry. He lives with his sister at the end house. We talk many times and I find he is a chess player. So tonight we play chess.'

Roland and Mara exchanged glances, hiding their pleasure at the prospect of another evening alone. Time was their treasure. Unspoken between them was the acknowledgement that this interlude must come to an end, that there was no future to the idyll. For ten minutes while they ate their stew all they could hear was the ticking of the old kitchen clock, a battered refugee from the dining room which still kept good time.

That night and on every subsequent night the bed opposite Pieter's remained empty. Roland only returned to the room to retrieve items from his case, or exchange a civil word with Pieter about some event of the day, either at work or in the wider war-torn world.

By the end of January Beatrice had established herself as one of the best workers on her section and was moved across with Mary on to the more dangerous section, to work alongside Josie and Esme. Her fingers, made deft by fine embroidery and stitching, adapted well to this delicate work. She was still quiet, taking her time in getting to know people, seen as quaint among the robust, forthright factory girls. However, like parents of a foster child, they cheered each sign of development in their protégée: the new short hairstyle; the dancing, which she took to; the experiments with smoking, which she soon abandoned. There was a conspiracy among them to get her to one of the dances at the Gaunt Valley Hotel where 'all the lasses went', and where you could meet some nice lads.

Josie was a regular dancer now, and could vouch for the good time. She was popular with the boys and had some bristle-necked, new-uniformed boy to walk her home every dance night. She would let them have one short-lived kiss on the lips and no more.

As she wriggled away from some over-eager soldier boy she would sometimes get a quick image of herself and Alex, shrieking and laughing over their contortions at the house called Beaconsfield. Once, as she turned away from the night's soldier boy, her mind imprinted the Beaconsfield rose window on to the glass over Bessie's door.

But there was no new Alex among these soldier boys.

Despite this, she encouraged Beatrice. 'Blokes from Killock Camp get to the dance. From all over England, they are. Even further. Canadians and Australians, half a head taller than Durham blokes.'

'They'd suit you Beatrice,' said Mary seriously. 'You can find yersel' a lad to look up to.'

In February, the talk was all of the Valentine Dance. Luckily it would fall on a Friday this year, so there would be a dance on the very night. On Tuesday dinner time Beatrice was sitting round the canteen table with Esme, Mary, Josie and three of the others. Swigging off the last of her tea, Esme bashed on the table to stop the chatter. 'Here's a Valentine's Day game,' she said. 'We all have ter tell when was the first time we—' A shriek went round the table. 'No! Cheeky buggers, not that—kissed a lad. Proper, like. Not playground kiss-me-quicks. If we think it's true you get a penny off each of us. If we think it's false, you owe us each a fag.'

The table settled down, all eyes on Esme, who took charge. 'Now, Josie, you first. Can't be so long ago for you.'

Josie grinned. 'Sure, it'd be a pleasure. There was this lovely boy. Funny and clever. Thought he knew everything but it was all out of books. So we were playing, kind of, hide and seek in this bombed-out house in Coventry, see? An' didn't I make him kiss me, see? He didn't know the first thing about it! But he was a quick learner. Couldn't stop after that.'

431

They roared with laughter at this and threw pennies in her direction.

'Me now,' said Mary. 'I was walking to this dance at the Gaunt Valley Hotel and a big car stopped beside us, one of those low ones, a racing car. And this feller leans out, he says, "Could you tell of the whereabouts of the Gaunt Valley Hotel, miss?" So I tells him and the car roars off. Then later, I'm coming down this big staircase at the Gaunt, yer know the one by the balcony? And there he is, six foot tall in his RAF uniform, just waitin', looking up at me. An' he asks me to dance an' we dance all the dances, except for the Barn Dance, when we sit out and he tells me he how many Huns he's shot down. Then he takes me home in this car, and there, parked beside the netties at the bottom of our street, he kisses me so hard you'd think the world was on fire...'

She was interrupted by hooting and howling and demands for their cigarette forfeit. She threw a packet to the centre of the table and turned to Beatrice. 'You now, Bea.'

The furore died down and they all looked at her. 'No, not Beatrice,' said Josie, 'she's only...'

Beatrice had taken a deep breath. 'That's all right, Josie.' She looked at them, from one open, eager face to the next. 'I was seventeen, a bit older than Josie, but not half so wise. I'd been to Market Day at Priorton on messages for me mother. I was walking down Gypsy's lane. You know the one between Priorton and Carlton? Well, this feller came alongside us, a big feller with side whiskers. I'd never seen him before. He started to talk to us, some dirty talk about pub-women in Priorton. Then he grabbed me. Kissed me and worse. First time anyone kissed me. And last.' She paused. 'He's dead now. I thank God every night for that, in my prayers.'

Then there was a silence, finally broken by the relief of the whistle to start work again. On their way out, one by one as they passed, the girls placed a penny beside Beatrice's plate. As they walked back to the changing rooms, Beatrice was linked on one side by Josie and the other by Esme, who said fiercely, 'I'll get you to that bloody Valentine Dance, Bea, if it kills us.'

Krystof had completed his factory drawings. He had had letters from London suggesting the possibility of his having exhibitions in the North and in London to celebrate the human aspect of the war effort. So now he was working at home transforming some of his factory drawings to paintings and mounting and framing the remaining drawings. Min sometimes worked on her own drawing alongside him in his attic. Sometimes, excited by the project, she helped him to select and mount the best of his drawings. They never discussed the fact that their relationship had moved now in an almost seamless fashion from passion to friendship.

In the room below Lizza could hear their footsteps and the murmur of their voices and felt isolated. She walked out into the town less as the months progressed. It was cold and sometimes slippery underfoot and she was very bulky now with the baby. Much of her time was spent reading, or working at the desk on her stories, going over them time and time again until they were pared down just to the essentials. Most of them were stories from the early days of her nursing training, the heroine being a young girl not unlike herself. But she had given her her own name and very soon she grew into her own self, not unlike a very interesting stranger.

One Saturday at midday dinner Krystof looked at her across the table. 'Lizza, I was thinking it would be good if you could see the work as it is now, before the final decisions are made.'

'Yes, you must see it now, Lizza,' Min chimed in too enthusiastically. 'The collection's coming together.'

Krystof turned to Bessie. 'And you, would you like to see my factory pictures, Miss Bessie?'

Bessie shook her head. She had been very subdued lately, very worried about May Lynn, who had still not returned from her Christmas saunter. Lizza had been pressuring her to go to the police and get them to make enquiries. It was more than two months since she had gone for her walk. Bessie still demurred, saying May Lynn would never forgive her for 'setting the pollis on her trail'.

Now Lizza urged her to come to see Krystof's pictures. 'Look, Bessie, if I can make my way up those stairs, you can.'

Bessie said, 'Nah. I'll mind the bairn.' Liam

434

was playing with his soldiers under the kitchen table. 'You go.'

Lizza insisted that the other two walk in front of her so she could take her time getting up the stairs. 'I feel undignified enough without getting stuck on the stairs with you two behind me.'

In the attic, the midday winter light was flooding in from the skylights. The framed drawings were hung in a line from a joist and the oils, still not dry and as yet unframed, were leaning against a set of chairs which Min had purloined from the next-door attic which Bessie called the 'glory-hole'. On the easel, one painting was still in progress. It was a half-completed image of Beatrice, before her hair was cut. She was standing looking serenely out of the canvas, like some biblical maiden. The top of her body was foreshortened so that it dominated the space. She was holding shell-cases, spread across her forearms like a shining bouquet. Only one arm was completed in colour, the other was sketched in, as was the broad bench where she worked.

Among the drawings were images of the women walking into work on a dark morning; sitting around the canteen table; loading waggons; driving trolleys; fixing lorries. It was remarkable that, despite the uniform of overalls and turbans and the mechanical nature of the tasks portrayed, Krystof managed to show the variety of character from morose to comic, the difference in age and personality. The overall image was not one of automata making their contribution to the war effort, but diverse human

435

beings brought by the accident of war to one place and one kind of task.

Lizza was relieved to see he had not included his drawings of Coventry, the city on fire. She looked up at Krystof, who was studying her reaction. 'You're very clever making the girls so very human, Krystof, when what their work produces is, in the end, so destructive. They're not just full of valour, but full of character.'

He smiled slightly. 'They are heroines, Beatrice and her friends, and I wish to show that. They risk their lives doing this work.'

'Which is your favourite, Lizza?' asked Min eagerly.

Lizza shook her head. 'I don't know. They're so different.' She glanced at the portrait of Beatrice. 'It's so difficult.'

'You need to see them more,' said Krystof. 'You are welcome to come and see them any time. I will welcome your views.' The thread of pleading in his voice was just discernible.

She lay a hand on her stomach, shaking her head slowly. 'I would love to, but...'

'When's he due, the baby, Lizza?' asked Min.

'Somewhere about the twentieth of March, to my reckoning. A month or so.'

'Then you must bring him here to see the work as soon as he's born!' said Krystof, rubbing his hands. 'The portrait of his Auntie Beatrice, which is to be the centre, will be just about finished by then.'

436

'Come on!' Josie was marching ahead.

Beatrice pulled back against Esme's arm. 'No, Esme. I really don't think I can.'

The pavement leading up towards the Gaunt Valley Hotel was thronged with people, many of whom she could feel and smell, rather than see, in the black-out.

'Come on, Beatrice,' said Mary on her other side. 'Wait till you get inside. It's lovely.'

Beatrice weakened and let them drag her in, through the double doors and heavy green velour curtain. She could smell Sunlight soap and one-day-old perfume; cigarette smoke and half-washed clothes. She blinked in the twinkling light from the glass chandelier in the foyer and hardly dared to step on to the rich turkey red of the carpet.

Images of hell, read to her by her mother, came unbidden to her mind.

They paid their money to a woman dressed in black, sitting behind a table with a tin cashbox for the money. Men and women, in separate groups, studiously ignoring each other, thronged the foyer. The scraping strain of violins trickled towards them, filtered through double doors at the head of a broad staircase.

'We put our coats in here,' said Esme, leading her to a side room with long racks along one side for coats and a line of oval mirrors, some crackled with age, along the other. Beatrice watched as Esme carefully outlined her lips with lipstick, then handed it to Mary, who did likewise. Josie grabbed it from her and smiled at Beatrice in the mirror as she mimicked their actions. Beatrice was shocked at how it made her look grown-up, emphasising her fragility to a point of bright, transitory beauty.

Josie held the lipstick out to Beatrice, who shook her head, smiling slightly. 'No thanks, pet. I feel as if I'm three steps down the slippery slope already. If I put that on I'll feel like I'm in the very entrance-place to purgatory.'

Esme grabbed the lipstick and tucked it in her bag. 'She's right, Josie. We worked a bloody miracle to get her here at all. We can't expect her to do everything at once.'

The band dais was halfway down one side of the ballroom. Scratched gilt chairs were placed against three walls and at the far end were a few round tables set with the same chairs. These were full: women queued an hour before the ballroom opened for the privilege of a table seat rather than a wall seat. As this was the start of the evening, the chairs around the hall were occupied by women only and the men clustered in small groups near an aperture in the wall, through which they could buy beer if it were available, or a kind of homemade barley water if it were not.

Beatrice sat between Mary and Josie wondering miserably why she had come. Her despair was not because she was the oldest there; there were many as old or even older than she was, some of them very well made-up, teetering on very high heels. No, she might be innocent, but she was not ignorant of the different figure she cut, among these worldly-wise women. And it was all so noisy. The band was bashing

438

away and the level of chatter was high: the speed of talk, even from her friends, seemed impossibly fast.

She watched the band: a fat woman with trailing sleeves pumped away very effectively at the piano, an old man was playing a rather well-used set of drums, and a young boy no more than thirteen was playing the piano accordion. The woman called out in a booming voice that they should all take their partners for the waltz.

There was a clatter of leather on wood as the clusters of men broke up and one by one they made their way across the floor to find partners.

Mary was whipped away first, then Josie was whirled off by a boy in uniform who looked no older than the accordion player. Esme turned to Beatrice. 'You'n me'll dance this first one, Beatrice, so you can get used to the floor. It's better and bigger than the canteen.'

Just then, a tall fair boy with corporal's stripes tapped Esme on the shoulder. 'Are you dancin'?'

Esme cast a glance at Beatrice, who waved her away. She had never been to a dance but she understood the rule that no chance of meeting what might end up being a dream date should be turned down.

The chair beside her creaked as a thick-set man sat down. He was not in uniform, but wore a dark suit and a bright white shirt which sat uneasily on his bulky neck. Without looking at her he said, 'Yer canna dance, then?'

439

It was not too difficult to talk to someone who didn't look at you. 'I can dance, I think. But I've never been to a dance, to a ball-room.'

'Me neither.'

She looked at him directly, then. He was older than many men here, but perhaps only two or three years younger than she was: he had thick black hair neatly brushed and Brylcreemed back; he had high colour and his well-marked brows hung craggily over bright blue eyes, now looking hard into hers. 'Why d'you come then?' she said.

'Ah'm allus havin' rows with me da an' me brother cos ah niver get out. They mean the pub, like, not here. But ah dinnet drink. Dinnet like the taste. Ternight again they telt us ah should get out. Another row. So ah did. But ah wasn't gannin' to any pub.'

'You're still living at home?'

'Not in the army, yer mean? Nah. At the pit. Though they do say they might still call us up.' He put a hand out. 'Me name's Mick. Mick Stratton. I heard them lasses call you Beatrice.'

She nodded and shook his hand heartily. 'Pleased to meet you, Mick Stratton.'

Whether it was because he was younger than she was, or the peculiar nature of the evening anyway, she didn't feel in the least bit shy. 'Would you like to learn this dance, Mick? It's the waltz. It's very easy. I learned it in one dinner-time.'

'A dinner-time?'

'At the factory where...'

440

'Where you work with those lasses. Ah see...' He paused. 'Yer different to them. Chalk and cheese.' He stood up. 'Well, flower, if you can risk my size nines crushin' yer feet, I can risk mekkin' a fool of mesel'.'

They danced together most of the evening, except for the Barn Dance, which Beatrice refused, realising that she would be obliged to dance with all the men in the room, young and old. Mick Stratton was an apt pupil, concentrating fiercely on her instructions and moving lightly round the room despite his bulk. Beatrice enjoyed it more than anything she had ever experienced, and had a job to hide her delight.

At nine-thirty precisely, he brought her back to her seat and did not sit down himself. 'That was grand, Beatrice. Ah niver thowt ah could dance. But ah've gotta go now.'

She stared up at him, keeping her face very still. 'Oh well...'

'It's like this, see? I've got dogs. Greyhounds. They get a three-mile walk at half-nine whatever else is happening. It's my turn to walk them this week. They'll be clamourin'.'

'Well...' She settled back in her seat, smiling up at him too brightly. Mary was sitting at a table with her corporal, but Esme and Josie were standing close by, trying not to look too curious.

He hovered. 'Ah know this was the first time yer've been here, Beatrice. But you will be here next week, won't yer?'

She shook her head. 'I don't know.'

441

He looked across at Esme. 'You're her marrer, incher?'

Esme nodded.

'Mek sure she's here next week.' It was an order not a request. He turned on his heel and was lost in the crowd.

Esme was indignant. 'Cheek! What does he think he is?'

Beatrice looked from one face to the other and smiled quietly. 'He's straightforward, that's what he is. And I like him.'

Josie eyed her curiously. 'Will you come then, next week?'

Beatrice sat back and folded her arms. 'I think I will, pet. I think I will.'

And that is what happened. Each Friday, Beatrice would go with Josie and the others to the Gaunt Valley Hotel dance; Mick Stratton would turn up and dance with her, or they would sit out and talk—about the pit and the war—abstractions which allowed the avoidance of personal affairs. At nine-thirty he would go off to walk his dogs.

On the fourth Friday, at twenty-five to ten, Beatrice had to remind Mick of the time. He pulled out his watch and shook his head. 'Me brother's turn with the dogs this week,' he said. He looked at her directly. 'Ah was wonderin' if it'd be all right for us to walk yer home tonight.'

She shrugged. 'Don't see why not,' she said.

Later they walked slowly through the dark streets, twenty yards behind Josie, who had her own young escort. They passed them entwined

442

beside the stone gatepost of Campion House, both parties pretending they didn't see the other.

Standing beside the tall door, he looked up. 'Ah never imagined yer livin' in a house like this,' he said.

'I lodge here, with my sister, to be near to Priorton station for work,' said Beatrice. 'Our own house, at Bracks Hill, that's a pit house.'

He touched her sleeve. 'It's been nice, dancin' with yer,' he said. 'It was a new thing and ah liked it.'

'What else do you do, that you like, Mick? Is it just walking the dogs?' asked Beatrice. The dark seemed to permit the bold question. She was anxious to keep him here, despite the cold.

His hand caught at hers. Her heart leapt. She was used to the square power of his hand as it held hers to dance. But this was different.

'The thing ah like doin' most is drawin'. And paintin',' he said. 'Me da and me brother think it's a big joke.'

She squeezed his hand, trying to think of anything to say that would keep him there. 'Fancy that. There are two other lodgers here, who're drawers and painters. One's Polish.'

'Well, yer b...' He bit the swear word back into his mouth. 'Ah go to a class where there's this Pole. Krystof,' he said. 'A genius. Good feller.'

'The teacher of that class lives here, too. Min Roebuck.'

He laughed. 'Ah know her too. Yer gunna

443

tell us that you can draw next.'

'No. I'm not that bad with the 'broidery needle though.'

There was a pause, and he took the other hand. He coughed. 'Ah couldn't work out why a woman like...a woman your...'

'Age?'

'Nah. A bonny woman. Nice woman, didn't have her own man. Ah thought he must be in the Forces or sommat.'

She shook her head. 'No man. Never has been really. If ever we really get to know each other I'll tell you why.'

He looked at her steadily. 'Can ah kiss yer?'

She nodded.

His hands slid up her old grey coat to her shoulders and he kissed her hard on the mouth. As she returned the pressure she could feel the harsh bristles on his chin and thought in one part of her brain that with such dark hair he would need to shave at least twice a day to keep his beard at bay.

Then he released her so quickly she almost fell back. 'Yer'll go next week, to that dance, will yer?' he asked urgently.

She shook her head. 'I don't know. My sister's here and's just about to have her baby. I'll go if I can.'

He stood there staring at her. 'What if ah call here at this house at half-past six and walk there with you? Then, if this sister has her baby and you can't come, you can tell me to me face.'

She looked at him and nodded slowly.

'Gangway!' Josie was coming down the path,

cheeks flushed, full of the night's good feeling. 'Gangway, you lovebirds. Sure, if I stay out here much longer won't me feet freeze to the path itself?'

They parted then and Mick strode down the path, ignoring both Josie and the young soldier, who was still hovering at the gate, cheated of anything more than a fairly perfunctory kiss.

CHAPTER 29

The reports on the wireless that weekend intoned the Luftwaffe's renewed spring offensive involving heavy bombing on London: Buckingham Palace and other London targets were bombed. Lizza's cosy little world at Campion House was punctured like a balloon. There had been many raids since the Coventry raid that she had endured, but this news that the Palace had been bombed swamped her with feelings that she had pushed to the back of her mind in the four months she had been at Campion House. Now, sitting in the kitchen with the others, around the tables where they always gathered for the nine o'clock news, she started to pour with sweat. Then she stood up, abruptly tipping her chair over, and then rushed out of the kitchen.

She went upstairs and sat on the bed, shaking and shuddering, sweat pouring down her face. She put her hands into her hair and started to pull it, rocking backwards and forwards on the bed. The door clicked and the bed creaked and she felt an arm round her shoulders. She stayed rigid, refusing to yield to the offered comfort.

'It is hard, Elizabeth, hearing that and remembering,' said Krystof. 'I feel it too. I felt it even when we were in Coventry and it was happening. I had the double feeling. I felt it as it happened and felt again what had happened to me from the time in Warsaw.'

Her hands came out of her hair and she sat still. 'I could hear the thump again and the cry buildings make when they crack,' she said dully. 'I could hear the people screaming. I could hear Rebecca crying in the centre of it.' She relaxed against him and he hugged her tight. 'And here we are up here. We've the black-out and the rationing and the families have their dead and dying soldiers. But we're snug here. They are not overhead bursting into our lives and killing our children.' She put her hand on her stomach. 'Now they've hit the Palace. What's the use? They'll come over and get this one. And the next and the next. What's the use?'

He turned her to him then, and kissed her on the brow and on the cheek and on the corners of her tense mouth. 'No, no, darling girl, sweet darling. Your King and Queen are safe. You are safe here. That is why you found yourself in this place. God has made sure you have a safe place...' She pulled away from him at that, and he firmly pulled her to him again. 'Well, dear Elizabeth, that is what I believe. And you are here. And you are safe. And you will have this baby in your own land, your own home country. And the land will wrap itself around you and your baby and keep you safe. If you believe any other, then that devil Hitler and his henchmen have won. That's what the bombing is about. To break you, to break a people at its own hearth.' He was pushing the sweat-greased curls out of her eyes, away from her sticky cheeks.

The door clicked again and Min came in with a tray which held two cups and a glass. Krystof stood up from the bed and Lizza's hands went up to her hair.

'Aren't you two cosy,' said Min brightly. 'Lizza, dear! Talk about the tale of the magic pinny! That Bessie has a magic pantry. The butcher's uncle must work on a coffee plantation. She's dug out some coffee, one for both of us and a glass of the Blessed Barraclough's twenty-year brandy. Just for you. Apparently being unpregnant and unpanicked, I don't qualify.'

Lizza smiled at her in a watery fashion. 'I don't want it. You have it.'

Min put the tray on the bedside table. 'No, I...'

'Ladies!' Krystof was by the door now. He bowed slightly. 'Elizabeth. I can see you are in good hands.' The door clicked behind him.

Min poured the brandy into one cup of coffee and handed it to Lizza. 'Hmm,' she said complacently, 'seem to have stepped on someone's toes.'

The alcohol in the steam from the coffee was going straight to Lizza's brain. 'What you want most in the world, Min Roebuck,' she said brightly, 'is to be perpetually, till you are ninety, the naughtiest girl in the school.'

And on that minuscule pretext they both fell into helpless laughter which dissolved into a hiccuping conversation about some of the worst exploits of Min's schooldays.

When they got to bed, Lizza went to sleep quickly then woke up an hour later and proceeded to have a restless night. Min, as had been necessary in the last month or so, was clinging to the edge of the bed and didn't get much sleep herself. When Min finally got up, Lizza was snoring slightly, snoozing at last. As Min was creeping round the room getting ready, the door creaked open and Liam crept in. Min put her fingers to her lips, then her folded hands beside her cheek to show Lizza was asleep.

He went and stood quietly by the bed with his own finger to his own lips, and Min went to the bathroom. When she came back he was lying on the bed beside Lizza poking at her eyelids.

'What are you doing, Liam?' whispered Min.

'See if Lizza's awake,' he whispered back.

'Come here!' whispered Min fiercely.

'No. Leave him,' mumbled Lizza. 'I'm awake.' She reached and pulled Liam under the clothes with her.

'Have you had breakfast, Liam?' asked Min. He nodded.

'Well, I'll go and have my breakfast and I'll come and get you for school. Then you can snuggle down again, Lizz.'

'I've to get up. Bessie needs a hand, with no May Lynn to help.'

'Get some rest. I wish *I* could, after the night I had.'

Lizza giggled. 'It must be like sleeping with a basking whale.'

'At the very least,' said Min grimly, then she winked at Liam and vanished through the door.

Liam lay quite still beside Lizza. She brushed the curls from his forehead and looked at his bright face.

Then he said, 'Where did my mammy go?'

Her hand stilled. 'Your mammy?'

'And the baby. Mammy and the baby.'

'Well...they had to go away.'

A tear like a pea welled in the corner of one of his eyes. 'I want my mammy.'

'Mammy had to go to...Jesus. He'll take care of her till you see her again. In another life. In...Heaven.' The words poured out. She did not know how she was saying this, these words that she did not believe.

'I want Mammy here. I want the baby here.' He was crying full pelt now.

She gathered him to her and held him tight. 'I'm here, Liam. And feel, my baby's here. In here. He'll be here soon and he'll be your baby, and...I'll be your mammy...Mammy number two. You're a lucky boy, Liam. You have two mammies. Your mammy who was Maeve and me.'

He sniffed. 'Mammy two?' he said.

'Yes. Yes. I'll be Mammy two.'

He was all smiles by the time Min came back, in her outdoor clothes, carrying a tray. 'Bessie says if you're down before ten she'll beat you with a yard broom.' She plonked down the tray, which had a bowl of steaming porridge and a dainty cup of tea. 'Now stay there, you!'

She lifted Liam bodily off the bed. 'Now, young man, you need all your scarves and mitts this morning. There's a perishing frost out there.'

Lizza sat up to attend to the porridge. 'Thank you, Min.'

It must have sounded very heartfelt because Min looked at her sharply. 'I don't know what it is about you, Lizz. You're quiet enough. But the whole of this damned house runs around you.' Then she grinned. 'And with some cause. Get some sleep. After the night we've had, you need it.'

At the door, Liam turned and waved. 'Byebye, Mammy-two,' he said. Min shot her another look and Lizza bent her head over her porridge.

Having scraped the plate clean she lay for a few moments listening, as was her present custom, to Krystof's movements in the attic above. She knew he painted in the very early morning. She wriggled to get more comfortable in the bed. Her stomach felt very hard. Not much room for Charley to move in there now. She had an uneasy feeling, a heaviness that she had not felt so far, despite her bulk.

She shook her head, then swung her legs out to drop out of the high bed. That was when the first hard pain came. She stayed very still

450

till it faded, then stood up. She pulled on the voluminous man's dressing-gown rooted out for her by Bessie and went to the bottom of the attic stairs and called for Krystof.

He came bounding down, his hair up in uncombed spikes, still in his braces, 'What is it, Lizza?'

'Go and tell Bessie I want her, then I'd be grateful if you'd call on the midwife for me. I think it's time.'

He stood very still before her, then put one hand on her shoulder. 'Are you all right?'

She smiled, then winced as another pain hit her. He held her to him.

'Yes,' she said. 'But I'll be more all right by tonight, I think. I'll be even better if you go and get that midwife. Bessie'll tell you where she lives. Go!' She pushed him in the direction of the top of the stairs.

By the time Bessie had made her way upstairs Lizza had stripped the bed. Bessie took the bedding from her. 'Here, hinney, yer shouldn't be carryin' that.'

'Yes I should.' Lizza took it back and placed it on top of a chest of drawers. 'Now, Bessie, where's those old sheets you told me about?'

Bessie went off muttering and was soon back with ancient sheets, past the ministrations of even her nimble fingers. So Lizza went through the familiar routine: drawer organised as a cot for the baby complete with baby-clothes; white enamel dish and muslin cloths to wash the baby; towels; layers of newspaper on the bed, topped with old sheets; extra pillows covered with old pillowslips; old top sheet covered by old rugs to keep warm.

The last time she had gone through this routine had been for Maeve Callaghan, when Anne-Marie had been born. The time before that, when her own Rebecca had been born. She caught hold of the bedpost as another pain struck.

Bessie was behind her, her hard old hand rubbing away at the small of her back. 'Wouldn't it be easier, hinney, if you was in bed?' she asked humbly.

Lizza shook her head, dumb with pain. Then the pain left as suddenly as it had come. She let out a long breath. 'I want to go to the lavatory, then I'll get in. Will you come with me, Bessie?' The pains were coming more quickly than she had thought.

The old woman put an arm through hers. 'Aye, hinney, anything. You just tell us.' On the toilet, the urge to bear down was almost irresistible, but she firmly took her mind away from it.

Back on the landing, she told Bessie to go down and put kettles of water on the range. 'The midwife always wants hot water. Bring the first kettle up after it's boiled, and bring some sharp scissors. Those sewing scissors of yours will do.'

She made her way to the bedroom and finally swung her feet up on to bed. She had been lying there for a second when she felt an enormous contraction. 'Oh, God help me.' She clung to the bedpost and tried to let the pain happen, bearing down with all her might, opening her knees wide. For a second she could feel nothing down there, then came the movement of the baby's head grinding through. Then the contractions took over and her body was doing its own work. 'Bessie!' she yelled.

Puffing and blowing, carrying a huge kettle, Bessie lurched into the room just as the baby was born. 'God in heaven, God in heaven,' she said, her eyes out on stalks.

Lizza, gasping and laughing at the same time, leaned across to pick up the baby who was already bawling his head off. 'A boy,' she said. 'Charles Hugo King.' He was covered in blood and had thick black curly hair, some of it on his back. 'Lungs are all right. Black hair, where did he get all that hair? Black curls!' She was laughing and crying at the same time.

Bessie put her kettle down and leaned on the bed. 'Hinney, yer'll have ter tell us what ter do. Ah've niver in my life...'

Bessie's need steadied Lizza. She took a breath. 'Bessie. It's all right. It'll be all right. Nature does the work, if we're lucky. And today I feel lucky. Now, just pass me that towel so I can wrap him up. Now, put your scissors in the kettle...that'll sterilise them a bit. Now that extra pile of paper, put that under me...'

Too busy to worry too much, they dealt with the afterbirth and with the cutting of the cord. By the time the midwife got there, the afterbirth and the worst top sheet was in its paper parcel for disposal and Lizza was lying back exhausted but triumphant, holding her baby to her. He was still yelling, his birth-blood seeping through the towel which held him. In minutes the midwife had the baby bathed and the bed changed and Lizza into a clean nightie. All this time Bessie was almost dancing about, crowing, 'I manidged meself like. Just did what young Lizza said. D'you know she'd been a nurse, missis? She knew she could trust me. Me a spinster lady and I did it all meself.'

The fat midwife caught Lizza's eye and they exchanged a smile. She placed Charley Hugo King at Lizza's side. His mouth was a large black hole and the noise emerging from it loud enough to wake the dead. 'Here, love, this one was born hungry.'

As the baby clamped himself on to her and sucked, her body tightened itself in response, just as it had in response to Roland on those now distant times when they had made beautiful, spine-tingling love.

The midwife watched with satisfaction. 'You've done very well, Mrs King.'

Lizza beamed up at her. 'I couldn't believe it. Three pains, one push. The other times...' Her smile faded and Charley unhooked himself and started to wail.

The midwife put his head close again, to remind him of what he was missing, and he started to suck again. 'Don't talk, pet, if it agitates you. If it agitates you it'll agitate him. Goes straight to him.'

Lizza took deep breaths and looked down at the little dark head and the red mouth sucking away so vigorously. How Rebecca would have

454

loved him. And the twins, what would they have been like if they had grown and known their brother? She looked calmly at the midwife. 'I had twins who didn't thrive. And a little girl who I lost in the Blitz. But he looks fit, doesn't he?'

'*Fit*!' the midwife almost bellowed. 'He must be nine pounds if he's an ounce. I've seen month-old babies with less on them.'

Bessie reached out and touched the perfect little hand which had escaped the swaddling. The fingers curled round hers. 'Ah never saw anything so young. Niver.' She looked round the bedroom. 'Old Barraclough'd be tickled. A bairn born in his own bed.' She looked hard at Lizza. 'The little lasses, all three of them, they took a look at 'im and left, grinning ear to ear, well pleased. Ah thowt ah'd tell yer. Ah see things but ah dinnet always tell. Now, ah bet you could do with a cup of tea, hinney.'

Lizza nodded and she scuttled off.

In another few minutes, Charley had finished his first meal and was dozing, so Lizza lifted him away and adjusted her nightie.

'Shall I get your husband now, Mrs King?'

'I wish you could. But he's in Scotland, or was the last time I heard. The post's erratic, with the war. The man who came for you was his friend, Mr Sobieski. But you could ask him to come. He will want to see his...godson.'

Finally, alone with Charley, she pulled back the shawl and looked at his small perfect face with its cloud of black hair. One eye opened, then shut again.

Krystof was beside her. The midwife took up the dish in which she had bathed the baby and the heap of soiled parcels, and vanished for her own ritual cup of tea.

'Look, Krystof, here he is!' Lizza was flushed and triumphant. 'Charley Hugo King. Named for Min's dad. I promised her.' She held the baby up. 'Here, take him,' she said.

He lifted the delicate bundle and put his face close to the baby's, almost smelling him. He fitted a finger into the baby's tight clasp. Then he murmured some words in Polish.

'What's that?'

'A little prayer for Polish heroes. A prayer for the future.' He handed the bundle back. 'Now he'll always in some part be mine, Lizza. You know that. In some way, since that night when we were locked together in the Blitz, I knew that he would always be partly mine. And God will take care of him.'

'I told you then. I don't believe...'

'That doesn't matter. I do. The prayer will fly to its true home. This baby is for the future, when the evil is gone. He will grow in a new world. Lizza...'

The midwife returned.

Lizza turned to him. 'Please Krystof, send a wire to Roland. A son! Fit and well. He'll love that.'

He clicked his heels and bowed. 'It is my honour, madame!'

That Monday morning Alice Bremner received a package through the post from Alex. In

456

it were three pairs of socks, holey and stiff with bad washing, and two large card-mounted photographs of himself in uniform, grinning out at the camera. His skin had a sheen from the white photo lighting and his teeth gleamed. The note which accompanied them said all was well and would she pass one of the photos on to Beatrice as he understood she wasn't in the house at Bracks Hill any more, but a working woman in Priorton. He hoped his Gram wasn't moping around and she was to be sure to visit Beatrice as she would be working all hours and the trip through would do Gram good. Gram was to give his love to Lizza and was she a mother yet? He hoped all went well this time. He had been up solo and Gram, there was nothing in this world like it. The skies were the place for heroes. Being up there made you see things clearly. And would she see what she could make of these socks as they had gone queer.

She took a duster and moved it over the already clean surfaces of the photographs. On the top one he had written, *'To Gram, all love Alex'*. On the other he had written, *'To My Mother, Beatrice, with love from her son'*.

Alice got a stool and lifted down the framed holy tract that had been beside Tom's picture since she had put it on the wall in 1917. She sat at the table and unfastened the back, struggling a little with the rusted clips. She did not remove the tract, simply placed Alex's photograph on top of it. Then she put the frame, with its new image, back up on the wall.

She poked the fire, then took her needles and wool and settled down in the rocker and cast on the first sock. She glanced across at the two images on the wall, side by side. 'Belong there together, the pair of you. Like as peas in a pod. Always said so. Now I'll have to go and take the photo to our Beatrice, Alex. Don't know where you think all this money's coming from for all those bus-fares. And yes, our Lizza's due about now. Another bairn into this unforgiving world. Food on ration, world exploding, dead faces looking out at you in the paper and she has another bairn. Always, always going her way. A dreamer, they said at school. A good scholar and a dreamer. But this dreamer's hard, feedin' her dreams with those books, determined always on going her own way. Always was. Beatrice's not like that, Alex. She listens to reason. Our Bernard away, and Renee, and our Jonnie behind wire: just me and Beatrice and you. But then Lizza and the war took her away from here...' Her needles clicked away as she talked to him, his bright face gleaming down at her from a place beyond her reckoning.

Min and Liam, back from school at four o'clock, informed of the news by the crowing Bessie, raced up to visit the new baby. Liam ran across and scrambled on to the bed, then stopped uncertainly. 'Is he eatin' you?' he said.

Lizza looked down at Charley, who was feeding voraciously for the fifth time that day. She laughed. 'No. He has his dinner like this till he gets bigger. I'm his mammy so I have milk in me. He had it when he was inside and now he has it when he is outside. Can't you remember it with your other mammy and Anne-Marie?' She put out a hand. 'Come on, Liam. See your new little brother.'

He turned and ran away, bawling and crying for Bessie. Lizza looked up at Min, standing gingerly on the threshold of the room. 'Oh dear. Are you going to run away crying or will you come here and see your godson, Charley Hugo King?'

Min walked slowly across. Lizza unhooked Charley and fastened her nightie. She held him up. 'Here, take him.'

Min took him and drew him close to her face in wonderment. Her hands were trembling. He opened his eyes and looked at her and gave her a look as old as time. She thrust him back hurriedly at Lizza, who laughed.

Min straightened the quilt, avoiding looking at Lizza till the tears cleared from her eyes. Then she looked at her directly. 'You'll think I'm more of a lunatic than usual, but I swear he has a look of Charley...my father.'

'Babies are mirrors, moulds; they take on the look you wish for them. Just in these first days. Then they become themselves and you can't do that any more. Good thing too. There, he's asleep. Will you put him in his drawer? Bessie says there's something better in the glory-hole but this'll do for the time being.'

Min took him and tucked him in tightly. He looked like a chrysalis with a dark curly head.

'Where did he get that black curly hair from?'

Lizza shook her head. 'Roland's a blonde. My mother had dark hair, so have Beatrice and Bernard. But straight as pumpwater, no curls.'

Min took off her coat and her schoolclothes and pulled on a pair of slacks and a jumper. 'Talking about hair, sit near the edge of the bed and I'll brush yours. It's a mess.'

Lizza edged over and Min leaned against her back, brushing and combing her hair with hard, efficient strokes. Lizza talked dreamily about how easily it had been with Charley, how he had been no bother at all. Then she talked of the twins, and how very hard that had been, and Rebecca, which was not much easier. 'But Charley, he was no trouble at all.'

Min finished off her hair with a green silk scarf. 'There, you look human again. Here, put on that green Barraclough dressing-gown. That'll cover a multitude of sins. There'll be more visitors soon. You're just about bursting out of that nightie with all that built-in nutrition.'

Lizza looked at her. 'What do you think of it, Min, really?'

'I think it's a miracle. But,' she said vehemently, 'I'll never have one. I haven't that kind of courage.'

Lizza reached up and kissed her on the nose. 'The courage comes when you need it.'

'Never!'

There was a clattering noise overhead and footsteps and scrapings on the landing. 'That'll be Krystof. He's sorting some kind of travel bed out of the glory-hole and is taking it down in

460

the study. I'm to be there for a month or so, till Charley stops shrieking in the night. Can't have him keeping us both awake.'

'See? See?' said Min, smiting her brow with a wide-sweeping movement. 'That monster Charley Hugo King has come between us, come to take away my playmate already!'

By the time Josie and Beatrice came in from work, Lizza was installed in the study on the camp-bed. Krystof had carried her down the stairs as though she were a feather and Min had carried Charley down in his shawl and tucked him into the wooden cradle which Krystof had also found in the glory-hole.

Lizza had just settled back, exhausted, on the narrow bed, when the door creaked, but no one entered. Lizza started to talk to Charley. 'Now this is Campion House, Charley, which belongs to Bessie Harraton. And I live here with my family, the best one of whom is Liam Callaghan, your brother. He's a bit shy but he's very good at playing, so as soon as you're big enough you'll be able to play with him...well I never, here he is!'

Liam was walking towards the cot deter-minedly, holding in front of him, right away from his body, a battered red ball. 'A present for Charley,' he said.

'How very kind. Your best ball. Can you put it near his feet for now, and then perhaps you can keep it for him till he gets bigger? That's nice. Now, can you shake hands with him? A good thing for brothers to shake hands. That's nice.' She opened the blankets. 'Now would you like to come in with me for five minutes? I've been missing you all day.'

He flew into the bed and clamped himself at her side and was still there at six-thirty when Beatrice and Josie came in wearily from work.

Lizza watched Josie's face as she held Charley and noted the faintest shadow pass over it. She thanked the fates that Josie had lost her baby through a natural miscarriage, rather than by her own and Beatrice's fumbling machinations.

Josie finally grinned at her and said, 'He looks nothing like you nor Mr King.'

'Some would say he should be thankful,' said Lizza.

'Sure. I don't know. Neither of you is that bad lookin' for oldn's.' Josie dodged Beatrice's ghosted blow. Then she turned to Lizza and said quite seriously. 'I thought he might look like Rebecca, but he doesn't look a bit like her, either.'

Lizza shook her head. 'Bessie said that Rebecca was here, then went when she saw Charley was safely here.'

'She's a queer'n that Bessie,' said Josie.

Beatrice took the baby from Josie with some deliberation and stared down at him with deep wonder. 'He's lovely, Lizz. Really lovely.' She held onto him for a good half-hour until the door opened yet again, and in walked their mother, wearing her best coat and Sunday hat.

'Ma!' The sisters spoke in unison.

Alice nodded, then looked over at Lizza. 'You all right, lass?'

Lizza nodded.

Alice put one package she had been carrying beside Lizza on the bed. Lizza pulled it apart and a finely worked baby shawl fell out. 'Ma, this is lovely.'

Alice's face was visited by the faintest of smiles. 'I thought you'd be too busy with your head in a book to knit.'

Lizza smiled back, for once not feeling the slightest need to defend herself.

'An' this one's for you,' said Alice to Beatrice. 'From our Alex.'

Reluctantly, Beatrice surrendered Charley to her mother and took the parcel. When she saw the inscription her face went fiery red. 'What is it?' said Lizza, holding out her hand. She read the inscription and handed it back. 'Well, maybe being up in the sky makes you think more clearly. 'Bout time he called you mother.'

Beatrice looked from the photo, to Charley still fast asleep in her mother's arms. 'Funnily enough, I've been thinking lately it must be nice to have a baby of your own,' she said. 'Now, Ma, can I get you a cup of tea?'

Later that evening, when Krystof had walked Alice through the blackout to the bus-stop, and Liam and Min had paid their very last visits, Bessie brought two cups of cocoa into the study.

'Sit down, Bessie,' said Lizza. 'I wanted to tell you what a brick you were. I couldn't've managed without you. You were wonderful.'

Bessie stayed standing, fingering her cup. 'Yeh'd a manidged. Big manidger, you. I allus

463

say that, whoever asks.' She moved from one foot to the other.

'What's worrying you, Bessie?' Lizza felt very tired and longed to go to sleep before hungry Charley woke up yet again.

'Ah saw that bairn o' yourn an' got thinkin' about time. He lives to my age an' he'll be on this earth twenty sommat, never mind nineteen sommat. An' that made me think about May Lynn. An' when your ma was here, I went down the pollis an' told'm about her, about her walkin' off.'

'What they say?'

'They said ah should'a gone to tell'm months ago. Ah said May Lynn worried about the pollis. They laughed. Rude, they were. Anyway, they're comin' round here fust thing to ask questions.'

Lizza nodded. 'Good. Then they can find where she is and Min or Beatrice can go and bring her back. You're not happy without her, are you?'

'Ter tell yer the truth, when that lovely thing happened this mornin' with yon bairn, I wanted that hard to tell May Lynn you could a' carved that want right outta the air.'

'Well, Bessie, you did the right thing. The police'll get on to it and they'll find her.' Lizza handed over the empty cocoa cup, snuggled down, and Bessie tucked her in. She yawned. 'They'll find her, Bessie.'

Ten minutes later she was sitting up, wide awake, trembling with fear. She had gone to sleep thinking about the last time she had seen May Lynn, when she was going off into the

464

night, tucked into the big green cloak. Then she had fallen instantly into a dream where Theo Callaghan, dressed in the green cloak, had leapt at her out of the dark, and this time there was no chair, so she could not stop his raping attack.

Charley started to wail, and she leaned over to pluck him out of the crib. She undid her nightie and put him to her breast, but he was restless and not so content, latching into her growing worry and new concern about May Lynn: not just about her whereabouts, but about her safety.

CHAPTER 30

The girls at the factory were eager to know all about the birth of Beatrice's nephew. They were sitting round the table in the canteen, having eaten mash with, according to Esme, some sausages that had been nowhere near a pig, rather nearer to a bloody sawdust machine. 'Can't see why they don't call them *sawdustages* and be done with it,' she had said.

Now she was leaning forward, lighting her cigarette from Josie's Woodbine. 'Did she have a bad time, poor cow?'

Josie glanced at Beatrice.

Beatrice was quite relaxed, pleased that this dinner-time at least she did not have to fence off questions about whether or not she really wanted to go with Mick Stratton. And whether he had kissed her. And if he had, just what kind of kisser he was. She had been thinking of that photo of Alex, and how next time she saw Mick, she might show it to him.

She shrugged. 'I don't know what kind of time she had. Wasn't there. Our Lizza said she had an easy time. What she said was, "Three pains, one push and he was there." ' Beatrice tried to think what had happened in those hours just before Alex had burst from her, all those years ago, but that slot of time was wiped from her memory.

'No such thing as an easy time,' announced Mary. 'I'm not gonna have any kids meself. It kills yer. Me ma had six and it killed her. Died at thirty-six. Then me da goes and gets another one and she's had three already. So he's busy killing *her* now.'

'Aw,' said Esme, 'you can't say that, Mary. If all of us thought like that, that'd be the end of good old Britain all right. There'd be no need for old Hitler ter bomb us out. He'll just have ter wait, hang on for a while.'

'Well,' said Mary defensively, 'me ma used to say if the men had to have them there'd be only one child in every family, even Catholic ones like ours.'

'Hey!' said Esme. 'Did yer see that Mr Bevin, our beloved Minister, thinks we're the jewel in his crown? And he wants more like us. A hundred thousand.' She scrabbled in her bag for her paper. She stood up and put her fist up to her mouth, little finger in the air,

466

to cough. ' "...*I want them, look-you, to come forward, look-you, in the spirit, look-you...*" '

'I bet he's not Welsh,' spluttered Mary. 'It's the other one...'

Esme glared at her through beetling brows ' "...*look-you...to come forward in the spirit that they are going to suffer some inconvenience...*" '

'Inconvenience!' shouted Josie. 'Like yer hair turning yeller...'

'...and yer eyebrows gettin' blown off...' said Mary. 'And worse.' The laughter died a little. Then the whistle went and they laughed again and gathered their things together for the afternoon shift. Josie nipped out her half-smoked cigarette and tucked it in her hair-roll.

'You shouldn't do that,' scolded Esme. 'You get wrong for doing that.'

Josie laughed. 'Look who's talking. Who else is it that's desperate for a fag the second they're off the line?'

They walked out of the canteen and down the long passage to the changing room, in a long line, arm-in-arm.

Late on Tuesday morning Lizza had a wire from Roland. 'WONDERFUL BABY CHARLEY STOP TRUST ALL WELL STOP LETTER FOLLOWING STOP ROLAND.'

She was sitting up, fully dressed, on the camp-bed. She smoothed the paper on her knee and looked across at the crib. 'That's your daddy, Charley. Pleased about you. But he's busy with his aeroplanes and is not likely to be down on the next train. But he's a nice

467

man, Charley, and I think you will like him. He's very good at graphs.'

She closed her eyes and tried to summon up Roland's face but she couldn't. She could see his figure crouching over those interminable graphs he used to make, but she couldn't see his face. She closed her eyes even tighter but still it wouldn't come. She scrabbled in her handbag and took out a photo, the twin to the one he had on his works identity card. Yes. Yes. Of course, fair hair. Nice direct look. 'See, Charley, he's nice-looking, your daddy, really nice-looking. And he's doing a very important job for the government. On an island up in Scotland. That's a long way from here.'

She heard the doorbell and there were voices in the hall. The heavy sneering tone of a man boomed out and Bessie's protesting squeak.

'Bessie!' shouted Lizza. 'Bring whoever it is in here.'

Bessie came into the study with the man whom Lizza recognised as the policeman who had taken Krystof off for investigation.

'The poliss says his name's Morgan. Wants to know about May Lynn and I telt 'im about it an' he says how do I know what I'm sayin', an old woman like me.' Bessie was clearly upset.

Constable Morgan eyed Lizza. 'Sorry to disturb you, missis, in your condition.'

Lizza swung her feet on to the carpet, stood up and looked him in the eye. 'I am fine, thank you, *Mr* Morgan. What do you want to know?'

'The name's Constable Morgan, Missis. An'

I want to know all about when she went from here on Christmas Eve.'

Lizza shrugged. 'She had been here just as usual. She helps Bessie. She's her friend. It was a cold night.'

There was a pause while the Constable wrote this very slowly down in his notebook. 'What was she wearing?'

'She only had a shawl. So we wrapped her in a cloak from this house and she went off home.'

'And you expected her on Christmas Day?'

'Yes.'

'And she didn't come?'

'No.'

'Didn't you think that was, like, a bit funny? The old woman here didn't seem to think too much of that.'

Lizza glanced at Bessie, who was wringing her pinny into a twisted rope. 'We did. We all did. But *Miss Harraton* here,' she paused, 'Miss Harraton, she knows May Lynn very well. They are very old friends. And Miss Harraton knows that May Lynn's done this before several times. Just walked off for a few weeks. Once at Christmas five years ago. She was from a travelling family and Miss Harraton said she had itchy feet.'

There was a silence while his pen scratched away at his notebook. Then he looked up. 'She should still have come to tell us straight away.'

'Miss Harraton knew that May Lynn would be mortally offended if she sent the police after

469

her. May Lynn, like many travellers, has certain views of the police. So Miss Harraton waited. And she's come to you now that so much time has elapsed. She's an old lady and there's no point in harassing her.'

He clipped his pen on to the notebook. 'There's no question of harassing anyone, Mrs King. The facts have to be verified.'

She looked him hard in the eye. 'Well, *Mr Morgan*, now you've verified your facts, perhaps you can start looking for May Lynn.'

He fastened his cloak and adjusted his bicycle clips. 'Yes. Well. I'll see myself out.' He did not so much bang the door as shut it with a definite click behind him.

'Are you all right, Bessie?' said Lizza anxiously.

Bessie's purple knobbly hands were smoothing down her apron. 'The poliss. I hate 'em. Me da, he hated 'em, the poliss. I remember that, even though I was a bairn of ten when he fell off his roof. This very roof.'

She stomped out and Lizza sat down hard on the bed, suddenly tired out with the drama of the thing. Charley cried to be fed, and it was only when she was in the middle of feeding him that she remembered the dream she had had, which somehow connected Theo Callaghan and the green cloak. Rocking backward and forwards, she wondered whether it was worth confiding these half-formed ideas to the taciturn Constable Morgan.

'You should go and see that baby,' Mara Laine

looked up from her book at Roland. Since the arrival of the telegram she had been different with him: courteous but essentially neutral. He had tried to broach the subject directly with her. 'What is it, Mara? The baby?'

She shrugged. 'We...you should not stay away from your son.'

'But you knew about...'

She put up her hands. 'I am selfish. I thought of me...us. Now I think of the son.' She looked straight at him. 'I had no babies. He did not think it...appropriate. He did not permit.'

He did not need to try her bedroom door to know the ancient key had been gently turned on the other side. He was sleeping again now in the room with Pieter Vann.

The third night after the telegram they were sitting at opposite sides of the table, working. She felt his gaze on her and looked up. 'You must go now, Roland. Go and see her...and him.'

He pushed away his papers, and took off the spectacles he had found necessary in recent months. He saw now that this was all some kind of test. A game, the rules of which were a mystery to him. 'I was just thinking the same, Mara. I'm sure Pieter Vann can spare me today and tomorrow. That leaves...' He consulted his battered diary. '...Sunday the sixteenth, when I would be off work anyway. I'll be back then. Just check with Pieter when he gets back.'

Pieter was rarely at the cottage now. He had started keeping company with the fisherman's widow, who was the sister of the chess-player.

He had lost some of his weight and was looking younger and more carefree by the day.

Roland put his glasses back on his nose. 'There are things I need to sort out with Lizza,' he said quietly.

'You should try to move down into County Durham.' Her voice was still sickeningly neutral. 'There are shadow factories down there, aren't there? Or other work so that you could be with them? Your family.'

He laughed shortly. 'I couldn't, even if I wanted to. I'll definitely be under these rules of Mr Bevin's about essential work. We're tied now just as if we signed on for the army.'

Her eyes were straying back to her book. 'Will you get a travel warrant?'

'There'll be no problem with a warrant. But the trains are erratic. There's this new man who's arrived at the plant with a motorbike. I'll see if he'll lend it to me and I'll make my way down on that.'

Mara pulled her colourful shawl round her, gathered up her book and went out of the room, barely looking at him as she said good night. The next morning he made his own breakfast and there was no response when he knocked on her door and said goodbye. The sadness that he felt at this was more profound than any he had felt in his life, even when his daughter died.

The journey was ill-fated. The borrowed motorbike was wiped out under him in Clydeside, as his attempt to get through that area coincided with Scotland's heaviest raid of the war. The vehicle was thrown fifty feet and he was flung into the air an equal distance. He came on to a stack of sandbags, with the world once more in flames around him. He might just have been back in Coventry. It was as though the months between had been nothing. Buildings were still tumbling and the scream of sirens and false jollity of fire-engine bells still cut the air. He lay there and, for a second, he thought he was still in Coventry, and that all between—the island, the new plant and Mara Laine, the new baby in place of Rebecca—all that had been a dream, a dream of delight and despair in equal parts. Then, as he felt his limbs and his head to see if he was injured, he knew this was different. The island and Mara Laine were still there. And would always be.

He hauled himself to his feet and limped through the blazing streets, dodging friendly traffic and exploding enemy action alike. He kept walking through that day and the next, hitched lifts on waggons, army and civilian, and didn't stop till he got back to the ferry. It was still Sunday evening when he got back to the house on the harbour. The house door was open but Mara's bedroom door was firmly shut.

He knocked hard, twice, before there was a sleepy reply.

'Mara. Open the door!'

Another sleepy reply.

He battered the door with his fist, then kicked it with his boot. It opened very quickly. She was in a warm dressing gown. Her thick hair was in a single plait over her shoulder. She was furious. 'What do you think you're doing?

...My goodness, what happened?'

She pulled him in. He was filthy, almost asleep on his feet, his eyes half closed. He was mumbling. 'No further than Glasgow. A raid...' He collapsed on to the bed.

'I heard, but I hoped, hoped you had missed it.' She was kneeling at his feet, unfastening his boots.

'Couldn't find a way through. All that fire, clashing, the tenements crashing down, dead bodies, people crying...Coventry again. Motorbike blown from under me,' he mumbled.

She stood up and put her arms around him, pulling his arms round her waist, pulling his head to her breast. 'Ssh. We heard, saw, even from here.'

'Just like Coventry, Mara. Hell. Hell on earth.'

She lowered him to her bed and lifted up his feet, then loosened his trousers and pulled them off, loosened his collar and removed his tie.

As she pulled up the blanket he caught hold of her hand. 'I'm not going away, ever again...stay here with you...the island. You and the...'

She remained there, holding his hand for the next three hours. Every time she made a move, he clung on to her. Finally, she crept into bed beside him and pulled the quilt over herself to keep warm. It was three in the morning when she felt him wake up and slip out of bed.

When he came back he was wearing his pyjamas and smelled of carbolic soap. 'Mara? I meant it. I'm here now. For good. I'll not go back, ever.' He gathered her to him and kissed her and they made love tentatively, slowly, showing power and celebrating life, in deliberate denial of the destruction just visited on them.

On the Friday night that Clydebank was bombed Michael Stratton called at Campion House to take Beatrice to the dance. Josie, dressed up herself for her Friday night out, led him into the kitchen, trying desperately hard to suppress her smiles. 'Here's Mick Stratton for Beatrice,' she announced. 'I'll just run up and tell her. She was just sewing on a button, when I was up there.'

Lizza stood up, still holding Charley, and shook his hand. She surveyed him curiously. 'Hello, Mick. This is Bessie Harraton, our landlady, who keeps us all in order, and this is Liam, Josie's brother.' Liam looked up from the mat where he was crayoning on paper made for him by Min from carefully flattened sugar bags. Mick tucked his folded cap in his pocket, eased his trouser-creases and squatted on his haunches. 'What's this then?'

Liam looked at him for a judgemental second, then said, 'Aeroplane.'

'Would yer like me ter draw yer one?'

Liam nodded and held out his precious crayon.

Mick took it and a fresh flattened sugar bag from the pile and his hand moved across the paper and with powerful strokes drew a young pilot climbing out of the cockpit of a Spitfire. Liam clapped his hands with delight.

The door opened and Beatrice came in, followed by Min.

Mick straightened up and smoothed his hands down his trousers. 'Hello.' Liam stood up beside him.

Beatrice nodded to him.

Min smiled mischievously. 'Michael! It *is* you who're...Beatrice's dancing partner.'

He nodded, then he looked at Beatrice. 'Are yeh ready?'

She nodded.

'But you can't go till Krystof's said hello,' said Min. 'Come up and see him in his lair.' She glanced at Bessie, who put her head on one side then nodded. 'Come on, Beatrice, we'll take him up there. There's a portrait of you which is just...well, come and see.'

They left the kitchen, trailed by Liam. Lizza sat down in the vacuum of silence left behind them. Bessie looked up at her over her stitching. 'Sometimes, hinney, it all seems like it's happenin' to someone else, doesn't it?'

Lizza had been wishing she could bustle up there with the others, give her opinion on the paintings which Krystof was assembling now, for their exhibition in Durham City. Sometimes, with Charley on her knee, she felt invisible. She shook her head. 'Bessie, you never miss a thing.'

'Folks on the edges never do. It's when yer in the middle when yer canna see the whole of the pattern.' She held up the quilt in the gaslight, turning it this way and that to throw the continuous line of stitches into shadow and reveal the depth and complexity of the design.

Lizza looked hard at the old woman. Her face was whiter and sharper than usual; her eyes seemed more deep-set. 'You've got May Lynn on your mind, Bessie.'

The old woman shook her head. 'May Lynn, she first came ter this house fifty, mebbe sixty years ago, sellin' pegs. Still on the road then, with her man. Kept comin', mebbe twenty years, reg'lar as apples in autumn. Fine pegs. Then her man died of the cold one winter, an' she got on with a man at the abattoir an' she came *in brick,* into a house, like. An' she came in this 'ouse now an' then and give us a hand with the spring cleaning an' that. Old Barraclough never knew. Then her next man turned up his toes, after too much beer on Market Day. She would'a gone back on the road then, but for me. Nowadays, it's just now and then she goes on her walking.'

'So that's what's happened this time,' said Lizza eagerly.

Bessie straightened the quilt across the table and shook her head. 'Nah. It's not that,' she said quietly. Then she sighed a weary sigh. 'Wherever she is, ah need ter find her. Police'll be deein' nowt, busy worryin' about who's showin' light in the black-out.'

Lizza tucked the sleeping Charley into his pram, which was stuck awkwardly behind the kitchen table. 'Why don't you and me go and look for her tomorrow, Bessie? It's Saturday. Min's off school, so I'll ask her to mind Charley. Then we can go across to May Lynn's house

477

and, kind of, try to find where she might be. We could do that. Couldn't we?'

The next day they walked the mile to Copton Gaunt, the hamlet where May Lynn lived. Copton Gaunt had once been a thriving pit village whose streets housed the families which serviced two pits. After the pits had been worked out, the houses emptied as people moved, scattered across the North-East and further in search of work. The houses, primitive and ill-serviced, were let out at a very low rent to anyone who would occupy them.

May Lynn's house was a centre one of twelve set round three sides of a square with a block of coal-houses and communal privies making up the fourth side. They peered through the window, then Bessie fished the key up on its string through the letter box and they went in. The single living room was sparse and fairly tidy and had a sour smell about it. The narrow window was curtained with a bright fringed shawl. The fire was long dead but there was a kettle half full of water standing on the hob. The food cupboard beside the fire was empty, only a trail of sugar and flour on the shelf showing what had been there.

Lizza climbed the ladder which led up into a hole in the ceiling. When she was halfway through it she could see, by light lipping through the tiles, the small bed in the cramped space and a large wooden box with the edge of a skirt or dress trailing through.

She came back down, relieved. 'She's not there.'

Bessie was straightening the cloth on the centre table, putting the random collection of plates and jam jars in a dish which stood on a box under a tap by the back door. 'She never come back,' she announced.

'What?'

'After she was at the house. She never come back.'

'How do you know that?'

Bessie looked Lizza full in the face. 'Ah know it. Ah can tell, standin' 'ere. An' she wouldn't go off walking without comin' back here to this ken to see things straight. Ah know that too. She was tidy.'

Lizza put a hand on the frail shoulder. 'I'm sorry, Bessie.'

Bessie shrugged off her hand. 'Give us a bit help here, sortin' it out. May Lynn wouldn't want it left like this.'

When they came out, blinking, into the daylight, May Lynn's next-door neighbour, a narrow-faced young woman in a dingy turban, was lying in wait for them. 'Are you friends of 'ers? The poliss was here too, asking for 'er,' she announced.

'Do you know where May Lynn is?' asked Lizza.

She shook her head. 'Went off some time over Christmas,' she said. 'Never come back. But like I says to the poliss, she did that sometimes, went off. An' she owed me a cup o' sugar. Never know where ye are with these gypsies.'

'Ah see ye helped yerself to the sugar. Flour too, as ah can see,' said Bessie sourly.

'Ah've a right to what's me own,' said the girl. 'Anyway, like ah said ter the poliss, what're ye gonna do about her dog? They did bugger all, like. But ah canna keep it off me doorstep.'

She pulled a string from behind her. Cringing at the end of it was a very thin whimpering dog, a rough-haired mongrel with many signs of whippet in it. 'It vanished for two days when she went, then came back, an's been hangin' round here ever since. Ah kept it, cos ah thowt it'd be worth half a crown of anybody's money.'

Lizza looked down at the pathetic creature. Then she made to take the string from the woman. The woman fought her for it. 'Half a crown, ah said. Ah've bin lookin' after it all these months.'

Bessie put her hand into her coat pocket, pulled out a two-shilling piece, lay it in her palm and held it out to the woman, who grabbed at it and released her hold on the dog.

Lizza pulled at the string, and the dog leapt, trembling, into her arms. She grabbed Bessie's arm and walked determinedly away from the woman. When they were at a safe distance, she said to Bessie, 'You shouldn't've given her money, Bessie. She did nothing for this poor little thing.'

'She needs it,' said Bessie briefly.

'She'll just spend it on beer.'

'How do yer know that?'

Duly reprimanded, Lizza stroked the dog as they walked along. The trembling stopped.

'Polly!' announced Bessie. 'That's its name.'

The dog leapt out of Lizza's arms and started

to strain ahead. Lizza hung on to the string as the little dog fought to get away. 'Come here, come here!' she shouted desperately.

'Foller 'er lead,' said Bessie. 'Foller 'er lead. Ah'll come after.'

Running after the dog, Lizza soon drew away from Bessie along the winding lane. The dog dragged her off the lane, through a gap in the hedge and down a track which still had sleepers for a narrow railway line. The lane was sticky with mud from the recently melted snow and Lizza was pleased she'd had the forethought to put on her galoshes. When they were nearly out of sight of the lane she started to shout at the dog, to pull her back. Then she fell over her, stopping on her haunches beside a wedge-shaped hole in the ground.

In the middle distance Lizza could see tumbled buildings and the rusty support struts for a conveyor: familiar signs of a worn-out pit. Polly jumped up at her and whined, her fine-boned, wide-eyed face somehow at odds with her rough, matted hair.

'What is it, Polly?'

The dog started to scrabble with her paws at the edge of the hole, then she leapt forward and Lizza's hand burned as the string whipped out of it and the dog vanished into the black space. In a second all she could hear was Polly whimpering and scrabbling far below. She looked back and saw Bessie in the distance coming through the hole in the fence. 'Polly's gone down a hole,' called Lizza.

Bessie scurried across the field and knelt at

the edge of the hole, her head on one side, listening to the yelps. 'She's not too far down. Ah can see her string on a root. Hang on ter me heels.'

Lizza found herself kneeling beside Bessie, clinging on to the old woman's belt for dear life, as she leaned further and further into the hole, shouting and crooning in a language Lizza didn't understand.

'Huh!' Bessie gave a grunt of satisfaction and sat back suddenly, sending Lizza flying. The dog started yelping at a higher pitch and Bessie pulled her out of the hole by her string, like an angler landing a fish. The dog did a somersault and landed on her feet.

Lizza scrambled to her feet and squatted down beside the dog, which growled, guarding an object she had in her mouth.

'Leave!' said Lizza in as hard a voice as she could muster.

Polly looked up at her, her lambent eyes gleaming in the thin March sunshine. Then, very gently, she lay a sodden rag at Lizza's feet.

'Good dog. Good dog.' Lizza patted the fragile head then picked up what looked like a piece of black cloth. She handed it to Bessie, who was standing very still beside her. The old woman took the cloth and squeezed slimy black water from it. Then she shook it out and held it up in the sun. The rotting cloth was not black but green.

'The cloak,' said Lizza. 'I wrapped May Lynn in the green cloak before she went off.'

'Yer'd better get up, lass. We'll have ter get down there and tell that poliss. May Lynn wants nothing in a dirty pit-hole an' no prayers said for her. I'm gettin' that poliss.' Bessie was stalking back across the grass and Lizza had to pick up the trembling Polly, and run after her.

As she did so, she ducked down quickly as the heavy drone of aeroplanes filled the skies and she could make out a formation of black bombers making their steady way further north. Polly barked at them. Bessie stopped a second to look up at them, clutching Lizza's arm. 'What with getten' blawn up and drownin' in dirty pit-holes, hinney, it's a wonder any of us is spared. Any one at all.'

CHAPTER 31

When Lizza and Bessie got back from the police station there was chaos in the house. Charley's penetrating wail assaulted them from somewhere upstairs. Min was at the kitchen sink, washing the knees of a howling Liam, who had fallen head over heels on the frozen gravel outside. Polly pattered across to him and started to howl in unison. Liam stopped instantly, his eyes out on stalks at the sight of the moth-eaten dog.

'This is Polly,' said Lizza, tying the dog's string to the table leg. 'She was May Lynn's dog.'

'Was?' said Min.

Lizza glanced at Bessie, who was holding the crusted black kettle under the tap. 'We found May Lynn's coat, well, Polly did, didn't she, Bessie? Then the police found May Lynn...she had fallen into a pit-hole on the common beside the Copton Gaunt path. She must have wandered off, on her way back home on Christmas Eve.'

Then she left them, going off in search of the distressed Charley. She leapt up the stairs two at a time, and was breathless when she reached the attic. Krystof's hair was awry and his colour was high. He smiled his relief when he saw her and thrust Charley into her arms. 'Thank God you're here, Elizabeth. This boy is very desperate for something.'

The yelling lessened as she took Charley, but he continued to cry. 'He's hungry. I should start him on bottles.' She looked around.

'Here, let me help you out of your coat.'

As she moved Charley from one arm to the other they peeled her coat off between them. Instantly Charley was nuzzling, feeling his way into her.

'I'll have to go down,' she said.

'No! Sit here!' he said, his tone peremptory. He grabbed a pile of papers from the iron bed which doubled as his sofa. 'He is too hungry to wait. I will work.'

He plumped up two pillows to put behind her and pressed her to sit down. Then he turned his back and tacked up a new sheet on his makeshift easel. She loosened her blouse, then shared with Charley his relief at food being on hand at last. As he sucked away she closed her eyes, trying to work the events of the last few hours into her understanding of things. May Lynn must have wandered off the track somehow on Christmas Eve. She frowned, trying to remember the weather that night.

'Don't frown,' said Krystof.

Her eyes flew open and she blushed. Charley whimpered but she settled him back, soothed him. 'Krystof you...'

'Forgive me. You are so...lovely there with Charley... You make me think of my wife and my sons...that same cry, that same beautiful solution. Please may I...?' He gestured towards the empty sheet before him with his charcoal.

She took a deep breath, then nodded, adjusting the edge of her blouse with more effective modesty around Charley's head. She allowed herself to watch Krystof's work: the wiry strength of his shoulder and upper arm; the strong supple hands; the hair allowed to grow too thick on his neck so that the thickness took on a hint of a wave; the depth of his gaze as he glanced and kept glancing at her. Then she started to think of those hands when they had been above her on the beam, the sinews inside the wrist bulging as he kept his weight off her in the big raid. Her glance moved down his body and she closed her eyes, allowing her body to need him just for a moment.

Then she shook her head. She had to stop this. 'There's something I can't understand about you, Krystof,' she said.

He glanced over at her and smiled. 'Just one, Elizabeth?'

'You've seen some terrible things before you came to England. We saw some terrible things together in Coventry. There is what is happening to Pieter Vann's family...your wife. You've...lost your sons. You've no idea where your wife is...I lost my twinnies and then Rebecca. And now He's let poor Mary Lynn wander off on Christmas Eve, and take I don't know how long to die in a black hole on Copton Common. Bessie's breaking her heart down in the kitchen. He's taken her friend.'

He was staring at her.

'And yet you still believe there's a God, Krystof. You mention Him all the time. You go to your church on Sundays.'

'And you don't? You were not taught to believe?'

She rolled her eyes. 'Took it in with my mother's milk. She talks to Him every day. Chapel three times on a Sunday. *"Jesus saves"* on the morning, and *"Hell-and-damnation"* on the night. Ma sees Him as this wise man with a great beard, the father she never had, who looks on the terrible things with sorrow and understanding. I see nothing.' She paused. 'No! I do see something: a kind of cosmic conspiracy for destruction, for reducing man to a kind of helpless, dangling object...' The familiar despair was invading her now, and tears were pricking her eyes. Charley whimpered. She cuddled him closer.

Krystof put down his charcoal and came to

486

sit beside her. He took her hand and started to stroke, almost massage, the back of it with his thumb. 'I have to tell you the beauty in my church in my home village was my first vision of beauty: the colours, the forms, the stillness, the intricacy. The weaving sounds and the storm of words assaulted my senses. A person cannot release, cannot forgo that sense of wonder, of beauty and order that is absorbed by your soul as a child.'

She leaned down to kiss the top of Charley's head. 'But all those things, they were made by men and women. People imagined a God and made the things for Him. People need a superior kind of audience for their images, their words. What it was, was the best of themselves. Their skills; their poetry; their fantasy.'

He nodded slowly. 'So it is.' Then he looked around the long attic, now a forest of paintings and drawings accumulating for the Durham exhibition. 'But I cannot account for how, when I paint, new things creep in, which I had not conceived. I don't understand how people, seeing my paintings, see far more in them than I understand. There is another dimension, extra to human intention, and in there lies my idea of God: not a man with a beard, maybe not even a man, although I take care not to let priests hear me say it. It is something outside, a creative thing.'

'And my Rebecca, those dead and dying people we saw in Coventry, your boys, those people in the factory in Germany?'

He shook his head. 'It is a hard equation.

If we are free to create we have to be free to destroy. A merciless freedom. Like the beautiful objects, the heavenly music: such things are men's creation.'

She shook her head.

He stood up. 'You're too polite, Elizabeth, too secret to show your disagreement. One day you'll throw pots at my head.' He leaned down and kissed Charley's head, his cheek only an inch from the heat of her breast. Then he turned towards his easel, and as he turned away, he said, 'I love you.'

Or she thought he did. Her brain cartwheeled for a second with images of bright Eastern churches, the flare of fire over Coventry. Her hands started to shake. She wanted to shout at him, 'What did you say? Say it loud!' But she couldn't. Then Charley slipped off her breast into his post-prandial sleep and she was busy with her blouse again and there was no easy way of pursuing what he may or may not have said.

'So when is this exhibition in Durham?'

'Three months' time. There is much to do, to get everything ready.' His head was down, his voice distracted.

She stood up. 'I'd best go and see how Bessie is. She's cut up about her friend May Lynn.'

'I can see she will be.' His shoulders were hunched as he concentrated on the central section of the drawing. He did not turn round as she left the room and she made her way down the stairs in a daze.

Min caught her on the landing, shepherded

her into the bedroom and plonked her on the bed. 'Sit there for five minutes and talk to me. You're always bustling by. This house is so full of people: Beatrice, Josie, Krystof, Liam. Now that little monster on your hip, even if he is called Charley Hugo.'

Lizza grinned at her, adjusting Charley's shawl. 'What's the matter, Min? Not the centre of attention?'

Min blushed. 'There you are, that's what I mean. I need you to say things like that to knock me off my pompous pedestal, to laugh with me in the night. So I want you and Charley to come back here. You don't need to stay on that rickety cot in the study.'

Lizza looked longingly at the high soft bed with its comfortable mattress. 'Charley wakes at least twice in a night, you know, and his screams penetrate the thickest blankets.'

'I don't care! He's my father's namesake and I'm used to his day-time howls anyway. I don't care. Come on, Lizza. This bed's so, forgive-my-French, bloody cold.'

Lizza laughed and stood up. 'Yes, yes. All right, Min, if you can stand the howls. I wouldn't mind my night's sleep broken if I was on a soft bed instead of that army thing. Now I've got to see how Bessie is.'

Min smote her brow. 'See what I mean? This house is too full. Like the Tower of Babel.'

Beatrice and Josie were in the kitchen. The cold of the night air was still on them from their walk from the station. Lizza told them about May Lynn and asked where Bessie was, but they hadn't seen her. Beatrice took Charley from Lizza so she could go off to search the downstairs rooms, but Bessie was nowhere to be found. Lizza finally tracked her down in her little maid's bedroom in the back of the house, lying on her narrow bed with her face towards the whitewashed ceiling. For a heart-stopping second Lizza thought she was dead.

She touched her arm. 'What is it, Bessie?'

Bessie turned her face towards her. 'May Lynn wouldn't go off the path, hinney, not on the darkest night. An' ah could feel her there, tellin' me that. An' ah could hear her shrieking like a demented crow against the feller draggin' 'er across that common.'

Lizza stood very still trying to pull out something which was niggling away at the back of her mind. Then she shook her head. 'Look, Bessie, we'll go to the police station tomorrow morning to tell them what you think. In the meantime, you can't lie up there. There are people in this house who need you.'

'They dinnat need an old woman,' Bessie muttered, closing her eyes again.

Lizza shook her shoulder. 'Yes they do. We do. And I'm staying till you come. Even if Charley screams and Liam yells, I'm staying here.'

Bessie swung her thin legs to the floor, her feet feeling for her old leather slippers, grumbling about folks who couldn't look after themselves. But she did allow Lizza to walk downstairs with her arm through hers, and she did tidy her hair in the hall mirror before she went towards the hubbub in the kitchen.

They didn't go to the police station the following morning. Constable Morgan came to the house to tell them that the body of the deceased had been examined and there were signs that the death was due to more than a simple 'death by exposure', come about through an old woman straying off a path. He would, he said, be returning early in the following week, to pursue his enquiries further. This perked Bessie up no end and she went about her evening tasks singing in her wavering voice.

In the next few weeks Liam and Polly became inseparable. Polly was the first thing Liam looked for when he came in from nursery school and the last thing he saw at night, as Polly, fatter and sleeker now, slept under a window in the room he shared with Josie. At first Liam pulled her around the house and down into the garden on her string, but that became very quickly unnecessary: the dog never left his side, and her eyes surveyed his small figure with slavish love.

They had occasional neutral reports from Constable Morgan about the investigation, but the recovery and examination of the body and its final surrender—this seemed to be the limits of any real commitment. 'Too busy persecuting people who've happened to lift a curtain,' said Bessie.

Everyone except Lizza and Charley went to May Lynn's funeral. Even Amos Silkin put in an appearance at the chapel, and turned up at the house afterwards to drink his old friend

491

Barraclough's brandy, and to talk to Bessie about the blessings of friendship.

The next day, when everyone else was out, Bessie asked Lizza if she'd come with her to do something for May Lynn. 'Leave the bairn with the Russian and come with us.' It was a tone which brooked no refusal.

She smiled. 'He's Polish, not Russian, Bessie.' At least Charley would take the occasional bottle now, so it would not be the same as last time.

Bessie sniffed. 'He's from across there somewhere and anyway, like ah telt yer at fust, he's like that feller in the book. That Pierre sommat.'

There was a cart piled with wooden boxes at May Lynn's door when they arrived, attended by a narrow, wall-eyed man with a horse. Lizza glanced at Bessie. 'How did you fix this up?' she said, as they opened the door.

'That Silkin feller sorted it. I telt 'im it had to be done.' She looked round the room. 'She didn't have much, poor lass. Anyway, we need all of this on the cart.'

They heaped all May Lynn's things into the boxes and the carter nailed the boxes down and loaded them on to the cart. Bessie climbed up to sit beside him and reached down a hand to help Lizza up beside her.

'Where're we taking them?' asked Lizza.

'You'll see,' said Bessie, settling her skirts. 'The gypsies. They all do this. May Lynn would want it.'

The cart stopped beside the break in the hedge where May Lynn must have run from

492

her pursuer. The carter lifted the boxes down and heaped them into a kind of pyramid on the far side of the hedge, away from the road. Then he put paper kindling under the four corners of the pile and lay two old rakes to one side. He looked down at Bessie. 'Is that all, missis?'

She opened her steel-clasped purse, drew out a crisp ten-shilling note, and pressed it in his hand. 'Thank you, Silas. Ah'm for ever in yer debt.'

He tipped his cap and climbed back up. They watched him ride off.

'Now what?' said Lizza.

'What d'yer think?' said Bessie, thrusting a box of matches in her hands. 'We burn it. The lot. It's the custom.'

It took a very industrious half-hour to get a good blaze going. It was a relief then, just to stand and watch the flames licking up around the boxes, and hear the cackle and the soft plop as one box collapsed into the next. It took a good hour of poking and raking together to reduce it to a heap of grey ashes. Lizza thought of the healing resolve which fire could bring, as well as savage destruction. Then she realised that it was days since she had thought of Rebecca. And even now when she thought of her, at last there was no pain. As she and Bessie worked together the task took on an air of celebration, and they smiled at each other as they prodded the fire with their rakes. When they got to the very last burning Bessie grinned across at her. 'Meks yer feel better, disn't it?'

When they returned they met the dinner-time

postman, who handed Lizza a pile of post, including a letter from Roland, which she did not read until she was alone in her bedroom. She had not heard from him for some time, although she wrote to him every week with edited accounts of their life at Campion House. The contents of this letter were quite perplexing. He thanked her for the photo of Charley, thought he was a fine baby. He hoped they were both well and they were receiving their money regularly. Work up in Scotland was going well; the Ministry was pleased with their progress. It was a beautiful place and he had taken to going for walks to blow the cobwebs away. A new habit which he enjoyed. Pieter was well, keeping company with a widow from that place. He sent his best wishes to her mother and Beatrice and hoped young Josie had settled down at work. She read it twice. It might have been a letter from a kind uncle or distant brother.

Very deliberately she put it back in its envelope and pushed it to the back of her underwear drawer. Beatrice came in with a snoozing Charley in her arms. 'I thought I'd put him into his cot,' she whispered. 'I'm getting ready to go out now.'

They left the bedroom door ajar. Lizza lingered with Beatrice at her bedroom door. 'Are you going out with Michael?'

Beatrice blushed. 'Yes. He's taking me to the King's Hall for tea.'

Lizza hugged her. 'Have a nice time.'

Beatrice shrugged her off. 'No need to make a fuss. It's nothing.' She had already refused

Josie's offer of a lipstick and Min's offer of a green silk scarf. But she knew this occasion was more than nothing. It could be her very last meeting with this gentle man who made her feel special. She would be sad if that happened. They had only ever held hands and kissed but she felt that between them there was a great deal more than that.

Mick was waiting for her, cap crushed in his hand, outside the café.

'You should 'a waited inside,' said Beatrice, walking in beside him.

'No saying yer would come,' he said gruffly.

She sat down and looked at him. His hair had been smoothed down with water and was flopping now on his brow. 'If I say I'll come, I'll always come,' she said, looking at him very directly. 'But after today you might not ask me to come.'

He frowned at her. 'What d'yer mean?'

She reached into her capacious bag and pulled out the photo of Alex. 'I wanted to show you this.'

He frowned down at it. 'Who's this?' The boy was young, perhaps ten years less than himself. Too young for...

'Turn it over.'

He read the inscription and cast an involuntary glance at her ringless finger. She blushed.

'He's your lad?' he said slowly.

'I had him when I was seventeen. It was because of a...an attack by a man I didn't know.'

Mick went red; his powerful hands became

495

fists on the white tablecloth. 'I'll kill him.'

'You're too late. Some Nazi pilot got him a month or so back. Bombed him in the middle of one of his own fields. That one that was in the paper. I thanked God for that. Till then he had me pinned down, the whole of me life, just as sure as he had me pinned down in the lane.'

'I wish he'd come alive again, so I could kill him again,' he said through gritted teeth.

Beatrice glanced round the quiet café. Their waitress was coming towards them with a loaded tray. 'Mick, leave him. I'm free of him now. Don't you take him on your back.'

He uncurled his hands and put them on his broad thighs as he waited in agonised silence while the woman put the teapot on the table, and the cod and chips before him. 'Will it mek any difference, Bea?' he said when the woman padded back to her station.

'Any difference to what?'

'Ter you and me when we're wed?'

She blushed scarlet. 'I didn't know anything about us getting wed and what do you mean any difference?'

'Will that happenin' mean you won't want, well...yer know what ah mean...when we're wed?' he said determinedly.

'Would it make any difference?'

He shook his broad head and put one hand across the table, palm up. 'Ah'd want ter wed yer even if ah slept in the kitchen an' you slept in the attic. Ah really like yer, Bea. Have since the minute ah saw yer.'

She put her hand in his and he gripped it

496

hard. 'Seeing as you ask, although I haven't said I'd wed you yet: seeing as you ask, as far as I can tell it'll make no more difference than if someone had stabbed me eighteen years ago. Cause that's what it was—a cruel stabbing, an attack.' She smiled at him. 'Anyway, what about family? Don't you want us to have any family?'

He put his other hand over hers. 'Give us time. Ah want you first. Then mebbe a littl'n. A lass. Ah fancy a little lass. Ah could teach her to draw... But now,' he picked up his knife and fork, 'let's get these chips before they're cold. Ah canna stand cold chips.'

CHAPTER 32

Beatrice's engagement ring, chosen by Michael Stratton from a jeweller's in Priorton High Street, caused restrained but admiring comments at home and shrieks of delight in the factory. When she noticed the ring in the changing room, Esme leapt across, clutched Beatrice's hand and gave her a smacking kiss on the cheek. 'Why, yer bugger. Just fancy you, of all of us, the first ter get a ring on yer finger.' She pulled the finger with its ring nearer, to peer at it with an expert eye. 'Hey, them's *diaminds* round the garnet! I thought that lad yer gannin' was with a pitman. Where's a pitman get money for a ring like that?'

Beatrice laughed. 'What if he is a pitman? Me brother and me father were pitmen before they went off to save this country. An' me granda was a pitman too, and he left a thousand pounds in his will in 1932. An' I've another brother diggin' coal for the war effort in Cornwall, not short of a bob or two.'

'Aye but that one...' said

'Works hard, doesn't drink, doesn't smoke, doesn't gamble. An' has greyhounds that win races.'

'Min says he's a brilliant drawer,' volunteered Josie, lighting her cigarette. 'Mebbe he's sold one of his drawings. And he an' Krystof's gonna show their paintings at Durham at a big exhibition.'

Beatrice shook her head. 'I don't know whether he's sold one already. I didn't ask about that.' In the weeks since she had known him, Michael had made few protestations of affection but seemed to think after the first kiss it was all inevitable. She felt that same certainty, so she moved along with him: he knew without saying that she had time, wasted time, to make up.

'Well, I've only one thing to ask you,' said Mary, who had been watching all this with interest.

'What's that?'

'Does he have a brother?'

The others nodded and laughed their agreement. 'Come on, come *on* cut the cackle!' Mrs Armitage bustled into the changing room. 'At this rate the shift'll never start.'

498

After work Beatrice had to go straight from the train to meet Michael, who was to take her home for the first time to meet his father and brother. The ordeal with her own mother would be the following weekend. She had already put a note in the post telling her she was coming and the reason for the visit.

So Josie walked home alone. She looked up at the sky, at the brightness of the June day turning with reluctance towards night. Alex crossed her mind briefly, and she wondered whether he was flying on his own yet. He would like it, being up there, looking down on the world as though he were Gulliver. Her mind passed on easily from that, and she thought ahead, rehearsing the fruitful conversation she would have with Min, about the dreadful fact that she hadn't a thing to wear for the Barrack Dance at Killock that night.

She saw the man coming towards her but did not recognise him; it was his voice which brought her up short. 'Josie?'

She frowned. 'Daddy! Sure, I didn't recognise you.' He was wearing a fine coat in smooth wool, a trilby and a thick military-cut moustache. 'Have you left the army now?'

He laughed, took her arm and walked alongside her. 'You might just say the army's left me. Given me long-term leave, as long as they don't catch me.' He pulled her to a stop just outside the Gaunt Valley Hotel. 'I've got rooms in here, Josie. Quite up to the mark. I was sitting there thinking about your mammy and Anne-Marie, overcome with sadness, you might say, with no knowledge at all about what happened that night. I'd this icy little letter from Mrs High-and-Mighty King, of course. But nothing, nothing to tell me what really happened.' His eyes were glassy and there was a plaintive note in his voice. 'So I thought I'd come and ask you on my bent knees—*bended* knees, Josie—to tell me of those last moments of your dear mammy's life.'

She allowed herself to be led through the double doors, and then the busy foyer (where preparations for the Gaunt Valley Hotel Dance were in hand), up to his little sitting room. She sat down wearily and sighed, accepting a cigarette from his silver case. He selected a cigarette for himself and lit it with a heavy lighter. Then he leaned over and lit hers. 'Ain't we a big girl now?'

She drew on it deeply. 'What're you doing up here anyway, Daddy?'

'I was in Newcastle, then Darlington, delivering some...stuff...for this man I work for in London. An' didn't I think I might call to see me own sweet daughter, an' me little boy who I miss so much? Sure, I know that that Mrs King has a downer on me and'll be poisonin' your minds against me.'

She sat on in silence, confused by his emotional outburst.

'You're thinking I'm after money,' he said. 'But you're wrong there. Look.'

He pulled a hand out of his pocket, clutching a wad of notes as big as a pork-chop. 'Sure, I've got money. Look, you can have some.' He peeled off four fivers and thrust them into the breast pocket of her jacket. Then he slipped out of his long overcoat and threw it over a chair. 'Now, how about a kiss for your old feller being so kind?'

She shook her head.

He went through to the bedroom, returned with two rustling packets and threw them on her knee. 'Stockings, Josie. Pure silk. Can't get them for money, but you can have them for love.'

She fingered them. One pair would make a nice engagement present for Beatrice. The other, treated with great care, would see Josie herself through the summer.

He was standing right in front of her, his hand in his pocket. 'Now, how about a kiss for your old man?'

She stood up and edged to one side to put some distance between them. 'I thought you wanted to know about Mammy.'

'Yes, yes, that after,' he snapped. 'A kiss first.'

She edged towards the door. 'I'll have to get back. Mrs King...'

He moved to block her escape. 'Mrs King! Mrs King! Sure, that woman is the most milk-and-water, stuck-up bitch I've ever met. You want nothing living with her.' He barked out a laugh. 'She nearly had her just deserts last time, only she sent some old woman out in her coat an' the old woman got it. No, Josie, you come to London with me. I've this nice place, very central. Money. A car. Lots of new clothes for you. Some friends that'll spoil you. Sure, there's no shortages at all, in the bit of London I live in.'

She ducked her head towards him. 'Sure, it sounds like the Black Market's payin' very well, Daddy. But I'd rather fill cartridges for guns to kill the bloody enemy any day, than live with you. I'd rather take a gun and shoot them meself, come to think of it. Now let me by.'

He grabbed her from behind as she tried to force her way past him, twisted her arm up her back and chuckled when she squealed with pain. He talked into the back of her neck. 'There now, calm down, baby. Don't be a naughty girl. All Daddy wants is a little kiss.' Then his voice changed and he bit into her neck and the pain shot right to the centre of her brain. She closed her mouth and held the pain in.

'Good, good. Now you're learning.' He marched her through the doorway to the bedroom and threw her on the bed. He wrenched up her skirt and knelt above her, loosening his belt. 'Now!' he said. 'A little kiss for Daddy.' His mouth came on hers and she wriggled and wriggled to try and get away from his mouth.

Down below she could feel the horrible soft thing being pushed against her. He lifted his mouth from hers as he grunted with the effort of achieving an erection. Then she started to talk to him, her voice low. 'It was the aeroplane, Daddy. It came down really low. Alex and me, we could hear the noise of the aeroplane. Can you remember Alex? Him and me made love once in a bombed-out house. He was lovely. Such a big...'

Theo Callaghan groaned, pushing and rubbing away to no avail.

'Well, Daddy, we heard the plane screeching over. An' we heard the guns cracklin' an' the people screaming. But Alex wouldn't let me go back. See, he looked after me like a...but I can't say like a father cause that's not good enough, is it? But I went afterwards and I saw them, when they'd been hours dead. Mammy with a big gash in her face and blackening blood on Anne-Marie's shawl. Dead there, with lots of others. I saw her. You should have been there and seen her, Daddy, cos you liked to see her bruised and battered, didn't you? Loved that, didn't you, Daddy? I remember you laughing about that. An' her crying. But even you couldn't do what that bloody German did, Daddy. Even you couldn't hurt her that much. She had this great big hole in her face, Daddy...'

He rolled off her and groaned. 'Get out, you little whore, get out.'

She stood up, pulled down her skirt and pulled up her socks. Then she gargled in her throat and spat at him where he lay, saying, 'There ain't no need to hope you're not in hell...*Daddy*...because I know you will.'

He turned his smeared face away from her. The back of her neck was throbbing, where he had bitten her. She started to walk steadily down the stairs, then, hearing him behind her shouting her name, she set off to run.

She ran all the way and as she let herself into Campion House she was sobbing and retching for breath. She went into the sitting room by the fire to calm herself down, before going into the dining room. She could hear them all laughing and joking there, over their tea.

Lizza, who had heard the heavy door swing to, came in search of her. 'What is it, Josie? What on earth has happened?'

Josie was white and wide-eyed, but there were no tears now. Her voice was grim. 'I met me daddy, Mrs King. No, he met me. He's staying at the Gaunt Valley Hotel. He...' She gulped and pulled back her coat collar and turned her head.

Lizza looked in horror at the deep purple, blood-potted circle of tooth-marks on Josie's neck. 'He did this to you? Your father did this to you?'

Josie looked her in the eye. 'And worse. He tried to...you know, the other thing. Nearly did it too,' she smiled very faintly, 'but I talked to him about Mammy and Anne-Marie and he couldn't...manage.'

Lizza put her arms round her and hugged her, rocking her to and fro. 'That's horrible for you, love, horrible.' She gulped back the desire to tell Josie that she too had suffered that same thing. The child had enough on her plate.

Josie pulled away and looked at her. 'There's something else. He was raging on about you, and he said something about you nearly having your just deserts last time, only you sent some old woman out in your coat an' the old woman getting it. It's been buzzing through my head

504

all the way home and all I can think of is May Lynn.'

Lizza sat down and closed her eyes. May Lynn. She should have thought of it. The cloak. This was the something which had kept niggling away at the back of her mind like a gnat, ever since May Lynn went missing. The feeling had come back more strongly when the little dog Polly had brought her the fragment of cloth from the hole where May Lynn had lain all those months. She should have made the connection. She stood up, pulling Josie with her. 'We'll have to tell Bessie. Come on.'

When they told her, Bessie's eyes gleamed with satisfaction. 'Ah knew he'd turn up, the beggar. Ah knew he wouldn't be let get away with it.' She grasped her stick. 'Haway then, lassies. Let's gan across there an' get him.'

'No, go to the police station,' said Min. 'He's too dangerous to tackle yourselves.'

'Ah'm gunna get'm,' said Bessie stubbornly.

'Min,' said Lizza, 'you go to the station and tell Constable Morgan and get him to the Gaunt Valley Hotel. We'll go straight there.'

'Me an' Polly come,' said Liam, looking from one to another, not knowing what was happening.

Min looked at him and held out her hand. 'No, sweetheart, you can stay with Krystof. He'll have to keep an ear open for Charley. You can help him. He's up there banging about, framing the last of his pictures. I'm sure he has a little hammer and a little nail for you.'

When they got to the Gaunt Valley Hotel,

505

people were streaming in for the dance. Lizza was directed by the woman at the ticket table to the manager's office.

'Mr Callaghan?' he said, eyebrows raising. 'We have no guest of that name here.'

'He's an Irishman,' said Josie. 'With a thick moustache and a big wool coat.'

'Ah, Mr O'Connor, you mean? Well, Mr O'Connor left half an hour ago. Said his business here was over, and went off in that plush car of his.'

Bessie swayed and had to clutch her stick to keep her balance.

'Did he leave no address? Is there one in the book?' said Lizza.

'Just a post office somewhere in London. Said he was just here from Australia and had no address.' He gave a knowing wink. 'Trouble is it? He wasn't too pleased with me, to be honest. Tried to pay me in Black Market stockings and cigarettes but I insisted on cash. Never deal with the Black Market meself. Smart Alecs the lot of them. Too risky all round. O'Connor paid with bad grace and stumped off.'

'Can we look at his rooms?' said Josie. 'There might be something there about where he's gone.'

He stroked his chin. 'Don't know about that.'

'Look,' said Lizza. 'Our friend has gone to the police, so they'll be here soon and they're sure to look.'

He shrugged. 'Busy night. Dance night.' He reached behind him. 'Here's the keys. First

506

floor Suite Three. Help yourself. Don't be long, mind!'

The rooms were empty except for a single tie dangling on the back of the wardrobe door. Lizza turned it over and read the name of the Savile Row tailor. 'Pure silk,' she said.

Bessie snatched it from her and held it close to her face. She sniffed it. 'This one'll come to nae good end,' she said. 'He'll be colder'n wetter than May Lynn, then dried out in the fires of hell.' She spat on the tie.

Lizza shuddered then, but Josie punched Bessie lightly on the shoulder. 'Attagirl, Bessie! You curse him. Ain't no better than he deserves.'

Constable Morgan, when he finally arrived with Min, was unimpressed by the empty room and the sketchiness of their story. However, sighing audibly, he took Josie's statement down in his laborious hand, and said they would look further into it. His ears pricked up at the mention of the Black Market and he started to ask sharper questions and write faster. 'I make no promises,' he said. 'But I'll pass this information to Darlington and Newcastle and they'll see if connections can be made. Now, if you'll excuse me, ladies, we are very busy at the station just now.' And he put on his bicycle clips and marched out.

'They were very busy drinking cocoa when I dug him out,' said Min glumly. Then they all laughed and their laughter echoed in the empty room.

Back at the house, Lizza went up to check

on the sleeping Charley, then up to the attic to collect Liam to get him ready for bed. He was sitting on the floor beside the stove, contentedly knocking big nails into a piece of wood with a small hammer.

Krystof smiled. 'We will make a joiner of him yet.'

As she told him of their fruitless visit to the Gaunt, she looked around. The long room was like a gallery now, with the framed pictures hanging three deep in places. 'The framing's done?' she asked finally.

He nodded. 'Just about. Three to go, then the fine finishing for all of them. So they should all be ready.'

'When is it?'

'At the end of July. You will be coming?'

'I think we all are. Min's got us marshalled in support. Beatrice's keen enough because Michael has some stuff in it.'

'Michael Stratton is a very talented man. And he knows it, though he is modest enough in the English way.'

Lizza nodded. Krystof missed nothing, quiet as he was. 'According to Min, who's in cahoots with the organiser, that Shirley Littlejohn woman, they're to be sold,' said Lizza.

He nodded. 'They're doing no good hanging in here. Half the profits will go to the Spitfire fund, half to the painters. It seems very fair.'

She wrested the hammer from Liam's hand and turned to go.

'Elizabeth.' His quiet voice came from behind her.

As she turned, he handed her a small drawing in a heavy gilt frame. 'This is for you. I got the frame in a junk shop, like some of the others. This one had a picture of a little Scottie dog in it.'

Moving Liam to the other hip, Lizza held the picture closer to the lamp. It was the drawing of herself feeding Charley. She frowned. She knew, always had known, she was no beauty. But in this picture, leaning down over Charley, she looked beautiful.

'You do not like?'

She beamed at him. 'It is lovely. But I must say I think you flatter me.'

He shook his head. 'I only draw what I see.'

'Thank you,' she said. 'I'll treasure it. But you know I will.'

'And if you bring me the drawing of Rebecca I will frame that too. There is a matching frame. That had a King Charles Spaniel in it.'

She nodded and hurried away in case by any action or look she betrayed her real feeling. That night she sat up late in the study, trying to write a reply to Roland's brief, cold letter. After three attempts she tore the sheets up and gave in. She had nothing to say to him. Nothing at all.

The following Saturday Lizza went with Beatrice and Michael to Bracks Hill to see their mother. Beatrice insisted they should take Liam and Charley with them for 'extra cover'. Alice made them welcome in her cool way, shaking hands with Michael without looking at him too closely. She did reserve a measure of warmth for the children, remarking on Charley's growth, and remembering Liam's liking for oatcakes. She even sat with Charley on her knee and allowed Beatrice and Lizza to put out the tea.

'Beatrice telt us yer son worked at Calton Old Pit afore he went into the army, Mrs Bremner,' said Michael, sitting awkwardly on a chair too small for his bulk.

She was forced to look at him then. She nodded, then returned to smoothing the dark curls over Charley's ears.

'Ah wus there mesel' six years back. Hewin'. Worked marrers with a man called Colin Barras.'

'Barras? I remember that name. Our Jonnie was there then,' she said. 'You might have known him. Jonnie Bremner.'

'Jonnie Bremner?' Michael laughed. 'Ha! Why, he worked marrers with Hunter Nattras, cousin to Colin Barras.'

Her daughters came in and started to unload the tray of tea-cakes and pies from the tray on to the table. Alice opened the cupboard door so that Liam could crawl in and pull out Alex's old toybox. Then she shot a glance at Michael that would have pierced a stone shield. 'You're thinkin' o' marryin' our Beatrice then?'

'Aye.' He nodded.

'Yer too young for 'er. Yer know that?'

He shook his head. 'That's for me to say. She's a grand lass. Special like.'

The clock ticked in the silence.

Then she said, 'What do yer own ma and da think?'

'There's only me da, an' me brother. An' they think she's a grand lass too.'

'Where'll you live?'

'We'll get a pit house,' Beatrice put in, moving beside Michael. 'We'll manage very well. We don't want to miss out on having a family of our own, Ma.'

Alice stood up and hitched Charley more safely on to her hip. 'I've no doubt that's true, lass. Mebbe it's about time. Now, can we give the feller tea or he'll think all the women in this house live with their nose in the book like yon.' She nodded at Lizza, who was calmly pouring tea.

Lizza smiled at her. 'Now Ma, don't start on that. I'm getting impervious now to your slings and arrows.'

Alice cocked an eye at Michael. 'It's been like that since she was born. Half the time I've no idea what she's on about.'

They all sat up round the table, Liam on cushions up on his own chair. Bea put her chair deliberately close to Mick's, and Alice refused Lizza's offer to relieve her of Charley. It was a quiet meal. Beatrice asked questions about neighbours in Bracks Hill and Alice told of the neighbour's son who was in the desert fighting Rommel who, they all agreed, was doing better than he should at present. Alice read out a letter from Alex saying he was definitely on his way to Canada for further flight training and he thought he would take his leave in London, seeing as he'd never been there. 'Always for himself, that one,' said Beatrice, smiling slightly.

511

No one disagreed with her.

Uniquely in that house, there was no tension in the air; they all knew Michael was accepted, and his status would be unremarked from now on.

At the end of the meal Beatrice said to her mother, 'Our Lizza needs you to do her a favour, Ma. Michael has a painting in this exhibition in Durham in a week's time and Krystof, who you met once, he has lots of pictures in it. It's for the Spitfire Fund. Maybe to get our Alex an aircraft. Well, I was wondering if you'd mind these two bairns for her, so she can go.'

Her mother looked Lizza full in the face. 'And why do you want to go, lass?'

'There's Michael's paintings to see. And Krystof's, Roland's friend. And there'll be pictures of Bea there, and Josie, Liam's big sister. I want to see them. I can take the little ones with me, of course, but it'd be tiring...'

'No need to bristle, lass. Always bristlin'! I'll watch them,' interrupted Alice. 'But I'll get the bus across to Priorton to watch them.' She glanced round the kitchen. 'There's times I get sick of the four walls in this house. I'll come.'

Liam clapped his hands and shouted, 'Come-come-come!' and they all laughed.

When they got back from Bracks Hill, Bessie met her at the door. 'There's a woman here ah want yer to see. It's about yon Russian feller but he isn't here. He's in Durham with the schoolteacher. Sommat about that show they're doing. Me and 'er 'ere was just talkin' about them Russkis fightin' tooth an' nail with that old beggar Hitler now...'

'I was explaining to your...to the lady here that things don't look good on the Eastern front...' The woman, in an unfamiliar dark uniform, held out a hand to Lizza.

'But ah telt 'er she should watch them Russkis. So should old Hitler. They'll be the death of him...'

The woman's eyebrows were nearly into her neatly cut fringe. 'My name's Cordelia Sallis. I am afraid...'

'She 'as a letter for the Russian but ah wouldn't tek it off her,' said Bessie, stationing herself by the door.

Miss Sallis handed Lizza a large open packet with two letters inside. One was a poor thing, battered, with one corner torn off, the writing on it quite faint. The name was unmistakable: *'Krystof Sobieski'*. The other letter was crisp and official-looking, carrying the Campion House address. The woman sighed. 'It's taken us months to trace him, through the War Office, then right down to where he worked in Coventry, then back up here. This came to us in York and, as I've visits for other reasons in this area, I was asked to deliver it.'

Lizza lifted the letter up to see it more clearly. The ink had bleached out, but the writing was shapely and well formed.

'Are you close to Mr Sobieski?' asked the woman, her voice neutral.

'He's a good friend. My husband and myself, and probably the people in this house now, are the only friends he has in this country.'

'Well, he'll need you now as he never did. I don't know what's in the small letters. But its circumstances are these. The wife of Mr Sobieski was in a camp and this letter was passed to a Swiss associate of ours who was making a visit. It was not passed by Mrs Sobieski, but a woman who had known her and become close to her, before she died. She had promised to get the letter out if ever she could. So that Mrs Sobieski's, and our colleagues used these words, was *"not another unmarked death"*.'

Lizza held the package close to her chest. 'I'll tell him that, Miss Sallis.'

The woman pulled on her black leather gloves, her mouth tight. 'There's no good way to present bad news, only less bad ways. Can you get Mr Sobieksi to write to acknowledge receipt? I must get on.'

Lizza glanced at Bessie, who was standing twisting her apron by the door. 'Can we offer you some tea?'

She shook her head. 'No. No. Your...the lady here offered me something. I am well behind schedule already. I've another call in Darlington before I catch the train.'

'Another call like this?'

'Something similar.' She smiled faintly at the look on Lizza's face. 'No, it's not easy. But, like a lot of things in this blasted war, someone has to do it.'

Later that evening Lizza sat quietly through supper with Min and Krystof gloating over the 'wonderful hall in which the exhibition was to

514

be held, the good light, the stretches of wall space...'

Krystof finally put down his fork and beamed all round. 'Well, I had better get on with the finishing. There is still so much to do, and I am now even more inspired.'

Lizza put Charley to bed and read to Liam before he would settle down. Beatrice had gone straight out to the pictures with Michael, Josie was at the Killock dance with Esme, and Min had just gone off to Darlington in a car with her friend Shirley, to meet another artist who was to show his pictures in the exhibition.

Lizza came back downstairs to a kitchen finally clear of bodies, and Bessie busy at the sink in the scullery. As Lizza took a cloth to help Bessie to finish, her glance fixed on a sealed pickling jar on the tiny window-sill. She peered closer. It was filled with murky water and had stones in the bottom. Inside, almost rippling in the flickering light of the scullery candle, was Theo Callaghan's pure silk tie. 'What's this, Bessie?' she asked.

'Ah telt yer. He'll have no better fate than May Lynn, that murderer. An' ah'm wishin' it on him.'

'Bessie, I don't think...'

Bessie, stacking the last plate, looked hard at her. 'Ah think it's time yer telt that Russian, flower. Showed 'im 'is letter. Better out than in.'

Lizza smiled bleakly, putting Theo Callaghan and his fate from her mind. 'He was so happy when he came in. I didn't want to spoil it.'

'Gan on.' Bessie sat down beside the kitchen fire and picked up her quilting. She squeezed her eyes together to thread the needle, then looked over it at Lizza. 'Tell'm now, flower. Like that lass said, there's no easy way. Just a less bad way. An' I reckon yer'll be good at that, you.' She paused. 'And 'im.'

CHAPTER 33

Krystof's welcoming smile faded as he saw the expression on Lizza's face. 'What is it, Elizabeth? Charley...'

She took his hand, pulled him to the bed that served as a couch and sat him down beside her. She put the packet in his lap. 'A lady from the Red Cross came. She'd have waited for you, but I told her I'd give the letter to you.'

He tipped out the contents of the packet, looked first at the battered little envelope, then opened the official letter accompanying it. He read this in silence, then stared at the little letter before carefully slitting it open with a penknife from his pocket. He held this towards the light and read it two or three times, handed it to Lizza, then slumped back on the couch.

Lizza turned over the thin page: the same looped graceful writing, but shaky and without vigour. She sat closer to him, so that their thighs and shoulders were touching. 'Will you read it to me, Krystof? What she says? I wish I could

516

understand it myself.'

He took it from her and in an unsteady voice started to translate. ' *"My dear husband. If God is merciful, as I believe he is, he will make sure you see this. I have endured in this place by the grace of good friends and the thoughts of the good years we had together before our boys went from us. I wish you to remember those good years and not concentrate on any bitter and unnatural endings. I want you to remember the good things and wipe out any disagreements between us as though they never happened. I want you to draw and to paint, to show with your gentle craft that each destruction is rendered impotent by a mountain of images which show the indestructibility of the human spirit. It's not with guns and whips or even bold words that victory over time is achieved. I wish you to look forward in hope, not back in bitterness. Make a new life, Krystof, a new family, and render all this destruction impotent. May the memory of your youthful passion always be a warm mantle around you..."* '

He was sobbing as he turned to Lizza. She put her arm around him and drew his face to her breast, stroking his hair. 'I'm so sorry, so sorry, Krystof.'

When the crying had faded and he was still, she pulled up his face between her hands, saying, 'Tell me about Wanda, Krystof. What was she like?'

He pushed his fingers across his eyes to get rid of the tears, sat back and stared at the ceiling. 'She was very tall.' He smiled weakly. 'I sometimes teased her about it, saying she

517

had grown so she could look down on a poor artist. Her family were very strongly Jewish. Grandfathers on two sides had been rabbis. Very brilliant people, and she inherited that great brain. She was beautiful, like a blazing torch. Marrying me was her great revolt against them: a great gesture, choosing a poor teacher and artist, from a Catholic family, in this generation at least. My grandfathers on both sides had been Jewish.' He shook his head. 'All highly unsuitable.

'We married young and had our sons. We had many quarrels. She was highly intellectual, always at meetings, very popular with people who were at the forefront of action—against anti-semitism, against social injustice...I think she saw me as lazy and uninvolved, only interested in the exterior form of things, not what is at their heart. She loved the boys very much but they were not enough for her. I think she was relieved to see them on to that train, away to her cousin in America. Then after the accident she was in anguish, blaming herself, blaming me for letting her do it...'

'When she was taken?...' ventured Lizza.

'We were still in the same house, but she had another...friend. One day I came back from the university and they had both been taken. Poor Wanda. That lovely bright torch.'

Far below in the house they could hear the front door slamming and the sound of voices. Lizza eased her arm, which was now in cramp. He caught her hand. 'Don't go. Stay with me. It is a long time to be alone. A long time.

518

Together just now we can render destruction impotent, just as Wanda says. So her death, as the woman said, does not go unremarked. She needs me to remember the bright torch, like this, in this action. Not...in that hell-hole.'

She breathed out and stayed still. He leaned down and kissed the skin that showed above her open-necked blouse, then her neck. Then he was kissing her eyes. 'Please, please,' he said.

She drew his face down and kissed him, gently at first, then lifting herself up to pull him closer to her, to line her body against his. He groaned and put a hand in the small of her back to press her closer. She could feel his hardness against her. The base of her stomach tightened as she felt her body quickening with the desire for even greater closeness. Her lips parted under his and he murmured with pleasure as their tongues moved against each other, playing, miming, anticipating the later sharing.

His hand was on her knee, then on her bare thigh above her stocking, his fingers moving on to stroke away at her mound of hair, then slipping and stroking their way inside. It was her turn to groan. 'Lovely, lovely,' he murmured against her lips. 'You are so lovely.'

She dropped back and they were lying very close, sideways on to each other. Her hand went down to his penis, which was straining hard against his trousers. 'Make love to me,' she commanded. 'Properly.'

It was two hours later when she came down the narrow steps and went to the bathroom to wash herself and brush her teeth, before letting herself quietly into the bedroom. She went across to check the snuffling Charley in his cot, then removed her clothes again, this time to put on her demure nightie. She stroked the flannelette sleeves down her arms, remembering his kisses, and felt the stomach-tightening again. He had admired her body, ignoring her laughing protestations about her sturdy frame. He had kissed her breasts and run a gentle finger over the down on her arms. She sighed, curbing the desire to race back upstairs and demand that they start all over again.

'Well, we have had a nice time, haven't we?' Min's voice came from the bed and she swung round.

'Don't know what you're talking about.' Lizza climbed into bed and pulled up the covers. Min sat up, her silk nightie slipping off one shoulder. 'He's good, Krystof, isn't he?'

'I don't know what you're talking about.'

'Oh, come on, you two've been walking around with your tongues hanging out for each other for weeks now. Don't tell me you've been up there all this time looking at his etchings.'

'Sometimes, Min, you're really vulgar. It must be your naval background.'

'But he is good, isn't he?'

'Mind your own bloody business!'

'Ah, but he was my business a few months ago.'

'If you must know, nosy Miss Schoolteacher, he had a letter today from his wife, who died in a camp late last year.' Lizza's tone was cold. 'He was telling me about her.'

'Oops! My foot in there again. Sorry, Lizza.' Min jumped out of bed. 'Well, perhaps this'll make it up to you. I brought a surprise for you. That's why I was sour, you not being here to greet it.'

She turned up the gas light, went to the narrow table by the window and whipped off a silk scarf which was covering a bulky office typewriter. 'See what I've brought, just for you! To transfer your blasted stories so that you can send them away for us to see in print.'

Lizza leapt out of bed. 'Min, for me? Where did you get it?' Gingerly she pulled the lever, pressed the keys. 'I want one of these. I really want one. Wherever did you get it?'

Satisfied, Min smiled broadly. 'I squeezed it out of Shirley Littlejohn. It was sitting in a dusky back room behind her office doing nothing, so I cadged it off her.'

'Min, it's wonderful. I never thought...'

Min put up a cheek. 'You may kiss me to indicate your complete gratitude.'

Lizza kissed her and Min grasped her. 'You do like it, Lizza?'

'Yes, Min, I love it. I'll start on copying those blasted stories tomorrow.'

Min reached up and kissed her on the lips. 'You know, Shirley Littlejohn was quite mad at me about the fuss I made getting it for you. She's quite jealous of you.'

Very gently, Lizza unclasped the hand that was clutching her. 'Well, my dear Min, there's no need for her to be jealous, no need at all. Now let's get to bed, as there must be only two hours now before Charley there'll want his breakfast.'

Lying quietly beside Min, who had taken herself to the very edge of the bed, Lizza thought of nurses she had known who had had the kind of loving friendship Min had hinted at: some of them elderly pairs who had been together all their lives. They had seemed happy enough. Then she thought about the electric effect that Krystof Sobieski had just had on her. And the adventurous times she had had with Roland in the early days. 'It's not for me, Min,' she whispered to herself. 'Not for me.'

The next day, on her way out to work, Josie was given a letter by the postman. She recognised her father's clerkish hand and pushed it deep into her pocket. Sitting on the toilet in the dinner-break, she ripped it open and read it. It was threatening in tone, saying he was her father and had no intention of giving up on her, and she was to look behind her all the time because one day he would be there ready to get her. Her instinct was to flush it down the toilet but she tucked it carefully into the corner of her bag to show Mrs King, and lit herself a cigarette while she thought for the fiftieth time about the way he had been, in the Gaunt Valley Hotel.

At the dinner-table she was so quiet that the others commented.

'Ten ter one yer in love,' said Mary.

Josie lit another cigarette. 'Don't talk rubbish.'

'That ciggy must be your third this dinner-time. It's getting hold of you now, little'n,' said Esme, lazily. 'It's quite a sight, seeing you gasp for one at the end of a shift. Across the changing room like a little whippet to get your first drag.'

'Ain't it you two taught me to do it? Never satisfied, that's your trouble.'

After they had changed and were walking back to the line, Mrs Armitage called her to one side. 'Give me that!' she said sharply.

'What?' said Josie innocently.

Mrs Armitage pointed. 'That cigarette behind your ear. I can see the shape through your turban.'

Sulkily, Josie extracted it and handed it over.

'Now come with me!' She turned and strode away, so that Josie had to trot along after her. In two minutes they were back in the changing rooms. 'Now take off your turban and your overall.'

'No,' said Josie.

Mrs Armitage folded her arms. 'You take them off or you get the sack, easy choice.'

Josie yanked off her turban and ripped at the buttons on her overall and then stood there shivering in her brassière, knickers and socks.

'And socks.'

Josie raked her feet along the floor to take off her socks.

Mrs Armitage picked up the clothes and examined them minutely, holding the hems and seams up to the light. 'Now, turn round.'

Josie stood rigid as she felt her brassière being pulled out. Even the elastic waist on her knickers. She felt the back of her hair being lifted up, then the woman pushed her on the shoulder. 'Get yourself dressed.'

She avoided the woman's gaze as she put on the overall; her fingers fumbled before they managed to fasten the buttons. She went to the tiny mirror to tie her turban, then turned to face the woman.

Mrs Armitage glared at her. 'Lucky for you you hadn't any more on you. I should sack you anyway for that one. You have endangered us all. If you ever carry anything...anything...like that into that building again, you'll be sacked where you stand. Do you understand that?'

Josie nodded her head.

'What did you say?'

'Yes.'

'What else?'

'Sorry, Mrs Armitage. I won't do it again,' she muttered.

She crept back on to the line, fighting hard to keep back the tears. Esme and Mary looked at her with sympathy. Beatrice said, 'Did you get a tellin' off, pet?'

She nodded, hitched herself on to the stool and picked up her tweezers.

'Old cow,' said Esme, her hands busy.

'She needs showin',' said Mary.

Mrs Armitage walked into the shop and all three of them glowered at her. Josie scowled after the older woman. 'Ain't it a free country? Way she goes on she'll need jackboots next.'

Mrs Armitage heard this but ignored it and kept going, her red hat bobbing up and down.

Esme grinned after her. 'Like a bliddy pouting pigeon, that one!'

Later, just before they went home, Josie was at the mirror, tidying herself up and putting on a smear of Pond's lipstick. She ran her finger through the sausage-like curl that her hair made, tucked up round her stocking-top bandeau. 'More ways than one, of killing a pig,' she said, but Esme's back was turned and she didn't hear.

That night Josie showed Lizza the note from her father and Lizza laughed heartily. 'Here, give it to me, Josie. Don't you fret. I'll burn the thing. He won't come back. Don't worry about that. He won't dare come back. He must know now, we're all on to him.'

'Pictures!' shrieked Esme. 'Ah thought we was goin' to the proper pictures.'

Heads on the bus turned.

'Sssh, Esme,' said Beatrice.

'Ah thought we were gunna see the pictures, you know, Charlie Chaplin an' that.'

'You thought nothing of the sort,' said Josie. 'I told you it was that Polish feller who stood there drawing us, and Beatrice's boyfriend. His drawings of the pit.'

'Huh! Who'd want to see pictures of a mucky old pit?' said Mary.

'Min says he's a genius,' put in Lizza, luxuriating for a short while at having no baby tugging at her breast or her skirts. 'Makes you look at the pit in a new way.'

'If I were a man,' said Esme, 'I'd rather be

525

in the desert with our lads' army than in the pit any day. Anyway, do we have to go and see these mucky pictures of us flogging ourselves over bullets or some man in a dark hole in the ground?'

Josie shrugged. 'It ain't compulsory. Me an' Mrs King an' Beatrice is going. You suit yourselves.' Her mood wasn't too good these days. She had found herself looking everywhere for the lurking figure of her father, even on this bus as they got on today. And she knew she was smoking too much, which was eating away all her pocket money.

'You just have to glance at the pictures, then go and have a good time in the town,' said Beatrice reassuringly. 'You can have a look at the Cathedral...'

Mary and Esme groaned in unison.

'According to Min,' said Lizza, 'when they were in last week, the place was full of soldiers.'

Esme grinned. 'Now you're talkin',' she said.

Min had gone off in the early morning with Krystof and Michael. Her friend Shirley had come to get them, and the final pictures, in her lumbering Ford. Lizza had peered through the curtains at Shirley, interested to get a glimpse of this woman who, according to Min, was such a dynamo in harnessing the arts in aid of the war effort. And who was taking up all Min's time these days. She was surprised to see a tall, slender, rather fragile-looking woman wearing a headscarf knotted under the point of her chin.

'What about this one?' Esme was saying now.

'Have you heard this one? *"Mareseatoatsanddoes-eatoatsanlittlelamseativy"*...'

'What?' shouted Josie.

'It's all joined together, see? *Mares... eat...oats...and...does...eat...oats...* You try!'

By the time they got to Durham, Esme had the whole bus singing it, even the three old women in the back seats with large market baskets.

It was market day in Durham and the city teemed with its ancient bustle, despite the war-time shortages. The second-hand clothes stalls in particular were going well, as clothes were now properly on ration. Min's promise of lots of uniforms on the streets was fulfilled, with servicemen from local camps making the most of their free time.

It took all Josie's time to drag her friends through the streets to the exhibition hall. 'Come on, Esme, come on! We only need go in for five minutes then we can come out here for the rest of the afternoon.'

They had to pay sixpence to get in at the entrance, which was plastered with posters showing Spitfires and photos of famous Spitfire pilots apparently having returned from successful missions. Inside, a hubbub combined subdued talk and the shuffle of feet, as people made their way from picture to picture. There were some interesting images of people at work, in factories and shipyards, in schools and army camps. Michael's three paintings of men working underground shone out like beacons, showing as they did the terrible way in which, in order to

527

harvest the earth, the men working there had to pay a toll so terrible it verged on beauty.

Krystof's paintings, in a central position, were in two groups: one where he showed the character and pattern of ordinary people playing their industrial part in the war effort. The paintings and drawings in the other group showed the perverse beauties of form engendered by destruction. When people came before these pictures, they stopped talking, and stared in a combination of alarm and reverence.

Down the centre of the hall was a row of wooden chairs, standing back to back as though set up for a game of musical chairs.

The girls stood before the picture showing Beatrice and clapped her on the back. 'Nearly like a film-star,' asserted Mary.

Beatrice blushed. 'Don't talk rubbish,' she said. 'An' didn't you lot say you wanted to get out into the town?'

'Can we go now?' said Esme.

'Go on with you!' said Lizza. 'We'll see you back in Priorton. Don't you miss that last bus!'

She and Beatrice sat down on two chairs facing the pictures, and watched the three girls snake through the crowd.

'It's very good,' said Beatrice, thoughtfully, 'but that's nothing to do with me being in it.'

Michael came up and threw himself on the chair beside her, making it creak protestingly. 'Ah thowt yer'd never come,' he said. 'Ah've been drowning in a sea of big-wigs.' He nodded to the head of the hall where Shirley Littlejohn and Min were at the centre of a group of people, some in suits, some in uniforms of high rank. 'If jawin' could save the country that lot'd sink Hitler in a day.'

'Your paintings look really nice,' said Beatrice, not knowing quite what to say. It was the first time she had seen them.

'They're very good,' said Lizza.

'Ah know they are,' said Michael indifferently. He looked at Beatrice. 'Now, is there any place we can get a cup of tea? Ah've been here listenin' to this lot blabber since nine o'clock an' ah'm parched.'

Beatrice looked at Lizza, who told her to go and find the poor man some tea. She would just sit here and contemplate. Watching them thread their way through the room arm in arm, she thought how important Beatrice had been to her in her life, giving her the unquestioning affection not forthcoming from their mother, and, with her quiet admiration, supporting her in the 'lazy' enterprises of reading and writing.

'Here she is, dreaming again!'

Min was in front of her, her arm through that of Shirley Littlejohn. Lizza stood up to be introduced. Shirley only offered the very tips of her fingers and her eyes, a bright blue edged with green, were cold as ice. Her lips formed a sweet smile. 'Min tells me you're something of a writer, Lizza. We'll have to see if we can...'

Lizza's cheeks were fiery red. 'Min tells you wrong. And she knows me well enough to know that what I do is my own business.' Lizza looked round. 'Now I promised to meet our Beatrice. Where is she?'

Shirley watched her burst her way through the crowd after Beatrice, then put her hand on Min's. 'Quite the prickly pear, darling, your little friend.'

Min looked up at her. 'My little friend... darling...could buy and sell you twice over, in terms of talent, sensitivity... But'—she turned her head—'she's not half as good as you at getting things like this going. Now is that Colonel Blackett waving? Don't you think his idea of not selling individual pieces and taking the whole exhibition on to other cities, then London, is simply super?'

The heavy door creaked as Lizza slipped into the Cathedral. The bright afternoon light only filtered through occasionally here, a long sunbeam cutting through the grey air to play on the fine black carving of the screen behind the altar. The fluting voice of a single boy sent a shiver down her spine. She sat down and, almost reluctantly, allowed her eyes to move up the sturdy circular columns to the arched roof. For a split second she could see men with rush baskets and wood-branch scaffolding, the flash of summer sun on strong backs and straining muscles.

All made by man: the graceful high arches; the massive columns; the intricate carving; the heart-wrenching beauty of the boy's song. What had Krystof said? Put together, it all made something more? Showed a power outside and above the mere contrivance of men and women? She knelt down, closed her eyes and tried to feel that 'something more', to look inside herself for the power to see or feel that other thing. She felt nothing, but stayed where she was. It was so quiet in here, so restful with her eyes closed. That was when she heard Rebecca's whisper. 'Secret, Mammy, a secret. A secret for Josie.'

It was the hardest thing in the world for her lips to move, to frame a response. 'What is it, sweetheart?'

She could feel the soft child's lips on her ear now, although she dare not open her eyes. 'Lots of places to play here. Lots and lots.'

Then she felt a small hand in hers, and her hair lift with a rush of wind.

'Lizza, Lizza, wake up!' Her shoulder was being shaken.

She looked up into Krystof's face. 'I was asleep?' she said.

'Yes. I have been shaking you for minutes now.'

'I must have been dreaming,' she said.

'What was it, this dream?' he said, sitting down beside her.

'I can't tell you,' she said. 'I think it's a secret. Anyway, how did you find me?'

'I was walking through the streets and then suddenly I knew you would be here.' He looked round. 'It is so beautiful, so tranquil here.'

'I was thinking about what you said about your churches when you were a child. The feeling you had, about the man-made beauty and another creator.'

'Did you feel it?'

'I don't know. I felt something.'

They sat quietly for several minutes, then she grasped his hand. 'Let us think about Wanda, and all our children,' she said. 'That their passing may never go unremarked.'

The boy started singing again and they waited for the song to end.

Krystof pulled her hands together and put his hands over them. 'And let us think about our two selves, two halves of a whole, who will never be apart.' He lifted her hands one by one and kissed them, and then she took his and did the same.

Someone coughed behind them and they jumped to their feet and stumbled out past a fat man in a long cassock who was eyeing them with a quizzical air.

They held hands on the bus all the way home and Krystof told her the high praise the paintings had received, and the proposal to send the exhibition on a tour.

'You mean, not sell the paintings? All that hard work.'

'Oh, they'll be ours to sell eventually, and the Spitfires and ourselves will benefit. As well as that, one man, who owns mines in the north of the county, was talking about commissioning a painting from Michael for his boardroom. And I've had one or two requests.'

Lizza laughed. 'I've got a feeling that Michael wouldn't do that, or anything else, to order.'

She was just walking along the street, shoulder to shoulder with Krystof, thinking what a very good day it had been, when she saw a familiar car parked outside Campion House. It was the Morris, Roland's pride and joy, which she had last seen without wheels in the garage of the Coventry house. It had wheels on now, and the dust of many miles of travel on its once highly polished bonnet.

CHAPTER 34

Roland was just opening the door as they got to the house. He was carrying Charley and wearing an old green Fair Isle pullover that Lizza recognised. Her heart flipped and her face lit up, all the instinctive feelings from the good parts of their shared history coming to the surface.

'Lizza, Charley and I've just seen your mother to the bus,' he said, putting out his free arm to embrace her as she ran forward, then handing her the baby. He lifted his gaze. 'And Krystof. How are you, old man? Been keeping an eye on my family for me?'

Krystof bowed slightly. 'I hope so, Roland. I hope so.'

Lizza took Charley from Roland so he could shake Krystof's hand. 'You look well, Krystof,' he said. 'This Durham air must suit you. You're quite changed. You look younger.'

'And you also look well,' said Krystof.

It was true. His old green jumper was just

533

about the only thing that had remained the same. His townsman's pallor had gone. He was bronzed, almost weather-beaten, his hair was sun-bleached, and his eyes looked extra blue. He looked fitter and, curiously older.

Seeing him with a stranger's eye, Lizza remembered again just how attracted she had been to him, in those early days. Then her heart came to her mouth and fear nibbled at the edge of her consciousness: fear that the recent closeness with Krystof was a wild dream. She shook her head slightly. These good feelings for Roland were a faint echo from history; no threat to what she felt for Krystof. They were something from the deep past. All that part of her life was as surely in the past as the twins and Rebecca, as the war to end all wars which had killed her father.

Krystof cleared his throat. 'Well, my dear friends,' he said. 'I must now go to see Miss Bessie. She promised to show me an old shawl she has, a gift given to her by her father when she was a child. I want to persuade her to pose in it for me by her fireside. I thought it might bring out the gypsy side of her. She has a wonderful face, Roland, and this will be another drawing in my series on her.'

Lizza grinned at Roland as she led the way into the sitting room. 'He's a funny one, Krystof. Thinks if he captures us all on paper we are somehow his.'

Even on this warm summer evening the fire was flickering, offering its gentle welcome in the crowded room. They sat together on the overstuffed sofa and she lifted Charley on to Roland's knee. 'So what do you think of this one?'

Roland blew into the baby's face, making him chuckle. 'He's a fine boy, Lizza. Does you credit.'

'Does *me* credit? So you had nothing to do with it?'

He looked at her over the baby's head. 'Well, I haven't been here, have I?'

She waited a few seconds before she said it. 'No. I imagined there'd be a reason.'

'I did try to get down once, then got tangled up in the bombing of Clydeside, so I had to turn back. Did I write to you about that?'

'Can't remember.'

Her own guilt was turning to anger against him. 'You'd think you were talking about coming from Occupied France, or the North African desert. It's a free country here. A person can get about, even in war-time.'

He stood up and moved towards the deep bay window, peering out at a garden still dappled in the late afternoon sun. 'The work up there is as crucial as fighting in the desert, you know.'

She looked at his back. 'I know that. You know I know that. Anyway, what brings you here now? I see you've got the car, so you must've been down to Coventry.'

'Yes. I've the chance of some concessionary petrol for journeys between factories in Scotland now. So I thought it worth getting it.'

'Poor Coventry. It must be in an even bigger mess after the April raids.' Curious how she could say that now, without the sense of personal loss she had brought with her in those early months up here. The war made great changes in such a short time: messing about with time itself, wreaking changes in months which would take a lifetime without the hothouse of war.

'The city's in a mess full stop,' he said. 'Although it's quite something, to see how the people there are hanging on and keeping going.'

She came up behind him in the bay and put an arm round his waist. 'Well, however you've come, Rollie, it is nice to see you now. Nice for Charley to see his daddy. He has to know who you are, after all. Now we should go through to the kitchen. I'll have to help Bessie get the tea, there's a houseful to cater for here.'

He turned and grasped her arm. 'I brought the car because I thought I could take you and Charley back up with me. It's as safe up there as it is here. The odd bomb...'

'Come with you?' Lizza froze.

'Yes. The island's a beautiful place. You'd love it. You could write your stories to your heart's content there.' His face was rigid with the effort to sound utterly sincere. He had promised Mara just this. 'I've got the car. We can pack you and Charley and all your things in an hour. Be up there in no time.'

'What's wrong, Roland? What's wrong? There's something wrong, isn't there?' Oh yes. There was something wrong. Their marriage was slipping away before their eyes.

'Wrong?' He shrugged. 'You tell me, Lizza. I've had no letters from you in these last weeks.'

'Letters? I wrote to you every week, every blessed week. And what do I get? Cold notes that you might send to the Ministry of Supply.'

'It's hard for me. Writing comes easily to you...'

Her anger rising, she walked away from him, towards the door. 'Why not take Charley for a walk round the garden? Get to know him. I'm going to help Bessie.'

Bessie, cutting the last carrots in the scullery, refused help. 'That Russian came and wanted to draw us again, and ah telt 'im he could go fly. He wants nowt wi' drawin' an ugly old woman.'

Lizza put a hand on Bessie's shoulder. 'He knows a lovely thing when he sees it, Bessie. Proper artists do.'

'Gerraway with yer.'

Lizza's eye rested on the empty window-sill. 'I'm pleased to see you've got rid of that horrible tie.'

Bessie looked at her sideways, gimlet-eyed. 'It's not got lost. It's put away. Anyway, have yer seen that man o' yours? Seems like a canny enough *gadgie*.'

'He is. He wants me and Charley to go back with him. Up to Scotland.'

'Yer want nowt wi' that. This is yer own land. Yer belong here. With this lot 'ere.' She wiped her hands on a tea-towel and picked up the colander of carrots. 'An' dinnet think yon lad's straight thinkin', 'cause he's not. He might be canny, but he's not straight thinkin'.'

Lizza followed her through to the kitchen, wondering if, in her Cassandra-like ramblings, Bessie was ever quite conscious of what she was saying.

Later, at tea, Roland was on good form, talking of his work, and speculating about the war: regretting the heavy naval losses off Crete and the disappointments in Greece, but optimistic about the sound of sabres rattling in America.

Beatrice was pleased to see him and introduced him to Mick. She had always got on well with Roland, but thought his visit here was very overdue, and was concerned that Lizza appeared not to miss him.

Roland flirted with Min in a manner which Lizza didn't recognise, and he reported back to an interested Josie about the current state of play in Coventry.

'Ain't no point in going back then?'

'Not just now, Josie. After the war, though. Even now they're talking of big rebuilding schemes. Wait and go back then.'

'I was just tellin' them all here, Mr King. About you an' Mrs King bein' such good dancers.' Josie looked at Bessie. 'What about a bit of a dance, Bessie? Can we dig out the old gramophone again?'

'All right with me,' said Bessie.

'I'd have thought you'd be going to one of the dances in the town, Josie, or down at the barracks,' said Beatrice.

Josie blushed. 'Well, Esme an' them are going to the Gaunt an' I didn't fancy it.'

Lizza looked at her and felt a surge of anger against Theo Callaghan, who, without even being here, was still haunting his daughter. 'A dance! Good idea, Josie,' she said. 'Let's have a little dance to celebrate Roland being here.'

'I will buy beer,' said Krystof.

'There's pies,' said Bessie.

They all set to with a will, clearing the room and getting the records from the dining room. Josie put one on straight away, turning up the volume so they could barely hear themselves speak.

Shirley Littlejohn called for Min to go to the pictures, but Min told her that the pictures were cancelled and she had to come in and dance.

Lizza and Roland started off the dancing, managing a very graceful foxtrot before Min tapped Lizza on the shoulder and swept Roland away. Michael would only dance with Beatrice, warning them dourly that he had to go off and walk the greyhounds at half-past nine. Beatrice said she would go with him; she quite liked a nice long walk.

Krystof poured the beer, danced just once with Bessie, then took duty by the gramophone.

Lizza and Josie danced the St Bernard's Waltz together. 'You don't want to worry about your father, Josie,' said Lizza. 'There's nothing he can do to you. Nothing.'

Josie shuddered. 'He's got in me head, somehow, Mrs King, know what I mean?

I'm dreamin' about him now. Anyway, I got a knife now, ain't I?'

Lizza stumbled to a stop, then set away again. 'A knife? Where from? Josie?'

'I got a soldier to give me it. A sheath knife. Exchanged for three kisses and a quick feel.'

'Josie!'

'Well, it was worth it. I'd like to see that old...*bugger*...trying it on again.'

'Anyway, don't you worry. I think Bessie has him under a spell.'

Josie laughed. 'Trust her.'

Krystof changed the record to a foxtrot. Shirley Littlejohn asked Roland to dance with her and Min danced with Lizza.

'I've set up the truckle bed in the study, Lizz. I can sleep in there tonight,' said Min, watching her closely.

'No need to give up your bed,' said Lizza. 'Roland can sleep on the truckle bed.'

Min stopped dancing, led her to the couch and sat down beside her. 'What's happening here, Lizz?' Her voice was serious, without the fizzy tone which she had adopted since the time she realised that Lizza had supplanted her in Krystof's affection, 'I know there's something with K—'

Lizza put a finger on her lips.

Seeing the gesture from across the room, Shirley moved in closer with Roland. 'You're such a beautiful dancer, Mr King...Roland, if I may.' She looked over his shoulder around the room. 'It's an odd collection of people in this house, don't you think? The decrepit

540

old woman who owns it all and this rag-bag collection of people... Normal people like you and me seem somewhat out of place...'

Roland executed a perfect dip and then, as they came up, he smiled sweetly at her. 'I can't for the life of me think what you mean, Miss Littlejohn...Shirley, if I may.'

Min watched them with narrowed eyes. 'There she goes, trying to make me jealous, always trying to make me jealous.'

'And does she? Does she make you jealous?' teased Lizza.

Min picked up Lizza's hand and landed a smacking kiss on it. 'Dear Lizza, the boot is very much on the other foot. Very much. Now, to important things. Is it goodbye to Roland this weekend? Is it all over in favour of our lovely you-know-who?'

Lizza shook her head. 'I don't know. Roland's like a stranger. It'd be like having a stranger in my bed. Something wrong about it.'

In the event, Roland had the choice of two sleeping places. When Michael and Beatrice stood up to go at twenty past nine, Shirley stood up and yawned. 'I simply must go. I'm on duty at the exhibition first thing tomorrow.'

Min stood up with her. 'Early shift for me, too. Don't suppose you could put me up in Durham tonight, Shirley? A lift in your car tonight would save me that awful bus journey tomorrow.' She dropped one eyelid, in the merest shadow of a wink, in Lizza's direction.

Shirley blushed with pleasure, but she said,

coolly enough, 'No trouble at all, Min. Happy to be of service.'

They bustled out in a draught of expensive perfume and the clatter of high heels. Roland raised his eyebrows at Lizza who smiled slightly in return. 'Min can be a very big tease when she wants to be,' she said.

Bessie then announced that it was her bedtime and told Josie and Krystof to gather up the records and gramophone. And she'd show them just where they should put them, ignoring the fact that they had got them from there in the first place. Lizza and Roland, she said grandly, could put the room straight.

When they had finished, Roland made Lizza sit down. 'We've got to talk, Lizza. I have to go back to Scotland tomorrow. We have to talk tonight.'

'I am too tired tonight to go through all that, Roland. There's just one thing I'll say. I cannot, I *am* not, coming back with you. As for the rest...let's leave it till the morning. You're tired and so am I,' she said. They retrieved his rucksack from the kitchen and she led him through to the study where Min had left the little bed, neatly made.

'You can sleep here,' she said.

He stared at her. 'Here?'

She nodded.

'Right.' He leaned over and kissed her cheek. 'Then there is no "rest" to talk about tomorrow, really, Lizza, is there? Nothing at all.'

He pulled back the blankets.

'Don't forget to turn down the gas,' she said

542

from the door. 'Sleep well, Roland. I am glad you came, remember that.'

'You're a funny girl, Lizza. Did I ever tell you that? A funny girl.'

'Not lately,' she said. 'You used to, but that hasn't happened lately. Not lately. A lot has happened since you said that. Too much.' And she closed the door behind her with a distinct click.

She pulled Charley's blanket back up over him, then lay in bed and listened to the creaks as Krystof moved about in the attic above her. She put a hand over the empty space beside her and thought of the cool dark interior of the Cathedral, and Krystof with his head down on the rail beside her. She wondered briefly if all these thoughts were blasphemous. Then she went into a deep and dreamless sleep.

She was awoken the next morning by the sound of Roland turning the starting handle of the car outside. She opened the window and leaned out. He was wearing his jacket and his rucksack was on the ground beside him.

'Roland!' He turned his head and waved a hand, the other still cranking away.

'You're off?'

He nodded.

'Wait for me.'

She pulled on old Barraclough's big dressing-gown, picked up Charley and went downstairs.

'Were you going to go without saying anything?' she said.

'You said it all last night,' he said.

'What is it,' she said, 'that's made us like

543

this? That's made the change?'

'The war, I think. We would have trundled along quite happily without that.' At last the car started to purr. He stood up.

'I wouldn't want to trundle along, ever,' said Lizza vehemently.

He rubbed his hands on a rag and put them on her shoulders and kissed her on the lips. 'Me neither, Lizz. Best friends?'

'Best friends always.'

She held out Charley to be kissed. 'Don't forget he's yours as well, Rollie. Come and see him. Keep in touch.'

He got into the driving seat and leaned out of the window. 'I will, Lizz. There is a letter. I left you a letter.'

She was walking into the house with a light heart when she bumped into Krystof in the hall. 'What's the matter with you? Krystof? You looked dreadful.'

'What's the matter with me? I am awake all night because I see Roland and think what a good man he is, and I know you will see it and go off with him...'

It was the first time she had ever seen him angry. She shook her head. 'Bessie says I have to stay here, in my own land.' She smiled, putting a hand on his arm. 'And it's her house, so I think I'll have to do what I'm told, don't you?'

He looked at her through beetling brows and started to laugh with her. 'I think you always, always do just what you choose, Elizabeth.'

'Here, take Charley in to see Bessie, will you?

Roland's left me something.'

Roland had typed his letter on the typewriter, folded it and left it neatly on top of her steadily growing pile of stories. It was a long letter, for Roland. How much he had always loved her. How unique she was. How the war had put its fingers into their lives and made them both change. How the island had made him change, think of things afresh. He had thought if she and Charley had come to the island, then she would feel its magic. But perhaps her instinct not to come was right. Part of the impact of the island had been this person who had made him think and feel differently. This person had said he must come to get Lizza. But in his heart he knew that was not right. He would always love her, and growing up together as they had, they would always be part of each other. But things changed, and now were changing faster than ever...

In the kitchen Krystof was giving Charley his bottle and Bessie was stirring porridge on the range. She cocked an eye. 'Yon lad's gone then?'

Lizza went across and kissed Bessie on the cheek, only to be casually shaken off. 'Yes, back to Scotland, back to another life.' Her eyes were on Krystof. 'It's funny, but ever since we were young, since we first met, me and Roland have been in tune. We went out of tune when I lost my twins and Rebecca. Now we're in tune again.'

Bessie stood up, her hand in the small of her back. 'Yer ma was tellin' us that yer allus talkin'

545

in riddles, an' ah wus tellin' her ah agreed with 'er. Now can yer tek this spoon an' stir the porridge? Ah'm not feelin' too grand. Ah've bin feelin' strange all night. Ah think ah'll gan and have a little lie-down.'

Lizza looked at Bessie's lined face with alarm.

She knew this had something to do with Theo Callaghan and his silk tie.

CHAPTER 35

In the days of Bessie's illness they all realised just how much the old woman had done to keep their lives running smoothly at Campion House. In those days Lizza's workload doubled. When he was not out doing his drawings, Krystof worked alongside her, brushing and dusting, pegging clothes out, cleaning windows, or minding Charley while she 'got on'. Beatrice, Josie and even Min did chores after work. All this, so that when Lizza went in to sit with Bessie in the evenings, she could answer 'yes', when Bessie asked if all the usual jobs had been done.

There was a feeling of strain right through the household. Krystof had kept his distance from Lizza since Roland's visit. He was working on new Ministry commissions now, and was his normal warm and polite self in public. However, she waited for other signals in vain. In the crowded household she felt unable to make any move herself. Every night she would lie in bed, ignoring Min's punching and poking and chattering, and listen to his footsteps overhead, feeling almost beside herself with longing.

Josie was more subdued than usual. The incident with her father had cut deeper than she would admit and she finally started to mourn her mother. She was eating very little. Her face had become narrower and sharper, and she was bad-tempered with Liam, a thing Lizza had never seen before.

Bessie was no trouble to take care of, but day by day became worryingly more frail. Amos Silkin visited her every few days. Hearing the murmur of their voices through the bedroom door, Lizza imagined them to be talking of the days when old Barraclough held hearty suppers at Campion House and Bessie, standing as she always did, joined in their laughter.

One night Bessie asked Lizza to send Josie to see her.

Lizza met Josie coming back downstairs just minutes later. She raised her brows.

Josie shrugged, but in her eyes was the first flicker of humour, the first glimmer of the old Josie, that Lizza had seen for weeks. 'I'm sent to get the gramophone and some records an' we're to listen to them. Ain't she an old duck?'

One afternoon Alice turned up and went upstairs to see Bessie. Then she came back downstairs, took Bessie's apron from its hook in the kitchen and wrapped it round her middle. 'Yon gypsy woman says you're worn out. You look it too. Go and get a lie-down. I'll see to the bairns and things down here.'

Lizza hesitated. The image of her mother and Bessie in cahoots was almost unbelievable. 'Ma...Bessie. What do you think of her?'

Alice tipped the potatoes into the dish and picked up a knife. 'I might have lived in a little pit town all me life, Lizza, an' I've never been in any big city, but I know a good woman when I see one. Even if she is a gypsy. Now go, or she'll be down here after me in her bedclothes.'

Lizza was smiling when she let herself into Bessie's little bedroom.

Bessie opened one eye. 'Oh, it's you. Ah telt yer ma ter get yer ter lie down afore yer fell down.'

'I thought I'd come and sit with you. That's as good as a rest.'

Bessie closed her eyes. 'Ah canna be bothered with nae talk.'

'That's all right. What if I read you the paper?'

Both eyes opened now. 'Yer can read me one of them stories of yer own that yer keep clackin' away at, if yer like. Ah'm sick of that paper. All about rationin' an' the war an' the ships sinkin' an' the poor old Russians runnin' away. An' them Yankees sittin' tight.'

'But Bessie, they're still hanging on, those Russians, waiting for the winter. Remember old Bonaparte?'

A faint smile passed across the worn old face. 'Aye,' she said. 'Anyway, get on. Get one of them stories.'

Lizza was on the third story when there was

548

a polite knock on the door. It was Amos Silkin. Lizza gathered up her sheets of paper and squeezed past him.

'Come in, Mr Silkin,' said Bessie, her voice quite strong now. 'Yer should hear these nursin' stories of Mrs King's, they should be in the paper. They should really be in the paper.'

Lizza did go to her bedroom then. She lay on the bed and went straight to sleep, only waking again when her mother shook her. 'Lizza. That lawyer of the gypsy woman's wants to see you.'

Amos Silkin was sitting, with the relaxation of long custom, in the study. He stood up as she entered. 'Mrs King, there are two matters about which we must speak. One, on Miss Harraton's instructions, is regarding the affairs of this house. I have drawn up papers which she has signed today. These transfer the house and its contents, by deed of gift, to you.'

Lizza sat down very hard.

He put on his glasses and took out a sheet from his small document case. 'There are special conditions...' He peered closely at the paper. '... "that in perpetuity there will always be a home at Campion House for Miss J Callaghan, Miss M Roebuck, Master Liam Callaghan, Master Charles Hugo King and Mr K Sobieski. And herself, Miss Bessie Harraton, till death."'

'I can't believe this,' said Lizza.

Silkin cleared his throat. 'It is unusual,' he said. 'However, I have known Miss Harraton for more than half a century and know that her brain, though unlearned, is as sharp as a knife,

549

and her wisdom is unbounded. And to her, you are now the family she has never known. This makes a very logical act.'

'I can't believe it,' Lizza repeated.

Silkin rooted in his case for another paper. 'I fear my second errand is less...pleasant. I have had a letter from your husband Mr Roland King asking me to call on you and invite you to consider instituting proceedings for a'—he cleared his throat and a ruddy stain blotched his left cheek—'divorce. He tells me here that the fault is on his part and he will furnish any evidence appertaining to that...'

'Stop!' said Lizza. 'That's enough. You may write to him, Mr Silkin, and tell him I'll think about it. You may also tell him that I'll not write to him myself on this matter but will come to see you.'

'Very well, Mrs King. I must say I am mortified to be the carrier of such...'

'Don't worry, Mr Silkin I had an inkling. There are *faults* on both sides. And about the first matter, would it be all right if no one knew about it except you and me and Bessie?' Any talk about this could bring complications and dramas she could do without.

'Miss Harraton said you would say that. And yes, that is perfectly in order. Moreover, she requests that you do not refer to this matter with her.' He smiled slightly. 'Precisely, she said it was "nowt to make a fuss about".'

Despite the stunning nature of Bessie's gift, it was the communication from Roland that was uppermost in her mind as she showed Amos

550

Silkin out. Trying not to hurry, she made her way up the back stairs to the attic, her heart thumping.

Krystof was bending over a table under the large skylight, working on the final stages of a shipyard drawing he had made on Tyneside the previous week.

She walked up to him, pulled him round to face her and kissed him. He murmured and started to return her kisses, his hands on her face and in her hair, on her shoulders and in the small of her back. Then he pulled himself free. 'What's this, my dearest Elizabeth, what's this?' His eyes were glittering and he was breathing heavily.

'My ma's downstairs doing the teas and Bessie told her to make me come upstairs for a lie-down. So I thought I'd come and have a lie-down with you.' She took his hand and led him across to his couch, which was pulled into the shadow under the eaves, just out of reach of the band of sunlight which was quartering the dusty floor. She sat down on the couch, took off her cardigan, folded it neatly, and lay it in the dust. She looked up at him. 'That is, if you don't mind?'

Playing the records for Bessie, as she did now some nights after work, seemed to cheer Josie up. Beatrice was particularly pleased to note the girl, now her very special friend, was much more like her old sparky self.

The morning Lizza received her news from Amos Silkin, on the train on the way to work, Josie had questioned Beatrice closely about Mick. 'Sure, he loves you like mad, that man! Shines out of every pore of him.'

'I should think so. He bought me a ring.'

'What does he say when he tells yer he loves yer?'

'He never tells me.'

'I notice he never says much. But how d'you really know if he doesn't tell you?'

'I just know. You just told me you could see it yourself, anyway.'

'Aren't you dying to get married?'

Beatrice smiled at her. 'Yes, seeing as you ask.'

'You're gunna get a wedding dress? You can have my coupons if you like. How many do you need?'

Beatrice shook her head. 'No need for that. We'll just go, one day, to Priorton Registry Office, and it'll be done.'

Josie scowled. 'Ain't I gunna be bridesmaid then?'

She shook her head again. 'No. Not even a witness, flower. You have to be eighteen to be that, according to Mick.'

'So you wanted me then?' Josie sat back, satisfied that they had wanted her. 'That's not so bad, then.' She lit a cigarette. 'I was talking about love to Mrs King once, a long time ago in Coventry. She took me to this caff for some tea. The last time the old town was still there. Last day it was. I said then, that the love thing was important for after-the-war. I believe that. So you and old Mick are on the right lines.'

'What about you, Josie? Have you no sweetheart on a string at present?' Beatrice knew very well Josie hadn't, as she had been out of the house so very little in recent weeks.

Josie shook her head. 'These boyos you meet at the dances, they're only after one thing. Those soldiers, always pleading sudden death tomorrow, to get into your knickers. Can't stick them.'

'Josie!' Beatrice looked around the crowded compartment, but no one was taking the slightest notice of them.

Josie went on. 'There's only been one real one so far and that was your Alex...don't worry, I ain't carrying no torch for him, any more than he is for me. But that week or so in Coventry, playing about with him, it was such a lark. P'raps we did love each other a bit then. First time I thought any of *that* could be...nice after I'd seen what my daddy did to my mammy. No, I wouldn't a' missed that with Alex, even given what followed. Sure, I loved them all, those games I played with Alex.'

Beatrice frowned at her. Josie sounded as though those events were all in the very deep past, almost as though they had happened to someone else.

Beatrice had not heard from Alex in months. As far as she knew he was in Canada for flight training. He probably wasn't giving any of them a single thought. He had always been so very good at keeping his full attention on himself, had Alex.

Her mind turned to its favourite subject.

Mick had said Alex could live with them when the war was over. He would always have a home. So long as he didn't mind the dogs. Mick was getting very urgent now, about them getting married. They confined their embraces to kissing, but she could feel him reining himself back like a great battlehorse longing to run. The wait was building up in her too, and she was amazed how she longed to experience that act which for so many years she had banned even from her thoughts.

Soon. They would make it happen soon.

Josie stood up to open the door when they arrived at the station, then pulled back quickly, treading on Beatrice's foot as she did so.

'Ouch! What you're doing, Josie?'

'He's there, can you see him?' She put her head out of the window.

'Who?'

'My father.'

Beatrice pulled her to one side and looked out. 'No. He's not here. Look! No one even slightly resembling him. Come on, Josie, you're holding us up.' She pushed Josie ahead of her out of the train. Josie held Beatrice's hand as she looked in every direction, at and through the hurrying figures. But Beatrice was right, there was no one even slightly resembling Theo Callaghan anywhere to be seen.

Josie was sullen all morning, not responding to Esme and Mary's jokes or Beatrice's gentler attempts to cheer her up. Running back from the canteen to the changing rooms after dinner, she turned round a corner and charged full pelt into Mrs Armitage, sending her red beret flying.

There was a titter from the girls. Mrs Armitage struggled to her feet, almost spitting with fury. 'And what do you think you're doing, lady, charging round like a hoyden?'

'I ain't doin' nothing. I was just...'

Mrs Armitage planted her beret back on her head and stormed off, shouting, 'You watch yourself, lady! I've got my eye on you! You watch yourself!'

Esme put her arm through Josie's, chuckling. 'There now, Josie, you put a fox in 'er chickens.'

Josie wrenched her arm free and walked on, ignoring the calls of her friends behind her. By the time they got to the changing rooms, she had her overall on and was standing at the little mirror carefully threading a cigarette and a single match into the neat roll of her hair, where it turned over her stocking top.

'She'll get you for it!' said Mary.

'You mind your own bloody business,' said Josie, stomping out. 'It ain't got nothing to do with you. Nothing at all.'

Towards the end of the day Beatrice had built up her tally sufficiently to make time to go to the toilet. Josie waved her away, grinning, her good mood restored by hard work and the passage of time. 'Don't you worry Beatrice. Have one for me. Sure, I'll do a few for you if there's a lag.'

The explosion, when it came, rattled the glass in the toilet windows. Beatrice pulled up her clothes and started to run. She was stopped by

555

Mrs Armitage and a uniformed security man, twenty yards from the section. They had already set chairs across the space and were not letting anyone through.

The air was hot. Around them people were moving away from a certain centre, like sand thrown on a spinning wheel. The certain centre was the section where Josie, Esme and she herself worked.

Beatrice grabbed the woman's arm. 'Who is it, who is it?'

The woman put a hand over hers. 'Were you at the lavatory, love? You were very lucky.'

Beatrice pushed away at her. 'Let me see them, let me see them.'

The woman put her arms around her, tears in her own eyes. 'There's nothing, love, nothing left. Mary, and cheeky little Esme. And your Josie. Gone. You can't go back there.'

Beatrice knocked her down and started to run towards the mess. The security man chased after her, swept her off her feet, threw her over his shoulder and carried her back. He set her quite roughly on her feet. 'Stay where you are, flower, unless you want to be blown to kingdom come too.'

Beatrice stood there, her hands limp at her side, and wept. For her son, for herself now and herself at fifteen with everything destroyed before her, but most of all for the bright spark who had helped to bring her out of her own dark place and had now gone from them all.

The workers on the whole of that section were ushered out of the building and sent home early. They were reminded that all events at the factory were confidential and not to be shouted abroad. This would be a comfort to the enemy. Mrs Armitage was detailed to go all the way home with Beatrice to make sure she was all right, and to help her tell the girl's family.

At the gate, a man got out of a dusty car and came towards them. Beatrice recognised Theo Callaghan and pulled close to Mrs Armitage, who said, 'Who's this?'

Beatrice spoke through stiff lips, from a face lumpy with crying. 'It's Josie's father. She is, was, afraid of him. She thought she saw him this morning but...'

Theo looked round suspiciously. 'Where is she, my daughter? Where have you hidden her?'

'Are you Josie's father?'

He nodded, very warily.

'She's dead,' said Beatrice flatly. 'It blew her up, the stuff we worked with.'

Theo sagged a little, then stood up straight. He had come to warn Josie not to talk about him to people. To give her a good shaking up. Now at least she couldn't...

'Can I offer you two ladies a lift home?' he said unctuously. 'You must be devastated by this...'

Beatrice clutched Mrs Armitage's hand. 'Just put me on the train will you? You go with him if you want.'

Mrs Armitage shook her head. 'They said I'm to take you home Beatrice. And that's what I'll do. Mr Callaghan, if you want any more information, the manager Mr Clarkson'll give you the necessary details.' She knew he wouldn't. The details of these incidents stayed within the factory walls, or in government files.

That night Theo Callaghan had as good a time as he'd had in years, consuming pint after pint in Priorton pubs, milking the natural sympathy of other men for his great personal tragedy. He ended up with a woman called Marjie Allyns, drinking in the Prospect, a dark hostelry on a high point over the River Gaunt on the other side of the Priors Bridge.

Marjie had been picking up men in the Prospect all night and Theo was to be her last. One of those men, who would get his cut, had told her the Irish feller had a car, so there must be a bit of money to be had there. A car was better than the alleyway, and she might even get double from such a man, then she could get home to the bairns and put her feet up.

'So where is it, this car of yours?' she said, after she had sympathised for the tenth time about his poor daughter and tolerated his hand under the table creeping up her bare thigh. She winced as his hand gripped her harder, his nails digging into her flesh.

'Outside the Blue Bell, on the other side of the bridge.' He was leaning over her; his speech was slurred; his shirt was open at the neck and his tie was around his shoulders. Marjie eyed the tie. That would do just nice for her cousin Alf, who'd done her a few favours lately.

'They said no one came across here except

558

folks from this side of the town. They said not to bring the car across here cos this place was a den of thieves.' He looked round. 'An' they were not wrong.'

'Oh, you are a clever man.' She stood up. 'Aren't ye gunna show us this car of yours then?'

'How much'll it cost us to show you me car, then?'

'Ten bob.'

He hooted with laughter and leaned towards her. He fingered the hem of her skirt and said quietly, 'For an ugly worn-out whore? Ten bob is it? I've shown it to better whores than you for sixpence.'

'Suit yourself.' She pushed his hand away from her. It was part of their fun, part of what they paid for, this sneering and slagging at you before they jumped or fell on you. But she was tired. It had been a long night. She buttoned her coat over her cleavage. 'I'm off.'

He stood up. 'Aw, don't be like that. Here's a man who's lost his only daughter today and you're quarrelling over shillings. Five bob. What about five bob?'

'All right,' she said. 'Let's get on with it.'

In three places along the Prior's bridge were deep niches where, during the day, you could stand directly over the swirling water and view the Priory. Theo grabbed both her wrists and pulled her into one of these. He transferred both wrists to one hand and started to kiss her and bite at her neck, pulling at her clothes with his free hand.

She got her mouth free and screamed, 'The car, you said the car!'

His hand had reached her knickers and he was pulling at them. 'That car's too good for you, whore, I wouldn't let you soil it. And if you think you're getting five bob for this lot...'

That was his mistake. In her time Marjie had ensured a lot, to get her just payments, and she had her own ways of dealing with quitters. With practised expertise she pulled her knee hard up into his groin. He yelped and released her hands, which she raised to his chest to push him with all her wiry strength against the parapet.

The grinding noise of stone against stone filled the air and her push was going further than she thought. Theo Callaghan screamed, 'No!' his hands grasping her arms, then her hands, as he fell backwards over the breaking parapet. She heard the splash as he fell in the water, then further splashes as the stones continued to fall. She could hear his voice calling from below. Somehow she had caught his tie as he fell and it was still in her hand. Silk. She could tell by the feel of it. But she decided not to keep it. She had met a few bad men in her time and this was a very bad man. She lay the tie just where the parapet was broken, and secured it with a small stone.

The voice was still calling.

'When will you men learn that the labourer is worthy of 'er 'ire?' She said the words out loud. Then she made her way home, looking forward to the broth that her eldest, Henry, would have left on the stove for her.

CHAPTER 36

It was a sombre evening at Campion House. Mrs Armitage was surprisingly kind, insisting on coming in with Beatrice and breaking the news to the others, who gathered in the sitting room to hear it. 'We don't quite know what happened,' she said. 'These are dangerous, volatile materials we work with. The possibility of accidents is high.' She looked round helplessly. 'It's the war,' she said. 'It asks for sacrifices in the most unexpected places.'

Lizza, carrying Charley who was bawling because his feed had been interrupted, showed her out, thanking her for her kindness.

'Kindness?' Mrs Armitage exploded, stopping in her tracks. 'It would be a kindness for these girls not to have to do this. With every one of these...' She went pink. She had orders not to talk like this. '...With every one of these accidents I feel responsible myself, that I didn't check properly.'

Lizza shook her head, not knowing what to say, still numb with having to understand herself that Josie was not here any longer, that she wouldn't come bouncing through the door, scooping up Liam and spreading her particular light in their lives. She would no longer go up on her hands once a day to keep herself right. She would no longer play records with Bessie.

She would no longer try her very best to shock them with the tales of her exploits.

Lizza took several deep breaths before she went back into the sitting room. Min was sitting on the sofa with her arm round Beatrice, and Krystof was showing Liam his reflection in the ornate mirror over the mantelpiece. Lizza took the bottle. 'Here, Bea, you feed Charley before he yells the house down entirely. I've to go and tell Bessie what's up, or she'll think the war's over.' She put Charley on Beatrice's knee, placed her numb hands round the bottle and popped it into Charley's mouth. He stopped yelling and started to suck. Beatrice wriggled a little to make Charley comfortable and was forced to relax just a bit. Min smiled slightly and nodded up at Lizza.

'I will take Liam and walk round to Michael Stratton,' said Krystof. 'He will want to be here with Beatrice now. I know it.'

Lizza smiled at him in watery gratitude. 'Thank you, love,' she said. Min and even Beatrice looked up at this open endearment.

Bessie, sitting up in bed sewing her quilt and looking surprisingly well, seemed unshocked by the news. 'Poor bairn,' she said. 'But she wouldn't suffer?'

'No. The woman said it would be absolutely instantaneous. But Bessie, Josie's too young for this, a little girl.'

'She had extra time, didn't she?' Bessie put down her needle.

Lizza sat on the bed and shook her head. 'What do you mean?'

'If it weren't for knowing you an' that lad o' your Beatrice's, that Alex, she'd a' died with 'er ma, wouldn't she? So nearly a year that lass's had, to know joy and bring it, afore she took her turn to gan to the land. An' the little lad, Liam, he's saved for a lifetime. You mark me. A lifetime.'

'How do you know these things, Bessie? What makes you so sure?'

Bessie spread out the quilt in front of her, right across the bed, forcing Lizza to stand up. 'Well, hinney, when ah'm sewin' this, ah move this way an' that with me needle. It might seem a mess to you, a muddle. But when you see it laid out larger, you can see the pattern. Look, the turns here is exactly the same as the turns there, though ah didn't plan it. An' that bit here is mirror image to this bit ower here. Oh, mebbe ah'm that old, ah can see the big pattern. Ah just know. An' sometimes voices tell me. Old Barraclough reg'lar...'

Lizza remembered something. 'I was in the Cathedral once, and heard my Rebecca's voice giving me a message for Josie.'

'An' what was that, hinney?'

'She said to tell her there were places to play where she was.'

Bessie nodded with satisfaction. 'There!' she said, her eyes gleaming.

Lizza's eyes were filling with tears. 'You and your "gannin' to the land", Bessie. Then Krystof and his greater pattern. But Josie should be here. I miss her, and I miss Rebecca...'

Bessie reached for a snowy handkerchief from

563

the pile on her table. 'Hinney, ye wouldn't be given it, if ye couldn't bear it,' she said tenderly. 'Now, dinnet let them tears drop on me quilt or it'll pucker all the edge.' She thrust the handkerchief into Lizza's hands and picked up her needle. 'Think of the livin',' she said. 'Dinnet worry about your Beatrice. 'Asn't she got that canny lad to look out for 'er now? Dinnet worry about the schoolteacher or that man in Scotland. They'll gan their own queer way without yer. Dinnet worry about your ma. She's a good woman, fully grown. She can watch out for herself. Dinnet worry about the bairns, the little lad and your baby, as every breath yer breathe guards them without yer knowin'.' She put a knuckle underneath and plunged a needle in the fabric. 'Ye can worry about that Russian if yer like, hinney. Mek yer pact with 'im an' get things settled. Took me ten years to mek me pact with Old Barraclough: a cruel waste.'

Lizza stayed there for five minutes, quietly pulling herself together and watching Bessie sew. When she got back downstairs Michael was there, holding Beatrice's gloves while she put on her coat. Liam was crying, asking where was Josie. Where was Josie?

Beatrice put her hand in his, fighting back her tears. 'Josie's gone to play with Rebecca, pet. Can you remember Rebecca? They're having a nice time playing together. Now you and me, we're going down Mick's allotment to feed his dogs and his chickens. You'd like that, wouldn't you?'

The house was hollow and empty when they had gone. Lizza went up to put Charley in his cot. When she came back down Min was presiding over Bessie's Napoleon brandy and three glasses. She sloshed a large measure in each and handed one to Krystof and one to Lizza. 'Shirley's coming for me in a minute. We've planned a weekend at the coast in her mother's cottage. I'll go with her as I don't think you need me here, even in this crisis.' She shook her head at their protestations. 'So I want my say. And I want to say it to you two, whom I love more—no, don't say anything—than anyone since there was just me and my dad at home after the loony mother went. No one'll mean this much to me, ever,' she said vehemently. 'My dear ones. I hope we'll all be friends always. I wanted to say this to you. There is this terrible distillation going on all round us. It's going on out there and we've no power over it. But here in this house, we're all survivors: you two and me, Beatrice and Liam, Bessie the greatest survivor of all. Let's hope the distillation is as fine and full of promise, as full of life and promise as this.' She held up the glass, and in it they could see, threefold, the image of the gas mantel above the fireplace. She swirled the brandy and broke the image and took a great gulp, and they followed suit.

Krystof raised his glass. 'And I will give you Josie. A bright spark in our lives.'

They drank.

'Josie,' repeated Lizza, her lip trembling yet again.

Then they were hugging each other, their mingling tears as much for themselves as for Josie. The clang of the doorbell relieved the tension and they unclasped themselves with some relief. Min picked up her bag and coat in the hall and walked out without letting Shirley over the threshold.

Krystof put a finger on Lizza's cheek. 'You look worn out. It's quiet now. Have a little rest. We all need you to be fit, and tomorrow will be a hard day. I will listen and wake you when Beatrice returns.'

She allowed him to lead her upstairs and held on to him outside her bedroom. 'Come and rest with me,' she said.

He wavered. 'I will. Just wait for me.' And he was gone.

She went into the bedroom and with a tranquillity which amazed herself put on her nightdress and one of Min's silk wraps. Then she lay on the bed and closed her eyes. She did not open them when she heard the door click, or when she felt the bed creak as it moved with his weight.

'Elizabeth, I have something here for you.'

She opened her eyes then. He was holding a ring of ornate orange gold set with dull turquoise stones. 'I have been looking for a proper moment to give you this, ever since the time in the Cathedral. To seal the bargain we have made there. It is my mother and my grandmother's ring.'

She put out her hand and he slipped it on over the narrow band which Roland had given her. 'I love you, Elizabeth, and always will, whatever becomes of us...'

She shook her head. 'We're safe now. We are what Josie described as after-the-war. The people who love each other. Not Josie, though. Not Rebecca.' Her voice started to tremble again.

He pulled her to him. 'No, no, my dear love. Do not cry.' He kissed her damp lids and cuddled her in. 'They wouldn't want you to go on crying.'

They lay like that, quiet and comfortable for half an hour, then suddenly she wanted to kiss him, and she reached up and pulled his head round so that she could. His lips opened under hers and his hand went to her breast, over, then inside the wrap, pushing it further and further off her shoulders. She burrowed with her face on to his chin and down to the hollow at the base of his throat. Her hand pulled at the buttons on his shirt and he helped her remove it, and the rest. In seconds they were naked. 'A fresh start,' she murmured. 'For Josie, who liked the idea of love.'

Then they were kissing and stroking each other, weaving their way across the bed as they played all kinds of games to delay the moment. When they finally did come together, Lizza's senses throbbed to the outside edges of her skin and for a split second she knew all about Josie and Rebecca, and the twins, and her own father, and Min's father, and all of Min's pupils, all playing on the 'other side'; on this side she was flying above the clouds with Alex and walking the heather with Roland; she knew about the passion in this very place, between the younger Bessie and her young Barraclough. All she could feel was life, not death. She could feel Josie urging her on, too bright a spark to cast a shadow on their lives even now. Josie was about life, not death. Josie, like Rebecca, would be folded in her heart for ever, a bright core of smiles and laughter. Lizza knew she wouldn't make her mother's mistake and sanctify the dead with misery. Josie and Rebecca would be remembered in light.

Lizza and Krystof were just rolling away from each other, still breathing heavily and sweating, when a sound hit their ears from across the corridor,

Blue Moon
I saw you standing alone
without a dream in my heart
without a love of my own...

—sung mournfully by some crooner, to the straining violins of a large orchestra.

They lifted themselves up on their elbows. 'Bessie!' said Lizza. 'The gramophone!' Then they laughed, clutching at each other in delight.

And across the corridor, Bessie smiled.

The next morning Lizza took up the *Northern Echo* to read to Bessie. She checked every single page but there was nothing in it about the explosion, nothing at all.

She peered closer. 'But here's something, Bessie. Josie swore she saw her father yesterday, and that disturbed her. Now listen to this.' Then she read out a piece about an Irishman who had been found dead in the River Gaunt. He had papers on him in the names of O'Connor and Callaghan. His car had contained a considerable amount of stockings and cigarettes, which the police were investigating. It was feared that O'Connor or Callaghan had survived in the water some time, being trapped by branches swept down in the recent high water. Eventually Mr Callaghan or O'Connor must have lost his hold and drowned.

Bessie sat up straight and grinned at her, a malevolent, ancient grin. 'No more'n he deserved. Now May Lynn has her right reply.'

'Wait,' said Lizza. 'There's more. It says here that the police have his tie, caught in the stonework which broke as he fell.'

'Yes, they would have that. The tie was part of it,' said Bessie. Then she swung her legs out of the bed and stood up, swaying just a little. 'Now, where's me pinny? We'll be ter dig outer this 'ouse.' She cackled at the look on Lizza's face. 'Did yer think ah was gannin' to the land too, like that poor bairn? Nah. Ah've work to do yet. There's them Russkis ter watch, ter make sure they burn that beggar Hitler off, an' them Yankees, ter make sure they come to heel properly. 'Ere, lass, help us up will yer?'

Lizza picked up the quilt which had fallen to the floor. As she folded it she saw that there was indeed one quite small corner of the quilt as yet unsewn. It would take Bessie at least till the spring to complete that. She was right. There was work to do. For all of them.

This Large Print Book for the Partially sighted, who cannot read normal print, is published under the auspices of

THE ULVERSCROFT FOUNDATION

Other MAGNA General Fiction Titles In Large Print

FRANCES ANNE BOND
Return Of The Swallow

JUDY GARDINER
All On A Summer's Day

IRIS GOWER
The Sins Of Eden

HELENE MANSFIELD
Some Women Dream

ELISABETH McNEILL
The Shanghai Emerald

ELIZABETH MURPHY
To Give And To Take

JUDITH SAXTON
This Royal Breed